NOONDAY
FLOWER

NOONDAY FLOWER

Carla C. Ohse

Published by Carla C. Ohse

Edited and Designed by Girl Friday Productions
www.girlfridayproductions.com

Image Credits: Cover (field) Delcroix Romain/
Shutterstock; (dove) Elena Maximova/Shutterstock
Map p. 22 © Audrey Schreck

ISBN (Paperback): 9781733510509
e-ISBN: 9781733510516

Second Edition

Printed in the United States of America

*This book is dedicated to a champion—christened
Margaretha Katherina Jenny Johnson—who hit home runs,
bowled perfect 300 games, caught critical balls in fast-
pitch, and made winning shots in basketball. Athletic "Peg,"
as Margaretha came to be called, knew no fame, and chose
to be a "champion" in marriage and motherhood as well.
Thank you, Mother*

Author's Note

This book is neither sensational nor humdrum but remarkably true . . . *and* guardedly fictional. A mix for you to discern, chapter by chapter, what is true and what is not. My name is Carla C. Ohse, alias Maggie Johnson Dunn Millgard. I'm a Western Michigan native and former teacher who promises one thing: Lake Michigan sunsets will rival any sunset across the globe.

I

The Birth

Long ago, I remember hearing rumors about a young black woman living in Walhalla, Michigan. Now I know they were not rumors, after all.

The young woman, named Marla Jean, was with child. No one in Walhalla, or nearby, knew it until she became weighty and swollen. Not long before, she was yet a girl. But deep in the pangs of birthing, the young woman was fast becoming a mother. The pain was intense, so hard she likely couldn't think back to a time before the pain. She couldn't think of anything but the pain. It was bad, permanent, stuck.

The young woman's muscles kept screaming for her to push, but the tightness of her womb had become stubborn. The pain tormented her like a force, an unknown force, rising up with no end to it.

Her birth canal was miraculously expanding to make ready its delivery. All womanly instincts, with awesome respect, were trying to move toward an ultimate conclusion—to receive a God-given creation of life.

☙

I never met Marla Jean. She was a hard worker, and many Walhalla farmers were witness to that. Lizzy grew to love her, as evident in her kindness and fair treatment of the girl. I vaguely remember the narrow-minded talk around the village about a black woman living with the Schrecks. I grew up with a devoted mama and pa west of Walhalla and far enough from the Schrecks to have seen Marla Jean now and then, and wished I had taken the time to get to know her. I never wondered whether it was good or bad that she lived and worked in an all-white community. Still, with the information given to me by Lizzy Schreck and Vita Mavis, I feel like I found out enough to write Marla Jean's story in the most honest and authentic way possible.

Even though I lived at a farm nearby, being young myself, I knew little about Marla Jean living in Walhalla. Years later I heard the full accounting of the birth from two wonderful and caring women, Lizzy Schreck and Vita Mavis, who were there.

Vita, who had been at the birth as a midwife, began, "Maggie, it was so long ago, but I remember the day like it was yesterday."

Lizzy added, "Maggie, I will never forget that day, either. Vita and I talk about it, time and again. Maybe we should of done more. No sense in thinking 'bout it now."

The women's telling of this day filled my heart and mind with story. I knew, because of its importance, it had to be written down.

☙

Though not a midwife, a white woman hovering over Marla Jean was trying to help. The small-boned, delicate older woman, named Lizzy Schreck, was sweating; her hands were trembling, unsure of what to do next. The Schreck farm had their animals give birth before but never a hired hand. As Marla Jean screamed again and again, it was clear the birth was near. Yet, it was like a locked vault that refused to reveal its combination to the older woman.

Marla Jean opened her eyes and called out, "Oh, Miz Lizzy, helps me! Lawd, helps me! Please, helps me!"

"Oh, Marla Jean, I'm sorry. I don't know how to hurry the baby. I don't know what's wrong. Oh, oh-oh my, *o-o-oooh* my." Lizzy leaned close to her friend. "Old Doc ain't coming, but I called after Vita Mavis, she'll know what to do. She's coming. Hold on, Marla Jean, she's comin'." Lizzy looked up and away and asked, "What's keeping her?"

It must be frightening and exhilarating to give birth with such pain. But Marla Jean, who was frightened beyond exhilaration, began to reel in and out of consciousness, having hallucinations. Did she imagine her body breaking into two parts, a severed right and left, and her baby lying between the two? Did she imagine her baby crying out, "Mommy, Mommy," but couldn't put herself back together to pick it up?

A pink dawn brightened the windows in the east. Lizzy looked out but abruptly turned back. Again, Marla Jean screamed, turned, and gripped the edge of the bed, nearly to the point of rolling off. "Oh, oh! It hurts. Oh Lawd, I'm hurting. Oh, Miz Lizzy, I'm hurting bad."

"Marla Jean, you got to stop that fussing." Lizzy pushed her to the center of the bed and looked where, generally speaking, no one looks at another. "Ooh my. I can't see a baby. I can't see it. Stop, stop! Hold still."

"I can't, *I can't*," screamed Marla Jean. "I can't do this. I can't do this."

Gasping, Marla Jean's eyes rolled back into her head. The bed jerked as a seizure gripped and heaved her mighty form. Clutching her teeth, grasping for breath, the young woman rocked as the pain imprisoned her abdomen. Lizzy grabbed her friend and held her down. Presently the pregnant woman became still. Lizzy let go of her. She stood, wiped her brow, and uttered a prayer questioning a higher authority. *Why is this birthing taking so long? What's wrong?*

Checking Marla Jean again, Lizzy prayed loud and hard. "Dear Lord, help us. Oh, merciful Father, see our trouble. Please. We're needing you, now!" Pleading, she prayed even more loudly, until her prayers reached the pitch of the pregnant woman's screams. "Oh, oh, oh God, can't you hear us?"

"I'm bad, Lizzy. I'm bad. Help me. Oh, oh Lawd, help me, ahhh . . ."

"Oh God, oh God!"

Two tiny feet became visible as Marla Jean lay motionless with her body exposed, legs limp and lifeless, far apart. Pulsating blood gushed out onto the patchwork quilt while a veil of uncertainty covered Lizzy's face.

Lizzy looked down the front of her shapeless dress and saw blood there.

As a woman who always wore dresses that didn't complement her figure, Lizzy never lent herself to gossip or cared what others thought. On this day, she wanted desperately to help her friend regardless of the stains on her dress or reputation.

Should I go ahead and pull that baby out? she asked herself, standing over the bloated young woman. As she bathed Marla Jean's shining brow with a cool rag, she looked quizzically into her face. Too frightened to realize that the young woman had fallen down into a dreamlike state, Lizzy entered into her own state of meditative prayer.

"Our Father who art in heaven, hallowed be your name . . ."

☙

In her delirium, Marla Jean may have viewed the tale of a black swan swimming among the reeds in a serene pond.

Content with flies and fishes, seeds, and the roots of lily pads that floated on the water's edge, this black swan lived peacefully in the lagoon. Suddenly, white swans appeared and sneered at the bird with its rare flowing black feathers. They met at the center of the pond, and clear and shrill clamoring filled the air as they flapped their mighty wings. The splashing water, like a raging rain, settled in huge ripples around them, and the black swan retreated to a far side of the pond. Marla Jean's delirium may have sensed a winter of rare, extreme cold whereby the great pond froze. The swans did not escape the quickly crusted-over pond and died a chilling death from the uncompromising temperatures. Living and dying, the full circle of life became measured, not by the total circumference of the great pond but by its shallow, divided parts. At that, Marla Jean awoke screaming to pain—the undeniable pain of flesh bearing flesh.

❦

The Mavises' place was a stone's throw from the Schreck farm just down Walhalla Road, but the Schrecks' driveway meandered, making it a great deal farther. On foot, running like a deer, it was much closer. Vita Mavis considered the shorter route but did not take it, mostly because of the morning fog. Her husband drove her in their 1930 Ford. He dropped her off but didn't stay.

"Come back around noon, Carl," Vita called out as she jumped from the sputtering vehicle. Quickly, Vita Mavis stumbled through the door into the kitchen and found her way to the little room off to the side.

The room was tiny; its only window faced the railroad tracks. The wallpaper bubbled on the walls, the paste giving way after years of hanging vertically. The old iron bed, painted over, encircled a concave mattress where the pregnant woman lay. A mending basket in one corner overflowed with holed socks, and a cheap, oval braided rug covered a worn section of the floor's linoleum. Vita Mavis appeared, not expecting to see such grievous particulars of birthing. Marla Jean responded woefully to the midwife while the woman took charge.

Marla Jean pushed so hard you could see the bright-red flush in her black face and the protruding veins in her neck. As the need to push came more often, Vita realized that the two little feet amid the sappy edges of Marla Jean's vagina were not moving farther out.

Something's awful wrong, she thought. *Maybe the cord's 'round the baby.*

Lizzy Schreck stood close by, her hands tightly together pointing upward in desperate prayer. With Vita now in control, the older woman fought the temptation to leave the room.

Marla Jean was working hard to bring her baby into the world. Her eyes made known her inner soul, the extraordinary soul of one who'd never denounced her servitude to others. Marla Jean lay on the brink of death, asking for something, although asking was something she had never done before in her short life.

She pleaded over and over. "I'm dyin'. Oh Lawd, I'm dyin'. Get my baby out, so it can live. I'm askin' you."

Vita muttered to herself, "Where's the dam'd doctor? Why ain't you here?" She knew Marla Jean didn't have much strength left. She had to do something now.

Looking up at her neighbor with desperation, Vita said, "Look here, Lizzy! Now, I want you to do exactly what I say, you hear?"

"What? What, Vita?"

Before Lizzy realized it, the midwife was instructing her to get on the bed and straddle the black girl.

"Sit on her. Don't hurt her, just hold her down. Go'wan, do it!"

Lizzy looked at Vita like she was out of her mind. Vita grabbed her, pulled her over to the bed, and motioned for her to get on. "Now!"

Lizzy kicked off her shoes, pulled up her dress, and reluctantly got on the bed over Marla Jean. "I don't know why I'm doing this, Vita."

"You gotta help me. You gotta hold her still, hear?" For one brief moment, the room breathed in an unusual silence. Vita closed her eyes and took one deep breath. Opening her eyes, she immediately worked her hand and arm up into the birth canal. A scream, the likes of which had never been heard before, shocked the little farmhouse, the two women within, and the village beyond.

"Oh, Vita! Marla Jean! Oh God!" Lizzy shouted, still holding the convulsing body.

"Hold her, Lizzy. Hold her!"

Marla Jean thrashed violently and then went limp while the midwife concentrated intently on what she'd started. Once she made the intrusion, she had to continue.

Perched over her body, Lizzy was crying, "Hold on, Marla Jean."

Minutes flashed by.

Lizzy looked at Vita. "Please hurry, please, please, oh, eeee! Vita, hurry!" Lizzy screamed, "I can't do this no more!" Her voice cracked with terror as she looked down at the unconscious young woman. "Oh, Marla Jean—Marla Jean, I'm sor-ry."

Though it was cramped, Vita managed to feel the baby's throbbing torso. Buried in soft flesh, her hand felt the twisted cord, tight around the unborn child's chest.

Oh, dear God, I'm needing you now. Help me get this baby out, Vita prayed. *Please, allow me to do this.*

Lizzy took Marla Jean's face into her hands. "Wake up, girl—wake up!"

Marla Jean remained still.

Madness lay in the silence.

Lizzy toppled off Marla Jean, almost falling to the floor. "She's dead. She's dead! Oh—oh-oh, my Lord, I think Marla Jean's gone! Look, Vita, she's dead!"

"Shut up, woman, jus' shut up." The midwife disregarded her friend's hysteria. She had to. She was sweating and dizzy with anticipation. Standing nearby, Lizzy closed her eyes, believing her lack of vision would take her away.

With one hand, Vita pulled on the tiny feet, at the same time trying to ease the cord. For several agonizing minutes, she pulled on the legs and worked the cord free. "Lizzy, I got the baby. I think I can pull it out."

At once, Vita realized she could not feel a pulse. *The baby's not going to make it,* she thought.

Marla Jean lay unconscious, life literally leaving her body as her baby was being born. Lizzy looked on with despair as Vita pulled the baby from Marla Jean's bloody womb. The birth canal was now a stretched gorge, deeply bruised and limp at the edges. The bloody parcel was finally delivered from between the mother's legs, along with the cord that bound it to its mother. It didn't kick or wave wildly with its first breath of air. "Oh, Vita, the baby is dead, too. Oh, oh, oh, what'll we do?" Lizzy cried.

"Quiet, Lizzy! Help me! Get a towel."

"It's gonna die, isn't it? It can't breathe."

Quickly, the women tended to the silent infant, wiping it off and looking intently into its tiny, blank face. The infant had a perfect little torso covered in blood and tissue with the cord now cut and dangling from its small belly. Right away, Vita rubbed the baby's feet, and then slapped them, one after the other. "Cry, little one. Breathe, breathe. Please, breathe. Don't leave us now. Cry, little one!"

"Oh, Vita, it's dead." Lizzy started to sob.

Vita grabbed the baby like a little burlap bag and held it upside down, patting its tiny buttocks. Finally, she laid the baby down next to the warmth of its mother and, instinctively, started to blow into its tiny mouth and nostrils. She held the little one with her able hands, blowing, wiping, and blowing, again and again. An eternity of seconds passed. Then, Vita felt—movement.

Incredibly, the miracle of life burst forth. Like the force of thunder announcing a storm, the baby gasped its first breath. Rapidly, its little chest began to heave up and down, giving it life sustained by its now beating heart. Vita backed up as the infant cried loudly and desperately. Vita and Lizzy looked at each other.

Lizzy exclaimed, "Thank you, Lord Father!"

The exhausted midwife handed the girl-child to Lizzy. "Take her," she said and then turned to Marla Jean. Already, the after-birth was discharged, along with a vast amount of blood—too much. Vita's fear was evident as she started to revive the young mother. "Please wake up, you poor thing," she pleaded.

The young woman's body, relieved of the complicated birth, was trying to overcome the damage. Even though Marla Jean was young, the midwife remained fearful. As Vita put her head to the young mother's chest, she could still hear her heartbeat. It was not strong. Marla Jean's life was rattling the cage of death too soon.

II

The Death

The issue was no longer saving a new life but saving the underprivileged and unnoticed life of the baby's mother.

Vita kept wiping Marla Jean's ashen face. A great weariness overwhelmed her. She feared the worst. The new mother was bleeding inside. Vita Mavis had done only what she knew how in a situation that required more knowledge than she had. The placenta eruption, which had caused the internal bleeding, couldn't reverse its course.

At last, the debilitated young woman opened her eyes. Her parched lips smiled when Vita reported to her that it was over. "You gave birth to a girl baby. She's perfect."

Lizzy returned with the baby wrapped in a muslin cloth. Its little face peeked through the opening. The pug-nosed, dark-skinned beauty squirmed in Lizzy's arms. Soft, coal-black curls surrounded the newborn's little face. Lizzy showed the baby to Marla Jean. Tears glistened in the new mother's eyes.

Lizzy declared, "You made this beautiful child, Marla Jean."

With a whiff of a whisper, Marla Jean asked with concern, "Is the big star lightin' up . . . the heavens . . . today?"

"Yes, the sun's shining today, my dear," Vita answered, looking over at the window and its reflected glare.

"When's . . . the sun burning . . . most hungry to lick the ground with its yellow tongue? When?" she asked.

"Now, noonday, sun's straight up. Why, Marla Jean?"

A faint look of importance crept over her face. "I want my baby named . . . Noonday . . . she be shining . . . like that best star . . ."

Not fully understanding, Lizzy asked, "You wanna name your baby Noonday?"

". . . Noonday. My Noonday . . . be somethin' . . . someday. Str-aight up and shin-ing."

Amid the disorder of the day, the dying woman smiled, her manner perfect. She nodded, then turned and looked, for the last time, at her precious wee daughter. Unbelievable sorrow captured the women who watched from just inches away. Many may never grasp or understand their long, hard fight to save this young woman. Marla Jean died ten minutes after noon on September 30, 1932.

III

The Life

This may be a proud and happy time indeed, and normally neighbors with gifts applaud new mothers. But the new black mother was gone, so no congratulatory jar of jam was even thought about. The villagers, many of whom didn't even know Marla Jean, wouldn't think of offering a jar of jam to a black mother anyway. Oh, eventually, the word did get around, but no one cared to question the hows or whys. The black baby remained in Walhalla, and Vita Mavis, with an air of assurance, and without a doubt as to whether she should or not, took complete charge of the baby's care. A perfect doll baby she turned out to be, who settled in with the white family simply as a new daughter and sister to love. She never cried much. She smiled and cooed and ate and slept like newborns do. The happy baby, content in her little makeshift bed behind the big black cookstove, thrived, and Noonday Flower was her name.

And God was there.

Noonday was a joy to the two families in this little corner of the world near the shores of the big lake of Michigan. The little village of Walhalla in remote northern Michigan had US Highway 10 running east and west through it, and Walhalla Road crossed it southward.

Lizzy Schreck lived in the village of Walhalla with her husband, Henry, on a twenty-acre homestead. Marla Jean hadn't started out living there. It was a gradual happening, and most people didn't understand the circumstances.

Lizzy and Henry reared two boys. Hank, not too ambitious, still lived at home. William was born with an obvious cleft palate. He was the younger and brighter of the two. Hank considered Marla Jean his servant and wouldn't leave her alone. Hank got along quite well with Marla Jean, as long as he did the talking and she did the listening. She learned from him, though, and he respected her in a careful way, although he never knew it. William, on the other hand, liked Marla Jean because she was black and he was white with a face only a mother could love. He could relate to being stared at, just as she was. Each of them was looked at by many who were curious and many others who were repulsed.

"Hey, Marla Jean, you know how many zeros are in one million dollars? Do you?" Hank asked Marla Jean.

"Lots of 'em, I 'pose."

"Well, you have to know, cuz someday somebody is going to make that much money, and it's going to be me. I'm going to be the first one in these parts to make a million dollars. What do you think about that? You believe me, don't ya?"

"Ten dollars is a lot of money to me."

"Lots and lots of tens make a million. More than you can count. When I'm rich, I'll have lots of coloreds working for me. Maybe even you and your baby. Come here and I'll show you how many zeros are in a million dollars."

Marla Jean walked over to the kitchen table and watched Hank write out the big number. He looked up at her and said, "See, there? Six. I'd pay you better than my mama pays ya, but you gotta do extra for me. You know what I mean?"

"You ain't got a million dollars yet, Hank. 'Sides, I work for your mama. Every day, I think about working for her and about my baby coming, that's all. Not no stupid zeros. Not no million dollars."

"What you think you are, smart-mouthing me? I'm gonna be a millionaire."

She walked away and softly sang, embellishing the words of a William Cullent Bryant poem: "Where are the flowers, the fair young flowers. The flowers that stood in the bright light, the gentle noonday flowers, where, oh, where are the flowers . . ."

She never had the time to sit around, listen to the stock-market report, and figure out how to make a million dollars. Hank was a dreamer, and fanciful dreaming for farming folks was usually limited to their slumber. He was no farmer, either. He knew nothing of the meaning of hard work. Over time, Marla Jean had become indispensable to the Schrecks. She was their hired *man* and knew how to work hard.

When she first arrived at the Schrecks', Marla Jean slept in the barn. She awoke one morning with Hank beside her. She stared at him, wondering how and when he'd come to her.

"What are you doin' here, Hank?"

"You nice and soft, Marla Jean. How ya gets a baby growing in ya?"

Marla Jean sat up and jerked away. "It's none of your business. Now, git outta here and don't come back."

"This is my barn, Marla Jean! Who planted the seed in ya, huh?"

"Hank! I'm calling your mama if you don't get goin'."

"Oh yeah? Not if I hold your mouth shut."

"How can I tell you, then?"

"I'll tie ya up 'til ya tell me and—show me."

Frightened, Marla Jean got up. "Get away from me, Hank."

William burst into the barn, immediately jumping over the bales of hay and grabbing Hank. He beat Hank, one punch after another. His anger was obvious and frightening to Marla Jean. She must have thought that if William didn't stop, he would kill his brother. And who knew who would be blamed. Finally William stopped and looked up at Marla Jean as if to say, *He won't bother you anymore.* Then he left the barn as fast as he'd come in. Hank was lying down, bleeding, moaning, and clutching his stomach. After several minutes, Hank slowly got up. He looked around, tears running down his battered cheeks.

Marla Jean waited, then spoke. "Hank, how many zeros are in a million? Tell me again."

He stopped and weakly replied. "You know already." Suddenly, he shouted, "I told ya a million times."

"Let's go to the house—okay?"

"All right, come on. I'll show ya again." Marla Jean followed Hank as he left the barn.

A month later, as Marla Jean's time came to its fullness, Lizzy moved her into the large pantry room off the kitchen. They carried all the staples and canned goods onto the back porch and squeezed a bed into the little room. Hank never bothered her there, either.

William had developed a young boy's crush on Marla Jean. She likely knew it and appreciated his shy way of showing it. He was more like his mother than Hank, who was more like his father. When William went away to school, she may have missed him more than she thought she would. He was book smart but also quick to learn from others. He was honest about who he was and expected the same in return. Marla Jean was surprised she liked who he was; he was a white boy, but also so much more.

Henry and Hank were home in the early morn of Noonday's birth but moved out of earshot by choice.

"I'm not liking that screaming, Pa. I can't hear the radio."

"We'll go where we can't hear it. Come on. You gonna help me in the barn today. Marla Jean can't help."

"But I don't wanna. Can't ya just wait 'til Marla Jean gets her baby?"

"Hank, Marla Jean won't be able to work even after she gets her baby—for a while, anyway. You're gonna have to help, so quit your fussing."

"Not now, Pa, the stock report's on. You can listen, too."

"We can't hear with the screaming. Come on."

"Listen, Pa. I think the baby is coming out now. Marla Jean's screaming real loud."

Henry grabbed Hank by the ear. "I'm gonna pull your ear off. Then ya won't hear half the screaming."

The two walked through the kitchen to the front door, and Henry marched right out.

Hank lingered, covering his ears and calling out, "You better hurry it up in there, Marla Jean. And cut out that screaming." He ran over to the pantry door and hollered through it, "You hear me? Cut out that screaming, Marla Jean!" He ran out of the house, slamming the door behind him.

Henry turned to make sure it was Hank who'd slammed the door. When Hank was beside him, he asked, "What do ya think, Hank? Why'd God give woman such a pitch in her voice that'd drive a good man from his own house?"

Hank responded, "Ya, you're right, Pa, why'd God give woman a mouth like a big ol' bitch hound dog?"

Like many men, Henry Schreck believed birthing babies was up to the woman, or the midwife, many of whom were as knowledgeable as the doctors. A man not immune to the ignorance of the times knew about the birthing of cows and the bedding of his woman, but not much else about reproduction. So, this day, while thinking about it, a subject he'd never given much thought to before, he guessed everything entered the world the same way according to the laws of God and nature. His wife never hollered when she gave birth. His cows didn't, either. Let the Almighty take care of it, he likely concluded.

Henry's woman was still womanly in her sixty-sixth year, although he took no notice of it. Even though her appearance revealed a face over which time plowed many a furrow, one could see the seeds of character planted there. The scents of her baking bread and the fresh Fels-Naptha line-dried laundry distinguished the woman as a dutiful wife and mother. The sweet pea and Sweet William bouquets from her flower garden dressed her meager home with floral grace as well. During the months Marla Jean worked for the Schrecks, it was Lizzy Schreck who bonded with the young black woman, a relationship that was totally unheard of at the time, as whites and blacks went separate ways and led separate lives.

Lizzy wondered about the young black woman who worked for her. She had grown attached to the bright, friendly, ambitious young lady who could and would do just about anything for her.

While Marla Jean stayed with the Schrecks, she suppered with the family, but afterward, she always retired to the barn. Every night, Lizzy walked to the barn with her and saw to her comfort by bringing along feather pillows and comfy quilts. She loved the girl, and often stayed in the barn talking and dreaming with her as the sunlight faded through the old barn wallboards. Marla Jean confided in Lizzy and told the woman about her former life in Idlewild; some of the bad parts shocked Lizzy, and the grandeur of the place shocked her, too. It was only in Marla Jean's ninth month when she moved to the house. As her baby came to full term, the anticipation of a child coming into the world turned their evening conversations into much happier talks.

"I love this child. My baby going to the Bell School and do more book learning, more'an me. She'll be something someday,

I know it," Marla Jean had said one night, then looked up at Lizzy for affirmation. The older woman smiled and nodded in agreement, like she always did.

The young woman, with her bright visions, continued. "I'm sure my baby's tomorrow will be a heap better than my yesterday. Ya know what I'm saying, Miz Lizzy?" Having the knowledge of her years, Lizzy knew what she meant. Marla Jean wanted her child to have what she would never have: schooling and the opportunities that accompanied it.

Where are the flowers, the fair young flowers that
  lately sprang and stood
In brighter light and softer airs, a beauteous
  sisterhood?
Alas! they are all in their graves; the gentle race of
  flowers . . .

And then I think of one who in her youthful
  beauty died,
The fair meek blossom that grew up and faded by
  my side.
In the cold, moist earth we laid her, when the
  forests cast the leaf,
And we wept that one so lovely should have a life
  so brief:
                          —William Cullen Bryant

The flower and the grassy knolls together,
Let your eye and mind appreciate
And let no blade touch its grandeur.
                          —Author Unknown

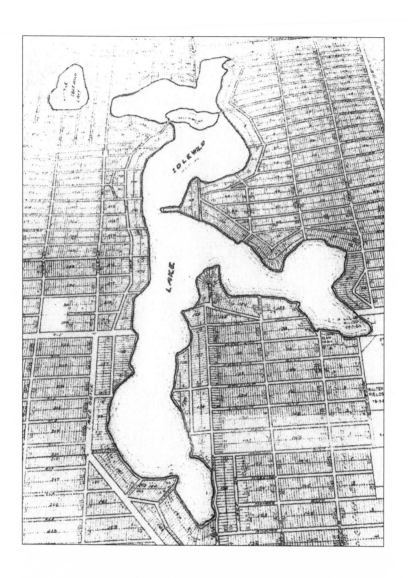

CHAPTER ONE

Idlewild

Idlewild, from where Marla Jean had come, was unlike Walhalla in every respect except in size. Located along US 10, about fifteen miles to the east of Walhalla, the marvelous and magical resort exploded on the scene in the 1920s and 1930s despite prejudice and segregation throughout the rest of the country.

From the 1920s forward, many blacks found this place in Michigan a getaway as precious as gold. It became the primary resort for middle-class and wealthy black people from across the United States, and was the biggest and best black resort in the Midwest. It was an escape from bigotry, and so blacks found this place a paradise. They returned, many of them, year after year. Why would blacks go to Las Vegas and be refused entry except at the back door (and even then, only to work) when they could go through the front door at a place in Michigan that offered big-name entertainment and facilities that were nothing less than plush?

During its peak, Idlewild was nestled in one of the wealthi-
est counties in Michigan. In the late 1920s, Idlewild was known
throughout the Midwest, and by the 1930s, its fame had spread
throughout the country. The names of the people who owned
lots there read like pages from the index of a black-history text.
The summer residents were doctors, businessmen, bankers, and
Chicago politicians, and the locals were sweet, strong women
and keen-witted men, with few exceptions.

Idlewild's glory was not written down in books but rather
told from one to another. Lee-Jon's Soda Bar was the center of
town, and became the meeting place for locals to gather and dis-
cuss Idlewild's growing popularity and the reason why of it all.

Two older men always sat on the great porch of Lee-Jon's,
and anyone who came to buy a magazine, cigarettes, or a soda
was captivated by the two men and their stories. Old Black Joe
and Sam Siggers were the ringleaders of all the conversations at
Lee-Jon's. The others there threw in whatever they knew, but
mostly they just listened to the wealth of information from the
mind pictures Joe and Sam created. The men allowed all to share
in their "thought pictures," and the children especially reveled in
Idlewild's history as they sat on the porch steps, making colorful
enlargements from the men's descriptions. The womenfolk did
not gather on the porch but always listened in as they meandered
inside to buy cream or milk and chat with Queenie, Sam Siggers's
wife, who was actually a more reliable bureau of information but
did not have the flair for "just a-sitting and a-talking."

I learned of Sam and Joe through residents who were present
at Lee-Jon's Soda Bar and had heard the stories. The following
script is my interpretation of some of Sam and Joe's dialogue.

One woman spoke out as she entered the store. "What's all
this talk 'round da porch? Why do they think 'bout things so
hard? If'n they worked just as hard, things might get done."

"Oh yes, is true what you say, dear, but I like the whooping and hollerin' and the belly laughin'. It's powerful good," Queenie answered her.

"Uh-huh . . ." the woman uttered as she walked closer to her.

Queenie explained, "If ya listen, even the words teach the young'uns about who they are and where the black men come from. Is good."

Through the opened window, they listened as Sam started one of his tales.

"You hear about old Gin Face burying up his coins years back?" Sam asked.

"I hear'd some. Where 'bouts he bury 'em?" Joe asked, knowing Sam was getting started on a story.

"Says it's a treasure. Uh-huh. Gin Face buried them treasures before the porch was made. Now, he can't get at 'em. He's gotten to be a big tub a lard, you know. Can't get at his treasure— cuz he can't fit under dat porch." Laughter burst out. The women in the soda bar heard it, too, and shook their heads and rolled their eyes.

"He's just too fat, and mean, too, but his wife just ignores him," Sam continued. "What he do? Just leaf it buried?" Old Joe asked.

"He didn't want to, but—he hadda think on it a spell. Uh-huh, ol' Gin Face, he's a thinking man."

"How come you call him 'Gin Face,' Mister Siggers, sir? That his real name?" a child asked.

"Well, now, I's tell you how come . . ." Sam sat back and reflected upon his telling. He cleared his throat and said, "He's got the face of my ol' Vir-ginny home where Queenie and I come from. Yup, his mouth is like that valley there, and his nose is as big as the mountain from behind where I lived." Again, laughter filled the porch. "Yup, just like my ol' Vir-ginny home. If I'm feeling homesick, I get on over and visit him a spell."

Sam stopped, took a sip of his soda water, leaned back, and closed his eyes. His eyes didn't open soon enough to suit his anxious listeners.

"Well? What about them coins, Sam? Did Gin Face ever git at 'em?"

"Hold on, and I'll tell ya . . ." Sam thought about his story and soon spoke again.

"That ornery cuss made his young'uns fetch 'em. Yup, first 'twas the oldest who crawled in there. Then . . ." Again, Sam paused.

"Well, did the boy find them?"

Sam smiled. "Naw, he didn't. Now, this is what happened . . . God's honest truth." He paused. "That boy crawled under there, all right, but he backed up outta there so fast, a-pantin' and heaving and not black no more. He was white with fright."

"How come? He run into a varmint under there? Did it cold-cock 'im?" The group laughed.

"No, sir! I's been told . . . now, listen up good." Everyone looked at Sam as he continued with his now serious declaration.

"*He done found a human carcass under there.* Not the whole thing, mind you, just the . . . head. Yup, someone rolled it under ol' Gin's porch. Probably aiming to get even at him for his double-crossing ways."

The youngsters who were gathered on the porch steps stared into midair, the whites of their eyes boldly circling their black irises, their eyelashes curled back to their foreheads.

"Stop your foolish talk. You's scaring the young'uns!" Queenie yelled through the opened window.

"Hey, I'm tellin' the truth," Sam said, looking to the window that connected the store and its porch.

The woman mumbled as she left the store with her purchase. "Uh-huh. Human head, treasures—marvelous talk, uh-huh . . ." Silence surrounded the woman as she waddled off the porch, her abdomen leading the way. Wishing her a speedier stroll, the group watched as the woman walked out of sight. In unison, everyone turned back to Sam, anxious for him to continue. "A real head? *Really!* A head of a real human bein'?"

"Yep. Now, that young'un of Gin's a-fixin' to leave. Says he waked up the dead, and now the 'spirits' not leaving him alone. None of Gin's other children wants to go after those coins, nohow, even if ol' Gin offers to give 'em some. No siree. Last I heard, ol' Gin's a-fixin' to tear down the old porch. But now, his wife's a-hollering about how they gonna git into that house. She's a big one, too. No siree, neither of them can jump *that* high!"

Again, laughter burst out on the porch. Old Sam Siggers, the ringleader of the porch congregation, was Father Confessor and a humorist to boot, with facts tried and true and some not so true. He was Idlewild's history book, and when opened to the pages of actual fact, he was still hard to believe.

In time, an inquiring child asked Sam, "How'd this fine place get so fine?"

He smiled and nodded. "Yes, indeed, is fine, mighty fine."

He looked at the child and once again started to tell Idlewild's story, always remembering to add the latest to its notable history.

"Well, I know'd all about it from my older sister, Lela, God bless her soul. She was my mama's first child. She, Lela, was at the start of it back in the early days. Then it was an Idlewild Resort Company. A few decades ago, they turned everything over to the all-black Idlewild Lot Owners' Association, which my sister headed up."

Old Joe broke in. "That resort company was headed up with white men, ain't that right, Sam?"

"Oh ya, but they weren't hogs. No siree, they were good men. They had know-how to sell, but we got our share, too."

"Too bad us blacks and them whites can't work together like they did back then."

"Ya, you's right, Joe. That's a cryin' shame of it, ain't it? I still worry seeing a white face come 'round."

"Mister Sam, why we got schools just for us niggers and then schools for just the white childs?" an older youngster asked.

Unusual silence enclosed the porch as everyone looked to Sam for the answer.

"Don't rightly know, child, just the way it is. We have our own way to get where we're going. We get going to our own schools, but there's no reason I can think of, why you can't go to the white school, if'n ya want. Someday you will."

"I love it here. Is glad your sister bought this town," another child remarked.

"Well, now . . . she didn't do it all alone. Ya see, it all started way back in the year of nineteen hundred and thirteen. In Chicago, you know that fine town, south a-here? There was a big con-ven-shun, of sorts, called 'ex-po' somethin' or 'nother. That's where the white men made a miracle happen! They sold lots to Negroes! Getting the finance help of Wilbur Lemon of Chicago, and getting the good brothers, named Adelbert and E. G. Branch, to carve out the plots, it happened. Lela boarded a train to White Cloud, Michigan, where those Branch brothers met 'em and took her and other buyers over yonder to have a look. Adelbert and E. G., the Christian men that they were, sold the land cheap. I remember a Charlie Gass, who sold properties from his stand as a shoeshine man, imagine that? After that, Lela and Charlie and others like 'em became what they called de-vel-o-pers. Lela sold lots for the association for thirty-five dollars each. Yup, just thirty-five dollars. Or if that was too steep, you could buy for six dollars down and one dollar a month with no interest on it. Then, Lela's income was paid to her either in cash money or with property. So, she chose property."

"From that point on, this place exploded into a place for our people to va-ca-shun—ain't that right, Sam?"

"Yup. It started over yonder on the island, with the good, good fishing. The carp caught over there was as big as this here." Sam extended his arms far apart. "And those fish was gold all over. Ya had to cover your eye for the pain of it. And they had scales on 'em as big as half-dollar coins."

"Old Ma Buckles was the first lady on the island. Then the others came. Joe and me built the Purple Palace, a fine place with the color of the ripest plum. Remember, Joe, the first entertainers?" Sam laughed and Old Joe nodded with sweet recollection.

"It was a four-woman band and, boy, could those ladies roll out the tunes. One played on the piano, one on the drums, and one played the horn."

"What that other lady do, Joe?" Not waiting for Joe to answer, Sam continued. "Oh ya, then we hadda build them doghouses."

"Why? Was there too many dogs?" a child asked.

Sam looked over at Joe and the two chuckled. "Uh-huh," Sam said. "The dogs started coming 'round. Lots and lots of dogs." The two old men laughed wholeheartedly.

"We're meaning the two-legged dogs. They came from far and wide. They wanted lodging for little or nothing. We called them doghouses 'cause they were so small, just big enough for a dog or two. And the rent was cheap."

Sam stopped talking for a moment, then, with a long drawl, said, "Yup, it all . . . started . . . over there . . . on the island." Dreamy-eyed, he continued, "And soon, Idlewild had a grocery store, eatin' cafe, trinket shop, and with the Hotel Casa Blanca built up, we's still growing."

"Got a post office now and a dress shop for the ladies, and Lee-Jon's Soda Bar. 'Member, we built it, just Sam and me."

"Yup, I 'member, Old Joe, I do 'member . . ."

Sam looked at the children, then pointed to Joe. "This here's a good man, and he's not seeing so good anymore, but he drove in 'bout every nail you see here. Yes siree, he help build near everythin' in this town, starting with them doghouses. He can hear real good, so don't ya ever try putting anything over Old

Joe. He can tell how many of yous are here on this porch right now. Right, Joe?"

Old Joe nodded.

"He hears you come up the steps and keeps the count in his head, ain't that right now, Joe?"

Old Joe nodded again and proudly said, "There's nine of ya here right now, counting me and Sam."

"Then, after the island, and the rest of the place started building up, wow-de-wow! Did the entertainin' begin?" Sam said.

"Like what kind of entertaining you mean, Mister Siggers?" asked a youngster.

"Like the Chitlin Circuit, and we be proud to be part of it. Pigmeat Markham and Lottie, the Body Fantastique comes here and puts on a great show."

"'Member Peg-Leg Pete, Sam?" And Big Maybelle?"

"Roy Hamilton, Art Prysock, and LaVern Baker. Those are great guys—mighty talented."

"Oh ya, they brought the crowds in. The people was as thick as the sand on Idlewild's beach—and Paradise's beach and Watermill's and Tank's beach, too."

"All the sands on all the beaches," Old Joe added.

All the children looked at the two old men and marveled at their knowledge. Everyone returned to their homes full of pleasure and knowledge that the black race was well and good and worthy of the opportunities afforded them. Prosperity abounded in Idlewild when segregation policies in the rest of the country limited black people's options for traveling, entertainment, and lifestyle. And so the stage was set, and for forty-odd years, this small Lake County village flourished as a mecca for top-name black entertainment. Idlewild burst into a showcase of big-name entertainers and never-ending parties. It became a jumpin', thumpin', summer-long Mardi Gras in the woods.

Whenever Sam had a crowd gathered around him, his mind was always working, whether he was talking or not. And even in his sleep, he relived his past, remembering vividly his beloved Idlewild. Sam Siggers possessed more information in that head of his than even he knew what to do with. He became a showman, typical of his surroundings, and his elaborate display of telling Idlewild's history always drew a crowd to the porch. One day, all at once, a bunch of thoughts ran through the caverns of his mind and spewed out the tunnel of his mouth, revealing the actuality of Idlewild's fame.

"It's a hubbub here, all right. And the people, they keep on coming. One time me an' Joe counted up to a hundred people, then we lost our count. Plunging into nonstop partying, some reach a breakdown, then there is no stopping 'em. Even after the liquor can't be sold anymore, the die-hards carry their bottles with them to the late-night joints like the Club El Morocco or The Hippy Dippy and order a bowl of ice, ginger ale, or club soda. The setups, along with their own shots, keep them going 'round the clock. The singing and dancing and partying gets to be so loud, I heard even the fish were jumping one night to Ol' Bill Doggett's 'Honky Tonk' song."

"I'm obliged to know you children sleep through it. Yous don't need to know 'bout this late-night stuff," said Sam.

"'Member when they called up the National Guard to help direct all the traffic? That was something!" Old Joe remarked.

"Who is it who comes here, Mister Siggers, sir? You know'd them all?" asked a young child sucking on his peppermint stick.

"Oh, let me see—Dr. Dan . . . Dr. Daniel Hale Williams. He bought land here. He's a doctor, for the heart. Yes siree, he was the first doctor to open up the heart and fix it, and close it up and it beat good as new. He's a black man, and he was the first doctor to do that!" Sam sat tall in his rocking chair and leaned forward as he proudly continued to speak the words everyone hungered for.

"Then, too, there is Mr. W. E. B. Du Bois. He is another early buyer. He is a man full of figuring. He started the club of the National A-ssocia-shun for the Ad-vance-ment of Colored People. He is a social activist for us colored folks. Mr. Web, I call him, is a smart, right-good man. Another good man, Charlie Chesnutt, comes here, too. Right, Joe?"

"This here's a everybody-knows-everybody town, ain't that right, Sam?"

Sam lifted his hand in the air and pointed his finger at Joe. "An' a drinkin'-whiskey, kicking-up-your-heels kind of town. I heard it tell that we made a town ahead of our time."

Sam's eyes widened. "I heard a poem by a writer name of Mr. Dunbar. It goes like this: 'If ya ebber want to git to hebben quick. Come here to Idlewild.'" Sam winked at Joe and said, "Ain't that the truth, Joe?"

"Yes siree, Sam," he said. "And I know'd a lady who cured her ailments here. It was our waters that did it. She waded into the lake, and just like that, her room-a-tism was gone. That's rightly so, rightly so."

Sam snorted, inhaling a laugh, and when Sam laughed, everyone did.

"We don't need the white folks comin' 'round here. We can do just right by ourselves," an older child boasted.

"Hush your mouth, child. We outta take our hats off to those white men who started it all. They did not squeeze the lemon dry. They give us that lemon with enough left to make lemonade. We just added our own sugar. You young'uns know this. They were open, square-minded men. Understanding the past and understanding the why of things takes a heap of thinkin'. You never sit in judgment. That's the Good Lawd's job." Again, Sam leaned forward in his rocking chair and stared intently at the children.

"You give credit where it's due, but always be proud you is black, all of yous. Is not true that us black people are just branches in the wind with no connection to the tree. Be proud of the tree you are a part of. Is a strong tree with deep-in-the-ground roots. The white people have their own tree of self-respect, and we have it, too. Just think of the great black people before you. They were doers, not just 'wish-washer wishers.' They felt their freedom beneath their feet. Naw, it never came easy. Time and time again, the black man, the black woman, their branches tossed every which way, but their feet, like the roots of the tree, stayed planted on the ground. They found the way to a proud life. Pride rules the black man's will. So—you angel faces smile and jump over your gloom if'n ya have it. Though I see no gloom in you, that's good. You is black, it can't be denied. Be humble 'bout it, but be proud. So, don't be a lazybone; work hard in school and be proud of who you be."

As the years passed, one day nearing the end of the Lee-Jon's era of history lessons and storytelling, Old Joe turned eighty years old. Sam Siggers himself, nearly seventy, saw folks gathering together at the far end of town.

"What's Jackie Wilson and those kids conjuring up now, some kind of marchin' parade?" Suddenly, they could hear music in the distance, and it soon drew closer to the porch of the soda shop.

"I hear 'em, they's comin' this way," Old Joe remarked, looking upward, since it was his ears informing him, not his eyes.

Jackie Wilson, a veteran Idlewild performer, gathered up all the children from the beaches and parking lots to sing a tribute to the oldest member of the village. Many joined the parade as they meandered to the center of town. The large group of singers stopped in front of Lee-Jon's, and Jackie Wilson led his glee club in a moving rendition of "Old Black Joe."

> *Gone are the days when my heart was young and*
> *   gay;*
> *Gone are my friends from the cottonfields away;*

Gone from the earth to a better land I know, I
hear their gentle voices calling,
"Old— Black —Joe," I'm— com—ing, I'm—
com—ing, For my head is bending low;
I hear those gentle voices calling,
"Old— Black— Joe!"

Within the group, a young teenage girl, Trixie Siggers, whose lead voice guided the others in a performance, moved the town to heartfelt tears. And Old Joe, whose eyes were sightless, could clearly see the music coming from deep within those heart-shaped boxes—the voice boxes of Idlewild's kind people.

Talented Trixie Siggers was Sam and Queenie's granddaughter, a bright and spirited young girl. Her mother, Sam's only daughter, had left home for the big city a long time ago. Only once did she make it home again, and that was seventeen years before when, as quickly as she'd come, she'd left, leaving her newborn with Sam and Queenie.

A great sadness dwelt within their hearts; they hoped for their daughter's return, but after a time, Sam and his wife concentrated on a beginning with their new granddaughter and, to their surprise, Trixie filled that void. So, when Trixie started talking about going away, about wanting a career in show business, the Siggerses became alarmed.

"You wanna get into show business, do ya? Well, you ain't gonna run off to any New York City or Hallywood, like your mama. You can get into show business right here, and that's all that's comin' outta this here mouth on that subject."

Sam didn't know Trixie had a boyfriend named Johnny Flower.

When Trixie finally introduced him to her grandfather, Sam frowned with squinty eyes and said, "Where'd you come from with a name like Flower? You're pretty enough, but you're no magnolia, maybe more of a weed. You better not be planting yourself here."

Sam paused, then asked, "You in school?"

Trixie was infatuated with Johnny, and her affections were returned. Talk of running away together evolved into a promise that, when she was ready, he'd take her to California to find her mother. Johnny hung around Lee-Jon's more often than Sam wanted him there. Sometimes Sam didn't notice him as the boy stood off in the shadows of the porch. Johnny patiently waited for Trixie to see him so she could sneak away and join him. Inevitably, Sam found them. Sam called her foolish, and she called Johnny exciting. This went on for a good part of a year, and then, from what this writer understood, Trixie saw the light, and their last rendezvous tells the tale.

Johnny pleaded, "Come on, Trixie, let's just go. You've saved up money. I have a little, and we'll find work if we run out."

"Oh, find work, yah? We are working now! I thought we were going to save enough money to go all the way. Think, Johnny, who is going to hire a black couple and feed us and house us, too?"

"Trixie, you know my dad takes the money I earn in the fields. I can only take back what is mine when he is drunk. I have to convince him the next day that what is left is all we earned."

"Yes, I know. I'm sorry, Johnny, but that tells me you are weak."

Trixie and Johnny stopped seeing each other. Johnny still came around, but Trixie did not yield to his suggestions that they start seeing each other again.

☙

In deciding to write all this down about Idlewild and its good people, I would like to add my interpretation regarding the differences under which each of these young teens lived: Johnny, abused; Trixie, loved. The reason for their breakup became pretty clear. Trixie loved her grandparents, and because she knew their love for her would never fail, she decided she'd never hurt them by leaving like her mother had. Johnny, on the other hand, lived with a father who controlled him and, at the same time, failed him in every respect, unlike Trixie's family.

I bring fresh showers for the thirsting flowers,
From the seas and streams;
I bear light shade for the leaves when laid
In their noonday dreams.
From my wings are shaken the dews that waken
The sweet buds every one,
When rocked to rest on their mother's breast,
As she dances about the sun.

—Percy Bysshe Shelley

Heavenly seen, a cloud serene.
Heavenly homed, our Marla Jean.

—C. Ohse

CHAPTER TWO

Marla Jean

And so, Idlewild's history developed throughout the 1920s and 30s, although many, at the time, disregarded its importance, and nothing was written down. Some of the blacks wanted to share in Idlewild's wealth without contributing. Some thought it was free or that it was their due. Thanks to Sam and Joe, Idlewild's history remained alive. After Joe died, Sam slowed down. The stories of Idlewild's prominent history were put to rest within the caverns of the old man's mind.

Sam and Joe were not known in Walhalla. Neither was the greatness of Idlewild. While some white folks found their way into the clubs and heard the great music, many did not. I knew of Sam and Joe through research later in my life. Much of what they shared on that porch many years ago was true.

☙

I was born and raised in Walhalla. In the beginning, even though I lived so close to Idlewild, I knew very little about the resort. Now that I am old—a retired schoolteacher whose past years echo like some long-forgotten time, the true bits and pieces of Idlewild have come together. Some facts I found easily, while others have come to me from other people's reminiscences. Noonday Flower, my daughter in every respect but legally, and Robert Olie Brenner, a special neighbor and friend—my former students—are both principal in my composition of facts with prose worthy of writing their stories. I hold dear the revelation and repetition of the stories of Idlewild and beyond.

One thing is certain, if anything is certain: Maggie Johnson Dunn Millgard will recollect and share with you one story at a time.

৵৩

Marla Jean lived in the middle of the best of times in the wondrous place of Idlewild, although good fortune, short-lived for Marla Jean, was a mystery to many black people. Marla Jean was nearly twenty when she died. Although she was a married young lady who had come from Idlewild's woods east of Walhalla, little was known about the young woman's husband and their life together. No one except Lizzy Schreck knew very much about Marla Jean, and no one in Walhalla knew very much about Idlewild, including Lizzy Schreck. The young black woman had come to the white community to find work. Many people questioned why she had come to Walhalla to work when a job in Idlewild would have been preferred. Many said she was a lost soul seeking more than work, or hiding from something, but what, no one knew or cared.

There were definite class distinctions, even among the black people in Idlewild, and Marla Jean was a part of the mix. The residents were all same race, but the wealthy were the upper crust, even though they were not stingy. They invested their money in the successful black resort, and successful it was. In addition to wealthy vacationers, entertainers, permanent residents, and sporting men, the poorer black community began to settle in outlying townships of Idlewild that weren't funded with investments, but they still wanted to jump on the bandwagon.

Marla Jean was fifteen when her family moved from Gary, Indiana, to Idlewild. Her father had lost his job and had heard of the cheap land and easy living in Idlewild. So Marla Jean, her mother, father, and four brothers moved into a basement house. At that time, there were many unfinished, cavelike structures in Idlewild's outlying townships. A finished upright, wood-sided home was a dream at most then, but in time, may have been realized. After the family's arrival, I believe Marla Jean's mother and father were looked down upon by the other residents of Idlewild. Their educational and economic background, as well as their inept social skills, were likely the reasons.

Most of the poor newcomers became permanent residents living on public assistance, working when and where they could. People earning as little as three to four dollars for twelve days of picking fruit and vegetables could not afford to go to the nightclubs or partake in any of the festivities in Idlewild. Marla Jean's whole family must have spent long days in the fields, picking beans, cherries, and peaches for cash. This money enabled the family to eat through the winter months.

The facilities at the farms were not fit for human use. Only one outside toilet was supplied for many workers. A diet of vegetables, rice, and salt pork was provided, but no milk or other meat. More than likely, the farmers themselves were poor, as the profits from their crops were often minimal, depending on the growing season and weather.

It was true that Marla Jean Atlas, along with her mom and dad—whose nickname was Attie—and four reluctant brothers, worked the Michigan fields day after day, year after year. One by one, the brothers left; some said goodbye, but some didn't bother. Finding work in Idlewild proved futile for every young black man who wanted the good jobs in the clubs. The waiter, parking-lot-attendant, and even the janitorial jobs were taken well ahead of any newcomers.

Marla Jean was sixteen years old when her last brother left. She had grown to be a pretty girl, and soon she was an attractive teenager with deep-brown eyes and dark yet golden-hued skin. She was not willing to join in with the other young female vagabonds and seek out the action in the village proper. Devoted to her parents and their needs, Marla Jean not only worked hard in the fields but also cleaned and cooked in a far-from-livable basement home far into the night, even after Moms and Daddy Attie had retired.

Many late nights, by candlelight, she retrieved her handwritten alphabet from beneath her pillow and recited the sounds over and again. This was indeed a hard life for a young girl trying to find her sense of direction while appreciating her daily bread and breath. After Marla Jean left Gary, Indiana, she did not go to school—not formally, anyway. The farmers did give the youngsters time to gather in the shade to rest and read to each other. The very young just slept while the older youngsters looked at the pictures in the books. They were tired, and reading did not seem important to them. Many did not make good use of the time and were called back into the fields. Every chance Marla Jean had, she picked up her favorite reader and began to read, not well, but well enough to grasp the meaning. Lizzy Schreck told me that she loved poems best for their rhyming melody. She cherished one poem in particular; its ending she knew by heart, repeating and repeating its rhythm of similar sounds.

> And then I think of one who in her youthful
>   beauty died,
> The fair meek blossom that grew up and faded by
>   my side.

In the cold, moist earth we laid her, when the
forests cast the leaf,
And we wept that one so lovely should have a life
so brief:
Yet not unmeet it was that one, like that young
friend of ours,
So gentle and so beautiful, should perish with the
flowers

Eventually, Moms became ill and bedridden. Marla Jean took to her bedside to tend to her. Moms was not an old woman, but work, poverty, and medical unknowns were taking their toll on her. Marla Jean knew Moms was burning with fever, so she bathed her with a cool cloth and read to her. One story in particular told of a lesson that many youth must learn, a choice between two roads. One road is hilly and rough, the other broad and smooth.

"[W]hile the lad stood in doubt as to which way he should go, he saw two ladies coming toward him, each by a different road.

"O noble youth," said one, "this is the road which you should choose. It will lead you into pleasant ways where there is neither toil, nor hard study, nor drudgery of any kind."

Marla Jean continued, engrossed in this tale of lessons to be learned.

"If you take my road," said the other fair woman, "you will find that it is rocky and rough, and that it climbs many a hill and descends into many a valley and quagmire. The views which you will sometimes get from the hilltops are grand and glorious, while the deep valleys are dark and the uphill ways are toilsome; but the road leads to the blue mountains of endless fame, of which you can see a faint glimpse, far away. They cannot be reached without labor; for, in fact, there is nothing worth having that must not be won through toil."

One fair lady in the story, named "Pleasure," and the other fair lady, named "Labor," intrigued Marla Jean. As she finished the story, she thought intently upon the youth's choice.

"I will follow your road, Labor, and whether I shall ever reach the blue mountains or not, I want to have the reward of knowing that my journey has not been without some worthy aim."

Quietly, Moms said to her beloved daughter, "You's my aim, my Marla Jean. You is my journey, and you is my reward."

Her last cough took her last breath and refused her another. The realization of her mother's death seized the young girl with terror.

Marla Jean wailed at her mother's bedside, "Wake up, Moms. Wake up! Moms, Moms, don't leave me!" She shook her mother again and again. When Moms did not wake up, Marla Jean slowly backed away. Staring at her dead mother, Marla Jean noticed Moms's vacant stare looking back at her. Then Moms's eyes slowly closed. Like viewing an apparition, Marla Jean may have witnessed her mother's soul in motion to a better place. Stunned with disbelief, she blinked continually to stop her tears, but it was to no avail; they fell like the torrent of a waterfall.

Marla Jean and Daddy Attie buried Moms just behind their basement house. No one else was there. Father and daughter began their improper burial of wife and mother without saying a word to each other. A feeling came over the young girl in a cold wave that rose up her backbone. Its shiver shook her, exhausted her, and she fell to her knees crying and sobbing, yelling, "I'm poor, I'm black, I'm empty, I'm numb—I'm dead, too!"

Daddy Attie backed away, unaware of how to comfort his wailing, grieving daughter, lost within his own muted self.

Depression took a hold of Marla Jean, and she didn't get out of bed for days. When she did, she sat outside next to her mother's grave and desperately talked to her.

"Moms, I'm scared. I'm no good without you. What do I do now?"

Looking around, she stared at the muddy ground that had become even more saturated from many nighttime rains. Trash lay everywhere, and there were broken bottles and cans scattered as far as one could see.

"Daddy is drinking more. All our money goes to making more brew. Our basement is flooded with smelly drink that his friends toss, saying it's bad brew. I'm drowning here, Moms. I don't know what to do." She paused, then quickly declared, "I want to be with you."

Voicing her plan aloud, she decided "it's the only way . . . I can't stay here. I can't live without you."

The young, impressionable girl stood. Then, suddenly, as if compelled to look up, she tilted her head back and witnessed the sun burst out from behind dark clouds rather quickly. It momentarily blinded her as she had to squint against its brilliance. Raising her hand to her forehead, she was able to shade her eyes to see more clearly. The sun was directly on top of her, and its warmth penetrated her, head to toe. The comforting sensation enveloped her, persuading her to linger outside.

Before returning to the house, a den of neglect and uncertainty, she instinctively looked back at her mom's grave. Immediately, she saw a dazzling reflection. The reflection was bouncing off something a few feet from Moms's resting spot. It seemed to be coming up from the ground like a plant that had just decided to grow. The reflection possessed the girl to get closer. She needed to dig a little, but several rainy days had helped wash away a lot of dirt. Rather quickly, she discovered the source of the bright reflection. She resurrected from the earth a small mirror attached to something she thought had to be the handlebar of a bicycle. Marla Jean found a second handlebar, and if she kept digging, she knew in her heart, she'd unearth a complete bicycle.

She may have thought, *Which brother saved enough money to buy a bicycle? Why was it buried, and for how long?* Immediately, she thought of her father and how mean he was to her brothers. She prayed that, wherever they were, they were well and happy.

Was it the sun or was it Moms herself releasing the sun's amazing reflection on the mirror for her daughter? Marla Jean walked back toward the house with a smile and said out loud, "You're here, Moms, you are! You're here with me!" It took days to unearth the bike, as the girl had to do it on the sly, then hide it again.

⁓

In my writing, I knew I had to include Idlewild's dark side. Years later, I'm attempting to write the truth of it, but I still struggle with writing about those who didn't want to appreciate Idlewild's success and would rather engage in more dreadful behavior.

Flowers brighter than the rose,
Bloomed in the blackest of the hearth for her;
Out of a sullen hollow in a livid hill-side,
Her mind could make an Eden.
                                        —Charlotte Brontë

Her mind could make a sinless Eden.
                                        —C. Ohse

CHAPTER THREE

Black Eden

Continuing with Marla Jean's background in Idlewild, even though I was not witness to these happenings, I have recorded interviews to cite their validity.

᰷

Marla Jean's daddy, along with others, convinced themselves that they needed an escape from boredom and the drudgery of their lives. Making their own alcoholic brew with a crude apparatus, assembled in Attie's basement house, they set their medical cures on course. On the days and nights the appliance was not in operation, it had to be disguised in the corner in which it sat. So Marla Jean told a few nosy neighbors that the curtained gray area was her bedroom.

The more Attie and his friends got together to celebrate the day's end or to numb their existence, the more Attie relied on his homemade brew. "To medicate my ailments," is how Attie explained his indulgence to Marla Jean and others. She hated it because of the drunkenness that inevitably followed. It scared her.

On the many nights Attie sat at home with his friends drinking the homemade brew, he never noticed, or didn't care, that a middle-aged man kept looking at Marla Jean. Dragging intensely on his cigarette, the man stared at her from beneath his puffy eyelids with narrow, slanting eyes. The more he drank, the more he looked at her. The heavily bearded man peered at Marla Jean through the black disks of his pupils. She was invaded by this man and, in truth, abused by all those present, including her own father.

The wretched men whom Attie spent time with referred to themselves as the Cavemen, and they were content with their wildcat ventures. No doubt the liquor made its way into stomachs, but more into empty minds. To the young, innocent Marla Jean, they did, in fact, look a lot like cavemen, and she worried that one day the man she feared most, the one who kept looking at her, would drag her off by her hair, a club in one hand and a drink in the other. She must have visualized the whole scenario and saw herself resisting the merciless Caveman, but inevitably he would knock her out and succeed in dragging her away. It was a frequent daydream, and Marla Jean tried desperately to put it out of her mind. Afraid to retire to bed on the nights when the Cavemen gathered, Marla Jean found her way into Idlewild.

"Hey, Attie, where's dat woman dawter of yours?" one Caveman asked as he took his first drink of the evening while looking around for Marla Jean. "You oughta get a hold of dat child and shut dat door. Allowing her to g'wan to town, you's asking for trouble. Yessuh, I know'd what ah'm talking 'bout. Them dogs gonna suckle her, yessuh."

"Don't rile me no more! Just lemme have my liquor. I know'd Marla Jean, she's good," Attie retorted.

"Ya mean she's too good! Ask her in the morning what she ketch!"

Laughter shook the place as the men drank more of the hell-fired spirits that razed the body and consumed the soul.

℃⁊

"Maggie, Maggie Johnson, get your tail back here," my father would yell at me. As a child, I didn't get far, even in my wanderings around the homestead. My mother and father were hardworking Swedish immigrants. We farmed and stayed within a five-mile radius, like a lot of the folks in the Walhalla area.

In these pioneering years of the 1930s and 1940s, Idlewild became a black Eden, although my mother and father knew little about it. If any in Walhalla had gotten over to see the place, they would have said it wasn't any different than the hundreds of nearby lakes being turned into white resorts and campgrounds. At a time when segregation knew no bounds, Idlewild became a welcome refuge. As described in a brochure, circulated among the blacks only, Lake Idlewild was "renowned for its sparkling streams of crystal waters"—and a whole lot more.

℃⁊

Subsequently, Marla Jean uncovered the whole bicycle when her father wasn't home or was drunk enough not to care what she was doing. As it turned out, she had a lot of time. Once uncovered, she worked on it every day and, in time, hid her only mode of transportation the best she could. This was what she needed because it distracted her from her present living conditions and gave her purpose to think about its usefulness.

The impressionable young Marla Jean found her way to Lake Idlewild on her bicycle, and she found her way to God because He was there. She could see the electric lights and hear the music in the distance. She reached the lake, riding along a wooden boardwalk surrounded by cottages and rental bungalows.

As Marla Jean meandered through the beautiful area, she noticed street names: Unity, Sincerity, Generosity, Kindness, and Patience. This was a town of glitter and gaiety, of sport and celebration, but also of warmth and love.

She stopped and paused, amazed at what she was feeling.

Wrapping her arms around herself, she may have said aloud, "Feel the air, look at the sky, Marla Jean. Like a soft blue blanket. The trees—the flowers. The water, so clear, with ripples for dreams to sail on. The sun, it whispers to me. The sun is my friend. Listen, I hear the songs of birds."

It was the most beautiful place Marla Jean had ever been.

᠀

Marla Jean still worked in the fields with Daddy Attie on the days he made it to work. Because he was older, and because of his addiction to alcohol, he didn't put in a full day's work anymore. And, many times, he had to sleep off his increasingly frequent drunken binges from the night before. So, whenever the opportunity presented itself, Marla Jean snuck away on her bike. Daddy Attie didn't pay much attention to his daughter, so she was free to do things on her own for the first time in her life. At almost seventeen, Marla Jean may have thought of herself as fully grown. I'm sure she was happy about this newfound freedom, even though money was a problem, since they were not working as much. And while Daddy Attie did make a little extra money selling his homemade moonshine, he must have kept that for himself.

One night, Marla Jean strong-mindedly grabbed her bike, peddled hard, and *did* venture farther toward the lights and sounds of the bustling village of Idlewild. It wasn't long before the music drew her in, and there was no turning back. Suddenly, people surrounded her. Men were dressed like mannequins, stiffly starched in their best attire. Women, dragging their furs, wore sequined gowns and sported their best jewelry. Marla Jean had never seen anything like it. Right away, she felt she was in a fairyland.

She stopped, holding on to her bike, and just stood there in the center of the village. She may have asked herself, *Where do these beautiful people come from?*

Handsome car-parking valets greeted smiling guests from big cities like Chicago, Detroit, and Cleveland. Handsome doormen escorted people into the club. Lights twinkled everywhere. Happiness permeated the fairyland as people were smiling and laughing, coming and going.

The girl, who felt out of place, got caught up in the charisma and glamour of Idlewild, the likes of which she had never seen before. Before she fully understood where she was or how obviously she stood out, a deep female voice, full of friendliness, spoke to her.

"What's yaw doin' here, girl?"

Startled, Marla Jean quickly replied, "Nothin'."

"Come here and get out of the way."

"Can I bring my bike . . . over there?"

"Yes, by me. Bikes okay."

Suddenly, Marla Jean thought the better of it. "Oh no. I'm—I'm sorry, I gotta go."

"No, you're not leaving now. You're in the way. You'll have to wait until everyone gets in."

Awkwardly, Marla Jean crossed the street with her bicycle. She stood like a statue, her bicycle lying at her feet.

The young woman next to her never stopped moving as she ushered people inside the anonymous building.

The pretty young woman asked again, "So, what are you doing here? Are you alone? Kinda late for you, isn't it?"

Marla Jean cringed at the questions. "I'm alone."

"What's your name?"

"Marla Jean." She paused and then said, "I . . . I wanna see
. . ."—she pointed—"this."

"Can't blame you there. I'm Trixie."

Soon, most of the people around them had dispersed. Marla
Jean didn't know what to say or do, so she quickly said, "I gotta
go now."

"Come on, I'll walk you out," the young woman replied.

The girls walked away together, one with a bicycle, one with
a fast step, and both with smiles at the start of the music that,
over time, would gain world-renowned fame. I'm not sure how
much more was said between the two teenagers before Marla
Jean got on her bike and left that night.

ↄ

It was the summer of 1928 when Marla Jean met Trixie Siggers,
Sam and Queenie's granddaughter. Trixie, over the course of
two years, had started working at the celebrated Flamingo Club
as an exotic singer and dancer. But all Marla Jean knew at the
time was that Trixie had to have been the most beautiful woman
in the whole wide world.

Over the next few months, Trixie and Marla Jean became
the best of friends. Trixie got Marla Jean a job at the club, and
when Trixie wasn't dancing, she helped Marla Jean wait tables.
It took Marla Jean a while to learn waitressing; it wasn't that
simple. Marla Jean couldn't write or spell very well, but Trixie
was always at her side to help her learn the club's shorthand.
Carrying a tray of drinks and food was not an easy task, either.

"What if I drop it, Trixie? I don't wanna drop anything.
They'll make me leave. I can't leave here, Trixie. I can't."

"Hey, you're not gonna drop anything. Don't be scared. Yaw
can't be acting scared, girl."

"Trixie, how do you spell 'martini'?"

"That's an easy one—o-l-i-v-e. You know. Just tell Manny 'the one with the olive behind the bar.'"

Trixie tried to teach Marla Jean to dance. They spent many an early-morning hour after the lingering crowds had gone spinning and turning with boas and beads, laughing and singing until the tears from their glorious fun ran down their faces. Marla Jean loved trying on all of Trixie's costumes. She had dresses and shoes that matched—dresses of velvet and coats with fur trim. Trixie had perfumes and talc and powder puffs with soft scents that smelled so good. She had colors for lips, and fake eyelashes that stuck to eyelids, and eyebrow color to shape and darken the brows.

"How do I look, Trixie Siggers? I'm a clown, I'm a clown . . ." Marla Jean sang.

"You're no clown. You're a moonflower. A beautiful flower of the night."

"I'm no flower, not no moonflower, either." Marla Jean blushed.

"Let me take yaw to the Flamingo. Yaw know it is not over 'til the long-legged pinkie bird sings." Trixie broke into song so loud and high that she placed her hand over the rise and fall of her chest to steady herself.

"Where did you ever learn to sing like that? You are so good, Trixie."

"I had lots of teachers. Great singers come here. I watch them, listen, and practice."

Marla Jean enjoyed being with Trixie so much. A sisterhood developed between the two girls, creating a bond of devotion unlike anything Marla Jean had ever known before. Some patrons soon knew the girls and liked their antics and clownish capers. The owners of the Flamingo Club liked the girls and let them do their own thing. The club's famed ambiance brought in business, too. But one thing bothered the owners about Marla Jean. She'd developed the habit of watching the shows. Trixie had to keep reminding her: "Mar-lala Jean, yahoo, girl! Get back to work."

Sometimes, she had to whistle at or pinch Marla Jean.

"Better keep moving and grooving!" Trixie reminded her.

One couldn't blame Marla Jean for being in awe of such talent. All the beautiful talent she was witnessing revealed a score of black memoirs in the making like no other time and no other place in history. One notable night, a woman named Dinah Washington performed. Marla Jean noticed how the singer's voice reached deep down inside her, unaware that she was listening to a talent that would soon be widely recognized. Another night, she heard Ella Fitzgerald perform with Chick Webb's band. With remarkable vocal control and with an uncanny ability to improvise, Ella sang, "A-tisket, a-tasket, a green and yellow basket . . ." It was a flawless rendition of a song that was later recorded and became a nationwide hit.

Marla Jean often stood there, in a trance, absorbing the wonder of it all. She had stars in her eyes, a reflection of the stars that were performing right in front of her.

"Marla Jean? Marla Jean, I need yaw to run on over to the hardware store for some ice, we're running out," said the bartender, Manny. Marla Jean left the Flamingo Club and pulled an ice wagon into the night. She headed down Harmony Lane to Joy Street where a hardware store stayed open all night to sell ice to the nightclubs.

The moon drifted under a canopy of clouds, and Marla Jean felt the darkness surround her. The shadows of trees laid down their ghostly silhouettes. A kind of water dust fell upon her head, cool and refreshing. Her two hands reached out to catch the mist, and upon rubbing her cheeks with it, she immediately became flushed with pleasure. Suddenly, an owl flew past Marla Jean in a buoyant manner, as if it were lighter than air. The startled owl did not scare her but rather excited her, and she began to dance. She moved with childlike glee and echoed the owl's song.

"Ooooo, hoot, hoot, hooooooot. You not scaring me, hoot owl. I can hoot and howl. Jes like you, hoooooot, ohhh!"

The song ended when the absentminded girl remembered her errand. On her way back with the ice, she decided she had better find a shortcut to the club. The wagon, burdened with its load, moved slowly over the soft fern path, a dark route that had known little travel. All of a sudden, her sense of wonderment disappeared. She questioned if she was alone. Or was someone out there in the dark, beside the owl, watching her? As she headed down a slope, she was forced to let go of her weighted cargo as it raced out of control. It sped past her and she jumped out of its way and gasped at her dilemma. She ran to the bottom and saw that the considerate wagon had not tipped over but sped to a stop right in front of the club's back door. Marla Jean delivered the block of ice and, in due course, Manny used his ice pick to change its shape forever.

"We thought that the boogeyman got ya, girl!" exclaimed Manny.

Quickly, Marla Jean grabbed her apron and put it on. "There's no boogeyman that lives 'round here." She smiled, her soul humming a tune to the beat of her heart.

Everyone who came to Idlewild loved it and got caught up in continuous partying, all day and all night. After the main shows—sometimes three a night—they'd go to Club El Morocco, an after-hours joint, and the shows would start up again. Many groups, including the Count Basie and Ellington bands, performed in Idlewild. Duke Ellington's "It Don't Mean a Thing (If It Ain't Got That Swing)" introduced swing to the people of Michigan. Many of the contributors to new innovations in music, without a doubt, were these talented Afro-Americans.

As for now, in this little village nestled in the heart of Michigan, a young girl was witness to this music—swing, jazz, and rhythm and blues—so expertly expressed by Etta James and Fats Waller and others. It was a wonderful time for Marla Jean.

She was enjoying life, she had friends, and she was learning to be
self-sufficient. More importantly, she was learning to laugh out
loud. Trixie laughed often, and the two girls laughed together,
infecting each other in healing proportions. Soon, Marla Jean
laughed herself out of her worries.

Marla Jean stayed with Trixie all the time. They did not
spend much time awake at Trixie's place, only sleeping. Her
place was a one-person bungalow, a doghouse. Her bedroom was
so small, she had to back into it and jump onto the bed, which
filled the room. The bathroom was equally small; shutting the
door while sitting on the commode required putting one's feet
in the bathtub. Marla Jean slept on the floor of the tiny cottage
with a quilt to cover her and many more beneath her.

"Trixie?"

"Yaw . . . ?"

"Are you sleeping yet?"

"No, girl. How can I be sleeping when I'm talking to you?
What's the matter, are yaw sick?"

"No, I feel so good I can't sleep. I feel so good my heart won't
be quiet. I feel so good my toes tickle. I feel so good . . ."

"Go on and feel good, honey. I don't wanna feel nothing. I
wanna feel nothin' but my Z's."

Marla Jean loved Trixie so much, she wanted to become
more like her. Trixie sang and danced with her whole heart. Her
body and spirit moved with the music as if they were one. The
love of her life was the total package of Idlewild. Marla Jean
knew that Trixie hoped to manage the Flamingo Club someday.
The talented woman was a match for her ambition, as determined as she was to hold on to a piece of Idlewild's good fortune.

At one point not long after Marla Jean moved in with Trixie,
a young man took an interest in Trixie that left her new roommate uneasy. Marla Jean never saw him, but she was nervous
that she would have to leave when or if he moved in. Trixie saw
him away from the resort and always came home alone.

One day, Marla Jean asked her friend about him. "Do you like him, Trixie? A lot?"

"I used to. He is not like the others who want, you know, right away. But he has no job and is controlled by his horrible father."

"My father is drunk all the time, but he doesn't control me, thank goodness."

"Ya, Johnny says his dad drinks, too, and maybe he'll become just like him someday. No thanks."

And so the girls, finding that they were of the same mind, became closer. They shared their stories of misfortune. Yet they believed God's Holy Spirit had been present with them in the past and would continue to do so in their future.

℀

One particular night, a larger table centered in the middle of the Flamingo Club bustled with activity. Between shows, Marla Jean and a fellow waiter, Tremont, tended to the service of the important clientele at the table. They were handsome men who laughed easily and fit well into the ambiance of the Flamingo Club, and tonight they appeared to be the center of it. One man, specifically, whose athletic prowess gave him an irresistible aura of attractiveness, stood apart from the others. Marla Jean brought him iced ginger ales. He always winked at her, as a man free of pretensions, and, in a softly spoken voice, he always thanked her. This man was most comfortable here in Idlewild, with people like himself who had money, but he never forget his poorer background.

When a recording of Memphis Minnie with Black Bob on the piano filled up the club with the exultant and happy song, "He's in the Ring (Doin' the Same Old Thing)," everyone stood and clapped. Then the most famous black man in America slowly stood, raised his arms of muscle and blood, and clasped his hands over his head. He demonstrated his winning stance and waved to all. The crowd cheered and whistled, encouraging the man to remain standing for a wildly long time. Marla Jean reached over and grabbed Trixie, pulling her close enough to ask, "Who's that? Ever'body sure do like him!"

"Oh yaw they do, honey! That there's Joe Louis, the prizefighter!"

❧

Thinking back to that moment in Marla Jean's story, I started digging around for more facts about the prizefighter. I found that many people in America couldn't name the president of the United States and yet they knew about Joe Louis.

❧

The impression that Joe Louis made on black culture (even its music) only begins to suggest the depth of Louis's penetration of black consciousness during the 1930s. Louis was called "the Detroit Negro." Louis's race inspired white journalists to come up with imaginative nicknames for the boxer. Those monikers that followed Louis throughout his career included the Dusky Challenger, the Brown Bomber, the Dark Destroyer, and the Mahogany Maimer, all referring to his race.

In Idlewild, Joe Louis could relax and be himself. Louis often disappeared into black communities for days at a time to escape his life, including his wife, managers, and especially white reporters. When not in training, Louis had a lot of free time. That night, Marla Jean noticed the celebrity watching her as she approached and circled the table, removing dinnerware and glasses and then inquiring of more orders. His gaze pierced her confidence, and ultimately, she dropped a glass from her tray of towering dishes.

Nervous and excited, she uttered softly, "I'm sorry."

They looked at her, and one man at the table said, "Don't worry 'bout that, doll. You's doing real good." And Joe Louis smiled and nodded in agreement.

Upon early-morning cleanup, after the shows with dinner and cocktails, Marla Jean noticed the tip Joe Louis had left her. It was a twenty-dollar bill, but upon closer examination, she found two twenty-dollar bills tightly stacked on top of one another. She stood there staring at the tip, stunned, her mouth open, and couldn't believe what she held in her hand. Those close to Joe Louis always knew he picked up the tab and tipped generously, giving no thought to an eventual bottom to his resources. Perhaps the others didn't care about his resources, either, as long as the drinks flowed freely while they were in his company.

Joe Louis's fame did spiral downward when the talented boxer started losing fights, one of which was years later, in 1951, when Rocky Marciano defeated him at Madison Square Garden. Everyone who watched the fight sensed it to be Louis's last.

After the fight, Josephine Baker, a famous entertainer at that time, waited in the corridor outside Louis's locker room. A corridor that would have been packed with well-wishers, reporters, and promoters not long ago, but this night it was nearly empty. Someone asked her, "What you doin' here? Louis didn't win. He blew it!"

She answered, "I just need to shake his hand. It's so important."

Dark an' stormy may come de wedder;
I jines dis he-male an' dis she-male togedder
Let none, but Him dat makes de thunder,
Put dis he-male an' dis she-male asunder.
I darfore 'nounce you bofe de same,
Be good, go 'long, an' keep up yo' name
De broomstick's jumped, de worl's not wide.
She's now yo' own. Salute yo' bride.

—*Author Unknown*

Marla Jean deceived;
Noonday Flower conceived.

—*C. Ohse*

CHAPTER FOUR

Black Eden, Continued . . .

Everyone loved Josephine Baker, and years later, I found out from others that Trixie adored her. Josephine Baker exemplified black talent at its best, with guts and a savvy spirit for breaking into show business at a time in history when only pretty and white women made it. Josephine was peppy, bouncy, upbeat, and full of energy. She attacked her audience with her talent for song and dance and delightfully shocked fans with her ingenuity. She advised Trixie: "Dance a lot, sweat a lot, and you'll sleep like a baby. Sleep's good for the eyes."

The people in Idlewild accepted the talented young woman as the ravishing black creature she was without a reminder of her pickaninny origin. She experienced a difficult beginning in America, especially when Fanny Brice was the principal draw of the 1930s Follies. So Miss Baker went to France, and the French embraced her in a way America would not—except in a resort in the backwoods of Michigan not far from a great lake with the same name. Josephine radiated talent and glamour that transcended skin color. Just as America was slow to embrace Joe Louis, America also took her time to appreciate Josephine Baker.

Marla Jean and Trixie watched with wonder as Miss Baker performed in Idlewild. A special Josephine Baker song, "Suppose," left many in the club awestruck. "Suppose" was half spoken, half quavered in the manner of Al Jolson and vaudeville. Her spoken introduction led her into a song that was as rich as Josephine herself, offering sugarcane to her audience. Baker performed marvelously. With her fabulous wardrobe, including some scanty, scandalous outfits, this woman embodied sophistication and captivated those in her audiences, including Marla Jean and Trixie.

One late night after closing, the Flamingo Club still flowing with the afterglow of honey music, the girls and Josephine sat talking and laughing while others were clearing off the tables. Even the broom pushers stopped to listen when the star spoke.

Josephine, sitting in one chair with her feet propped up on another, ran her fingers through her hair and, with a frankness of manner, talked inexhaustibly with the hired help. Trixie drew close and hung on to her every word. Marla Jean listened, quietly attentive, lending an ear to the singer's airy tongue, not wanting to miss one syllable. She was enraptured by the presence of this extravagant woman.

"In my childhood, I own'd no stockings, so when I was cold, I danced. I learned to dance to keep my feet warm. I've learned—I learned many things. One thing: I'm not intimidated by anyone." She looked around, making sure everyone understood. "Ya see, everybody—yes, everybody—is made with two arms, two legs, a stomach, and a head. Just think 'bout that!"

Marla Jean probably thought about that. She may have thought about how lucky she was to meet this woman and to live in Idlewild.

At this time, I think the people of Walhalla stood up and took notice as the news of Idlewild's Black Resort filtered to us.

Walhalla residents still stayed away, even with our piqued curi-
osities. I remember my father saying that the Flamingo Club
and the Paradise Club were every bit as impressive and elaborate
as any club in Las Vegas at the time. I believed it to be true,
even though I knew my father had never been to Las Vegas,
or even Idlewild. Idlewild's fame spread not only to Walhalla
but throughout the country, due largely to word of mouth and
a silent film from the late 1920s that promoted the resort in
many black theaters. The quality of black entertainers and black
patrons—and some white, too—combined with the low rate
of crime and the absence of urban congestion, made Idlewild a
flourishing haven, a frenzied hot spot, a black Eden.

☙

Marla Jean seldom saw Daddy Attie anymore. He must have
become a pitiful sight in the last days of his life. He gave up his
battle to exist and yielded to the drink that eventually sucks life
out of body and soul. No one knew exactly how Attie died, but
what resulted from his death was important. Marla Jean didn't
deserve the chain of events that turned her life back into the
misery she had known before.

Marla Jean turned eighteen the year Daddy Attie died, continuing to be confident and happy despite the uncertainty of her
future. Actually, I believe she loved life just as it was. Perhaps,
in the recesses of her mind, in that one spot where happiness
reigns, she prayed for life to stand still. Her reading and writing
remained important to her, but those activities had been diverted
because of her new life with work and friends.

Pretty Marla Jean looked older than eighteen, especially
when Trixie used her beauty know-how on her. Looking into
the mirror one day, Marla Jean blushed when Trixie pulled her
shoulders back, lifted her chin, and said, "Do you know this
beautiful woman, Marla Jean Atlas? She's got the world in her

hand! Why do you think she'd be named after that muscle man who holds up heavens an' earth?"

The girls laughed and hugged, and Trixie said, "Forget your childhood, you's a ripe, mighty fine woman now, mighty fine. Stick with me, Miss Lady Atlas, and the world's your playground."

"Welcome to the Flamingo Club! Hope you all enjoy the show. What can I get you?" she asked with confidence. Marla Jean's shyness faded away. She could greet guests with big smiles just as Trixie did.

℃

A new act was introduced on one particular night. It was a father, son, and uncle tap-dancing team. They tapped to the music and never seemed to tire. Their feet just whipped over the floor in magical blurs that escaped the eyes but not the ears of the audience. Those shiny black shoes with the big silver taps kept striking the floor at an astonishing rate, embracing the rhythm and causing the audience to stand and gyrate. Clapping and whistling erupted from the crowd as the dancers rejoiced in the heel-toe dance of their performance. Watching the youngest member in action, with his tremendously hardworking feet, everyone believed he was extraordinary. Talent radiated from the young man, and no one at the club, including Marla Jean, dared to dream of what was to come for this multitalented tap-dancing black man whose name would later be known to all: Sammy Davis Jr.

Night after night, the audience viewed talent after talent and did not realize they were witnessing stars in the making. Marla Jean had a special sense of it all. To her, the entertainers were a beautiful enigma. They were already stars in her eyes.

℃

One night, the partying at the Flamingo Club was excellent, as usual, but something was amiss. Because the forecast for a moonless night had proved to be true, it got dark rather quickly. Just the same, the shows were exciting, and I believe Trixie must have danced in perfect rhythm to the beat of her heart and soul. As always, the crowds were wonderfully receptive, gracious, and loud.

But unlike ever before, the most unfriendly circumstances invaded the famed Flamingo Club. Many were not aware of the intruder who entered from the rear door—most likely a substitute worker. He was clearly out of place in the establishment. The man carried a club-like implement, presumably to aid in his uneven gait, but maybe not. The activity of the crowd shielded Marla Jean from the unwelcome intrusion by this man. Soon after the unknown man had entered the club, a fellow worker approached Marla Jean. But she didn't notice him until he tapped her on the shoulder.

"What's happening, Tremont?"

"Marla Jean, there's someone askin' 'bout you."

"Me? Someone's askin' for me? Are you sure?"

"Yaw, I'm sure. He's plenty spooky. See, over there by the back door . . . the door workers use." Tremont pointed. "See 'im there by himself?"

Marla Jean didn't look where he was indicating right away. Her thoughts of *who knows me* and *who knows I'm here* hit her like a brick of concrete. *Attie's come for me,* she quickly reasoned. She felt the warmth rise in her cheeks as she strained to look through the crowd. Tremont pointed again to a dark, quiet corner, and Marla Jean immediately recognized the man as JD, a Caveman who often drank with her father. She felt herself stiffening, hopelessly anchored. Her heart pounded so hard its deafening beat reached the incessant rhythm of a drumroll. She couldn't speak.

After what seemed like forever, she shouted to Tremont, "He don't belong here! How he get in? Get Trixie!"

The Caveman spotted Marla Jean and moved toward her—a cold, calculating figure on his way to collect his due. Repulsive to all he passed, the Caveman walked along the back of the club through the crowd of cheap seats. Regardless, those ticket holders didn't like being a part of a show away from the headliner.

Marla Jean crouched down, trying to move out of his sight.

Tilting her head up again, she exclaimed, "Oh Lord, he sees me. He's coming . . . !"

She must have realized at that moment that she had no choice but to try and get him out of the club before he made a scene, which would result in her being fired. In seconds, the Caveman was beside her; his stench defined him, his presence was undeniable, and his glare mortified her. She grabbed onto him to try and direct him back the way he'd come. He stood firm, saying, "Attie's dead. You's mine now. You best come an' see 'bout things."

Suddenly limp, Marla Jean couldn't speak. The hard thing in her throat just stuck there. She tried to look beyond the upturned stares but couldn't see through the confusion that permeated her 360-degree vision. She searched for Trixie as the Caveman grabbed her arm and pulled, saying to her, "You's a bad, bad girl. Come home, bury your pa!"

She resisted. "You're lying. My daddy's not dead! You're lying!" She backed away and ordered, "Take . . . your . . . filthy . . . hands . . . off me . . . !"

With sweat rolling down her face, she pulled her shoulders back and called upon a strength she'd never known she had. "I'm not afraid of you, you stingy, good-for-nothing . . . drunk! I *hate* you!"

He moved closer, spitting out his words. "You's mine, an' I got paper says so. T'ain't nothing you can do but just com'on!"

The music was still playing loudly, and many in the audience hadn't seen or heard the vile man enter the club, but patrons in the back were beginning to move away from the ongoing commotion.

Marla Jean pushed him away again. "Let *go* of me, you fool! You gotta leave *now!*"

He leaned into her, almost falling onto her, and through his rotten teeth, he told her, "I'll kill ya right now, right here, if'n you don't come . . . *now*."

Before Marla Jean could say another word, someone else grabbed her from behind and forced her into a choke hold. The Caveman grabbed her other arm, and they began dragging her toward the door. At the same time, Tremont and Manny, one of the bartenders, sprinted after them, knocking down tables and chairs while patrons scrambled out of the way. In unspeakable chaos, the two kidnappers dragged Marla Jean across the floor and out the back door faster than the workers could reach them. Marla Jean was gone when Tremont got to the door and jumped out, Manny right behind him. The dark night and the heavy foliage aided the Caveman's plan of escape with his captive. Everything in the club stopped cold—the music, the laughter, and the joy of the evening. Trixie leaped out the back door screaming her friend's name again and again until her vocal cords couldn't support another scream for Marla Jean.

The rain to the wind said,
"You push and I'll pelt."
They so smote the garden bed
That the flowers actually knelt
And lay lodged—though not dead.
I know how the flowers felt.

—*Robert Frost*

Marla Jean knew how the flowers felt, too.

—*C. Ohse*

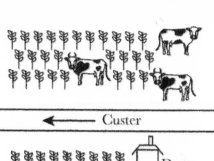

← Custer

U.S.

Dunn

Weldon Creek

Manistee
National Forest

Pere Marquette Railroad

Weldon Creek

1st Street (dirt road)

Brenner

Johnson

Pere Marquette River

© Audrey Schreck

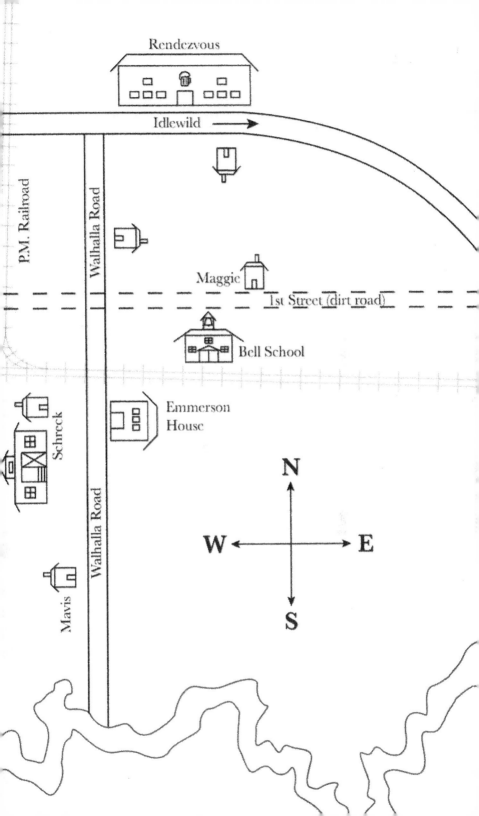

CHAPTER FIVE

Walhalla

Of course, I don't know the full truth of what happened after Marla Jean was taken away that night many years ago. Additionally, I don't know if Marla Jean ever told anybody about it. Trixie knew parts of it, as well as Lizzy Schreck. My written account of what happened falls between truth and fiction. I promise it will be an honest and astute judgment of Marla Jean's life-changing, and horrifying, turn of events.

❦

Marla Jean sat all night in a chair in her father's home. She remained there, shivering in a state of shock, with no tears, only confusion. The dark gloom of her confinement consumed her, although she knew she was not alone. She shook off the lethargy that bound her to the chair, and her whole body trembled with fear. She could see the dark outline of her dead father lying on the table not far from her. Her hand moved out to make contact with her dad. Afraid to feel death, she looked at her feet while extending her arm. Her hand fumbled but found the corpse, and, yes, the cold reality of her touch told her that Daddy Attie was dead. She fell back onto her chair and cried out, "Oh Lord, no! Please Lord, deliver my daddy."

At one point, Marla Jean slept. She may have felt herself falling from a high place, descending down a steep cliff into the depths of some kind of slumber. She slept pitifully and awoke to the morning light squeezing into the room from above. Marla Jean slowly recognized the place; it was the cave of her prior existence, the one from her dingy, lightless past. The darkness, despite the light of day above, hid the filth of the room. Little varmints scattered about with the slightest movement. The smell of decaying flesh, urine, and vomit filled her senses. Suddenly, the place lit up with a lurid glow. She could see the piles of dust-covered vomit and torn clothes scattered about.

Actually, to Marla Jean's surprise, the area of the room where the body lay was clean, somewhat. For a fleeting moment, she lost her feeble hold on reality. She stared, seemingly in a trance, but then not fully aware. It had been a long time since she had been back home.

Soon she snapped out of it. "Where are they? I gotta get out of here before they come back." She ran to the door but couldn't open it. No more than a minute after she had questioned her kidnapper's whereabouts, she heard footsteps. Before she knew it, the door flew open, and they were down the steps and beside her. She was awake in the middle of a nightmare.

Without saying a word, the two pulled her and led her to her father's side, grabbing her head and forcing her to look into his expressionless face. Opening her eyes with reservation and fear, she saw the sunken hollows of her father's cheeks. His lips, swollen with thin cracks, and his bulging eye sockets made his face nearly unrecognizable. His whole body was puffed up, and its heavy rotting odor consumed her. Marla Jean's mouth was so thick with dryness that she couldn't speak.

"Did ya ask old Attie how's he doing? He not sayin' much, I bet. What kinda dawter leave her old Pa and never come on back again? You is rotten, bad! You know that? A bad, bad girl!"

The Caveman struck Marla Jean. She wavered and raised her arms over her head, anticipating another blow.

The little man stomped his feet repeatedly, chanting, "Bad, bad, bad!" Then, with narrowing eyes, he looked at her, and said, "No matter, now. You is mine! You ain't never gonna run from me!"

A quiet moment followed as the three stood there looking at the dead man. Marla Jean noticed that her father's appearance was actually neat. It was as if someone had tended to the dead man's final showing, cleaning his fingernails, smoothing down his hair, and making sure his shirt was buttoned to the neck. There he lay, in pomp display, as if an actual funeral were about to take place. Of course, Attie Atlas was not a prominent man of the community, so Marla Jean was sure no one would come by to pay their respects. Suddenly, she spied the flower-edged plate lying on his chest.

The Caveman spoke again. "Sees that saucer we put on him? Nobody come by! See, there's no moneys in it to pay for his burying. Yaw see nobody care 'bout your pa! An' nobody care 'bout you, neither. You best know you's mine now. Attie's dead, see for your own self."

The man hit her again and again. "Bad, bad, bad-d-d. There's nobody gonna see to a bad girl but me. Got that?" He stopped, out of breath. His eyes bore into her. "Ya think you're goin' back to the fancy club? No, whore, you not. Yur own daddy's dead cuz you run off."

Finally, Marla Jean looked up. Looking squarely into the Caveman's eyes, she pressed her trembling lips together. She didn't speak; instead, in lightning fashion, she knocked the saucer off her father's chest. It flew to the floor and broke into pieces.

JD and his son may have been shocked at the gumption shown by the girl, because they said nothing. Immediately, she jerked away from the Caveman's hold and sharply spoke. "I'll bury my daddy." Then, loudly: "Where's the damn shovel?"

Outside, the digging started next to Moms's grave. Marla Jean's ruthless guards stood by, but they soon showed impatience when her digging slowed. So the Caveman ordered the younger man to dig, too.

"Johnny, get down dere. Help that bad girl. She's a weak, no good dawter. Go on . . ."

"Pa, I don't wanta. I told ya, we never should of taken her." Faster than his dad could speak, the young man jumped out of the way and into the hole Marla Jean had dug so far. He knew his dad could aim his walking implement directly at his head, and he did not want that. JD's walking stick had more uses than aiding his walk.

From the makeshift grave, Marla Jean heard the young man speak again. The words whispered out of his mouth, almost without sound.

"You bes' keep on a-diggin'. You don't want to rile old JD."

Stunned, the girl gasped. "You're . . . you're Trixie's friend, aren't you?" He turned his back to her. She grabbed him and frantically called out, "Help me!" And again, in a whisper: "Please help me, Johnny, please."

At that, JD hollered, "Slap her face, ya hear me, Johnny?"

"She won't talk again, Pa, or I'll slap her good," Johnny replied and then looked over at Marla Jean as if to say, *Don't say another word.*

When the hole seemed big enough, Marla Jean and Johnny fetched the body from the old kitchen table inside. Faintly, Marla Jean lifted her father's tethered bones and withering flesh. He was loose, yet heavy. The rising scent of the body was inescapable and nearly caused her to drop hold of him.

The young man cursed. "You hol' on, dang-blame it!"

She groped for a better hold of her father's feet. Anguishing that she might pull them off, she raised her scalding-red face up and away, took a deep breath, and managed to lift again. She dropped the body, but this time it was because the young man had lost his hold. Attie was heavy. The two looked at each other, perspiration flowing down their faces, but neither said a word.

For a daughter to be forced to bury her father without kindness, sympathy, and love had to be the worst experience of death and dying that any child should ever have to face. Being exposed to the death and burial of her father in this way may have helped justify the guilt she most likely felt for not having checked on her father in many months.

The hole was neither large nor deep enough, but they went ahead and squeezed him in anyway. They tilted his head off to one corner and then squished his feet into the opposite corner, forcing them into the earth. They squeezed his arms and hands in, and although Attie was a small man, his grave did not accommodate him well. The sweating diggers paused, unsure of what to do next. Quickly, JD threw a handful of earth onto the dead man.

"Dust to dust, ol' Attie, a good man. Is done. Is done, is good enough." The man turned and walked away. "I'm needin' a drink. My tongue's gone dry like a desert."

"Wait. Wait!" Marla Jean shouted, and before the man could blink, she'd disappeared into the dwelling, returning with an oil tablecloth that she placed over poor Attie's face and torso.

As she covered his body, Marla Jean began to sob. She stood and turned away, praying the young man would finish the burial. Light faded before her eyes, and her perspiring face turned chalky white. Surrendering to legs that refused to hold

her up, she collapsed into a wave of unconsciousness, ending her
father's burial.

℘

*As I learned more and more about the Caveman during my Idlewild
research, I thought, how ironic that this dirty skunk of a man had
a perfumed name: JD Flower. The J stood for "John" and the D, I
was told, didn't stand for anything other than D. In my own interpretation, the D clearly stood for "the Devil." Few people knew the
Flower father and son, but one who did said JD never became Marla
Jean's husband—but his son did. I was told the younger Flower was
a cocky sort, a good-looking young man whose inner life remained
hidden because of his father's power over him.*

℘

After burying Attie, the three walked several miles to the Flower
dwelling. Even though Attie and JD were neighbors, the dwellings in this area were far enough apart that no one neighbor
knew much about the other.

JD piled up everything worthwhile from Attie's place into
Marla Jean's arms, making her carry the items from one basement home to the another. He snarled, "And don't you drop one
thing, bad girl! Or else I'm gonna knock everything down on the
ground and make you pick it all up."

"Damn it, Pa, give me some!" yelled Johnny. "She can't carry
all that. You're hurting your own self cuz it's taking so long in
this heat."

"Oh, shut up. Take the fan. We don't want that broken."

And so a basement home became Marla Jean's domain once
again. She was the newest member of the fading Flower family,
although far from being a respected part of family life. Marla
Jean's lot was cast; she had become a servant in the Caveman's

dwelling. JD's wife had left, taking the younger kids with her. Marla Jean didn't know much about the woman and her life with JD. She had undoubtedly left with good reason. In all probability, poverty, lack of direction, and ambition played a part, not to mention the lack of love. The Flower husband and son never heard from their wife and mother. They had waited, sure that she would return.

"Where the old lady go, walkin' with two young'uns, and no money in her pocket?" JD questioned.

But Mrs. JD Flower and the children never returned. I think Marla Jean felt absolute sadness for them. She never met them, but now she had to live the life they'd left behind, right down to wearing the woman's tattered clothing. Marla Jean replaced her service to JD, and it was not cooking and cleaning that was important to him. It was hard to know what was important to this man besides having someone to abuse. He displayed no regard for human decency, and certainly not for a proper manner of living. It was decided that Johnny would marry Marla Jean to make it seem befitting, although JD figured she was his to keep, marriage or not.

"Get on a nice dress, girl, and look good. You're gettin' married," JD ordered.

"What? What did you say? No, I ain't getting married."

"You're gonna do what I say and put a smile to it, too. Get yourself pretty. Pretty enough, anyway."

"You can't make me get married. I'd die before I'd marry you!"

JD grabbed her hair and jerked her back. Tears sprang from her eyes.

"Oww. Ow . . ." she cried out.

"Then plan on dyin', cuz I can kill you an' bury you without anyone noticing. You ain't nothin' to nobody. Who'd know you was gone? Who?"

He let go of her hair and laughed. "But you ain't gonna marry me. You gonna marry Johnny."

Surprised, Marla Jean stood there. Quietly, she said, "But maybe he don't wanna get married, either."

"No matter. You and he are gittin' married and we're gonna be a happy family, you and me and Johnny."

He laughed and slapped her on the butt. "Now, smile for your daddy."

Abruptly, he stopped laughing and said with a snarl, "Get ready, whore."

Someone who owed JD a favor drove Marla Jean and Johnny to the courthouse to be married by a judge. They waited until the judge was free, as no appointment had been made. Marla Jean paced the second floor, JD and his friend on her tail. Johnny, though, sat with his head buried in his hands. Perhaps he was hoping that she could get away somehow. He may have said to himself, *Run, run, run, girl, you can run faster than JD.* Marla Jean must have thought of that as well. I'm sure she wanted to scream, "Help me," at the top of her lungs, but she never did, because both JD and his friend had guns. She'd felt the gun press into her side too many times that day.

A couple of "I do's" and it was over. She was married to a man she didn't even know. The saddest married couple in Lake County—with no smiles, no jubilation—took the shortest ride back to the basement house and a life of wedded, depraved bondage. Marla Jean became a Cinderella to the Caveman's family—everything but the fairy-tale ending.

The mocking bird echoed from a nearby tree.
And, when she glanced to the far-off town,
White from its hill-slope looking down,
The sweet song died, with a vague unrest
And a nameless longing filled her breast.
A wish that she hardly dared to own,
For something better than she had known.
She wedded a man unlearned and poor,
Children may play around her door.
But care and sorrow and childbirth pain
Left their traces on heart and brain
Her graceful ankles bare and brown
Rode the pedals to a newfound town.
                                    —*John G. Whittier*

Marla Jean, with certain sadness,
Found a way to simple gladness.
                                    —*C. Ohse*

CHAPTER SIX

JD and Attie

It remains a mystery how it happened that JD held claim over Marla Jean. The night he won her from Attie, the den of thieves must have been stirring like a pot of booze stew. The noisy activity must have included a demonic decision that went against the absent Marla Jean. She knew nothing of her peril. The outcome of a game of cards had put her future at risk. Attie, sickened by his own moonshine, became deplorably ignorant, totally dulled by the frenzied goings-on. Perhaps the cards were marked, or JD held an ace up his sleeve. Regardless, the Caveman's actions were cruel and inhuman.

"Attie, you's lost. Marla Jean's mine. Ha!" JD hollered.

Attie took another drink. "Naw, naw. We gonna play nutter hand." His head bobbed like a toy doll with a springy neck. His eyes closed. An effort to open them resulted in a slivered squint. He peeked at JD. "Naw, naw, Marla Jean's my kin. You can't have her. Play nutter hand."

"Oh naw. You the loser, Attie. You jus' a'cept it."

JD snapped his fingers. In record time, his son was at his side.

Attie's head hit the table, the cards flew in all directions, and his drink fell to the floor.

Finally, a third man at the card table got up. "You's nuts, JD! Game's over. I's goin'. Come on, Deacon."

The fourth man stood with such a jerk that his chair crashed to the floor behind him. The two staggered away—they did not want to be a part of JD's dirty shenanigans.

JD must have told his son what to do. Holding the pen in the drunken man's hand, Johnny moved the pen along to spell out Attie's name. Attie signed the ruffled scrap of paper that, according to an ignorant man's knowledge of the law, relinquished his guardianship of Marla Jean. Whether the note would have stood up in a court of law—probably not—one glum and sinister man believed that it would.

Not long after that night, Attie died. He didn't wake one morning, and no one knows if he died in his sleep or if something else happened. JD and Johnny found him and prepared him for viewing in hopes of collecting some money from his untimely death. When that didn't bring in any money, which they wouldn't have used for his burial anyway, they started out to find their illegitimate possession. Marla Jean hadn't been home for a year, maybe more, so she didn't see Attie in his last days.

❧

Now, immeasurable sorrow consumed Marla Jean. Months dragged by, and the young girl despaired. Trips to the privy out back gave her time to think about her situation. She thought of Trixie, the Flamingo Club, the music, the beautiful people of Idlewild—thoughts that gave her strength.

One day, Marla Jean heard a noise from outside like a motor running, possibly a car. She looked over at JD and Johnny, who both seemed occupied and had not heard what she had. Nonchalantly, she started up the stairs, calling down that she was going to the privy. JD, puffing on his cigarette, motioned with a wave of his hand for Johnny to follow. Johnny was probably getting pretty tired of being her jailer, so he took his time getting up to follow her. Marla Jean quickly slipped out the door and looked toward the two-track road but saw no one. Praying it wasn't her imagination, she walked over to the road and started walking away from the dwelling. She kept looking back, but no Johnny. Walking faster, she wondered if she saw something ahead. Right then, her heart beat faster than ever when she spied a car. As if on cue, the car stopped. Had the driver seen her in the rearview mirror?

Trixie flew out the passenger side, yelling, "Marla Jean, Marla Jean . . . Oh my God, it *is* you!" The girls ran to each other, embraced, each hanging on to the other, not letting go, feet dancing and tears flowing.

"Oh, Trixie, you found me! How did you find me? I'm so glad to see you."

"Yes, finally. Are you all right? How did this happen? Is it your father?"

"No, no. Oh, I have so much to tell you."

Trixie, anxious to leave, said, "Never mind now, hop in the car with Tremont. We gotta get the hell outta here right now."

But, in all the excitement, Johnny got to them before they knew it. Trixie screamed when she saw him, "You son of a bitch . . . You son of a bitch." As fast as she could, she jumped him, beating on him with fists and trying to scratch his eyes out, screaming, "How could you do this? You bastard, I hate you! I hate you!"

Johnny pulled her off and threw her to the ground, "Shut up, woman, shut up!"

Marla Jean ran to Trixie's side while Tremont started up the engine, yelling, "Get in, get in . . ."

Marla Jean cried, "Are you hurt bad, Trixie? Can you get up?"
Gunshots rang out from behind all of them.

Johnny screamed, "Get out of here now . . . *go!*"

All of them stopped cold when they heard the monster's
gravelly voice screaming at them, "You trespassin'? I's allow to
kill anybody trespassing on my property. Don't care if you're a
dirty rotten kid."

Then and there, everyone saw JD drop his walking stick and
lift his rifle with two hands to take aim. He didn't wait, but the
bullets flew high over his targets. Trixie took a hold of Marla
Jean's hand, both of them ducking the wildly flying bullets.
Trixie kept yelling, "Come on, girl! Come on, hurry!"

But Johnny, in a flash, grabbed Marla Jean away from her
and distinctly said, "She is *my* wife, Trixie, she stays."

"No, Johnny, you don't deserve her."

Johnny pulled Marla Jean to himself and yelled, "*Go!* He
will shoot you, Trixie!"

Tremont, still in the car, stepped on the gas pedal, and the
engine sputtered loudly. He screamed, "Get in, Trixie, get in!"

Marla Jean, sobbing, declared, "Trixie, I love you! I'm
sorry—"

With bullets still flying, the frightened girls, catching a last
look at one another, seemed to know that they would not be
leaving together. Trixie took off running, caught up, and jumped
into the car. Tremont revved the car's engine and took off as fast
as the old car could go. Out the window, Trixie yelled, "Marla
Jean, I'll be back . . ."

༉

Yes, Marla Jean did have people who cared about her and who
missed her and loved her. She gained strength in the months
ahead just knowing that. Something in this poor girl's favor, if
one could consider anything to be in her favor, was JD's nightly

drunken binges. His lack of sexual prowess benefited her in their time together. Even though she was married to Johnny, JD considered her his property to do anything with whenever he pleased.

"Marla Jean, get over here; get to bed, now," JD said.

"I'm coming, I'm coming. I'm scrubbin' the frier pan." She pounded the pan in the sink so JD could hear. Every muscle in her body tightened at the thought of going in to him. "I got more pans to scrub . . ."

"Come now, woman, or I'm gonna whip ya first!"

"I'm coming . . ." Her voice trailed off into a sob. She held it back, almost choking.

Waiting until he fell asleep didn't always work. More often than not, it was JD's attacks of flatulence that sent her to the far edge of the bed, but she got used to the smell of the man, the pawing touch of the man, and the obscene moans of this morally depraved excuse for a man.

Closing her eyes in prayer, she learned to work around his primary intention and made sure to avoid the sting of his foul, yellowed toenails as he mounted her. Once on top, he remained there, a dead weight. She must have felt deeply buried. Waiting, closing her eyes, she demanded her mind take her away. Perhaps her ability to remove herself from a repugnant reality went something like this: *She could feel herself running. She ran endlessly through fields of hay and through fields of wheat until she could see a home in the distance. It was aboveground, a white house with a green roof and a small child romping about in the yard.*

The liquor, along with the passing of time, rendered him useless in bed, so JD stopped trying. He passed out so routinely that Marla Jean could count down to the minute he would fall off her. She often had to move his head away from her face in order to breathe again. Again and again, she prayed that the night would end before he would wake and try again. She moved as far away from him as possible, sometimes to the floor. He had made their time together an abhorrent disregard for love—a rape. Her mind rejected the rape, and her body never received the seed of rape.

Good-looking, but ill-mannered, Johnny stood tall, muscular, cold, and lean, and he had an attitude of complacency about him. His arrogance revealed itself whenever he was in the presence of his father. He did his father's bidding, which molded him as if a deep-seated fear gave him no choice in the matter. Johnny was different when he was with Marla Jean in their many nights together. She felt that he had some decent feelings for her, but when he was around his father, he slapped and cursed her. She always questioned him with pensive eyes, but he avoided looking at her. Although the incidents became less frequent as time went by, Marla Jean didn't dare resist or fight back.

And so, when Marla Jean became pregnant, it was not JD's child but most definitely the younger Flower's baby. She knew it was very important to try to confuse JD by welcoming Johnny. When it was Johnny's turn with Marla Jean, she learned to work her wiles, remembering everything Trixie had taught her. Her survival depended upon her cunning deception to maneuver and lure Johnny to her. He accepted every sensuous minute of being with her without knowing a possible web she was planning to weave. She knew Johnny liked being with her, but what he didn't know was that she enjoyed being with him as well. When not drunk, Johnny was gentle and loving. Perhaps she yielded to the flesh, the sensual side of her being, and let her mind wean from sound reasoning. Nonetheless, her nights with Johnny made her days bearable.

During the quiet periods of her day, she sometimes prayed for the young Flower to come to her that night. She couldn't shake the daydreams of Johnny's firm, solid, smooth body next to hers. Thinking of JD jolted her out of her pleasant daydreams. It required effort to obliterate JD from her mind and bring Johnny into focus. She knew she needed to eliminate Johnny from her daydreams as well, but how could she when her time with him at night was so lovely?

Most nights, Johnny came to her smelling fragrant and clean, as if realizing the importance of cleanliness to closeness. She closed her eyes as soon as she realized it was Johnny and not JD who was to be her lover.

Please, Lord, let this be your blessing. Let him care 'bout me.

She felt erotically appealing as he pulled back the covers, looking at her brown body and eagerly crawling in beside her.

"Move over, baby doll, Johnny's here."

Sometimes, at first, he just held her, a need stemming from his infancy, perhaps. Although it wasn't very long before his lean body trembled with passion when he started to caress her.

"You is so smooth, like peach skin."

She responded as his hands and lips moved over her. He moved slowly over her smooth belly and the long lengths of her sleek thighs. He loved to feel her, to feel her respond, watching. He, alone, was making something beautiful happen, without his father, and in spite of his father. Soon, she reached for him.

"Johnny, Johnny . . ."

He maneuvered over her. She arched up and drew to him like a magnet. She felt she had the strength of many men as she held him, nearly breathless. The momentum moved them as one. Enthralled with each other's timing, they moved and never disconnected. Immeasurable energy burst forth, climaxing their union. Suddenly, he fell back, breathing in great gulps of air.

Loudly, Johnny exclaimed his passion. "Yaw got me, girl. Oh Lord, I loves ya!"

Doped with the fumes of their "bolt of lightning," he lay beside her. She stayed close, not wanting to accept the sudden disconnection.

He patted her head with sweet exhaustion. "You is good. Oh, you is fresh and good!" Later, before he fell asleep, he held her again, like she was a precious gift.

Together, they slept as dawn crept in the shabby room. Slowly, the light of day entered and revealed their nakedness. As their eyes unveiled the reality of daytime, each turned away from the other. It was over, the dream, the magic, and the rhapsody of their union in the darkness. They got out of the lumpy, disheveled bed without a word. Johnny quickly dressed, left the room, and waited at the old kitchen table for the usual breakfast to be placed before him. He may have had to force from his mind the feelings he had for this young woman. On most mornings, his zombie father was ignorant of his surroundings. He never knew that Johnny and Marla Jean came out of the same sleeping place almost every night.

ও

JD sneered at Marla Jean as if the words were assuring him of his possession. "Ya'all get to stoking that stove or I'll be breaking that wood over your head, woman!"

He stared at her with threatening, hungover eyes. "I's hungry. Git me my grub."

He sat down at the table and looked over at Johnny. "What ya'all looking at?"

Johnny hesitated. "Nuttin', Pa. I ain't looking at nothing."

He glanced up at Marla Jean and quickly looked the other way. He twisted uncomfortably in his chair. "But, I was thinkin'—"

JD interrupted him. "I do the thinkin', you ain't got no thinkin' to do. So, you quit your lookin' and thinkin'."

"I got eyes for lookin' and I got a head for thinkin', old man," Johnny shot back, "and I aim to do both if I have a mind to."

JD grabbed Johnny by the throat faster than anyone could believe he could move. "Not if I bash your head 'til your eyes pop outta your thinkin' head."

"Go ahead and bash my head. I don't care. I hate it. I hate we live like this. You're a thinkin' drunk and I'm no better. We're nobody, nothing! Do you hear me? Nothing!"

JD hit Johnny hard.

The young man looked him square in the eye. "Hit me again, old man. Go ahead!"

JD grabbed his hair and pounded him again and again. Johnny did not resist. Exhausted, JD let loose of Johnny's hair and plopped back down in his chair.

"You better shut up, boy . . . You better shut up."

At the stove, Marla Jean hung on to every word as she stood with her back to them, fixing grits for the two men—one she hated, one she loved. This was the first time she'd heard Johnny raise his voice to his father.

JD put his head down on the table, mumbling, "Son of a bastard, son of a bitch."

Slowly, the anger dissolved. With JD's head down, eyes covered, Marla Jean anxiously turned and looked at Johnny. She spied the stove poke near him, then looked at him again.

Johnny, grab the stove poke and kill him. Her blazing eyes added, *Now! Now!*

He responded by shaking his head as if to say, *I can't. I can't.*

Marla Jean walked over and picked up the poke. She moved quickly behind JD and raised the poke, and Johnny hurried to grab it from her. Just then JD looked up.

Johnny, hiding the poke behind him, said, "I better put more wood in the stove."

"Let the wench do it, you stupid idiot," JD ordered, looking over at Marla Jean. Back at the stove, she looked down at her hands, which were shaking uncontrollably.

Marla Jean served breakfast that day the same as she did every morning, then they both left. They never thanked her or even acted appreciative of all she did for them.

As Johnny left each day, she noticed his eyes looked everywhere but at her. Faith, hope, it didn't matter—it was fleeting. That tiny twinge of expectation was disappearing. She fell back into despair.

Marla Jean didn't know where they went and, for the most part, didn't care. They didn't tell her anything, of course; she was nothing to them—at least, nothing to one of them. She was nobody, just someone to do their bidding, to tend to their demands. She dared not complain or ask any questions. She wanted to believe there was something for her to hold on to, perhaps a beginning for her and Johnny. A small part of her yearned for a life with Johnny, but she knew it wouldn't happen, not with JD around. She may have thought of talking to Johnny about running away together, but she never did.

Johnny often spent time out back target practicing. He was able to purchase a powerful scope for his rifle and was proud of his ability to hit the bull's-eye more often than not. Accomplishing something that had nothing to do with his father must have given him a good feeling about himself.

When passed out, JD didn't know that Marla Jean joined Johnny out back. To have a conversation with Johnny in the daytime must have given Marla Jean hope. But they didn't do much talking. When the shots were fired, Marla Jean covered her ears.

"Johnny, will you stop and talk to me?" she asked him one day.

"Why?" he answered as he aimed and shot again.

"Don't you want to get away from your father? Why have you stayed here this long? I'm the prisoner, and you are in prison by choice."

"I'm just like him, good for nothing. I can't escape." Johnny shot again, and this time it didn't even hit the target. Angrily, he yelled, "Leave me alone!"

"I care for you, you know that. Go ahead and tell me you don't care for me."

"I don't know what to do with you, Marla Jean. You are the best thing that has ever happened to me. And to think I have to thank that horrible excuse for a human being, lying dead drunk inside, for you."

"Johnny, we can run away together. Yes, we can, we can . . ."

"No, we can't run away and live happily ever after. No, that's a dream, not for people like us. And I'm sorry, but I won't set you free, either." He looked her square in the eye and said, "You listen good: you will never be free . . . just like me."

"Maybe if he didn't wake up from one of his drunken binges, we could be free." Johnny carefully put down his rifle and walked over to Marla Jean and grabbed her. "Is it so bad living here?"

"My God, you really don't see how bad it is for me—and for you, too. You are a blind man, Johnny."

He let go and pushed her so hard she fell to the ground. He finished with, "He *will* die someday, just hafta wait."

Marla Jean, stunned, got up and walked away. She ultimately gave up all hope for a good life for herself with Johnny. She concluded that he was destined for destruction, as was his father, as Attie Atlas had been before them. She longed for a better life but couldn't quite convince herself she deserved it.

❧

Weeks later, Trixie and Tremont *literally* dropped off her bike one day. Fearful to stop completely, Trixie drove slow enough so Tremont could drop it carefully without stopping. Marla Jean heard them drive by and then the sound of the bike clunking down on the ground. Of course she knew who'd brought it. So happy to have her bike back, Marla Jean started riding around, though not going far at first. She wanted so badly to go see Trixie, but she knew JD would go after her in Idlewild. Instead, she rode her bicycle to her previous basement home. She wondered if anyone had moved in. It wasn't long before she could see the place from afar. No one was around, and the tall grasses that obscured the place told her it was uninhabitable. She dropped her bike and waded through the grasses to the back where her parents were buried. Pushing the brush aside with her legs and feet, she found the cross that identified her father's burial site. Letting out a cry, she fell down and screamed, "Daddy, forgive me, forgive me. I'm sorry I left you . . . I wasn't with you at the end. Please forgive me." She held her head in her hands and sobbed. Still on her hands and knees, she crawled over to her mother's grave. She sat, crossed her legs, and tightly grasped her hands together to pray.

"Dear God . . ." Suddenly, the words that came out of her mouth were not hers. Using Marla Jean's vocal cords, the words reiterated a message from her past. *In the brief course of your life, you've grown strong. You took Labor's road. Stay on it. Remember your worthy aim is ahead.* Her voice diminished, and the words ended with a whisper: *I will be with you always.* The young woman drew her hand up to her mouth, waiting for more words to come out, but they didn't.

Thinking on this strange happening while riding back on her bike, she remembered that she had read some of those words out loud to her mother the day she died. She prayed and prayed for a more specific reveal, like a road or path out of here.

When she returned, she walked her bike to its special place out back. She couldn't let go of it and held on longer than usual. She moved her hands over the handlebars again and again as though she were caressing a jewel. Perhaps she was remembering when she'd first spotted them peeking up from the earth. And how lucky it was that she'd found the bike in good shape. Ultimately, it helped her survive her imprisonment. All at once, she knew the bike had to be instrumental in her escape. She knew what she *had* to do.

Over the next couple of days, she carefully took time to study the actions, timings, and comments of Johnny and

JD. The first morning they both left the house, it didn't take her long to figure out how long it would take her to ride to Idlewild and back before Johnny and JD would return home. Then again, they might not come home at all, as happened sometimes. She hopped on her bike and took off. Her ride seemed long, so she peddled harder until sweat beaded up on her forehead. At one point, she stopped to wipe her brow with her sleeve. When she got close enough, she may have thought, *What if Trixie's not there? I'll have to look for her—but I don't have time.*

To Marla Jean's delight, her best friend surprised her. Sitting on her porch, Trixie saw her first and called out, "Oh my golly, is that you, Marla Jean?"

Marla Jean was so happy Trixie still lived in the same place. They didn't waste any time getting to each other and holding on tight. Upon release, they stared at each other and then laughed and hugged again.

Finally, Trixie said, "Are you free, girl? Tell me?"

"No, and I can't stay long, but I just had to see you." The girls embraced again, then Trixie pulled away and asked, "How *did* you get away?"

"I didn't. Really, I have to get back before they come home."

"What . . . You're going back there?"

Trixie didn't understand why Marla Jean stayed with JD and Johnny when she could just leave.

Marla Jean worshiped her friend, her best friend. She had dreamed of having a best friend like Trixie but had never believed it would happen. But it had, and she was grateful and wanted Trixie to know.

Marla Jean whispered, "I won't be coming back again, but I wanted to see you one last time and thank you for everything." The tears sprang from her eyes as she declared, "I love you, Trixie. You are my best friend in the world. How could I have been so lucky?"

Trixie held her and said, "There, there, it's okay, don't cry, we'll be friends forever. Who says we're not going to see each other again?"

The two continued to talk and even laughed a bit, but when Marla Jean had to get on her bicycle to leave, their goodbyes could barely be verbalized. Marla Jean knew she would never walk the beautiful streets of Idlewild again. It was a place that brought joy and happiness to her like she had never known before in her life.

✌

As a writer, I've wondered if Marla Jean told Trixie about her many nights with Johnny. That she stayed with him despite the conditions under which they lived. If she did, maybe she didn't emphasize how much she liked him, even loved him. Maybe Trixie didn't want to know everything, since she had once been lovesick over him, too. The young woman, in tears, rode away from her best friend that day, and her prediction that she would never see her or Idlewild again turned out to be true.

✌

Upon her return to the home she had known for nearly two years, she found it was just like she'd left it. She was relieved that JD and Johnny had not come home early, especially today. She spent the next hour checking the dwelling for anything she could take with her, hoping to find some money, and she was surprised and happy when she did. She packed up her few things and went out to attach her bag to the bicycle. Whether from instinct or not, she started to hurry, anxious to leave. She may have thought, *What will they do to me if they find me leaving, especially if they catch me stealing from them?*

Then the unthinkable happened. As she was walking her bike from the back of the dwelling, not yet in front, she heard the car drive in and park. She said a swear word and stopped cold, stood still, and wiped her sweaty hands on her pants. She waited, head down, heart pounding. It was early evening, not yet dark, and luckily JD, more drunk than Johnny, stumbled into his cave home unaware of the girl's presence on the other side of the dwelling.

But Johnny spotted her. He started toward her and then stopped. "What's you doing, girl? Where you think you're goin'?"

The two stared at each other for the longest time.

Grasping tightly to her bike handlebars, her head tilted down again and tears sprang from her eyes. "Johnny . . . I have to go."

With a half laugh, he questioned her: "You have to go—go where?" Immediately, he knew what she meant. "Okay—go. Go, girl, just go!" He waved her on, nearly losing his balance in the process.

"Johnny, I can't live like this," she cried.

"You're a dreamer. Go'wan, see if that damn club will take you back."

"I can't stay. You know why. You're never here anyway."

"Go! I never liked ya much anyway . . ."

"Johnny! JD's poison. He runs you. You know it, too."

"Yaw, an' maybe I don't care. Maybe JD's right. Maybe you is just a whore."

Marla Jean started to cry. "You like me—I think you love me. You know I'm no whore."

"Ya thinks I love ya? I'm telling ya to go'wan, ain't I?"

"Johnny—"

"Git on outta here. I don't ever want to see your ugly face again. And don't you come back, yaw hear . . ."

Just like that, he walked away from her. Her husband, for-lorn and alone, had freed her and then disappeared into the cave of his dismal existence.

Marla Jean hurried to the road and got on her bike. She peddled hard, the tears pouring down her cheeks. She stopped to wipe her face. Suddenly, she turned around. "I gotta go back. I don't know what I'm doing, where I'm going."

Just as suddenly, she turned again. "No! I'm not going back." This time, she didn't look back.

She traveled quite a distance to the west, fifteen miles or so, all the while questioning her escape. She knew that returning to Idlewild would put her friends in danger when JD returned to get her, and so she continued in a direction far away from her beloved town. Marla Jean crossed the picturesque Pere Marquette River and happened upon a small hamlet among many oak and pine trees. She didn't know then that she had ridden into Walhalla, the little settlement named by Indians long ago. A strange peace came over her as she continued to ride down the wide path into the center of the village.

And God was there, and He whispered to her: *Come unto me, and I will give you rest.*

Marla Jean saw the Emerson House, and it looked like a very old building to her, too old to be servicing its community anymore. But it had served Walhalla as the center for business for many years and, geographically, was still the center of the village. Situated on the south side of the tracks, it still served as a depot, post office, and store. The schoolhouse, a block away, would become very important to Marla Jean's child, although she would never know.

Three trains a day rumbled in each direction through the town, dropping off the mail and other cargo. For many years, trade was good for the Raes, the family who ran the Emerson House. Many townsfolk were trying their hand at farming around the area, as there was little work in Walhalla. Times were changing, lumbering was tapering off, cars were becoming a common sight, and the center of town was moving to the new highway and away from the railroad tracks.

When Marla Jean walked into the store in the Emerson House that day, everyone stopped and looked at her. It was unusual to see colored folks in the area.

"I need work, ma'am," she told the woman behind the counter. "You got work for me? I can work hard." Marla Jean could hear her own soft voice as she spoke, and it frightened her. It was as if the whole world had stopped to listen.

Mrs. Rae replied, "I'm sorry, but there's no work here. Go on—get on your way now."

Self-consciously, Marla Jean bowed her head. She studied the floor. I'm sure she hoped the floor would swallow her up. But it didn't, so she allowed her feet to take her out the way she'd come.

A petite, white-haired woman in her sixties gently touched her arm. Marla Jean jumped.

"You can come home with me, young lady. Don't be scared."

Those in the store who overheard the invitation raised their eyebrows in disbelief.

Marla Jean looked at the woman with a half smile, unsure of the kind invitation. The woman spoke to her again: "I'll fix you something to eat."

The black girl and older woman left the Emerson House together.

"My name's Lizzy Schreck. What's yours?"

I bring fresh showers for the thirsting flowers,
From the seas and streams;
I bear light shade for the leaves when laid
In their noonday dreams.
                              —*Percy Bysshe Shelley*

Clouds are predisposed for God's creations.
                              —*C. Ohse*

CHAPTER SEVEN

The Rendezvous

In 1935, a newly constructed tavern took center stage in Walhalla. The tavern, christened the Rendezvous, flourished, just as the black child christened Noonday Flower would flourish.

The Rendezvous' pine-log walls surrounded a horseshoe bar that was made of the finest mahogany. The mirrored wall behind the bar gave the illusion that the whole tavern was larger than the true measurement of the place. Its planked hardwood floor was suitably made to withstand the stomping boots of the many who danced there on Saturday nights. On the main, windowless wall to the north, a painting depicted the essence of the new establishment. It portrayed a contented fisherman in a sinking boat, fishing pole in hand, and floating beer cans surrounding him. The inscription read: "I like to sit and think and fish. And fish and sit and think. And think and fish. And sit and wish. That I could get a drink."

The people of the black community in Idlewild didn't visit the tight-knit white village of Walhalla. The black people numbered many, and stayed in and around Idlewild, fifteen miles east from Walhalla. The fact that Marla Jean came to Walhalla and worked for pennies a day remained unknown to many of the villagers. Idlewild was a high-class black resort, while Walhalla was a poorer, white-populated refuge for common folk. There was no need for a white influence in Idlewild, just as a black intrusion was not desired in Walhalla's newly built tavern. The communities respected each other and politely stayed away from one another. It seemed everyone wanted it that way.

My parents and I knew the hearts of our Walhalla neighbors. Even though I was young at this time, I can recall my parents speaking of our neighbors in respectful ways. Most Walhallans were simple people because they believed in what they had, not in what they wished for. I came to understand that the people of Walhalla didn't know they were living with prejudice toward others unlike them. Many did not recognize the ignorance that plagued their little village.

So why did Marla Jean venture from Idlewild into Walhalla, an unknown domain for her? When I learned of her escape to the small town years later, I anguished over her short life. This young girl worked in Walhalla day after day, month after month, content with a baby on the way, and found a thimble of peace and happiness despite all her ill fortune. Marla Jean had married Johnny Flower at eighteen, although many in Walhalla did not know she was married. After Marla Jean died, and as far as anyone knew, Johnny was only a phantom of a husband despite the fact that his sperm was indeed a reality. The union of these two young black people had created a living, breathing baby girl-child living in an all-white community, and this child was the subject of discussion for a lot of villagers.

My father, Oscar Johnson, had many occasions to visit the new tavern. He told my mother and me many stories that were shared among the gossiping townsmen there. After Marla Jean had her baby, the beer chatter in this new establishment was all about the colored baby at the Mavis's. This new development in the tiny village remained the subject of discussion, and, in time, not one male resident had failed to voice his opinion. Most of the men declared the black child none of their business as long as the child stayed out of sight.

"She should be taken back where her mammy come from," some said.

"Leave her be. She's not hurting nobody," said others.

"Yaw, she's just a child," my father remarked.

Segregation was rarely discussed in Walhalla, so no one really questioned it. It was accepted there just as it was elsewhere. From my schooling, I knew that, by 1900, Michigan had some of the strongest civil laws in the nation, as well as a supreme court to enforce them. But in Walhalla, and in rural areas everywhere, not many knew it. The talk of race stayed within the confines of homes, except at the Rendezvous.

"That's just the way it is," some said.

"The colored baby can stay here, just so too many of them don't come 'round," they agreed. And that was just about the end of it.

☙

I remember the stories my father brought home from the Rendezvous. They were entertaining and revealing, and helped me understand the simplistic lives of the people in Walhalla, my neighbors and friends. It wasn't until later in life that I realized their significance and jotted down their stories.

☙

Women of the village did not go to the Rendezvous. They were allowed inside but were not welcomed. Dance, sweat, smoke, and beer were not conducive to ladylike behavior. Even though the fine ladies of the town would have liked to join in the fun, they didn't let it be known. Some women did go, however: out-of-towners with no names who were referred to as "loose women." These ladies, just passing through, loved to frolic at the Rendezvous, displaying no regard for their good reputations, which they had clearly left at home. Looking for a good time, they liked the woodsy change from the concrete city taverns back home.

The Rendezvous, soon nicknamed the Rendy, became a rowdy honky-tonk where everyone could let down their hair on a Saturday night. Later, in the 1950s and 1960s, the farmers in the famed Stakenas Band set aside their plows and picked up their horns to blow the crowd into the wee hours of the night. Farmer Stakenas led the famed band with his golden saxophone. All who came through the doors had a good time. The music rang out and infected the crowd with inescapable rhythm. Quickly, the dance floor filled as the Rendezvous' signature polka roused everyone to take part.

> *Just because you think you're so prett-y!*
> *Just because you think you're so hot!*
> *Just because you think you got some-thin',*
> *That no-body else has got!*
> *You smile when you spend all my mon-ey!*
> *You laugh and call me ol' Santa Claus . . .*

"One, two, three, hop; one, two, three, hop; one, two, three, hop!" Feet synchronized movements with bobbing heads and dizzying turns. Everyone sang along, and the roof of the Rendezvous didn't physically rise, even though it seemed like it did.

> *I'm tell-ing you, bab-y, I'm through with you!*
> *Because—just be-cause!*

Loud stomps and a "yahoo" or two invited a second and third verse.

My father remembered one Saturday night when a woman, a troubled soul, came into the establishment and headed straight to the bar. She drank heavily, never removing her coat. She was a fine-looking woman with hair of gold and perfectly shaped eyebrows over uncertain eyes, which were glazed and saddened. Before long, a man meandered over to her and asked her to dance. As she stood, she backed away from the barstool, swaying to and fro, and removed her coat with great difficulty. Everyone within viewing distance looked and gulped. The bewildered man, uneasy about her unsteadiness, reluctantly followed her to the dance floor. When the woman started to shuffle and move about, her shapely silhouette could be seen through the flimsy nightgown that she was wearing. Her breasts seemed to enjoy their freedom. They bobbled up and down and followed her, one beat short, as she twirled around. Her well-rounded bottom filled the circumference of her gown, and her bare legs barely skipped a beat. While many male patrons whooped and hollered, others stopped and stared.

No one knew what to do about the nearly naked woman who continued to dance and dance and dance, even when the band lost all wind to blow their horns and beat their drums. Eventually, the woman was rescued by an acquaintance and returned to her home. The woman never remembered the incident, which was a good thing. Others have never forgotten it, and many patrons have analyzed it in detail, beginning with, "Remember the time when . . ." This was as close as the people of Walhalla ever got to seeing a strip tease or a burlesque show without leaving town.

The ladies of Walhalla didn't worry much about the playful tarts who came from nowhere to dance and flirt with their men until night turned to dawn. Women like Lizzy Schreck, Vita Mavis, and my mama were too busy with daylong chores to concern themselves with their husbands' playtime. The end of each day meant rest at last for the hardworking women of Walhalla. Of course, not all men needed the outlet the Rendy provided, either. The farmers especially didn't have the time to get over to the watering hole and contribute to the discussion of politics, taxes, or the colored baby down the road at the Mavises'.

℀

One Saturday night, long before the band had set up for the incoming crowd, a few of the regulars were *not* discussing the colored resident down the road at the Mavises'. They were also *not* discussing who was running for township supervisor or the big raise in property taxes. Rather, they were discussing the new outhouse that was built out at the Wanda farm.

"Did they dig a two-holer this time? How many young'uns they got now? Must be up to eight," asked Fritz O'Brick.

Norm Camfield, wanting to stretch out his saga of the new outhouse at the Wanda farm, started in again. "Did yaw hear about the outhouse party Mrs. Wanda was a-plannin'? Wanda tells me his old lady wanted to throw a party to celebrate their new two-holer."

"That so?" someone remarked.

"Yaw, she told Ol' Wanda that she wanted a party with music and dancing and all that stuff. She wanted lots of food and drinking, too. So everyone would have to use the outhouse."

"I never heard about the Wanda party. When was it?" another asked.

"Never happened," Norm said.

The bartender, listening, asked, "How come?"

"I'll tell you why. Now, listen up." Norm started to chuckle, then stopped to clear his throat.

"Mrs. Wanda said to Mr. Wanda that she was proud of the new two-holer, but she wanted to have some decent toilet paper for the party."

Norm laughed again. "So, Ol' Wanda put two dollars in an envelope and mailed it to Sears, Roebuck and Company with an order that says, 'Send me some toilet paper.'"

Norm laughed even harder. "So, Sears and Roebuck wrote back and said he's s'pose to order from their new spring-and-summer catalogue, and toilet paper is on page three sixty-five."

"Did he order that new, really soft stuff called Northern?" someone asked.

"No, he shot a letter right back to Mr. Sears Roebuck. He says, 'What makes you think this Swede would be so dumb as to order any toilet paper if'n I had your spring-and-summer catalogue?'"

The Rendezvous regulars roared with laughter. Some stomped their feet while others pounded the bar. They sighed heavily after their good laugh and finished up their beers.

Norm concluded with, "Poor Mrs. Wanda, she cried for a week and never had herself a two-holer party."

❧

Another Saturday afternoon discussion at the Rendezvous centered on a Halloween prank urged upon a fellow neighbor.

"I still don't know who done it," remarked Fritz. "Nobody will admit to it. Maybe some of yous had something to do with it?" The men at the bar looked out from under their eyebrows and shook their heads from side to side. "It took mor'an one man to do that job, for sure."

"You ain't never gonna know, either, Fritz." Norm chuckled. "I s'pose they gonna take that secret to their grave."

"I'd give more than two bits and my good mama's sweet apple pie to have seen Sweeney's face when he walked outside his house that morning after Halloween. There it be, a-balancin' on top of his barn. Clean on top. I mean, at the very top, a hay wagon full of apples, 'magine that. That'd be a mighty big old lightning rod, not to mention all those apple pies," Fritz dreamily informed everyone.

Sweeney must have dropped his choppers and said, "How'd the sam hill did it get up there?"

"I know how they did it." Auggie Haus spoke up, and the others turned to him and listened suspiciously.

"They took the wheels off, and then they took that wagon apart," he continued, slowly, "piece by piece."

"How'd you know so much about it, Auggie?" Norm asked. "Maybe you was there in the middle of Devil's Night decking Sweeney's barn with an old wagon? Why don't you confess?"

A big smile spread across Auggie's face. "Oh no, I wasn't. I was watchin' from behind a tree, I swear. I saw the whole thing. They took apart the front of that wagon, and the back, and the sideboards. They lifted them one at a time, passing 'em on up, from one to another, clean to the top. Then, they put it together up there. Ya, I'm telling you, I was watching and couldn't believe what my eyes was telling me."

The men around the horseshoe bar looked at each other in disbelief.

Auggie continued, pleased at having their undivided attention. "Then they passed one bushel of apples after another to fill the wagon up. It was a sight! When they was all done, they passed the bottle of spirits 'tween them and looked at each other, and looked at that wagon, and marveled at the job they'd done. Oh, they celebrated. You could tell they felt they was deserving a medal of honor!"

Norm added loudly, "Yup, people come from miles around to see that wagon on top of that big barn that was chock-full of apples. What a sight! People, oooh-in' an' ahhhhh-in'. Ya know, I think Old Sweeney liked it, being a celebrity of sorts."

Later in the month, all the talk was about the big wind that came along and blew the wagon down. It must have hit the ground real hard, because it broke up into splinters, and the apples rolled all over the field. They surmised that the deer had a feast, and then Sweeney had venison whenever he had a hankering for it.

It became a ritual for the tavern regulars to get together at the Rendezvous, have a beer, share their news, and tell stories that included a lot of belly laughing before it was time to get on home to their womenfolk and children. Sometimes the stories would get told so many times that, by the time they got around to everybody in Walhalla, the truth got lost in the telling.

❧

The Rendezvous was the scene of another incident that did not turn out to be a friendly one. A lot of travelers stopped in Walhalla to get gas and a bite to eat on their way through, so it was not unusual to see strangers. But it was more than unusual to see colored men stop there. It was a late morning, near noon, when only a few people frequented the bar aside from the locals. It was at that time when three black men entered the Rendezvous.

From Norm's description, I know for a fact that the older of the men was JD Flower. Of course, the regulars didn't know who the men were and didn't know the history between JD and Marla Jean. The bartender thought they had lost their way.

"You fellows heading over to Idlewild?" he asked.

"Hell no, we're just needin' a beer," one man loudly declared while the other man nodded.

"We got beer. What'll you have, a draft?" the bartender asked.

Norm, Fritz, and Auggie were seated across the bar from them. They stared at the newcomers and didn't say much, then one of the black men yelled, "What you guys staring at? Haven't ya ever seen a nigger before?"

"Sorry . . ." Norm said to them, and then turned to his friends. "We don't want curiosity to kill the cat, do we?"

Startled, one of the strangers asked, "Ya'all kill cat and serve it?"

The other asked, "Oh shit, is it good?"

Fritz and Auggie grimaced and said in unison, "No, no! Cat's not on the menu here."

Then JD opened his mouth. "Shut up! I have important business here."

Norm asked, "What kind of business you meaning?"

"We need some 'formation from yous fine white folks. We're missing a dear sister and thought you maybe saw her."

"What's her name? What does she look like? Is she like you?" The questions came fast and furious.

"She's black, her name's Marla Jean, and she's this tall." JD stood and raised his hand above his own head.

Immediately, the regulars looked one to the other and gasped.

JD saw the reaction and asked, "Had you seen her?"

The bartender declared, "No, we never seen that lady. He looked hard at the others as if to say, *Keep your mouth shut.*

It didn't take long for JD to motion for one of his thugs to grab Fritz and put him in a choke hold. JD got angry rather quickly, and asked, "You tell'n me the truth?" Looking at the man holding Fritz, he said to him, "Squeeze harder."

Fritz screamed, "Ah, ah, eeeowwww . . ."

Auggie ran out the back door in a flash.

"Don't say anything, Fritz," Norm yelled.

JD snarled at everyone, "I's heard Marla Jean's a slave to a white farmer 'round here, and you know where, don't ya? Tell me where she is, or your new bar's gonna be nothin' but ashes."

The bartender shouted out, "She is dead, she is dead and gone!"

Quickly Norm added, "She died, we're sorry, but none of us know more than that, sir." JD, stomping his cane, screamed, "Ya killed her? You sons of bitches, you gotta be lying!"

JD hurried over to Norm, grabbed him, and shouted in his ear, "Yaw better be tellin' me more, I wanna know more, where is she?" He looked over to Fritz, then swung back to Norm. "You want you' friend to die?"

The bartender had hit the alarm under the counter. Norm knew it and quickly responded, "You let him go and I'll tell you more."

JD nodded to his accomplice to release Fritz. JD raised his walking implement to strike Norm. "Now, you talk, bastard, or we gonna take you with us—throw you body in a ditch somewhere."

"She died giving birth, they both died, and that is all there is to it." Visibly shaking, Norm tried to end the confrontation. "You better get going now, or you gonna be arrested. You got your information. Now, get out of here while you can."

The bartender joined in: "Now! Get the hell outta here and don't come back!"

Hearing the siren, the two musclemen headed out the door first. JD, unable to move as fast, grabbed his walking stick and slowly walked to the door, cussing a blue streak. "Ya killed her— damn, no-good white trash—killed my Marla Jean!"

As it happened, new customers were coming through the door just as JD passed them. But he took the time to look back at the others and raise his fist and mouth his promise, "I be back." When the sheriff got there, he listened to all the witnesses, but because they all talked at once, and the sheriff couldn't write it all down fast enough, he gave up and concluded that no robbery had occurred and no one was hurt except for Fritz, who insisted that his neck was broken.

※

A frequent patron of the Rendy was Henry Schreck, Lizzy's husband. Short, round-faced, and flat-footed, Henry stooped a little in the shoulders. Henry had once operated the Walhalla coal dock, fueling the trains with coal for many years. The coal vault had to be opened at just the right time for tons of coal to be emptied into the coal car. It may not have seemed an important job to some, but to Henry it was. It was not so much skill as timing and precision needed to keep the trains running to and from Saginaw, a bigger town on the other side of Michigan.

Henry's hair and beard were touched with white, and his twinkling brown eyes looked out from under shaggy brows. Henry no longer shoveled coal into a vault but operated a doodlebug. He'd made over the car to work like a tractor. He was proud of his ingenuity in creating it. His workload was not as heavy as past years, but because of his age, it was just as demanding. He grew corn and hay on his twenty acres—not a substantial crop, but still it required preparation of the land, cultivation, prayers for sunshine and rain, and, ultimately, harvesting before this cash crop paid the bills.

Henry had accepted Marla Jean into his home without question. At first, he didn't pay much attention to her or the work she did around the house. When meals were on time, and the clothes were washed and ironed, and the floor was swept clean, she was accepted with subtle approval. But when she worked the doodlebug in the field, his approval of this young worker skyrocketed. When Marla Jean died, Henry missed the girl more than he thought he would.

"She sure was mighty fine . . . a darn good, good worker," he told the others at the bar.

The others listened with curious wonder as the man they respected told of the birth of one and the death of another. As he spoke, honesty shone on the man's face, and it caused a hush among the others who bent over the bar to listen. His voice was deeply calm as he told of the day that a black baby had been born into their little white village. He spoke with authority, and even though he had not been physically present at the birth, he acted as if he'd played a major role in it.

"Black or white, the birthing's the same," he said. "Ain't no difference, and the pain's the same. They all holler good and loud. Some dies. 'Twas a bad day, I tell you. That black girl was a good girl. My missus cries like a water faucet ya can't turn off. She sure does miss her."

The men sat for a moment in silence. An idea had been put to them that they'd never given thought to before: black and white people are the same.

"My land's sake, she could work a field better'n any man I'd know, except for you, Olie." Henry spoke directly to the tall man at the far end of the bar.

Olie Brenner dropped his head into one of his long, hard-working, callused hands and rubbed his face. His thoughtful eyes, set in a long, thin face, looked out from beneath an unruly thatch of dark-brown hair that crowned his head.

To the crowd around the bar, Olie said, "My boy is more than two now, and I helped birth him. Birthing is a miracle, all right. The wife worked harder than I have ever worked. He come out a slippery feller, all puffy, so little he was. I'll never forget it."

The men listened but couldn't look at Olie. They stared into their beers.

"Yes, sir, a handsome boy, my Bob, and some day, he'll be a fine farmer," Olie Brenner concluded.

෴

My father was there that day. He knew this to be true because the Brenners were our neighbors. What he didn't know was that some-day I would be young Bob's teacher, and no one knew that I would be the little black girl's teacher as well.

Young Bob was born and cast into the same mold as his father. Back then, sons grew up and did what their fathers did for a living. This youngster was lucky to have so bright a future, in contrast to the black baby down the road at the Mavises'. No one even bothered thinking about her future. It was as if she didn't have one.

❧

When Olie left the bar that day, the bartender remarked, "It's a darn shame there ain't more men like that Olie Brenner in the world."

Everyone knew Olie Brenner was good at everything he did—working in the fields, rolling logs, chopping wood, or taming bees: he could do it all.

The bartender concluded, "I don't know anybody who cares as much about folks and loving just one woman as that man does."

The men laughed with a welcome release from serious talk. After some lighter conversation, like the questionable weather forecast, the bartender again spoke of Olie Brenner. "Gotta say that Olie's the workingest man in the whole county, not like you guys." Suddenly disenchanted with the faces around the bar, the same faces week after week, year after year, the bartender declared, "Why don't yaw all get off your asses, get on home, and love up your woman?"

❧

Just as the bartender said, Olie was well respected in Mason County. Olie was a gentle giant of a man with a fearless and frank countenance. He did not frequent the bar much, only stopping by on occasion to say howdy to neighbors and friends. Olie worked hard on his eighty-acre farm, not far off Highway 10. The never-ending chores on the farm kept his family and him extremely busy. Besides his son, the apple of his eye, Olie deeply loved his wife, Mrs. B, as she was called. She was a simple woman, but behind her blank look, she had a mind full of kind thoughts. And, with a manner perfect for the wife of a common man, she bore Olie a fine son indeed. Honesty was present in the child's clear blue eyes, the only outward trait he'd gotten from his mother. Otherwise, the child grew to be the spitting image of his father, tall and thin with broad shoulders and large muscles.

A lucky boy, little Bob's parents reared him with love and abundant devotion. Father and son became a twosome. If you saw one, the other was nearby. The farmer took pleasure in taking the child with him wherever he went. It was not uncommon for Olie to have little Bob with him when driving the tractor. When the child fell asleep in his arms, he cautiously got off the tractor and placed his sleeping son in a bed of newly mowed hay along the fence line. Olie had to remember where he'd laid his precious cargo before he finished the field to go on to another.

And God was there.

In a year or two, when little Bob could run sure-footed, he chased after his daddy, repeating, "Take me, too, Daddy." Olie got so used to having little Bob with him that, in time, the youngster became a big help to him.

A rumored anecdote about Olie and his son was first told at the Rendy. Olie had stopped the tractor in the middle of a field. Being a pipe smoker and needing a smoke, he looked for a match to light his pipe, and when he discovered he didn't have one match in all his pockets, he shouted a word or two of regrettable obscenities.

"I'll get a match for you, Daddy." The boy eagerly ran to the house and back, short of a quarter mile, just to get a match for his father.

When little Bob turned five years old, he began driving the old B tractor, the only tractor on the Brenner farm. It was a slow-moving vehicle but a jewel of a machine for the farmers of the 1930s.

One day, Sophia Johnson, my mother, was working in our yard and saw the B tractor coming down the road with no driver. She told me she panicked and felt faint. Before she opened her mouth to scream for help, she adjusted her spectacles and saw that little Bob was driving the tractor, the boy barely able to reach its steering wheel.

As the years passed, little Bob grew up loving farm life. His father passed to him his love of the land, the planting, and the bountiful harvest. Little Bob also developed another love in these formative years: the love of books. When the five-year-old received his first reader, little Bob unlocked a door bigger than the Brenners' barn; it presented a whole new world to him.

As his teacher, it didn't take me long to realize the boy's potential. In time, this common farmer's son read books of strength and manhood, of hunting and fishing, of travel, wars, and of noble death in fight. He read of peace and plenty, and of equal justice in the land; the boy read on and on, wide-eyed and, I would guess, forgetful of errands for his mother.

In 1935, little Bob began going to the Bell School on First Street in the middle of Walhalla, a small, perfectly square cement-block building with windows on two sides of the structure. A big cast-iron bell placed high above the building sounded its metallic gong to the entire village at the start of every school day.

"I'm a big boy, Ma. I can go to school by myself," the strong-willed boy told his mother on the first day of school.

Over the river and through the woods he walked, not to his grandmother's house but to school to begin an adventure—one that books are made of.

I believe in the purpose of everything living;
That taking is but the forerunner of giving;
That strangers are friends that we some day may
        meet;
And not all the bitter can equal the sweet;
That's creeds are but colors, and no man has said
That God loves the yellow rose more than the red.
                        —Edgar A. Guest

A man's origin is unrelated to his heart and soul.
                        —C. Ohse

CHAPTER EIGHT

The Bell School

I was Bob's teacher his second year at the Bell School. I preferred that the children call me Miss Maggie rather than Mrs. Dunn. After all, I was not much older than my oldest student. I loved Bob from the moment he stepped into my classroom.

It didn't take long for my little neighbor to be a pro around the school. He knew all the kids' names and grades. He knew all the rules and obeyed me without question. He knew his spot in the cloakroom where he hung his coat, put his galoshes, and placed his lunch box. His desk was orderly with his books piled according to subject from the beginning of the day to the end of the day. He used a pencil until his little hand couldn't hold it any longer when it wore down to a stub. In second grade, Bob was already borrowing books from the third- and fourth-graders to read. After writing his spelling words ten times each, completing his arithmetic, and checking it twice, Bob's face, heart, and soul were in a book.

Many children have a penchant for mischievous behavior. So, when I was stoking the stove or tending to other business, one or more of the pupils would create havoc of some kind or another, but not Bob. Someone was always prodding him to do naughty things, but he never yielded to their persistence. Goody Two-Shoes became his name of taunt, but that soon gave way to Bookie Bob and then just Bookie. That nickname caught on and remained with Bob throughout his school years.

It is a difficult undertaking teaching all subjects in a one-room school. Children come in all shapes, sizes, and person-alities. Character is revealed to a teacher in a very short time, and so it is helpful for a child to come to school with pertinent values— exemplary behavior and respect for all people. It was no different in Walhalla.

I became keenly aware that some children soon sensed the differences between themselves and Bob. I think back and will confess that, without a doubt, Bookie was my most prized student.

Bookie was a loner, and books were his friends. I would often catch myself calling on Bookie to recite the lesson of the day. I knew him well, as we were neighbors and lived just a half mile from one another. I loved Bookie, and tried not to show partial-ity. I truly loved all my students, especially when they tried hard and showed promise. But Bookie was special, and I knew it.

I hoped I could challenge Bookie throughout his school-ing years. My private dream was that someday he would go to college. I knew the time would come when I had nothing left to teach him. But the hope that he would realize his potential and go on to higher learning troubled me. It was indeed a rare happening in those post-Depression years for anyone to go to college, even the gifted, and especially the poor.

Bookie kept reading and never tired of it, but, of course, he couldn't read all the time. There were weeks in the summer when he couldn't even pick up a book. Farm work was demanding and relentless, and it started before school let out in the spring and lasted until after school started in the autumn near the momentous harvest time of year. And so, Bookie's life was full, and he was happy and content, whether he was working or reading.

One day in second grade, Bookie met Noonday, a little person not unlike himself, as some people may have thought, but very much like him. It was the first time I saw her, too.

It was a warm afternoon for fall. I remember Bookie leaving his seat, quietly, of course. He wandered, probably thinking about the contents of his lunch box. He was so grown up for seven, and like a grown man with a boy's yearnings, he appreciated a good lunch. The boy sometimes longed to be outside because his love of the out-of-doors never lessened as his desire for learning grew.

Bookie looked out the window and saw a little black girl sitting under a tree. He had never seen a black person before and was intrigued by her stand-up pigtails and her little feet, which were white on the bottoms. He stared at her until finally she looked up and saw him. Their eyes locked for the longest time. Bookie turned away, probably to consider what he was seeing. He looked again, and the little one was still there. She was pleased when she finally saw someone in the window. More than likely, she had been sitting there a long while. Finally, Bookie pressed his face against the windowpane. His distorted nose and mouth all crushed up to the window made the girl giggle. The little girl puckered her lips and smacked a kiss on her hand and tossed it, airborne, right at Bookie. Startled, he turned to the classroom and said, "Miss Maggie, there's a dirty girl out here!"

With that remark, the students bolted from their desks, scurried to the window, and, one by one, peered out. I, just like my students, open-eyed and curious, looked, too. The little girl, delighted with her audience, began to dance and prance and move her lips to a tuneless song. The music was within her, the trees and grasses her stage. She delighted in her presentation until the laughter turned joy into mockery. She knew the difference when she saw one older child mouth the words, "Go home, nigger."

Suddenly, I was jolted into being a teacher again. I demanded my pupils take their seats, and when the bobbing heads retreated from the window, the little girl left. I was as interested as all my pupils in the mystery of a black child in our midst. Questions flooded my mind, and I regret not taking time to speak to my class of the first time Noonday danced into the schoolyard, and into our lives.

Bookie soon returned to the window, and for the first time, I was angry with him.

"Sit down, Bookie Brenner. No one is allowed out of their seats, and that means you, too."

A few students reacted loudly. "Bookie Two-Shoes is not so good no more."

"Now, look what ya did, Bookie."

"Bad, bad Bookie . . ."

"Hush, get your work done, or you'll all stay after school," I said.

Days passed before we saw the unfamiliar girl again. The next time it happened, it was during an outside recess period. Everyone looked up and saw the girl coming. She strolled into the schoolyard as if she knew exactly where she was going. It didn't take her long to find Bookie sitting under the same big oak tree she had sat under when they'd first seen each other. He was reading a book. She plopped down next to him and giggled like she knew she would be welcome.

"Hi, boy, whuts your name?" she asked without batting a beautiful brown eye.

"Why, you ain't gonna throw me a kiss again, are ya?"

"Maybe I do, maybe I don't. My name's Noonday."

Bookie laughed. "That's a funny name. Noonday is eating time."

"I hear'd your name is 'book'; that's more funnier."

"My name is Robert Olie Brenner—that's my real name, and Bookie is a nickname. What's your real name?"

"I'm the real Noonday Flower, an' that's that, whatever you're called, boy," she said proudly. "Misses Mabis says I'm a love child, good as chocolate puddin' and pumpkin pie."

"Can I touch you?" asked the curious Bookie.

"Why?" she answered, looking at herself.

"I wanta see if you feel different."

She proudly held out her arm, and he rubbed her arm, and then she held out her little foot, and he felt her leg and ankle.

"You feel just like me, no different," Bookie said out loud.

She giggled with an air of pride.

"But you sure got different hair. Sure is funny stickin' up like that."

"Naw, I do not. You got funny hair, like"—she fought for the right words—"like yellow corncobs."

He got up and said, "Oh, that right, smarty Noontime? You got hair like a cow's teats, right side up." He wanted to get in the last word before the bell signaled the end of recess.

"You wanta play wit' me tomorrow, Bookie? I can come back."

He looked back at her but didn't answer.

The next day and the next day, Noonday came over to the school at recess. Bookie accepted her without question. The two youngsters chatted and played games. The other children sometimes joined in. Bookie was so inventive that Noonday found it exciting to be a part of his adventure. A friendship developed.

And God was there.

༺༻

With a stick, Bookie drew in the dirt.

"Here's the door, walk in here."

"Where am I, Bookie?"

"You are in my castle. You are a princess now. Close your eyes. See the beautiful walls and floor. They're made of gold and silver. See all the windows with velvet drapes in the grand dining room. See the light from the windows shine on the table. Your place is set. A sunbeam is on your plate. It twinkles, says, come and eat."

Noonday smiled and opened her eyes.

"Oh, Bookie, I am a princess, I am." The two youngsters sat on the ground, and in the middle of Bookie's castle drawing, they shared his lunch.

Surprisingly, no one discouraged the friendship. But many people, especially the men, didn't pay much attention to the children. Those who did notice said, "They'll tire of each other; it's bound to happen. After all, it's against the laws of nature to mix company of race or religion."

I, being the adult in the situation, thought profoundly about this friendship. An infant begins his life humble and helpless and totally dependent upon his parents. From there, humility is sustained or it dies. The little girl and the little boy met on humble ground, each accepting the other's differences and finding the differences not even important. I knew God would give stern warning to anyone who would cause a child to stumble, to be offended, or to go astray.

So I decided: *I am going to help my students to accept this little black girl into the classroom. She is a person worthy of being taught like any other student.*

I continued thinking about this. Finally, my mind was made up. I'd write the school board and ask permission to enroll her.

"It's against school-board rules, Maggie, how can you even think about it?" one of my in-laws asked.

"Oh, Jena, think about it. Is it the law? If so, who made it?"

"It must be obeyed, Maggie. You'd be a fool to try to fight this."

"Then I am a fool!"

"Listen to me, Maggie. Listen to reason. Please leave it alone."

"What is the matter with you people? I am going to write the school board."

And I did, but within a month's time, I received a blatant reply refusing my request to enroll Noonday Flower, a black girl, living in Walhalla. I was outraged. I immediately resolved to reverse their decision, not realizing the complexities of it.

"How can I change their minds? Is there not anyone who can see the injustice in denying her an education?" I spoke angrily, hoping someone could enlighten me if it was possible. But I was alone as I had been for most of two years by then. My husband, Dugald Kelly Dunn, was in the armed forces far, far away. I knew he would be on my side if he could, and I knew he would help me fight this terrible wrong.

Some nights, I longed to be near my husband. Often, I slept with his clothes and held his pillow. Many nights, tears just flowed, I missed him so. By night's end, I had explored his pillow to where there was not a spot that I had not put to my aching cheek. Morning always came and, along with it, a dedication for teaching my young pupils. Once awake, I had to steer my mind away from craving my Duggie. Even while missing him, my desire for teaching grew stronger every day.

Each day when I stood in front of the class, I could see Noonday under the big oak tree, trying to look in. My heart told my brain, *This is an injustice that defies all understanding.* I ached, knowing that a little girl was out there while the rest of the children were in here. She was separated and didn't know why. Her joy came from spending time with Bookie at recess.

On one particular day after school, Noonday returned to the big oak tree in the schoolyard. I was unaware of it, finishing tasks inside. I felt weary from the long day's work, and I was eager to get home and do other things. Perhaps I would visit my parents or write to Duggie. I gathered my coat and belongings, left the building, and I was locking the schoolhouse door when I heard a sobbing coming from the play area. I looked up and thought, *Something is wrong.* Walking over there, I found Noonday crouched down, crying. Her tears dripped onto her outstretched arm, which she was fiercely rubbing with her other hand.

Pity filled me as I dropped my belongings and knelt. "What's wrong, Noonday? Are you hurt? Why are you rubbing your arm? Please stop."

The perceptive little black girl tearfully replied, "I wanna rub it off. I wanna be white like you and Bookie. I wanta go to the Bell School." The sorrowful child looked up at me. "Why won't ya let me in, Miss Maggie?"

Immediately, I gathered her into my arms and together we rocked as a hint of rain thickened the air. The distraught child clung to me, and I began to cry softy. We held each other for the longest time. Finally, I started to sing a simple song. The words came to me, and I couldn't believe my own voice. I knew God was there with both His children, comforting one and leading the other.

"Don't you forget that . . .

> *You are the Noonday Sun*
> *Shining on everyone.*
> *You are the Noonday Sun;*
> *You have only just begun.*
> *Honeysuckle frown; put on your Noonday crown.*
> *Believe in you.*
> *Believe in you.*

"Come, little one. I'll take you home." We stood, and Noonday grasped my hand. Together we walked down the road to the Mavis place not far from the school. A soft rain had begun to fall, and I remember that we walked around the newly formed puddles. Noonday looked up at me, and I squeezed her hand. I wanted so desperately to give hope to the small girl who felt different and didn't understand why. I tried to hide my tears. When the child looked up at me again, I explained that raindrops were falling on my face. It didn't matter that we were considerably wet when we reached the house. Vita Mavis was concerned and quickly took Noonday's wet clothes off and put her into a hot bath just off the kitchen.

"I was worried about my Noonday. She don't usually go off without tellin' me. I know she gets over to the school at recess time, but not after school's out. I hope she's not bothering you, Miss Maggie?"

We sat down in the warm kitchen where the aroma of evening supper filled the room. We talked in a near whisper so Noonday could not hear.

Vita said, "She really wants to go to school. I explained to her that she can't, but I can't explain to her why."

We looked at each other and shook our heads, indicating that neither of us knew why.

"I read to her at home when I have time. I don't read too good, neither. And I can't read to her as much as she wants me to. It's just hard," Vita explained.

"Well, I'm going to do something! I'll get Noonday in school. She has a right to go to school just like every other child," I said.

"You're right, but there's nothing you can do, Miss Maggie," replied the good woman.

"I have to try, Vita." Instantly, my eyes enlarged and my mouth opened. "I know. I'll go to the next school-board meeting. That's what I'll do. I'll meet with them face-to-face. Maybe I can get through to them."

"I don't know. I doubt it."

"That's what I'll do . . . I'll make them see . . ."

"Some on the board are blind and will never see. There's no good sense in the lot of them, Miss Maggie."

Vita was grateful for my interest in Noonday, but she believed there was nothing I could do. I was young and inexperienced and had only been teaching for a couple of years. What could I do? She knew the people of the village, and she knew the men on the school board, probably for many years. I heard her curse under her breath as she left the room to check on Noonday.

Vita invited me to join the family for supper, and I was happy to accept. For one, it meant I didn't have to find something to eat from my empty cupboard at home. We set aside the subject of getting Noonday enrolled in school and consolidated our thoughts on the evening meal. The Mavis men welcomed me at their dinner table, and the dining chitchat resulted in a good time—almost to the point of forgetting what had brought me to the Mavises' in the first place. By the time I left, the evening rain had stopped, and Noonday was smiling again.

"Time for you to go to sleep, little girl—off to bed. Say thank you and bye to Miss Maggie."

"Can I stay up little longer, Vita-Mom?"

Vita shook her head. "No . . ."

The little four-year-old hugged me and said her good nights. I remember her shuffling off to bed in her mashed-down bedroom slippers.

As I walked back to my home, a small dwelling on the east side of the school, I anguished over the sad, unjust situation in which I found myself. The night was heavy with fog, just like my heart. Anger swelled within my soul, and no method of reasoning stood out in my mind.

"How can I convince them? What can I say?" I said aloud. "'Right must not live in idleness—'"

I wanted so badly to lie down and dream. And dream I did, after an immense effort to free my mind from the day. I dreamed of Duggie—his arms around me, his hands caressing me, his eyes engulfing me, taking away my troubles and replenishing my spirit. I slept well, remembering our love—so real, yet a memory, a memory never to be tucked away, even in my mind, even in my dreams. His ever-present love was my reason for being. I loved him so much.

Peerless in beauty, yet untouched by pride,
Young, but untainted by frivolity,
In all her dealings goodness is her guide,
And humbleness has vanquished tyranny,
She is the mirror of all courtesy,
Her heart the very chamber of holiness,
Her hand the minister to all distress.
                                        —Geoffrey Chaucer

Teacher Maggie, restless at best.
Schooling Noonday is her quest.
                                        —C. Ohse

CHAPTER NINE

Miss Maggie

Dugald Kelly Dunn had been my neighbor, living just a half mile north of me on US 10. Everyone was your neighbor in as much as we all lived within a cattle call away in Walhalla. Before my birth, my parents moved to the western edge of the township and started to farm: three miles west of the Schreck farm, and one half mile from my neighbors, the Brenners, all on First Street. My parents were older when they had me. They had almost given up on having any children when I came into the world, an answer to a patient prayer like the Bible's account of Abraham and Sarah and their first child, but not quite.

Even as neighbors, Duggie and I didn't see much of each other until ninth grade in high school. Before we met, our interests were juvenile, separated boy-girl stuff. Each of us had been blessed with a good childhood, although Duggie's father died when he was fourteen. He lived with his mother and five older sisters. I believe the women in his life spoiled him, but not too much. Duggie learned quickly that selfish behavior was not to be tolerated and that discipline inevitably followed.

In contrast, my parents were lenient; they were older, and even though they loved me, they spoiled me, calling me their princess whether I was good or bad. Coming from Sweden, where sexual discussion was openly frank and young marriages were a normal happening, they gave me leeway to come and go as I pleased, but I never gave them reason to take that privilege away.

I loved my parents, many times sacrificing my own time for them. When they first came to this country, my parents settled in a small Swedish settlement northeast of Walhalla. My father, Oscar Johnson, worked for a company that lumbered acres of a fertile white-pine forest. Tragically, fire destroyed the entire settlement during a very dry summer coupled with a worker's carelessness.

Six miles west of Walhalla, Custer, another little village, housed a high school. Walhalla did not. Custer was a trifle larger than its sister village to the east.

I remember the first time I saw the suave Dugald Kelly Dunn. Standing in the corridor of Custer High School talking with boys his age, Duggie's lively manner added to his charm. I was immediately attracted to him. He was talking and seemed to be engrossed in amusing, nonstop conversation. Helpless laughter erupted from the others whenever he stopped to take a breath to rewind. At one of those intervals, I walked up to him. He stopped in the middle of a word, not realizing the full impact of my presence. "Craaazy, man—" Suddenly, he saw me. "Oh, hi . . ."

"Is this ninth-grade English?" I asked.

"Ya, it is. Are you in this class?"

"Yes, I am. Are you?"

"No. I mean, yes, I think so."

A couple of the guys shouted, "Hey, Duggie, you know you are. You flunked, remember?"

He didn't want me to see how embarrassed he was, so he turned from me and barked at the others, "Hey, you guys know more 'an me? Why don't ya shut up?"

I was not impressed with the all-boys club and their chatter. The young, snappy Dunn sensed this and pushed the boys out of my way. "Why don't you gentlemen let the lady pass by?"

I could tell from the corner of my eye that he watched and then followed me into the classroom, waving off the others.

At fourteen, I had slim, long legs; small, high breasts; and a waist a man's two hands could easily circle. My dark hair, cropped short in the back, showed my long neck. I always felt my neck was too long, even though I felt fortunate to have nice skin, a Swedish complexion for which I thank my parents. My eyes could change from green to brown depending upon my disposition and the light of day. I was okay with myself as a teenager, not smug yet self-assured.

I turned and smiled at Duggie, and the hollows in my cheeks revealed my dip-in dimples. I found out later that the first thing he'd wanted to do was grab me and smooch my dimples.

He sat in a chair next to me.

"Hi," he said.

"Hi."

"Hi . . ."

"My name is Maggie."

"Hi . . . Maggie." He wiggled in his chair. "You don't look like a Maggie. I mean . . . I know a Meg. You don't look anything like her." He made a face.

"My name's not Meg. It's Mag-gie. Are you going to tell me your name?"

"Oh ya, sorry. I'm Dugald, but everyone calls me Duggie."

"Do-what?" I giggled, but carefully.

"Dugald. It's Irish. What's so funny?"

"Does Dugald mean 'do-good'?" I couldn't help myself.

"No, it means Cool Dude. See you around, Mee-gie." And then he moved to another seat.

When class was dismissed, we found ourselves leaving the room together. "Nice meeting you, Do-Good. I mean, Cool Dude."

"Ya, you, too, Mee-gie."

He was a cocky sort when we first dated. I remember the first time he kissed me. He jerked me to him and kissed me so hard my teeth hurt. But with practice, our kissing got better and, in time, more frequent. He misunderstood my refusal to give in fully as a rejection of his manhood. "I won't be held off much longer, Maggie. Someday—"

"Someday what?"

"I'm going to carry you away to paradise. You'll see. You won't be able to keep your hands off me."

It was a roller-coaster courtship through our four years in high school, but a deeper love prevailed. Even at a young age, our love grew, and we cultivated a respect for each other and, more importantly, an exclusive devotion for just one person.

A similar friendship developed between our families as well. Each family adopted the other teenager, and in time, we declared our love and convinced our parents to let us marry. Both families accepted the idea of marriage and their child's choice for a lifelong companion. We needed to complete school first; there was no question of that. It was strongly stressed, openly, by both families.

Duggie and I married the summer after we graduated from high school. We settled down on my parents' farm. Although not an ideal place for newlyweds, we made the most of our time alone. Preoccupied with each other, young and self-absorbed, we had energy to spare. I remember that time well.

Not necessarily because of their age, but rather due to the farming way of life, my parents retired to bed early. My pa expected the young groom to rise with him each morning. It was hard to get to sleep when our lovemaking kept us awake far into the night. Every night, our loving reached new dimensions, although the curtain that hung in place of a bedroom door interfered with our total expression. And so, whenever Mama and Pa were out of earshot, or perhaps when they were away on their weekly pilgrimage to town, we reveled in uninhibited love games—in the barn, in the cornfield, on the kitchen floor—our passion knew no boundaries. As newlyweds, our first months together were beautifully busy.

One temperate early evening, we were instructed to fill the troughs for the anxious cows to feed. As we went through the motions, we exchanged teasing glances. I remember throwing the first handful of hay. I ran, laughing, with a farmer's daughter's invitation to follow. A chase ensued as he followed me up the ladder into the hayloft. I remember our roll in the hay like it was yesterday.

"You'll never catch me, Duggie."

"Oh ya? There's no place to run up here."

"Yes, there is. The rope, Tarzan, the rope."

"Me, Duggie-zan, you Maggie-Jane." He grabbed me and we tumbled, bouncing off each other into the hay. As the hay settled, so did we—in each other's arms—not noticing hay in our hair and clothes.

He touched me and I tingled all over. Together, we entwined our bodies and souls as one. I was openly responsive, not at all shy to restrict our love play to the darkness. When Duggie drew upon me, I was filled with a longing that matched his. Always, when I closed my eyes, he claimed me for his own. We were fulfilled. Afterward, we rested, breathing heavily, assuredly satisfied. Like he often did, Pa entered the barn just then, checking on us.

"Maggie, Duggie, are you up thare?" he asked pointedly.

"We fed the cows, Papa!" I called out, and immediately covered my mouth in a muffled giggle.

My pa, nearing seventy years old, could no longer climb the ladder, so he could not see our nakedness, but his age didn't prevent him from knowing what we were doing. But our love was our own. A proper, unadulterated love that penetrated every waking, and nonwaking, hour of every day.

But within our first year of marriage, Duggie grew restless. Dreams of "from this day forward" were found to be short-lived, with hard work and little time for fun and games. With motivation, as inexperienced as we were, we moved forward with the blueprints of our life together.

"I'm thinking of joining the navy." Duggie paused. "I'm going to be drafted anyway, Maggie. I'd rather choose than be drafted."

I didn't like hearing that plan, but at the same time, I had been thinking of a diversion for myself. Not committed to the farming way of life, we were of a new generation where an education was seen as a way to a better life. Though farming is a good life, on a smaller scale, it proved to be laborious with few monetary rewards. Modern farm machinery not yet on the market limited small farmers to farm or buy bigger fields. The work required seemed to take more hours than there were in a day and more stamina than the body could provide. The bigger farms in Michigan were located in its thumb and south.

"I want to be a teacher," I exclaimed one midnight. A cloudless sky of moon and stars peered onto the wakefulness of the two restless lovers. Throughout the late-night hours, we expressed our longings, individually, and for our future together.

"I think the navy will be good for me in a lot of ways," Duggie said. "I can save my pay. I'll learn things. Maybe training will help me get a good job when I get out. What do you think?" He went on. "It'll be so hard to be away from you. That part, I hate." He hesitated, not knowing how to explain. "But I need to go."

He stopped and looked at me inquiringly. We looked at each other from our respective pillows. Tears welled in our eyes while the moonlight danced in them.

"I don't want you to go. How can I live without you?" I lamented. "Giving you up, even for two years, I can't imagine."

I lifted my head and kissed the lips of a boy, now a man, whom I loved with all my heart. As if years of wisdom had forewarned me, I said, "I know you have to go. I've felt it for a while now."

In a month's time, Duggie left for navy training in San Diego, California. He had just turned nineteen. After training, Dugald Kelly Dunn and group were assigned to a ship in the South Pacific and later at the Panama Canal. Rumors out of Washington, DC, hinted that WWII was in the making.

I enrolled in the Mason County Normal School. At the time, and because there was a critical shortage of teachers, the school's special training afforded young ladies who otherwise could not have done so the opportunity to become teachers. Teachers trained in these county schools received certification to teach in rural schools only. A year later, I received my certificate, and the county school commissioner placed me in the Bell School in Walhalla. Prior to Bookie's first year there, and before my twentieth birthday, I realized my second love—teaching.

౷

A nip in the air indicated fall was giving way to winter. One early morning, my feet touched the floor but rose quickly again; the floor was frosty cold. It was my first winter alone in a little house of my own. I'd gained the teacherage after my first year of teaching along with a renewed contract of employment. Wages were not high, but I felt proud of my accomplishments. Living on my own next to the school suited me very well.

I'm a teacher, a real teacher. I often pinched myself at the thought.

Slippers were a definite must that morning as I started a fire in the old wood-burning kitchen stove. As warmth radiated throughout the tiny house, I busied myself with my morning routine—dressing, having breakfast, and preparing a lunch. Usually, breakfast included a bowl of oatmeal and a cup of Postum, but on this particular morning, I ate nothing.

I shivered not because of the early frost but because my upcoming confrontation with the school board invaded my morning. For days, I had practiced in front of a mirror and said everything I could to defend Noonday's right to go to school. Over and over, I spoke to the mirror, throwing my frustrated hands in the air.

I've got to say the right words. I'm doing the right thing, aren't I? I asked myself judiciously.

Many evenings, I had supper with my parents, and they had voiced their opinion of the big meeting everyone was talking about.

"Maggie, dear, don't do this. You might lose your job. Is it really your business?" Mama asked lovingly. They didn't want me to be humiliated. It was hard for them to understand. They were old and thought their only child was incapable of handling this altercation.

Angrily, I said, "Yes, Mama, it is! You need to support me. Too many people say nothing when something is wrong."

"I know, my dear, but we are afreed," Mama replied, trying hard not to further agitate me.

"I'm sorry, Mama. I—I love this child, and I want her to be in my school. She is black, so what? Why is it so hard to understand?"

My mother hugged me, patting my head. What I remember clearly of that night was what my pa said to me. He had been sitting in his favorite easy chair in the next room when his voice echoed, declaring to me the simple truth of the matter.

"You do vat you gotta do, Maggie girl," he said firmly. "You are vright."

Yes, my good papa was a wise man.

☙

The day was here. My nervousness revealed itself in school that day, and Noonday didn't show up for recess. Some days it was too cold to be outside. Even the schoolchildren remained indoors, playing games like duck duck goose or hangman on the blackboard.

"Let's play hang the nigger, like we gonna do tonight," one child spoke out, immediately regretting what he had said because it had not escaped my ears. Indoor recess was instantly over, and I drew a circle on the blackboard, where the child's nose remained for the rest of the recess period.

"Consider your nose hung, young man."

The end of the school day crawled to a close. The children were dismissed, and I was clearing off my desk when I looked up and saw Bookie.

"I thought you left with the others. What is it, Bookie?"

The seven-year-old got out of his seat and stretched upright, probably thinking it made him look taller and older. He smoothed down his unruly head of hair, and drew close to me.

"I admire you, Miss Maggie. I wish you the best a luck tonight at the board meetin'."

I smiled. "Why, thank you, Bookie!"

I looked at him, grateful for his words, which were wiser than his young years.

I walked around the desk and put my arm around him. "It means so much to have your support. You've made me feel better, my little man. I'll do my best tonight. Noonday needs to go to school, too."

The boy agreed, and we walked out of the schoolhouse together.

"Will your mama and daddy be coming tonight? I'd feel better if I knew they were coming."

"Oh yes, they are. I wanta come, too."

"No, but I'll see you tomorrow, Bookie. I hope I'll have good news. You get on home now before your mama gets to worrying."

Slowly, darkness crept in over the lake in the west. The early evening brought forth the board members, one by one. Two by two, the townspeople arrived. Many cars lined up along First Street, a rare sight for Walhalla except on a Saturday night at the Rendezvous. The schoolhouse filled, and doubt filled me.

"I think I'm going to be sick." I winced and prayed aloud, "Oh, help me, my Lord Father in heaven. Give me courage to wage this battle. Help me to know the enemy. These good people are not my enemies."

Then, I thought, *Entertaining hope means recognizing fear. Oh yes, I recognize the fear. But there is hope, I have to believe that.*

I walked across the road back to the schoolhouse. I looked around and saw no latecomers. Opening the door, I saw the schoolhouse was full—many were standing. I stood in the back, removed my coat, and held it. Upturned stares seemed to unclothe the rest of me. My heart sped up to an unbearable speed. I waited.

The meeting was brief. The minutes were read. The budget was discussed, which included the old issue of the leaky roof in the cloakroom. When the chairman asked for new business, everyone looked directly at me. Everyone in this small village knew I planned to submit a new application for the little black girl to go to school. Most people hadn't thought much about the black girl going to their school until now. It was already settled in their minds that she couldn't.

Fearful that the beating of my heart would expose me, I tried to walk inconspicuously to the front of the schoolroom. I placed my coat on my desk, turned to face everyone, and began. "Good evening, chairman, members, friends, and neighbors."

All eyes were on me. Most looked at me with stares of bewilderment as to my state of mind. Their eyes and ears waited with intense curiosity. The gentle-faced chairman with weary, resigned eyes said, "You have the floor, Mrs. Dunn."

I was so nervous, I didn't think any words could come, but they did.

"I respect you and the job you do. I come to you humbly with a request, not a demand." I looked from the men on the board to the audience. "I know most of you believe old values and rules should never be compromised. They were good enough for you, so they should be good enough for your children, right?"

Most nodded their heads.

"Sometimes, these values and laws need to become naked or—or exposed, so we can look at them closely. Change is a fact of life. So . . ." I stopped and everyone looked at me.

I heard someone whisper, "Naked, what she mean naked?" One older man cupped his hand around one ear.

I cleared my throat. "Yes, naked and—ah—okay."

After a pause, the words came out. "Let's have the courage to change laws that are no longer valid. Let's look closely at Michigan laws; by 1900, Michigan had some of the strongest civil laws in the country. But discrimination still exists, and Walhalla doesn't need to be part of racial unfairness."

"I thought we're here to talk about that little nigger going to our school!" someone shouted.

I said loudly, "We are well within Michigan law to let this child go to school here."

Many in the crowd scuffled in their seats, mumbling one thing or another, when the chairman yelled, "Order—order!"

Holding the gavel, he scanned the room. "Proceed, Mrs. Dunn, and stick to the topic."

I could see I was talking over their heads. Suddenly, my anxiousness threatened oncoming tears, but I held them back.

With determination, I spoke again. "Can't you see that there is no law that denies a child—red, yellow, black, or white—the opportunity to go to school here? A little citizen of our village wants to go to school, and she is black. If we discriminate against her and say no, she can't go to school, and we are faced with corrupting a young mind. It doesn't matter that her skin is different than yours—she has a mind." I looked around the room, noticing complacent, empty minds staring back at me.

"I teach minds. We study words, how to spell them, how to pronounce them, how to put them together. This results in reading and writing and speaking. *I do not teach how to color minds!*"

My nervousness vanished as I continued. "Education will fly away like a random wind if we do not teach all children regardless of what they look like. How can we explain 'with liberty and justice—and education—for all' to white children when there is a black child who is denied it? One is given it and the other is not because of the color of skin? What does the color of skin have to do with the person behind it? What happens to your skin when you are in the hot sun all day? Yes, it gets sunburned. It peels away or you become tanned: a different color, right? What happens to your skin when you are sick and feel faint? Yes, you turn jaundiced and yellow. Are you denied admission to the hospital? Prejudice is a sickness, and if you let it, it will jaundice your whole soul.

"How can you say a black child cannot attend an all-white school? I know it's continuing in the south, but Walhalla can do away with this. This cannot be resolved until you—all of you—check your conscience. How can you, in clear conscience, allow this child to be a second-class citizen, to be denied an education? Let your conscience speak to you. Discrimination is your worst haunting sin if you let it hide in your heart and mind. Tell me about your prejudice. Is your prejudice fear? Or disdain? You just want to be separated from blacks? Why? Think about it, and whatever your reason, is it fair? Are you being fair?"

Someone in the back answered, "I don't need to think about it. That black child shouldn't even be here, let alone go to our school!"

Yet another spoke up, and another and another.

"Yea, I'm better'n any black man, that's a-certain."

"What yaw doing, Miss Maggie, tryin' to mess up our heads?"

"If that colored girl goes to school, I'm taking my kid outta school."

Olie Brenner stood. "Hold on! Wait a minute, wait a minute. Let's think about what Mrs. Dunn is sayin'. She's right. She's making good sense 'bout old laws being old and not being needed anymore."

His words shocked the room into painful silence until Vita Mavis said in a loud voice, "Olie's right. I know this child better than anyone here. You better believe that she is as good as any of your children who go to school here." Again, the words shocked the full room.

Except for Noonday's guardian, Vita Mavis, Olie was the only one speaking up on my behalf. I think some were so frightened they didn't want to say anything, one way or the other.

I took a deep breath and uttered a prayer. But I knew my good neighbors were in the minority.

Olie stood again, explaining, "Mrs. Dunn says that there's no law that says that little girl can't go to our school. She's got my vote."

A voice called out, "What makes you such a nigger lover, Mr. Brenner?"

A big lumberjack from the back of the room laughed, declaring loudly, "We all know your son's got a taste for brown sugar. You got it, too?"

Olie darted toward him just as Mrs. B grabbed his arm. Without a word, she implied, *Don't go there, Olie.*

Again the big man taunted Olie. "What's the matter, farmer man, afraid to tangle with a real white man?"

The man took a couple of steps toward Olie. "Come on, let's get on outside and settle this. I wanna do you a favor and knock the nigger-loving crap outta ya."

Immediately, the chairman pounded his gavel. "There'll be no talking 'bout fighting at this meeting."

The chairman looked straight at the stranger. "You're not from here, are ya? You better get on your way, mister. We want no trouble here from any outsiders. We're civilized, not barbaric. We'll settle this in our own way, fair to all who live in Walhalla."

Olie remained standing. His big fists kept opening and closing, exposing knuckles as red as the blood that flowed through them.

The lumberman looked around. "Pantywaists, the whole lot of ya. Talking like a bunch of prissy women at a tea party—"

"We are fair-minded people," the chairman interrupted, "and we are not having a tea party. This is an important meeting that should be of no interest to you. Get on your way."

"But it *is* of interest to me, Mr. Chairman. I'll get on my way all right, but you don't let that little nigger go to school here. Otherwise, you'll know 'bout my interest all right."

The big man looked around, his eyes homed in on his comrades.

"Come on, let's get the hell outta this one-horse town," he said, pushing his way to the back of the schoolroom and mumbling obscenities until he slammed the door behind him. Two men tailed behind him. Nervously, everyone watched them leave. Silence filled the room until a vehicle with no muffler sped away, backfiring like it was the Fourth of July. It seemed like everyone thought it was okay to breathe again when Olie took a deep breath and faced the chairman once again.

"Fair? You talk about fair? I might better fight that man for a fairer way of handling this. We can't let the likes of that man scare us into doing the wrong thing. Fighting with fists is not right, either, but pretendin' you're being fair and not letting the girl go to school in the face of it is wrong, just plain wrong."

"I, for one, don't like what that man had to say, Olie," Norm Camfield remarked.

"Me neither," said another.

"I don't like what he said, either. But we got to stand up against threats. He had no right to come to this here meeting. He has no say in this matter," Olie concluded.

This time, no one replied. Faces stared at Olie, expecting more. Everyone knew and respected the man standing before them. Yet many were fearful, especially of the man who had just left the meeting.

I knew that if anyone could convince them to allow Noonday to go to their school, it was Olie. But I worried he might give up trying before he could convince them.

"I'm just a farmer, just a family man like the rest of you. I work every day to the best of my ability. When I go to sleep at night, I don't want nothing bothering me—I wanna clear my head, leave nothing unsettled. Walhalla needs to let the little girl go to school."

Norm Camfield spoke up. "What about that guy who was just here, Olie? We don't want the Klan coming 'round here."

Olie answered, "No, of course not. There's no Klan around here."

Quickly, Norm responded, "Remember when those blacks stopped by the Rendy with questions? They left saying they would be back. I was there, Olie."

Someone piped up, "Ya, and who knows how many more will come if'n we have a black child going to school here."

"Ya, how we suppose to keep her hidden if she goes to school here?" another asked.

Olie tightly pursed his lips together and shook his head.

A woman stood. "Olie, wouldn't it be easier for everyone if she went to school somewhere else?"

"Ya," many added. And another said, "Let her go back to her own kind. Maybe she'll never remember she didn't go to school here. Then we can all forget it."

Olie scanned the room 360 degrees, opened his mouth, and barked loud enough for all to hear: "Her own kind, her own kind, what do you mean, her own kind? You and me, we're her own kind. She's born here. She's settled here. She is a citizen of the United States of America same as you and me. And she is a citizen of Walhalla, whether you like it or not. Ya, it'd be easier to send her away, but we're not gonna do what is easier, we're gonna do what is right. She's staying here and going to school here." Olie's anger escaped. "She is going to go to Walhalla school, and that's all I'm going to say about it. Now, let's vote." He sat down hard and Mrs. B. patted his hand.

Then, like a hundred turkeys, the whole room started up again.

The meeting, out of hand, forced the chairman to scream over the crowd. "Sit down! Everyone take your seats. Be quiet. Qu-i-et!"

It seemed each person needed to express their opinion more loudly than the next. The gobbles finally abated, and the overcrowded room of people settled down. The chairman, proud of the stillness he'd created, quietly asked me, "Do you have any more to say, Mrs. Dunn?"

I tried to focus. I wanted to disappear in a poof of smoke. Instead, I felt myself a statuette unveiled, naked and cemented. I just wanted it to be over. I spoke softly, so softly that the people strained to hear me.

"Thank you, Olie . . . ah, I—"

The impatient chairman shouted, "Speak up, Mrs. Dunn."

Again, I tried to speak. "I'm sorry . . . I'm sorry that some of you . . . feel . . ."

Everyone was staring at me. I thought, *Oh Lord, let me get this over with.*

I lifted my head and focused on the ticktock of the clock at the back of the schoolroom. Finally, I said, "*I* want to escape this prejudice; *I* want Walhalla to escape this prejudice. That's what it is, you know: prejudice. Please help me. Change your unfair law. We need to link our conscience to a higher law, a moral law. Let's do what's right, and not be bound by history."

I felt like an idiot, rattling off words they didn't understand. I stopped.

I looked resolutely at the men on the panel. "Please allow Noonday Flower to go to our school."

The chairman allowed no more discussion before asking for a vote. The nays outshouted the yeas, and again, Noonday was denied admission to the village school. In actuality, the people automatically joined the will of the members of the school board, who had voted first.

I walked home. I spoke to no one. No one spoke to me. I listened as the cars pulled away one by one. I listened as the chatter of the walkers faded away. Soon, it was quiet.

I spoke to the night. "They expect Noonday to hide, and for us to pretend she doesn't exist—how ignorant, how pretentious! Did some feel it to be wrong? I bet some did."

I sat down as if my body was as heavy as my burden.

"I failed. I didn't make it clear enough. I guess they are afraid, but afraid of what? That bully lumberjack? But, then, he scared me, too."

Exhausted, defeated, I couldn't stop recounting my speech. Back home, my restless body wrestled with the covers as I tossed and turned in bed. Around three a.m., I turned to my last letter from Duggie to console and comfort me. I read and reread it as tears fell onto the paper, distorting his loving words. I thanked God for giving me Dugald Kelly Dunn to love. There was no doubt in my mind that he loved me, too.

Gratitude is the fairest flower
That springs from the soul;
And the heart of man and woman
Knoweth none more fragrant.
                                        —*Madame de Staël*

None could be more soulful than
Lizzy Schreck and Vita Mavis.
                                        —*C. Ohse*

CHAPTER TEN

Lizzy and Vita-Mom

The winter of 1938 came and went. In the spring of '39, Noonday discovered a grammama in Lizzy Schreck, and the summer months brought forth a newborn son to the Brenners. With the new Billy Olie Brenner on board, the Brenner household was even busier. Three months of farm labor brought in the best harvest in many years. It was a perfect summer timing for sun, rain, and a blessed birth. Bookie stayed busy all summer helping his father. He probably thought little about school until he spied me from across a field. He waved with a big smile, and I mouthed the words, "How's the baby?"

I moved in with my aging parents during the summer months to help out with chores around our shrinking farm. The Brenners purchased our better ground so my father didn't have the fieldwork to do. He still milked six cows and sold the milk and cream to a local dairy. The cows were pastured and the hay came from the Brenners, as part of our contract together.

And God was there.

Noonday walked down Walhalla Road and turned onto First Street nearly every day that summer. It wasn't far to the Schrecks'.

"Tell me 'bout my real mama, please, wouldja, Grammama?" she asked, looking up into Lizzy's kind eyes.

"There she is, my lil' brown peanut. How 'bout some lemonade, and some bread an' jam?" the oldster asked as they settled into an afternoon together. While the old woman strolled into the kitchen and slowly moved about preparing refreshments, she sang. Noonday learned the catchy tune, and while the two sang happily, they danced in the kitchen. Throughout the song, they looked at each other and, with a wave of the hand, let the other one solo the next verse. Their happy voices told of a bond more powerful than blood, the color of which they shared, even if their skins were different shades.

*Twenty froggies went to school, down beside a
   rushing pool
Twenty little coats of green, twenty vests all white
   and clean.
"We must be in time," said they. "First we study,
   then we play;
That is how we keep the rule when we froggies go
   to school."*

*Master Bullfrog, brave and stern, called the
   classes in their turn;
Taught them how to nobly strive, also how to leap
   and dive,
Taught them how to dodge a blow from the sticks
   that bad boys throw.*

*Twenty froggies grew up fast, bullfrogs they
   became at last;*

*Polished to a high degree, as each froggie ought to
  be,
Now they sit on other logs, teaching other little
  frogs.*

"I'm gonna go to froggie school," Noonday often declared.
"But maybe I can't—'cause I'm not green."

"Someday you will go to school. Grammama knows. You'll see."

Lizzy's husband, Henry, sometimes stayed around watching the two. He knew the little girl brought untold joy into his woman's day. Young Hank was still around, mostly with his ear to the radio trying to decipher the stock-market reports, still determined to make his million. William was living away and attending school. On each visit, Noonday learned more and more about her mother.

"You look like your mama," Lizzy told her. "She was pretty but not as delicate as you. Marla Jean worked hard. She wasn't afraid of work. That's the way she was. When you started up in her belly, she still worked. She talked to you all the time, telling you she loved you. She knew you was a girl, you see. She had a crystal ball in her head. 'I see her,' she'd say every time she closed her eyes and rubbed her belly. It was you, a girl-child she named Noonday."

Grammama continued rocking and talking. Both came easy for the cheerful woman. Noonday became attached to her and never tired of the long stories, even when the old woman got off topic. The girl hung on to every word.

"It took a brave heart for your mama to leave her people and come on over here. She was scared that first day she rode into town on that old bicycle. I brought her on home with me, and we were soon the best of friends. She worked more than we could pay her, but she always said, 'I can do that, Miz Lizzy.'"

When Noonday asked about her father, old Lizzy just shook her head. She pressed her lips together, revealing the deep lines at the corners of her mouth, and said, "I don't know about your pa. Your mama never talked to me about him. Once I remember she said that he was mighty good-lookin' but had an unsettled spirit of sorts. I don't even know what his name is, or maybe I don't remember." She hesitated, noting the disappointment in Noonday's eyes. "I'm powerful sorry, little one."

Lizzy Schreck walked with Noonday behind their place, a bit of a walk, and soon they came upon a small area of ground, well-groomed with flowers, crocuses, and tulips just showing their color around the slightly elevated plot.

"We buried your good mama here."

Noonday looked up at Grammama with the gratefulness of a child no longer innocent. For the first time, the black girl had a sense of identity, a sense of past, a sense of belonging. She had this kind old grammama to thank for that.

"I'm not lost no more," she said. "I know where my mama is."

"Yes, indeed, she is here." Then the woman paused for a moment and held her hand to her chest. "And here in our hearts, too."

The child knew exactly her meaning. She knelt and, for the longest time, sat cross-legged with her hands holding up her chin, staring at the grave.

After the first grave visit, Noonday went there often by herself. Not much happened there, but the least little thing caught the girl's attention, and she appreciated dreamily conversing with her mother.

"See the teeny ants, Mama," she said as she watched the little construction workers marching to and fro, some carrying minute crumbs to their sand hills, others working in synchronized groups building their empire. For a long while, she was lost in her study of the hardworking constructionists.

While she sat still, the birds perched close to her. She turned from the ant colony and examined one feathered friend. It intrigued her to see the bird up close, the beady eyes, delicate

feathers, this one with a bright-red breast. Soon, a butterfly with
the airy loveliness of transparent wings landed on her. A strange
feeling embraced the little one. When she spoke, the butterfly
remained fixed on her arm. "Is that you, Mama?"

A mother-child bonding resulted from these visits. From the
grave, the spirit of Marla Jean filled her child with love of self
from beyond the realm of earthly understanding. Rays of sunshine reached from mother to child, revealing its angelic message:
*Be prepared. People on Earth can be cruel to one another. Look to
the heavens for divine guidance. Look at the totality of humankind.
Differences are unimportant. Life is short. Time is fleeing. But love
is deathless.*

Noonday took away the message from visits to her mama's
grave: "I am me, and that is good."

∾

The days of summer brought an exchange of young and old in
Noonday and Mrs. Lizzy Schreck. Noonday helped make the
old lady laugh and forget her painful arthritis. Lizzy loved hearing Noonday rattle on about the Mavis family. One time, she
told of Mr. Mavis, who worked for the railroad, and the boys
walking all over the freshly mopped kitchen floor leaving a trail
of railroad muck from that day's rain.

The black child could imitate Mrs. Mavis's voice and gestures
in a way that eerily matched the good woman. "Vita-Mom was
screaming at those guys, and they just look like nothing's happening. They say to her, 'What are you yellin' about, woman?'"

Another day, she told of the time Gunner Mavis, her brother,
found a puppy, now the family dog.

"Vita-Mom say that dog was dropped off by some people
who don't care, don't care at all. Make her mad how the little dog
got here. Vita-Mom say, 'That Gunner set out to fetch that wild
dog. When he finally grabs him, he lifts that dog up to have a

good look. An 'fore he knew it, that varmint shook like a scared rabbit, and pooped right down his coat into his boots."

Grammama laughed heartily at Noonday's rendition of how the dog, Little Shitter, got his name. She finished with, "Gunner 'bout kill that dog. Vita-Mom say she don't like that dog, but she really does. He can't come in the house, oh no. She says, little or big, no shitter's coming in my house."

Noonday was effervescent. Her innocence unveiled an abundance of joy for a new day and immeasurable pleasure in each day that passed. Lizzy knew she was a remarkably happy child, a little one who couldn't get enough of her stories.

"Tell me about Mama again, Grammama," she pleaded. Even if she'd heard the story before, she'd listen as if it were the first time.

"I 'member one Easter Sunday, might be six years passed now," old Lizzy Schreck began. "Your mama and myself made up a fine dinner." She tossed her head back, remembering.

"As I recall, we made the most dee-licious dishes: pinto beans with green tomato sauce, baked ham with the sweet taters made sweeter with candied apples on the side. Marla Jean also made the beet greens, cooked just right, then covered in a sweet vinegar and bacon dressin'. And we boiled little red taters and baked a sappy bread pudding. And had fresh cream handy to put on top. Makes me wanting it right now. My daughter and her family were coming for dinner, so it'd be a good many 'round the table. We put in the extra leaves to make it big enough. Marla Jean and myself worked the whole mornin' getting it ready."

Noonday sat with hungry eyes and eager ears to hear more.

"Did you all eat? Did all the people get big an' fat?"

"Oh no, we didn't even have a taste of that fine food."

Noonday's eyes widened in disbelief. "Why not, Grammama?"

"Well, when we was all 'round the table, giving thanks to the Good Lord, my Hank had himself a 'brain fit.'"

The old woman recalled the day as if it were yesterday.

"Oh my, land sakes alive, he raised up like a bull in heat, and he bellowed so loud we all thought the world was a-comin' to the end. When we looked and realized what was happenin', his face fell frontward, and his arms swiped everythin' off the table, every which way. The food was a-flyin' all over, on the walls and on the floor, dishes, too. Hank, he stiffened straight up like a wild horse on his hind legs, and he started a-jerkin' and turnin' blue. He tightened his teeth and fell like a big oak tree that had just been sawed down. Your mama couldn't hold him up, so he fell right to the floor. Edna's family ran away, in all directions, like the spokes of a hay-wagon wheel. Little Buddy jumped out the window and ran full force to the neighbors, and when he got there, he was so out of his breath, terrified, too, that he couldn't even speak. The neighbors, fearin' the worst, hurried on over here. By that time, Hank was as good as new. Yup, God always waked him up and blessed him with a clear mind. He was just a-wonderin' where everybody went off to and said, 'When we gonna eat, Ma?'

"It was your mama and my Henry who turned Hank over on his side 'til it was done. Don't think my boy Hank is crazy 'cause he has fits. No, no, he's not. He is just like you and me. I'm white, you're colored, and froggies are green. And Hank has fits, just sometimes. We're all different, yet we're all the same."

Noonday, spellbound, remarked, "My mama was brave, wasn't she, Grammama?"

"She was, indeed, my child."

Noonday never tired of hearing about her mother. Lizzy Schreck told the child everything she could remember, and still the child wanted more. This continued throughout the next year.

On one visit to see Grammama, Noonday walked in on what seemed to be a family meeting.

"Hi, sweetie, you are just in time. We got a letter from William. I was about to read it to the family. Come over here and sit by me."

Lizzy explained to Noonday, "William loved your mama. Now he is out of school and joining the CCC camp."

"What is that . . . CCC?" the young girl asked.

"I was just telling Henry and Hank, it is the Civ-il-ian Con-ser-va-shun Corps."

Hank piped up, "Get reading the letter, Ma!"

Lizzy began, "Dear Ma, Pa, and young Hank, President Roosevelt signed a bill to make it a law so the CCC could start. I'm joining and will work with lots of guys to plant trees and take care of our country's forests. There will be many camps all over the country, in Michigan, too."

Henry spoke up, "Roosevelt's in a wheelchair, but he still works."

Hank butted in, "How much pay will the president give William? Not no million dollars."

Lizzy started reading again. "We get thirty dollars a month, and we have to send twenty-two dollars back home. They give us shoes, socks, underwear, a work suit, and a toilet kit with a towel. Got a cot and mattress, too."

"That's all he gets?" Hank yelled.

Lizzy resumed reading. "The most important thing is the metal we wear around our neck with our number on it."

Again Hank interrupted, "I want a medal!"

Lizzy turned to Hank. "Shush up, boy!" She began again. "A lot of guys don't want blacks in the camp. I often think about Marla Jean and know there are as many good black people as good white people in the world."

Lizzy looked up from the letter and smiled at Noonday and started reading again.

"Blacks and whites have to be separated because of the rules by the director. Because I work hard, he took a liking to me. He asked me to count the sick one day. I found one was sick and told him, and then he asked me if the sick one was white or colored. I told him I didn't know what color he was."

Lizzy stopped, looked at everyone, and said, "William is making a good point here. Just so we know the truth, black is not a color. Black blocks *all* the other colors from our eyes."

Noonday looked at herself and said, "Maybe I'm green or purple . . . but you can't see past my black skin to see the real color."

Hank replied, "You're a smart kid, just like your mama. How you get so smart when you're not even in school?"

"Hush now and let me finish William's letter," Lizzy said. A rare moment of silence filled the room.

Lizzy finished William's narration that read with a bit of humor. "We do have some fun at CCC. We get to go into nearby towns on Saturday nights to dance. I don't know how to dance, and neither do a lot of the guys. So we have lessons from the ones who know dance steps after work. I wish you could see, Ma, guys dancing with each other and joking around. We fight over who takes the lead and who is the girl. Lots of funning around. When we get to the dance, we're afraid to ask a girl to dance, so we stand around drinking punch and eating cookies. Finally, I was first to show them how to politely ask a girl to dance, and I haven't had one refuse because of my lip. Of course, it is dark, so maybe that helps. After all the guys dance, we notice that the girls giggle in a huddle. There are chaperones, so we can't do anything with the girls but dance. And no one has cars, so we have to pile into the back of trucks, even in the cold and darkness. If you miss a ride back to camp, you have to walk or hitch. One weekend morning, two of our guys were missing. We found them later in a tree. They said they had to climb the tree to escape the wolves, but in the light of day, they were still afraid to come down.

"P.S. I might be moving to Michigan to help prepare wood-lots by showing farmers how to thin wooded areas. Maybe Bookie Brenner would like to learn about it."

Lizzy finished by reading the salutation: "From your loving son, William."

The words got caught in her throat, and one tear escaped.

Right away, Hank shouted, "Ma, I wanta join the CCC!"

Before Lizzy could answer Hank, Vita walked in. "Oh good, Noonday is still here," she shouted.

"What do you mean? You knew she was coming here . . . maybe she stayed too long?" Lizzy asked, winking at Noonday.

Vita answered quickly, "No, no it's okay. I'm glad she stayed and that she is still here."

Vita took Lizzy aside while the others dispersed and whispered, "There is word going around that strangers are asking about Marla Jean again. The people in Walhalla are being tight-lipped about it, and I'm grateful, but . . ."

"Maybe it's her family? How do we know?" Lizzy questioned.

"Family is one thing, but knowing for sure if they *are* family is another," Vita answered.

Lizzy added, "I wonder if they know Marla Jean had a baby . . . and Marla Jean died?"

"I think we need to keep a better eye on Noonday until we know more."

"Yes, I agree. Let me know if you hear any more, and I'll do the same."

Vita hollered for Noonday, who was in the next room, and suggested, "As long as I'm here, Noonday, we'll walk home together, okay?"

How do I love thee? Let me count the ways.
I love thee to the depth and breadth and height
My soul can reach, when feeling out of sight
For the ends of being and ideal grace.
I love thee to the level of every day's
Most quiet need, by sun and candle-light.
I love thee freely, as men strive for right.
I love thee purely, as they turn from praise.
I love thee with the passion put to use
In my old griefs, and with my childhood's faith.
I love thee with a love I seemed to lose
With my lost saints. I love thee with the breath,
Smiles, tears, of all my life; and, if God choose,
I shall but love thee better after death.
                                        —*E. B. Browning*

Death: where noondays are no more,
No beginning of the day,
No end of the day.
                                        —*C. Ohse*

CHAPTER ELEVEN

Miss Maggie, Continued . . .

Every fall when school started up, Noonday joined the children during recess time again. She knew she couldn't go to school, but she felt, maybe, she could be a part of it by being in the school's shadow. Bookie looked for her every day.

"Find me, Bookie!" Noonday yelled as she ran into the wooded area surrounding the playground. It didn't take him long to find her, and the two chased each other until one stopped and pointed to a giant mushroom. The curious twosome carried it back to the playground, each holding on to it. The children gathered around to see the fungus.

I hurried out of the schoolhouse to warn them that berries or mushrooms should not be eaten until an adult said it was safe.

"Maybe we can have a lesson about mushrooms and other things that grow around here."

"Me, too?" Noonday asked enthusiastically.

"Yes, you, too," I said, hugging her. "We'll have the lessons outside."

But I knew it would take more than outside lessons to fully educate this child. I thought about the problem often. I was growing very fond of Noonday.

Maybe I could teach her myself, I thought. *No one needs to know about it.*

I smiled at the idea of private tutoring. *I'll make it work!* I thought. *Vita Mavis will agree, I'm sure.*

That night, I tried to set up my tiny bedroom as an extension of a schoolroom by placing a desk in one corner. It didn't fit well. "It'll work, I'll make it work," I said to myself. The next day, Saturday, I further explored the idea of tutoring Noonday. I knew it would create a strenuously long day with lessons for Noonday after school hours and on Saturdays. I thought how unnecessary this would be if she could go to school like every other child in the county. I recalled the efforts to get Noonday enrolled in school, and to this day I remain angry with the preposterous obstacles that prevented it. I sat down and reviewed, in my head, my failed petition for Noonday to go to school. *Could I have done better?* I asked myself.

Unbelievably, my thoughts were interrupted. I literally jumped up when I heard a persistent knocking at the door. Usually, my friends and parents just hollered and came in. Before I got to the door, which was but a step or two, the knock turned into such a pounding that it startled me to respond, "Who's there?"

"Open the damn door, teacher, or we break it down," a voice demanded.

More frightened than I had ever been in my life, I yelled back, "My father's here." More pounding. "I called the sheriff. You better leave . . . now!"

I heard a man talking to another, but before I knew it, the door was knocked down flat and the man grabbed me. "Hold still, woman, or you'll regret it."

I recognized him right away, the racist lumberjack, the rude, outspoken man who'd been at the school-board meeting.

I shouted, "What do you want? The little black girl is not going to school here. You and your hooligans made sure of that . . ." The lumberjack hit me so hard that I saw flashes of stars and thought I'd pass out if he did it again. He didn't. We both watched an older man, aided with a walking stick, slowly get out of the car. While the lumberjack held me too tightly, the other walked up and got right into my face, so close that his drool splattered on me with every word.

"Take me to that girl. We's all gonna get in the car and you gonna show the way."

At that moment, I wished I had close neighbors, but there was only the schoolhouse directly across from me and the empty town hall next door.

"*No*, no, I'm not going to show you anything of the sort, and you can't make me!" Again, the lumberjack, whom I'll call Jack, hit me again. I felt the blood ooze from my nose. Before I could wipe it away or say anything more, he pulled me to the car, shoved me in, and tied me up.

"You wanna die, lady? You better tell us where to go," Jack demanded as he got into the driver's seat and started the engine.

I didn't know at the time that the older man was JD, but I knew that, whoever he was, he was evil. Moving at a snail's pace, he got in the car beside me, and I felt I might pass out. The scent was unbearable, yet I had to dismiss it and concentrate on what to do.

"See this, teacher?" JD raised his cane in the air and demanded, "Show us where the girl is, or I'll break your knees and you will never stand up and teach again. Ya see, I'm her pa, and she needs to be home where she b'longs."

I was stunned by that revelation and did not believe it for a minute.

I had to say something but couldn't bring myself to give any directions. The Mavises didn't live far from me, just a stone's throw down Walhalla Road, but their driveway, through a wooded area, was just as long. I thought about the long driveway that may be muddy from yesterday's rain. Maybe I could get them to veer off the road and get stuck. I reasoned that this old car couldn't do what the Mavises' trucks do every day, hauling logs in worse conditions.

Stopping at the corner of First Street and Walhalla Road, I shouted, "Turn left, it is not far." I tried again to reason with the two would-be kidnappers. "She is happy here. We all love her and want what's best for her."

"Shut up, just shut up—white do-gooder know-it-all. She needs to be with her own kind. I know'd what's best for my own kin. Don't open your mouth again," he snarled at me, "jus' get us dere, and fast."

I thought about the Mavis men, praying they would be home, but I knew they worked on Saturdays, too. Maybe Noonday had gone over to Lizzy's for a visit, and I prayed for whatever reasons that neither Vita nor Noonday would be at home.

Finally, I had to say, "Turn here—take it slow, it is a long driveway." It was true, and the car moved slowly.

"Where's the house?" Jack asked.

"You can't see it until we get closer," I replied, knowing it was the truth.

The old car started slipping and sliding sideways, and I knew it could easily slip off and get stuck. That thought gave me hope.

Finally, Jack stopped the car and said, "How we gonna turn around to get out of here when we can't even go forward. I think we should walk from here and just back out after we grab her."

I wanted to swear out loud. It didn't take Jack long to figure a plan.

Right away, I said, "Untie me; I know a path through the trees where it is not so muddy." I didn't know what I could do, but I didn't want to stay tied up in the car. I thought I could at least scream bloody murder to warn them.

"Good idea, and you will walk with me and never move from my side," Jack said. When we all exited the vehicle, he pulled open his jacket to show me the gun in a holster at his waist.

Jack announced the plan: "We'll go in and get the girl, and you and the girl will walk back with us to the car, understood?"

Grumbling, JD followed behind us. It wasn't long before Jack spied the house; the chimney was smoking, a good indication that a fire was lit that day and someone was home. No one was outside except for Shitter the dog, and it didn't take his nose long to know that somebody was in his domain. He started barking, pacing back and forth. Jack pulled out his pistol, ready to shoot the dog. But the barking brought Noonday outside in a flash.

Jumping off the porch, she approached the dog and asked, "What's wrong, Shitter? Did you see a critter?" At the same time, Vita stepped out on the porch to check the yard, all 360 degrees.

I grabbed ahold of Jack's handheld gun, pushing it down. "Put that away!" I loudly whispered.

By that time, JD was by our side. Excitedly, he exclaimed, "Looky here, she's right here—couldn't be any easier—go get her, now."

At the same time, Vita called out, "Stop that barking, dog! Noonday, I want you inside right now!"

"But . . . why?" the youngster asked.

"Come on, now!"

Just then, JD walked forward, right into Vita's vision.

Vita shouted, "Who are you? What are you doing here?" She quickly turned to the girl. "Noonday, come here, come here, girl . . ."

Seeing the rest of us, Vita hollered, "Maggie? Maggie, what's going on?"

I yelled, "Vita, get inside, you and Noonday, lock the door."
Jack hit me hard, and the blow thrust me forward.

JD raised his walking stick to Vita and yelled, "I want my
girl back. She is mine; I have paper that says so." By the end of
his sentence, the dog was on him, growling and biting at his legs.
In a flash, Jack ran over, picked up the dog, and threw it to the
ground. Poor Shitter lay hurt. Noonday turned around, rushing
back, crying, "Why . . . you hurt my dog?"

I pulled away from Jack, yelling at Noonday, "Get in the
house now! Go! *Run!*" She hesitated, but finally ran, turning
around and yelling, "Miss Maggie, help Shitter."

But Jack was behind Noonday before Vita could get her
inside. Jack picked up Noonday, who was screaming and holler-
ing so loud that all of Walhalla may have heard. Immediately, I
got to Jack, pounding and hitting him and screeching, "Put her
down!"

Vita joined me, making it impossible for Jack to get away
with the girl alone. Jack had his hands full with the three of us,
but he still managed to pull out his gun and shoot; he got me in
the arm. At first, I didn't feel the pain, but then I saw the blood.
Vita grabbed my arm to check it.

Jack shouted, "You crazy women, maybe another bullet will
take care of you once and for all."

"Shoot the bitches!" JD ordered.

I cried, "*No*, please no . . ."

"You bastard, shoot me, I dare you," Vita said, hammering
him again.

Just then, Jack handed Noonday over to JD. "You decide
what to do, old man. Is she worth it with these females raising
holy hell?"

I could see that JD could hardly hold the girl and the gun, too.

Suddenly, no one was screaming or talking or yelling, possibly thinking about what Jack had said: *Is the little girl worth it?*

But I was hopeful. Maybe, just maybe, they'd give up and leave.

I was surprised to see how calm Noonday was in JD's arms. I think everyone else noticed that, too. Not accustomed to holding a child, and because she'd stopped wiggling, he let her stand but held on to her. I think she realized her skin color was like his, and that interested her. I think she wanted to know more about him. And she may have been worried about me being hurt, because she said to him, "I'll stay with you for a little while if you don't shoot Miss Maggie again or shoot Vita-Mom, and not Shitter, either."

At that, JD seemed to soften and said, "You're a darlin' girl. I's going to take good care of you. Come on . . ."

Then, for a split second, it seemed everyone remained in deep thought: *take good care of her* and *come on*. Vita and I watched Noonday walk away with JD. It was as if everything in the world started spinning except for them. Together, hand in hand, they headed toward the pathway of the woods. In a snap, Jack hurried ahead of them.

My arm warranted my attention, but I could see it had stopped bleeding.

Then, like an insane awakening, I hollered, "Vita, are you with me?"

Strangely, the air turned sick with silence. With every running step, I sensed another intrusion that could not be denied. I stopped.

Out of the clear blue sky—a powerful blast rang through the air that caused everyone to stop. Quickly, my hands came off my ears, and momentarily, I couldn't hear anything. I stood for a moment slapping my ears. At the same time, I realized a second blast may be next and possibly a third. My ears finally popped opened up, as did my eyes, in search of Noonday. Lingering smoke cleared just enough for me to stop cold, and for good reason.

A few feet ahead, JD lay flat on the ground face-first.

Jack, who circled back, yelled, "My God, he fell like a rock." He leaned over to see if JD was dead. But then he left as fast as he could run.

Noonday, with her back to us, stood like a statue, likely stunned and, I'm sure, afraid to move. Strangely enough, JD's hand was still clasped around Noonday's hand. Finally, his hand released hers.

When Vita got to me, thinking I was shot, she cried out, "Oh, Maggie, did he shoot you again?"

"No. Look, *look*, Vita!" I pointed to the dead body.

"Oh—my—God!" she exclaimed.

Both of us ran to Noonday, who turned around and, upon seeing us, announced, "That bad man fell down . . . He fell down, Miss Maggie."

If we hadn't seen it with our own eyes, we would not have believed it. It took a second look for each of us to register what had happened, and yet Vita and I were still in disbelief.

I loudly declared, "*Who* shot him? Was it Jack? No, no, it wasn't Jack's gun!"

Feverously, I called out again, "What direction did the shot come from? Dear God, we better get inside."

Hurrying back, Vita tossed her hands in the air and screamed, "What the hell just happened here?"

We grabbed on to Noonday, and dragged her into the house. This time Vita let Shitter come inside, too.

Because the shot was heard at the river and beyond, it wasn't long before the Mavis men returned to find Jack and his car stuck in their driveway.

I heard later that Gunner, upon seeing Jack's gun, jumped out of the big log truck and surprised Jack with a beating he'd never had before in his "know-it-all, big-shot" life.

The sheriff and deputies arrived with lights flashing and horns a-blaring and a crowd trailing behind them. Never before in this quiet village in Michigan was there such a ruckus, let alone an attempted kidnapping and murder.

For weeks, I'm sure, there were many villagers in Walhalla, Idlewild, and beyond who speculated about who'd shot JD. The sheriff already knew that the dead man had to have been killed by a rifle with a scope.

I kept my thoughts to myself, and, not to my surprise, JD's murder was never solved.

☙

It took me a long time to recover, not because of my arm injury, but more because of an injury to my core beliefs in the human race. A broad spectrum of good to bad lies at the extremes where very good and very bad reside. But I was finding that one extreme far outweighed the other, and it was called evil.

My parents insisted I move back home with them. I fought the idea but eventually did as they requested because the whole kidnapping-and-attempted-murder incident not only scared them but scared everyone. Nothing like that ever came close to happening again in our little village. Idlewild was not happy that someone who lived nearby the town, in an outlying area, had attempted a kidnapping and was killed in the process. And incidentally, months later, JD's son, Johnny, committed suicide. The whole thing left an unjust mark on the clubs in this magical place.

I was bored at my parents' and hated the fact that my dad had to drive me to school every day. Most days, I walked home, which turned out to be good because I got to walk with some of the kids.

"Miss Maggie, tell us again how you saved Noonday's life from those bad guys."

"Yes, they were bad guys. And there's a lesson here, and it is: 'Crime does not pay.' Just like you have heard many times and, now, because I was there in the middle of a crime, I can tell you for sure: 'Crime—does—not—pay.'"

Noonday added, "And I was in the middle, too, huh, Miss Maggie?"

"Yes, you were," I concurred.

And Bookie added, "And brave, too." Noonday walked a little taller after hearing that remark.

Every few yards, we'd lose a child to their home. "Bye, Miss Maggie, see you tomorrow," said one and then another.

We all spied Vita-Mom, who was standing at the infamous driveway waiting for Noonday like she did every day now. Noonday took off running.

The children called out, "Bye, Noonday. See you tomorrow."

I knew it would happen: the children already accepted Noonday into the group, and I was sure, in time, they would have accepted her inside the schoolhouse.

Eventually, it was only Bookie and me walking down a two-lane dirt road that was a less-traveled part of First Street. We were neighbors whose farms were the farthest away from the school.

"Bookie, how is your little baby brother?"

"Good. My mom is busy, but she is happy to have Billy for company, except when he cries. Dad and I are always outside with chores."

"It is never-ending work for a farmer, I know. Is that what you want to do when you grow up?"

"I like it . . . don't know what else I'd do. I never thought of anything else."

"I can think of lots you could do, Bookie. Let's talk about it sometime. Thanks for walking home with me. See you tomorrow." I turned with a wave to my prize student.

Every night after dinner, my parents and I shared the news of the day, which amounted to nothing like the news of a week before. I retired to the bedroom of my youth and wished I was somewhere else with someone else. I missed Duggie so much.

It was getting to be too long, too hard, for me to be without him. I wrote him all about the mayhem that had occurred and how, thankfully, the bullet had just grazed my arm. I continued writing about the whole botched kidnapping attempt, which resulted in the shooting death of a bad man. After finishing the letter, I scolded myself for writing about it when my husband, so far away, could be in a war where killing and dying were the norm. After prayers, sleep came easily, knowing our love was well and strong. I dreamed we danced the whole night through. And upon waking, I felt his presence like never before. It had felt real to the point that I awoke with achy feet.

℘

It was not long before I moved back to my own place in the little house across from the school. So the education of the only black child in Walhalla got its start again, despite the many obstacles that prevented it in the first place. Supplies came easily, some secretly, and lessons with Noonday progressed smoothly, even after my full day at school. She learned quickly, and her willingness and eagerness to learn made it easier for me. Still, the little girl asked for more reading, more writing, more numbers.

One day, near supper hour, Bookie came by with a welcomed aroma from a basket he carried.

"Your mama asked if I might bring you these eats, Miss Maggie," he explained.

I smiled. "Oh, my mama knows me well. I haven't got around to supper yet. Come in, please, Bookie."

Noonday bounced out from the bedroom.

Without a moment's hesitation, she called out, "Hi, Bookie." Then, with a crinkled-up nose, she blurted, "You stink!"

Bookie looked down at his manured boots and retorted, "Not me, it's my boots."

"Stay, Bookie. Leave your boots outside. Maybe you can help Noonday with her numbers."

"Okay," he said, eager to stay.

That evening was the beginning of many evenings of study and supper for the three of us. We enjoyed our time together; our mutual love of books created a bond between us that was never severed.

I read to them often, explaining the value of the written word.

"A good book is full of admiration for its subject, the characters, and the writer. A book is not a talked thing, but a written thing. It is written down to hold on to the talk."

Their young minds grasped the true meaning of the words more than many adults.

"Listen to Emily Dickinson," I said, reciting her poem.

> *There is no Frigate like a Book*
> *To take us Lands away*
> *Nor any Coursers like a Page*
> *Of prancing Poetry—*
> *This Traverse may the poorest take*
> *Without oppress of Toll—*
> *How frugal is the Chariot*
> *That bears a Human Soul—*

"Remember this," I said. *"There is a route to arrive at any good author's meaning. Use these tools: the sharpest pickax for learning and a smelting furnace for your thoughtful soul."*

᠅

The two youngsters squabbled a lot, but I respected their youth and expected my prize pupils to argue and compete. They were, after all, still young despite their still-blooming intellects.

The disagreements always ended in laughter, and their back-and-forth often went like this:

"I told you."

"No, I told you!"

"I knew it."

"Well, I knew that, too."

While I cleaned the supper dishes, the two scholars rolled on the bed, tossing pillows like weapons and disarranging the total order of the room. I made Bookie leave for home at an early hour. Every evening, I walked them to the corner of Walhalla Road and First Street where Bookie left us, running and waving until we couldn't see him anymore, then I walked Noonday home to her Vita-Mom and the Mavis men. I was exhausted but always satisfied with my full day.

Fall ventured into winter that year with a whiff of a rumor that I was homeschooling the little black girl. I waited to hear more, anticipating the worst, but I never did hear from the school board. And I didn't stop teaching Noonday. I wouldn't have stopped even if they had fired me. I made extraordinary efforts at the Bell School, so no fault could be found there. Every day, I taught my students to the best of my ability.

ℰↃ

The next couple of months flew by faster than I took time to notice. It was an unusually warm day for late fall. The children, restless to be outside, were more unruly than usual. My mind kept wandering, which challenged my ability to discipline. A strange fall fever was impersonating spring fever, and I watched from the window as I allowed the children a longer recess. I had an unsettled feeling, a longing I couldn't explain. *I am tired,* I thought. *Maybe that's it.*

Quiet, at last. The students and I were consumed with the last assignment of the day when a knock on the schoolhouse door broke the stillness, and all heads turned. The children watched me walk to the back of the classroom, but before I got there, Postmaster Overmeyer barged in with Noonday in tow.

"You're not suppose to be in here, Noonday!" a child called out.

"I know it. I have to show Mr. Overmeyer where Miss Maggie is," she answered justifiably.

At that moment, Mr. Overmeyer handed something to me.

"I thought this looked important, Miss Maggie. It just came in, so I thought I'd better get it right over to you."

I held what looked to be a telegram in my hand. I opened the ominous wired message, and at the same time, I pictured myself watching from afar. I could see myself—I was there and yet I wasn't.

The children looked on, more quiet than at any other time that day. A fearful silence filled the room. No one told Noonday to leave, so she found Bookie's side and, instinctively, placed her hand in his. Mr. Overmeyer must have sensed a grave revelation within that telegram; his eyes told me that. Despite their immaturity, the children sensed it, too.

I closed my eyes, thinking, *Duggie's coming home, that's it. He's letting me know.*

I desperately sought the news, but couldn't quite bring myself to find out. When I opened the telegram, I looked at the words, and they jumped at me, choking me, until my breath halted.

> *Dugald Kelly Dunn . . . killed . . . Sorry to*
> *inform the family . . .*
> *death of Private Dunn . . . death, death . . .*
> *November 9, 1939 . . .*

I screamed, *"No—no. Oh please—No!"*

I slumped against the wall, rereading the tragic message. *Sorry to inform . . . death . . . death . . . death of—Dugald Kelly Dunn.* Immediately, I denied its contents.

"It's not—it's not true, it's—a mistake. No—no—Oh my God!"

Mr. Overmeyer mumbled, "Oh merciful heavens."

He held me up as I cried out, "My Duggie—no, not my Duggie!"

My face went pale; my body bowed as pity surrounded me. I looked around. The stares pierced me. I pulled away from the postmaster and screamed, "Why did you bring this here!" I hit him with the telegram—it fell to the floor. "Why, why . . . why?"

He leaned over and picked it up. "I'm sorry. I'm so sorry, Maggie."

I didn't hear him. I walked like a zombie back to the cloakroom, and by mere force of habit, I put on my coat. Mr. Overmeyer followed me, assuring me in my semiconscious state that he would find out all he could—where the telegram came from, when it was sent, and from whom. I don't remember anything else as I walked out of the school with the postmaster. All the little people remained seated inside, subdued and solemn.

I imagined that an older child finally spoke: "I 'spect we can go now, too."

Slowly and mechanically, they must have marched out single file, each child going their own way. Noonday must have cried her heart out, running down to the Mavises'.

When they all got home, parents learned: "Mr. Maggie Dunn died in the war."

When Mr. Overmeyer left me, I wandered around the bungalow, picking up Duggie's picture, picking up his last letter, and the letter I had started the day before—my last to Duggie. "Oh, Duggie, don't leave me . . ."

I cried out, "Mama. Oh, Papa."

I was broken. I was torn apart. Walking out of my little home, heading down First Street, my body parts barely moved. When I reached the unpopulated area where the Manistee Forest closed in on the two-track dirt road, I started to run. Like a wounded, terrified deer, I ran. The wind whipped at me. Cold tears wet my face and veiled my eyes, and I couldn't see through them. My legs, burdened with the weight of my inescapable sorrow, shuffled and weakened. I fell.

I crawled in the dirt path, screaming, "Duggie—Duggie. Don't leave me, Duggie. I love you. I love you."

I wept and wept. I beat the ground with my fists and sobbed uncontrollably. With convulsive catches in my chest, I stopped breathing. I gasped and gasped. My crying, so far back in my throat, finally released a hissing noise. I breathed again, but I wanted to die.

I lay in the dirt road until my papa found me. My dear papa could not lift me.

Ultimately, I reached for him. "Papa—help me, Papa."

My father's love for me was never as apparent as it was at that very moment when he embraced me in the dust of the earth and tearfully uttered, "Maggie, girl, I got you. You are safe in your papa's arms." I sobbed as he lovingly held me, quietly crying himself.

❦

That winter, I did not return to school, and once again, Noonday's education ceased to be.

Who was Dugald Kelly Dunn,
Who bore the greatest price of war?
(Are wars ever won?)

—*C. Ohse*

To Maggie, he was the husband of her youth.
To Noonday, he was the sailor her teacher wed.
—*C. Ohse*

CHAPTER TWELVE

Coming of Age

"She's like Jell-O my mama makes."

"Ya, jiggle, jiggle."

"She's horrible."

"Yaw got that right, horrible Harrible . . ."

The substitute teacher, Mrs. Harrible, started each day with a ruler in one hand and a walking stick in the other, though many questioned its purpose. The children learned one thing very quickly: do not disturb the teacher whose hand held the staff of punishment. The sting of the ruler or the stick could be felt many days after the conflict. No child knew when the instrument would rear its ugly head and strike, even when a correction was not in order.

On her first day, the large woman leaned forward, placing her palms flat on the desk.

She spoke to the children. "Pay attention, young people, for I shall not repeat directions a second time."

The old teacher's heavy bosom lay on a shelf of her larger, protruding abdomen. A dress of gray covered her, and on it, a large brooch sparkled and held center stage. She had unfeeling, milky eyes, and her gray hair was severely pulled back into a knot that sat on top of her head, indicating a woman easily inclined to sigh and faint.

As an older woman, she was often plagued by constipation. Upon her desk sat a fine china cup filled with Milk of Magnesia, which she sipped with deep concentration throughout the day. The children stared at the ruffles of fat around her wrists every time she tilted the cup to her full lips. The heavy-fleshed teacher was often the subject of discussion among the children. From the first day she waddled into the classroom, the older children huddled together at recess and tried to solve the problem of Mrs. Harrible. "She's hairy, all right. See the hair on her arms? They're in little knots."

"Ya, like little balls."

"I'd like to rip one off and make her scream."

"Let's tell Owen to rip one off the back of her neck."

"Ya, when he's rubbing her."

"Ya, I never thought I'd ever feel sorry for Owen."

Bookie didn't like the antiquated woman, though he was smart enough to keep his thoughts to himself. She reminded him of old Bessie, the Brenners' cow, bulky and bossy.

Even though Mrs. Harrible developed a fondness for Bookie, sensing his superior intellect, he didn't return the sentiment.

"Bookie, dear, recount the lesson in its miniscule detail so that the others may perceive it like you have." He didn't like to be the teacher's aide, but when the woman stood beside him in front of the class, her hand on his shoulder, he respectfully did what was asked of him. At times, the old woman's eyes would close, enraptured with Bookie's logical habit of thought and correct use of language. When he was sure Mrs. Harrible's trance had carried her far away, Bookie's recitation flirted with ridicule. The children loved it and responded with silent laughter.

It happened more often at the end of the school day, when the weary teacher retired to her desk, ushering one particular child to come to her. She instructed the boy with the biggest hands in the class to rub down her fatigued shoulders.

"Owen, it's time," she called.

"Ya, ya, I'm comin' . . ."

"What did you say, my good man?"

"Yes, ma'am, I'm coming. I'm sorry, ma'am."

"Get over here. Work on my left shoulder and rub hard."

The big boy made his way to Mrs. Harrible's back side. "Okay, I'm rubbing, ma'am." He looked at the class as he wrinkled up his face, opened his mouth, and imitated the act of gagging.

With her head down, she continued to give orders to the youngster.

"Over to the left. Down a little. There, there. Okay, now up, up to my neck. Rub, Owen, rub."

"How's that? Is that good, Mrs. Harrible?" he said with a patronizing smirk.

"Oh yes, Owen, keep rubbing," she responded.

The other children had a difficult time concentrating on their schoolwork when the child standing behind the old teacher, massaging her fleshy muscles, became a comic, distorting his own facial muscles. The children barely contained their laughter. When the baroness looked up with one eye to check the scope of her classroom, all heads immediately clicked down as if on cue from a maestro with a magic baton.

"Thank you, Owen. That's enough for now. You have an A for extra credit today. Take your seat." Owen lumbered to his seat, smiling all the way.

In time, I learned that even those who didn't realize my significance missed me. I received many notes requesting my return, especially by two individuals who missed me more than the others—one in school, the other in the shadows outside the walls of learning.

Noonday's visits to the playground were few, but as winter yielded to spring, Noonday's presence became more noticeable to the substitute teacher. One day, when Mrs. Harrible decided Noonday was coming to the schoolyard too often, she openly expressed her disapproval.

After dismissing the class for recess, the prosy teacher asked her young prodigy, "Bookie, please remind the colored commoner to remove herself from the premises. I do not believe she is allowed to mingle with the white schoolchildren."

Shocked at his teacher's request, Bookie responded without giving a thought to his blunt retort, "I will not!"

And, as fast as he could, he ran out of the schoolhouse.

The visibly shocked old woman must have felt a torrent flow into her large cotton drawers. With her eyes closed, and squeezing her buttocks together, she may have tried to stop it. Holding on to the edge of the desk, she looked down, red-faced, as the puddle spread between her feet. Her awkward stance went unnoticed except by three older children. In the cloakroom, peering around the corner, the threesome watched, nearly unable to keep still.

"Look! Mrs. Harrible is peeing her pants," one whispered.

"Why's she lifting up one leg?"

"'Cause she was a Saint Bernard in her other life, dummy." The three quickly disappeared when Mrs. Harrible finally looked up, sighing heavily.

After cleaning up and regaining her composure, the vain woman's embarrassment abated. The teacher, immensely disappointed in her prized student, quickly sent the school board her notice for resignation of employment.

"Kids today! Incorrigible!" she exclaimed to her lady friends.

I'm sure at the next meeting the school board discussed the letter of resignation from Mrs. Harrible. One member was appointed to visit the school and inquire of her reason to leave so abruptly in the middle of her contract.

"We have no one else to cover for Mrs. Dunn until her mourning is over," the board member explained.

"Well, you know I am not a young chick anymore. I am unable to tolerate the sass coming from this brood of children today. I had never been as disrespected as I have been here. It used to be that a teacher was allowed to wash, with soap, the sass out of a child's mouth. And take the ruler to their mischievous hand, but a teacher is bound today with rules and regulations unheard of years ago."

The big woman motioned the man to the windows to view the children at recess.

Making sure she had his attention, she added, "And, look here, a nigger comes here every day and plays with the brood . . . no doubt she will contaminate them."

They both stood there watching Noonday with the children.

"I'll call them in, and perhaps you will speak to them about this," she suggested.

He quickly asked, "The black one doesn't come in *here*, does she?"

"Oh, heavens forbid, no!"

The man hastily replied, " I fully understand your concerns, Mrs. Harrible, and will report it to the board." He promptly headed to the door, turned to shake her hand, and said, "The board appreciates that you will stay until Mrs. Dunn comes back. We will contact her right away. Perhaps she will be over her grief shortly." He rushed out, passing the children as they filed in.

Regardless of the substitute teacher's problems with my class, my mind could only numerate my class as one. I could not measure its precious numeral content, one by one. I buried myself in my grief and selfishly didn't care about any of my students or even if the world fell off its axis. When sleep came,

I was at peace. Upon awakening, I wanted to curse world war. I read and reread, over and over, the official report of Dugald's death and still couldn't accept it. I wanted answers to questions that haunted me. At this time, World War II had begun with other countries, but the United States had not yet joined. I remember Dugald telling me that President Roosevelt declared the Panama Canal a Pan-American Security Zone where US naval ships escorted other country's convoys safely through the canal. A naval destroyer that Duggie was on was torpedoed after escorting a UK convoy through the canal. I didn't understand why his ship was torpedoed when the United States was not officially in the war yet. We were told that my husband and all the others who died gave credibility to the creation of this so-called safety zone called the Declaration of Panama, as if that could ease our grief. I also received a letter from the prime minister of England, Winston Churchill, for Dugald's sacrifice that aided in their early efforts in the war.

I continued to be private in my grief, not wanting to share it with my parents or anyone else. I rarely came out of my room after the funeral and spent all my time reading and rereading the beautifully printed thank-you notes and exemplary-service notes from people I didn't even know. Sympathy cards from family and friends meant more. I spend hours holding and caressing Duggie's personal belongings, the most important being his wedding ring. I spent hours sliding it on and off my fingers. Though it was still too big for my biggest finger, my tears also made sure it didn't stay on. I'm sure my mother and papa heard me crying every day. I know they were distressed at my condition and didn't know how to help me.

I found out later that Noonday and Bookie had long been planning to visit me. They tried to understand why I was staying away so long, but I think their minds didn't want to comprehend the hard reasons.

"Maybe we can tell her 'bout Miz Harrible," Noonday suggested.

"Tell her what?" Bookie answered thoughtfully.

"She stepped on your foot and didn't say sorry, 'member? An' she's so big, maybe she'll break Miss Maggie's chair."

Her eyes got big, and she grabbed Bookie excitedly. "Maybe she's gonna eat some of you children and fry you like chicken."

Bookie laughed. "We gotta have better reasons for Miss Maggie to come back."

The following Saturday, the two preteens met at the stone markers placed on each side of the Johnsons' long driveway. They walked up the driveway, nervously wondering if they should go any farther.

Bookie raised his arm to knock on the door, but Noonday beat him to it. Because she saw them coming, Mama opened the door right away, grateful to see the youngsters.

"Ya, little vuns, come in. You vant to see my Maggie, yah? I don't know, maybe."

I heard the children follow my mother into the large sitting room.

"I baked this morning, how 'bout a cookie?"

"Yes, thank you," they replied in unison.

Soon my mama knocked on my bedroom door and spoke through it, timidly. "Maggie, dear, you haf visitors. You come out and say 'hallo,' yah?"

I pictured Noonday and Bookie standing there, frozen, not knowing if they would ever see me again. They likely wondered if I really existed behind that door. I didn't want to come out and face them, but at the same time, I didn't want them to think that what I had taught them about acceptance, inner strength, and faith didn't matter. That I couldn't live up to my own teachings and rise up and overcome whatever adversities came my way, however unfair. I stopped to listen to myself. I knew, right then, I had to do what Duggie would have wanted me to do: live again.

Mama spoke again. "Maggie, be polite, yah? Come out, the children are waiting." After what seemed like a long time, I opened the door. I emerged, not at all like the children remembered me. Their surprised faces studied me from head to toe. I didn't smile; I just stood there. There was no pink in my cheeks and no sparkle in my eyes. I just stood in the doorway, disheveled, in a bathrobe, barefoot. Looking at the children, as they stared back at me, I suddenly became uncomfortable. No one said a word for the longest time. I moved farther into the room, straightened up my posture, closed my robe, and tried to arrange my uncombed hair.

I finally spoke. "Hello, children."

At once, it hit me: I had missed those two wide-eyed students standing in front of me more than I'd realized.

Noonday stepped forward first. "Will you come back to school, Miss Maggie?"

Surprisingly, she ran to me and hugged me, both arms tight around me. "Miss Maggie, I need you, I miss you bad. I'm so sorry you're sad."

I looked at Bookie, who at that very moment turned away, not being accustomed to feeling such empathy.

"Come here, Bookie," I said, choking back my tears. The two youngsters clung to me while I called out, "I love you both. I am so sorry I have abandoned you. I am sorry."

"We loves you, too. Don't we, Bookie?"

Bookie nodded.

Noonday added," We want you to come back to the Bell School, huh, Bookie? That Miz Horrible is mean to all the children, huh, Bookie? Will you come back, will you, please?"

The tears streamed down my face as I catapulted from one reality to another—from death back into life.

ↄ

In a week's time, I moved back into my bungalow and started teaching. Certain mornings, just getting out of bed was difficult. I did it, though. As the weeks passed, my days of hours began to fall into a routine. I was glad to gain some order to my life. Keeping busy was my salvation.

It wasn't hard for Noonday to keep me busy, and the two of us became each other's salvation. The girl brought focus back into my life. We spent so much time together, it wasn't long before she moved in with me. It happened gradually, so that most people didn't realize the transition. The girl was at my place most of the time anyway. Vita Mavis didn't advertise the fact but answered others by saying, "Oh, sometimes she's here. Sometimes she's over there."

Noonday was maturing faster than I could teach her. I soon realized that, in time, she would become an exceptional student, and it wouldn't have anything to do with me as her teacher.

The lessons at my bungalow started again after school, and on Saturdays. Bookie joined in whenever he could. He enjoyed teaching Noonday.

"I loves you, Bookie," she expressed without reservation.

"No, no, Noonday. I . . ." he spoke slowly, correcting her, "love . . . you . . . Bookie."

"No, no, Bookie. You . . . loves . . . Noonday," she corrected him.

Noonday and Bookie both enjoyed learning beyond the basics taught in the schoolroom. They learned quickly, as quickly as the year flew by.

They grasped everything I taught them. Together we read of the birth of time in the heavens, and of the dancing stars in God's universe; they learned of the oceans and seas, and of the air and fire by which God shaped the wondrous Earth. We read about treasures, jewels of the highest mountains, deepest mines, and the virtues of herbs and flowers, of grains, beans, and full ears of corn. And that was not all.

❧

When the farm work kept Bookie away, Noonday and I missed him as if he belonged to us. When Bookie's younger brother, Billy, could help on the farm, Bookie could get away more. Just the same, he didn't appear on our doorstep often enough. When he did, two faces beamed.

"Oh, Bookie, so glad you could come by," said one.

"Oh, Bookie, did you fall down a well? And finally crawl out?" said the other.

One day, when Bookie came by, he found Noonday sitting on the back step. She didn't bounce up and run around, talking nonstop with every beat of her heart, as usual. She just sat there thinking, her eyes looking one way and then the other. She was happy to see Bookie, of course, he didn't doubt that, but he sensed something of monumental importance going on.

"Where's Miss Maggie?" he asked.

"She's gone on to the store to get me something only woman wear," Noonday said with a telltale smile.

Sober Bookie purposely sat down beside Noonday to avoid facing her. He looked straight ahead.

"Miss Maggie taught me how to 'member the name on the box, Go-Tex."

Bookie thought deeply about these things. Momentarily, he remembered seeing pads in the wash. What a revelation knowing his mother wore them. She didn't buy Kotex but washed the rags over and over until she made new ones.

Noonday kept up her nonstop chatter. "I got my womanhood on me, Bookie. It's a sign from God. He is blessin' me. I can have children now. Well, not now"—she paused—"'cause we're not married yet."

Bookie continued to look straight ahead.

"I was thinking, Bookie, if you and me have children, what will they look like?" Suddenly, she blurted out, "I'm budding out

. . . here." She looked down at her chest and pulled out her shirt, noting all the room in there.

Bookie didn't speak, nor did he look up.

"Miss Maggie says I'll have to have somethin' 'round me to hold 'em up. Why do they call them cups? Nuttin' much to hold yet. I have A cup; they go A, B, C, D, all the way to Z, I expect. I sure hope I never get to cup Z. I'd be hanging down to here, like your cows, Bookie."

Bookie looked up, his eyes wide open. Noonday got up and bent over with her arms and hands hanging in front of her. She began to walk, lumbering from side to side like she was carrying a heavy load.

Pensive Bookie watched and listened. He truly loved being entertained by Noonday, but today he wasn't sure.

"Umph, maybe your cows should wear a bra-zeer—big Z cups with little holes for the teats to poke through so'n you can milk 'em. Maybe they feel better and smile a big mooooo smile and give you more milk." She was enjoying attributing human-female characteristics to her best friend's cows.

"Maybe you should have some polka music in the barn, too. They can dance. The cows would swish their tails and stamp their hoofs, and their big bags would giggle and wiggle, but with a bra-zeer on—it wouldn't hurt. See? You'd have ser-e-naded buttermilk, how 'bout that? Or, maybe even butter!"

With that, Bookie burst into laughter, declaring loudly, "Butter can't come out the teats, Noonday." He got in the last word just as I rounded the corner of the little house.

I carried a brown paper bag under my arm. Two of us, one just beginning her womanly essence, went into the house. Bookie went home thinking about these things.

He may have thought, *What will happen to me to make me a man?*

The two youngsters, fast approaching their teen years, were naturally curious about their budding bodies. The questions came fast and furious in regard to sexuality. I tried to answer their questions. I was frank and open with my "adopted" children, just as my parents had been with me. The two learned without embarrassment. Because I did not show embarrassment, neither did they. I tried to make it clear to my young pupils that everlasting love and marriage must precede the sexual performance.

"Love, precious and rare, is the blending of two bodies for one brief period of time. They come together as close as two human beings can be. The two become one; no one knows the one like the two who have come together. This is the deepest trust and the warmest love two people can share."

I remember well the day the two young people stared in awe as I, their teacher, spoke from my heart, remembering the love I'd once known not so long ago.

ℰↄ

Each passing year brought its share of joy and sorrow. The sorrow passed away, along with the Johnsons; my beloved mama and papa; and the Schrecks, Noonday's grammama and grampapa. The joy of these years revealed itself in the intimacy the three of us shared, despite our losses. As a threesome, we were together as much as possible.

When Noonday and Bookie entered the eighth grade, the final grade for Bookie at the Walhalla school and for Noonday at the home of her teacher, the two students matched each other intellectually. And with high school one year away, they may have concluded that black and white students still did not attend school together.

No one graduated from the eighth grade at the Bell School without memorizing the Gettysburg Address as a final assignment. This was a difficult feat for a lot of students, but I was generous with my soon-to-be graduates. I let each carry a copy in their hand to refer to if needed. Each year on Memorial Day, the class journeyed to the cemetery and joined others from the village in a solemn but significant ceremony to honor the dead.

Many flags adorned the area. Speeches were given from a soapbox stage preceding the annual address of Gettysburg. I chose Bookie, out of five eighth-graders that year, to recite the address at the program, an honor bestowed annually on one promising student. Without any thought to the contrary, I allowed Noonday to join in and stand with the eighth-graders that day. Everyone in the crowd noticed her, of course, and whispered among themselves, but no one openly objected.

"Look at the colored girl! What's she doing up there?"

"Miss Maggie's got her nerve. Merciful heavens!"

Mrs. B leaned forward from her seat behind the ladies. "The heavens are kind, indeed. Ain't she the prettiest thing? I hear she is real smart, too."

Bookie stood tall in his tweed suit and bow tie. He was already a handsome, strong young man with a delightful honesty, and a mind ripe for learning—a fine example to represent President Lincoln. He recited the profound address without once looking down at the written form in his hand.

"Fourscore and seven years ago, our fathers brought forth upon this continent a new nation, conceived in liberty and dedicated to the proposition that all men are created equal. Now, we are engaged in a great civil war . . ."

This time, the small crowd listened to the message because Bookie presented it with perfect articulation and with inflections at just the right time. He accentuated the right passages, praising the many sentiments in this historical piece.

". . . It is for us, the living, rather to be dedicated here to the unfinished work . . . dedicated to the great task remaining before us . . . that this nation, under God, shall have a new birth of freedom . . . and that government of the people, by the people, for the people, shall not perish from the earth."

A bugle sounded. Silence filled the air for what seemed like an eternity to Bookie. No one had ever heard the address spoken so well. Suddenly, applause broke the silence. He smiled, then bowed politely. Noonday ran up and hugged Bookie. He picked her up and twirled her around. Many gasped and walked away. Others shook their heads at the sight of it. Then again, a few turned to the Brenners with genuine praise and congratulations. Slowly, the crowd dispersed, and I turned to Noonday and said, "Now it's your turn, Miss Flower."

The three of us walked from the cemetery to the Schreck farm, where Hank greeted us as we headed back to Marla Jean's gravesite. He was excited to see visitors. He'd lived a lonely life since the loss of his mother and father, both dying within a relatively short time of each other.

"How many zeros in a million?" he asked.

"Let's see, one thousand thousand is a million. There are three zeros in a thousand, so one thousand thousand has six zeros, and that's the same as a million," Bookie figured.

"Wow, Bookie. You're smart for a kid. I don't even have three zeros yet. Someday, I'll have a million dollars with six zeros."

"When?" Noonday asked.

"When I go to New York. I'm goin' to the stock market. That's where it is . . ."

"Why don't you make your zeros here?" she asked.

"Cuz, I'm learning how to invest. That's how you make money fast. Working here's too slow . . ."

"Quiet now, Hank," I reminded him.

He looked at me and snickered. "E-nee, me-nee, my-nee, mo. Catch a nigger by the toe. If he hollers, let him go. E-nee, me-nee, my-nee, mo."

I whipped around and grabbed him. "What's the matter with you, Hank? 'Nigger' is not an acceptable word."

"I'm just funnin', Miss Maggie."

"Don't ever say it again."

"It's how I choose my stocks. E-nee, me-nee, my-nee, mo. Catch a—"

Bookie interrupted, "No one ever got a million dollars catching anybody by his toe."

Noonday quickly said, "I'm not a nigger, either, Hank. Isn't that right, Miss Maggie?"

"But, ya are a nigger, Noonday. Everybody knows it," Hank bellowed.

I grabbed his arm again. "That's enough! You better go back to the house, Hank."

Sluggish, he said, "All—right, Miss—Maggie." He turned to Noonday. "I know'd your mama, Noonday. She could sing real pretty."

Noonday looked at Hank and smiled. "Thank you, Hank."

Satisfied, he replied, "Well, I better go now—ya, back to the house."

He walked away, but suddenly, turned and called out, "Come see me again. I'm not gonna say 'nigger' no more. E-nee, me-nee, my-nee, mo. Catch a doggie by his tail . . ."

We watched Hank leave. Then Noonday walked over to the foot of her mama's grave. She awaited my signal, then took a deep breath and started her recitation. She recited it perfectly, just as Bookie had done one hour before. She beamed with satisfaction when she finished. There were no flags, no bugles, and there was no applause.

But God was there.

We grasped hands in private, prayerful celebration to honor the first black woman of Walhalla, who had so nobly given her life with the hope that her daughter might prosper in a kinder, more accepting world.

༄

After many days of careful thought, I had decided it would be better for Noonday to experience learning in a nonsegregated atmosphere, so I placed her in Baldwin High School fifteen miles east, back to the area where her mother had come from. The young people of Idlewild attended school in Baldwin, a town just two miles west of Idlewild.

Noonday settled into a school routine fairly well. It was a change, and although she would have preferred being in school with Bookie, she adjusted to this variation with gratitude and eagerness. For the first time, Noonday met black and white students alike, together in a school setting. Yet she seemed more eager to embrace her subjects than make new friends.

What did not change was her time with Bookie after school and on Saturdays. When Bookie came to my home, the lessons broadened as the two compared notes from their separate instructions of the day. Bookie attended school in Custer, where he embraced each subject with vigor. The teachers, amazed with his ability and progress, desired more students like him.

You might think that these two exceptional students would have drifted apart with new acquaintances and new school settings, but they didn't. Although separated by the physical confines of a building—one here and one there—in actuality, their lives drew closer. As their friend, as well as their teacher, I hoped to guide them into life's teachings beyond the limits of a structured education. A mutual affection endured these growing years between the three of us, despite unfair rejections and untimely deaths in our lives.

Youth is a quality of the imagination,
A vigor of the emotions;
It is the freshness of the deep springs
Of life.
Youth is a love of wonder;
a sweet amazement of the stars;
the undaunted challenge of events;
the unfolding childlike appetite for what comes
        next;
And the joy in the game of life.
                              —Samuel Ullman (Revised
                                excerpt from "Youth")

Youth is Noonday and Bookie,
And Maggie, too.

                                        —C. Ohse

CHAPTER THIRTEEN

Bell School at Last

Bookie attended the all-white Custer High School. He continued to enjoy school with its invitation to learning. He didn't appreciate the complaints from the other students who grumbled about everything. Learning required diligent effort and a persistent passion for new ideas. These thoughts never entered the minds of some.

"Idleness, frivolity, and ignorance can only be put down by education," I recited to myself, knowing full well the truth of it. At this time in my life, I was content knowing my prize students were as devoted to learning as I was to learning by teaching.

Bookie grew into adolescence as a tall, fine-looking young man. He had a charming, boyish eagerness about him. His hair glistened in the sun, and more often than not, he wore a cap that shadowed his forehead. With his cap off, the young man exposed a two-toned face, pale on top and suntanned below. His blue eyes gleamed with interest, intellect, and integrity, just like his famed father. His already muscular frame portrayed a beautifully sculptured, soon-to-be-strong man. Though a quiet young man, Bookie was well liked and respected by his fellow students and teachers. He never refused a request by a teacher, never failed to do an assignment, and never said a bad word about anyone. He was an ideal student who remained first in his class scholastically until the day he graduated.

Noonday developed into an exceptional young woman. Womanhood unveiled Noonday as an exceptional being within a body of willowy curves perfect in balance and harmony. She was no common sparrow but a ravishing raven with loosely tossed, curly jet-black hair. Her high-energy face enhanced her sparkling dark eyes, which peered out from behind a silken fringe of black lashes. Elegant bone structure shaped her cheeks and nose from her translucent dark skin to form a softly balanced face. She was strikingly beautiful.

In Walhalla, tempered with love and nurtured by the kindly impulses of Vita Mavis and myself, Noonday became a veritable young lady—a young lady clad in the armor of self-respect, and that self-respect became her energy, stronger than self-reliance, higher than pride.

She never lost her youthful vitality, which touched everyone at Baldwin High School, a mix of white and black students, although many did not embrace her fervent spirit.

The teachers at Baldwin High School recognized her potential. She worked on her studies like all teachers wished students would. Many students labeled her stuck-up because she refused invitations to extracurricular group activities after school and on Saturdays. She remained loyal to her late-day meetings with Bookie and me. And Saturdays were a day of pure enjoyment with the "family."

During the week, Noonday was in the company of black people on a daily basis. Her black and white classmates didn't like her attachment to the white teachers. She didn't realize how much she clung to her white upbringing. It took some time before she could relate to her black brothers and sisters. In the meantime, this young girl's first experience with structured schooling was a difficult adjustment. The other students, accustomed to each other, had a hard time accepting Noonday into their school life.

Though Noonday embraced her subjects, she did not have many friends. Her beauty and intellect became a distant, envious deterrent for friendship. Many taunted her every day.

As her troubled days reached my attention, I started driving Noonday to and from school. Though it seemed like the right thing to do at the time, it turned out not to be. Waiting for me at the end of the school day was, at times, lengthy for her. I needed to finish my own day of teaching before driving the fifteen miles to pick her up. Noonday patiently sat on the school steps or stood on the walk near the street. This made her too visible and, of course, once again, too special, since she was receiving a chauffeured ride to and from school. It wasn't long before it was rumored that Noonday had a white mother. This created a melting pot of prejudices, which reared its ugly head in cruel remarks aimed at this impressionable girl. For a time, Noonday lost her zest for learning, her bubbling personality, and her spontaneous love of life. Her smile faded, and I worried.

One day, just before the school's break for Thanksgiving, Noonday was waiting for me inside the building as a heavy rain began to fall. I had entertained a visiting parent, so I was late, and the cold rain made for slow travel to Baldwin. I could picture her peering out the front door as the teachers, one by one, exited the building with friendly concerns.

"Your mother's late today. Are you sure she is coming?" one inquired.

"Perhaps I can wait with you," the kindly principal suggested.

"Oh no. Miss Maggie will be here soon. Thank you very much."

Noonday told me she could hear the custodian sweeping in a far-off room, flicking lights off as he finished one room, flicking lights on as he entered another. And she said she was concerned about the cold rain icing the roadway and the car I was driving, my parents' old Dodge. As the light of day gave way to an early fall evening, concerned, I drove faster.

She set her books down and started pacing back and forth, stopping often to wipe the heavy condensation from the door's window to look for oncoming headlights. When that wasn't good enough, she opened the door and stepped out for a better look. No headlights. Just as she turned to go back inside, the door should have closed behind her but did not. In a flash, two men stormed in behind her. With accelerated momentum, they lunged at her. She tried to run, but the two were on her immediately and forcibly backed her against a wall. One on one side of her, and the other directly in front of her, they stood with pompous grins, surveying her entire presence. The one in front of her was close. His breath, heavy with odor, imprisoned her.

"Well, well, well, what do we have here?" He put his hand on the wall to brace himself as he leaned in closer.

Little Miss Brownie, Noonday Flower, waiting for her white mammy. Where'd yaw get such a stupid name, anyhows?"

Noonday tried to push him away. He immediately slapped her with such force that her head hit the wall. He grabbed her face and squeezed.

Through tears, she asked, "Why are you hurting me?"

"Shut yo' mouth!" He grabbed her, pulled her to him, and pushed her, again, against the wall. One hand cupped the girl's mouth, hard. The other hand freely groped her. The other boy joined the invasion.

At the same time, I was parking the car, thinking, *Where is she?* I got out of the car and hurried to the building. It was locked!

Immediately, I heard a muffled scream that bolted me to pound the door as hard as I could. I thought to myself, *Oh my God! Something's wrong.*

I kept pounding, screaming, "Noonday, Noonday . . . open the door! For God's sake, someone open the damn door!"

The custodian had finally heard the commotion from the other end of the building and came running. "What the hell is going on here?" he bellowed loudly.

He made a beeline to open the door for me just as the intruders ran past the two of us and out the door.

I was able to grab one, hitting him with my umbrella and screaming, "What did you do, moron? You will regret this, I promise you!" I hit him harder, but he got away from me.

The custodian was consoling Noonday, who had slid to the floor, gathered up her knees, and was crying uncontrollably.

"I'll contact the principal immediately . . . and the police," the custodian called out as he rushed to the office.

I crouched down in front of Noonday, shaking and crying as well.

"I'm so sorry, Noonday. I'm so sorry." We embraced as our tears fell across our shoulders.

"Why, Maggie, why?" she sobbed.

In the months ahead, Noonday had a hard time dealing with that lesson of life. She learned quickly that, unlike science and mathematics, life's teachings were not always the lessons we wanted to learn. Life's lessons about fairness could rudely awaken a young girl to a world where the color of one's skin determined acceptability. But in this case, it wasn't the color of her skin that had determined her acceptability at school. It was the fact that some black students had felt she had been whitewashed by her white upbringing.

It was a long time before the new student with the funny name was accepted at school. Noonday was black, but she lacked a history of her black heritage, and even though the blacks and whites at Baldwin High School got along well, she was different. (Even though differences run more than skin deep, distrust and ignorance can plague many youths when the color line is

continually drawn. For everyone, black and white, the hardest
lesson of all is accepting oneself for who they are inside. This
takes guidance and understanding—and time. Time to *see* each
other, colorless.)

Noonday's vulnerability revealed itself her first year in high
school. For the first time in her life, she questioned whether
attending school was a good thing. In time, she dropped her
shield, opened her heart to new people, and they, at last, accepted
and respected her.

Even though things became easier at school, her loyalties
remained in Walhalla with her white family. Noonday and
Bookie continued their studies together after school and on
Saturdays whenever possible.

⇛⇚

Life continued in our small corner of the world. Excitement filled
the bungalow the day the new record player arrived. Between
the records bought or borrowed, Noonday and Bookie came to
know music in all dimensions—vocal, jazz, rhythm and blues,
as well as orchestration and big band music. One afternoon, they
listened to piano music playing a sad but lovely movement. The
music crept over the instrument, like the calm flow of moonlight
in darkness. The two listened as interlude after interlude danced
on the keys. The finale left the couple almost breathless, uncertain. The marvelous wave of sound carried the almost man and
his orphan companion away on rustling wings, leaving them in
emotion and wonder.

Bookie, sprawled on the couch, and Noonday, on the floor
clutching a pillow, both with their eyes closed, hadn't realized
the music had stopped until the phonograph needle repeatedly
asked to be lifted from its finished work.

"Wow," said one.

"Ya, how did that Bee-toe-ven make music like that?" said the other.

"He was a genius," they agreed.

Bookie phonetically read the record title. "Let's play 'Moon-light So-na-ta' again."

Putting the record back on the turntable, Noonday declared, "I feel like flying."

"And I feel like jumping over the moon!" added Bookie.

"Let's run away like the fork and the spoon." She laughed.

Together, they moved with the music. Their impromptu dance evolved with twists, turns, leaps, and bounds, embracing and rejoicing in the magic of it.

☙

There came a time when my thoughts expanded beyond the scope of teaching. A certain gentleman entered my life, and my attention was rerouted rather quickly. I was still young, and hoped I was still attractive. I hungered for another relationship. I wasn't buried with Duggie, even though I felt I had been for a long time.

This man was a retailer of men's clothing—a man whose concentration on success led him to be part owner of the business. He knew about me, and explained later that he'd admired me, from afar, and my devotion to teaching, to unpopular causes, and my willingness to live my life regardless of public opinion. One Saturday, I met him on Main Street in Scottville, another small town west of Walhalla, and farther west from Custer. He introduced himself to me as I walked by his store. Not occupied with a customer, he ran out to help me with packages.

"Thank you. They are heavier than I thought."

"You're welcome. Maggie Dunn, is it?"

Surprised, I answered, "Yes, yes. And you are?"

"Theodore Millgard. I am pleased to meet you, Mrs. Dunn."

"No, no, call me Maggie."

He smiled and I looked at him again and said, "Did I look that helpless?"

"Well . . . no. I looked out the window and saw a pretty lady—with packages."

"Ha, yes. I appreciate your help. I shop in Scottville often."

"Yes, I know . . ."

"How come I've never seen you before?"

"I don't know. I've lived here a couple of years now."

"Well, I'm very pleased to meet you, Mr. Millgard."

We got to my car and continued to talk. We spoke politely about the weather and other small talk until Noonday and Bookie returned from their jaunt around town. The young people looked at this friendly intrusion with reservation. Despite my expressions of interest in the man, they seemed hesitant to accept his apparent friendship. On the way home, the twosome told me about what had happened to them at the soda fountain.

The twosome had entered the Five & Dime and headed straight to the counter where they served Coke-a-Colas, Green Rivers, and ice-cream sodas. Noonday sat down on the red-padded stool and twirled around with pleasure.

"Oooooh!" she said with delight. Bookie smiled at his inventive companion.

The proprietor behind the counter spoke to a young worker who wore an overly large apron, colorfully stained. "I'll handle this, Judy."

The timid girl retreated as the man spoke to Bookie. "Young man, if you intend to make a purchase here, you better have your friend wait for you outside."

Immediately, words flew out of Bookie's mouth. "But . . . why?"

Others in the store nodded, justifying the store's ruling as to whites only on red-padded twirling seats. Noonday stared at the man, then her eyes scanned the others.

She may have been remembering the two black teens who'd attacked her at school that past winter. She may have surmised that those bad boys would not have been allowed in this Five & Dime, either. I'm sure she didn't like being put in the same category as her attackers just because of her skin.

Dazed, Bookie took Noonday's hand to begin their lengthy journey to the front of the store. Bookie may have appeared sick with shame. He had been to this store before, not often, and never before with Noonday. I'm sure Noonday didn't want Bookie to feel ashamed, so she squeezed his hand, stopped abruptly, turned, and stuck her tongue out, then whipped her head back with her nose in the air. "Bookie, it smells bad in here, real-l-l-y bad!"

Suddenly smiling, he answered, "Ya, it does."

Then he said very loudly, "Yup, smells like a snake's pee-pee in a cow's crap!"

"Like skunk cabbage!"

"Ya! Like cow's slurry, too!"

"And leek breath, and belly-button gas," Noonday called out, looking from one gaudy person to another.

The women in the store puffed up and gasped.

The two hurried down the aisle, and Noonday touched everything she could, one after another.

"Oopsy-daisy! Sorr-y, sorr-y, oh-so sorry," she said musically. Together, they banged the door open and ran down the street.

Through his younger years, Bookie probably avoided the concept of prejudice. I think the thought of anyone rejecting Noonday not only perplexed him but hurt him.

❧

Mr. Millgard started joining us in our weekend get-togethers of study or play. I welcomed this man into my life. Because I did, the teenagers did as well. Our newest member contributed brilliant conversation and proper manners, revealing a personality of reserved charm. His large frame and his noble face revealed a high forehead with a head of hair swept back. Behind his small spectacles were searching eyes, disclosing an active mind with intense emotions, easily moved. But it was his good nature, his obvious best trait, that won us over.

He readily accepted Noonday and Bookie into his life and became genuinely attached to them. It seemed effortless for him to get to know them; therefore, he understood my devotion to my special son and daughter. Because he was continually kind and generous, I drew close to him in a relatively short time.

My courting companion and I often delighted in evenings of late suppers or a picture show. On most occasions, Noonday and Bookie accompanied us. *South Pacific* came to Ludington, a town at the west end of Highway US 10 on the shores of Lake Michigan.

South Pacific tells a story of a Frenchman falling in love with a nurse, in the navy, who is stationed in the South Pacific islands. The riveting music had us humming, but more, the story led us into a profound discussion after we left the theater.

"I don't get it. Why didn't Nelly want to marry Emile?" Noonday asked. "She loved him, right?"

I tried to explain. "Yes, but . . . her prejudice got in the way. What I mean—"

Mr. Millgard interrupted. "Let me, Maggie, if you will. I'd like to explain, if you don't mind?"

I nodded. "Yes, go ahead."

As we got into the car and drove away from Ludington and the theater, he said, "Remember the song, 'You've Got to Be Carefully Taught'? Listen—just listen to the words." The man opened his mouth and amazed us with his baritone voice.

> *You've got to be taught to be afraid*
> *Of people whose eyes are oddly made.*

And people whose skin is a different shade . . .
You've got to be carefully taught.

He stopped at a red light and turned to look at Noonday and Bookie. "You see, the Frenchman, Emile, wasn't taught to be afraid. He loved his children who were born from his first marriage to a Polynesian woman. Nelly couldn't accept that."

"Why not?" Bookie asked. "Why can a Frenchman accept this and an American can't?"

"America and France are very different in their attitudes toward race," Mr. Millgard explained further. "In today's world, only a Frenchman could believably marry a Polynesian woman. That's why Rodgers and Hammerstein put a Frenchman in that role."

"What about me? I don't live in France," Noonday added. "My skin is a different shade, but I'm as American as you, ain't I?" She looked at Mr. Millgard and Bookie, then me.

"You're right, Noonday. You are an American," I said emphatically.

Mr. Millgard added, "Noonday, Americans still have a thing with prejudice. I can't explain why. When I look at you, I see a bright, lovely young girl—that's all. The day I made your acquaintance, I became the fortunate one."

I smiled at my date, comforted by his words.

The rest of the ride home was spent talking about the show, the music, and the story that ended sadly, but beautifully, a tale of overcoming prejudice.

❧

As time signaled change, studies kept Noonday and Bookie occupied with each other. We became twosomes rather than a foursome. In this way, our lives went through a major change.

Even though we didn't feel the change, we accepted the new partnerships that flourished as two and two.

One evening, Noonday looked up from her reading and found Bookie staring at her. She looked around, to the left and to the right.

"What's wrong, Bookie?" she asked as she brushed her hair from her dark porcelainlike face.

Bookie, embarrassed, shook his head and answered, "Oh, nothing, nothing, really."

Noonday glanced up. This time she smiled as she caught Bookie looking at her again.

"All right, Bookie, you don't feel like studying or what? What are you smiling about?"

"You're so beautiful. Do you know that?" He quickly looked away, trying to shake off what he had just said. A minute later, they were both looking at each other again.

"I guess I don't feel like studying," he said, still troubled with persistent thoughts.

They talked awhile, not about any particular subject, school related or otherwise. Suddenly, Bookie moved to the davenport where Noonday was curled up with her book. Just as he had done when they'd first met in the schoolyard years ago, he asked, "May I touch you?"

She looked at him through jesting eyes and held out her arm. "Sure," she said, smiling.

He reached over and held her arm. Slowly, he moved up her arm to her chest, where he tenderly engulfed her breast with his muscular hand. They sat looking at each other, their eyes capturing each other's deepest longing. For the longest time, Bookie held her breast. He looked away, but his hand remained on the softest, most sensuous thing he had ever touched in his life. Noonday closed her eyes. She did not remove his hand.

A new attraction was born. From that night forward, Noonday and Bookie looked at each other differently. Feelings, never before felt, erupted. They felt good, but when their intellect told them, *No, you mustn't,* they did their best to obey.

The feelings didn't go away. In fact, they became more intense. It became a struggle of immature experimentation versus maturity. Despite their restraints, and frequent diversions, their desire for each other grew. In a loving situation myself, I turned a blind eye to the changes in my nearly grown daughter and son.

The studies continued. Mr. Millgard continued to call on me. The black girl and the white boy continued to look at each other with sexual longings hampered by guilt and apprehension.

The end of the school year was near. Noonday, despite her difficult adjustment at Baldwin High School, received excellent grades. Finally fitting into a structured setting, Noonday cherished school and the opportunities there. At school, Noonday put Bookie out of her mind and concentrated on her day's studies. She made friends and became accepted.

Noonday heard about Idlewild from students who lived there. She knew from Grammama Schreck that her mother had come from there. Being so close, Idlewild and its proximity spurred her to find out more. She questioned many at school.

"Do you know anyone with the last name 'Flower,' like mine?" she asked.

No one said yes. This saddened the girl who felt so lost when it came to her heritage.

The talk involving Idlewild centered on the word "fun." The weekend frolic in Idlewild remained unadvertised, especially to those closest in miles. They knew it existed, but the whites never talked about it or paid attention to it. Noonday wanted to know more about Idlewild—its music, its shows, and its partying. Knowing her mother had once been a part of it, she longed for any information, no matter how small. She relayed the talk of Idlewild to Bookie, who likewise became fascinated with the place, more because he could see how much it meant to his best friend.

It was around 1946 when big-box attraction *Gone with the Wind* played at the Lyric Movie House in Ludington. I was eager to see this masterpiece. Having read the book twice, I made plans to see the film. Noonday and Bookie decided at the last minute not to join Mr. Millgard and me. The two students were serious about their studies, I didn't doubt that, but I was hesitant to leave them for so long. The film was a record-breaking new length. Add the time traveling to and from Ludington, forty miles in all, and it meant returning at a late hour.

"You get on home before I get back, Bookie," I instructed.

He nodded affirmatively, and I had no reason to doubt that he wouldn't do as promised.

For most of the evening, Bookie and Noonday studied algebra, English composition, and general science. Bookie's science lesson touched on anatomy, leading them into a discussion of human anatomy. The study of the differences and similarities in the human body seemed to fascinate the young man.

"Did you know that you and I are made up of billions and billions of little tiny cells?"

Noonday was silent.

"It says here I probably know more about our human structure than the wisest of the early Greeks," he boasted.

"I don't think so!" Noonday responded.

"Our tiny cells can only be seen with a microscope, but our larger body parts can be seen with the unaided eye," he continued.

They curiously looked at each other, thinking about their privately covered parts, parts that could be seen with the unaided eye, unclothed.

Without hesitation, Bookie said, "I'll show you first."

Noonday thought about it without saying a word. After a few minutes of confident expectation, they agreed to analyze each other's body—for science's sake.

"Okay, we'll undress together, removing one piece of clothing at a time," Bookie explained, justifying the activity.

Noonday and Bookie found their way into the bedroom. They sat on opposite sides of the bed, with their backs to each other.

"Take off your shoe. Now the other," he said.

Noonday giggled with apprehension, totally focused on the procedure. They continued removing their clothing until they sat naked. Neither turned to look at the other.

"Now lie down on the bed. Don't look anywhere but straight up, okay?" Bookie directed.

When Noonday didn't answer, he asked, "Do you want . . ." He hesitated. "Do you want to stop?"

Noonday answered, "I'm already on the bed, silly. I'm not looking at you, either."

They laughed nervously. Two budding adults lay stiff on the bed looking straight up to the ceiling. One white perfectly shaped male on one side of the bed and one black perfectly sculptured female on the other side. They listened to each other's breathing for the longest time. Instinctively, Noonday reached, felt around, and found Bookie's hand. They touched and clasped hands.

"Can we look now, Bookie?" she asked.

"No, no, not yet," Bookie replied nervously.

She broke their silence with a confession.

"I think you're beautiful, Bookie. I don't even have to see you to know that. But, I want to."

"I thinks . . ." he quickly blurted out, "ah loves ya, Noonday!"

Noonday laughed out loud. "No, no, Bookie, say it properly. I—love—you, Noonday."

Ceasing to be aloof, he stammered, " I—I love you, Noonday. I do. I really do."

She looked at him for a fraction of a second, then squeezed her eyes shut. Without the aid of a microscope, he let her see the *anatomy* of his heart.

The two lay quietly, watching the cracks in the ceiling, thinking, smiling, and anticipating.

Back to business, Bookie instructed, "When I say ready, set, go, we'll look at each other."

Before Bookie could say those three words, they heard me drive up alongside the little house. The bare teenagers bolted upright. In lightning fashion, they reached for the clothes at their feet.

They were fully dressed when I entered the bungalow, even though I found out later that every bit of clothing had come off that night.

Surprised to see him, I scolded, "Bookie, you're still here? Get on home, right now." Immediately, I shoved him out the door.

Smiling, the young man walked out into the moonlit spring night. The air smelled of leftover perfumed sunshine. He sauntered along the roadway and entered the woods, noticing the trees laden with new spring leaves. Everything around him seemed to confirm his feeling of elation. He whistled as he continued his familiar trek home, and to his family's normalcy. Halfway home, he shouted, "I love her. I love her. I love her."

He twirled around and around, hoping someone, anyone, may have heard.

"I really do. I do. I do."

And God was there. He heard.

So proud of his love for the radiant Noonday, Bookie burst into a sprint that accelerated him all the way home in record time. He was still repeating, "I do, I do, I do."

We've a story to tell to the nation
That shall turn all hearts to the right
A story of truth and mercy
A story of peace and light.
For the darkness shall turn to the dawning
And the dawning to noonday bright;
And Christ's great kingdom shall come to earth
The kingdom of love and light.
                                    —*H. Ernest Nichol*

From morning to twilight, all noondays avail.
Let truth and mercy, and peace and light,
        prevail.
                                    —*C. Ohse*

CHAPTER FOURTEEN

Back to Eden

In the late 1930s through the 1950s, Idlewild exploded further into an entertainment showcase and a never-ending extravaganza. Veteran Idlewilders recall visits from Aretha Franklin, Nat King Cole, and Stevie Wonder, along with James Brown and Cab Calloway. Showstoppers like Lionel Hampton, T-Bone Walker, B.B. King, Jerry Butler, the Four Tops, and the Temptations performed there, along with Bennie Carew with his drums. Also, Della Reese debuted in Idlewild before she made it big on *The Ed Sullivan Show*. Great singers Lil Green and Ruth Brown, although not as well known, performed in Idlewild, too. Others like George Kirby, Jackie "Moms" Mabley, Stepin Fetchit, and Betty "Bebop" Carter filled the clubs with comedic drama. A happy haven to call their own, talented blacks, in the shows or running the shows, made Idlewild a flourishing, independent black community, which earned respect and acceptance from the white people of the county.

The era that gave Idlewild its reputation was an intensely bright but relatively short chapter in Idlewild's history. Marla Jean, a witness to its heyday in the 1930s, led Noonday to its height of prosperity in the 1950s. Noonday continued to question many at school about Idlewild, including teachers. Information came to her until enough facts indicated that a visit to the famed resort was essential.

Bookie, at sixteen, had recently acquired his driver's license. Although he didn't need a license to drive a tractor, the law required he have one to drive a motor car. He practiced driving the car in the fields around the farmhouse. He had been driving a tractor for years, so it did not take him long to catch on to the mechanics of driving a car. The day he received his license in the mail, he drove over to show us.

"Noonday, Maggie, get in. I got my license today!"

"Oh, Bookie, can we go cruising? Hurry up, Maggie, we're going cruising."

"Hold on, I'm coming . . ."

The older Buick roadster took us up and down the short streets of Walhalla, with Bookie stopping at all stop signs and looking in both directions like a model motorist. On US 10, where Bookie could rev up the engine to forty-five miles an hour, we agreed to be his first passengers for a spin on the highway.

Bookie sat tall behind the wheel. A sense of pride emanated from him. The well-adjusted, courteous young man accepted the privilege of driving with gratitude. I resigned myself to the competent driver's control and smiled at the excited teenagers while the wind blew our hair out the open windows. I looked at Bookie and Noonday from the back seat of the car and marveled at how quickly they'd grown. I loved them both and was beginning to see the fondness they had for each other. I thought of them as brother and sister, and was sure they thought of each other in the same way.

"Don't ever show off when driving. Never abuse your machinery, and it will always do right by you." Bookie respected his father's wise teachings.

During their sophomore and junior years, Noonday and Bookie continued their studies together and at the same time excelled at their separate high schools. Their love of learning was only surpassed by their deepening love for each other. They grew accustomed to seeing each other often. When a day passed that they didn't get together, they desperately sought each other out.

"Where have you been?" one asked. "Where were you last night? I waited and waited."

In the spring of 1946, the heavens opened up over Mason County with a deluge of water. Rain fell to earth with all its "cats and dogs," and the land lost sight of its boundaries. For days, the sun hid its face while Bookie and Olie looked up, desperately seeking a break in the thick blanket that covered them. Heavy rain was a real concern for planting crops, and it plagued the farmers. The fields became lakes, and the back roads became sinkholes unsuitable for driving from one place to another. Noonday and Bookie hadn't seen each other recently because of the persistent, inclement weather. It was the longest time they had been apart, but they maintained their togetherness over the telephone.

New to rural homes, the telephone sent and received news on a wire. Many marveled at its concept and loved to talk on the wire, considering it the best thing to come into the home since electricity. Other than news and pertinent messages, the wire carried a troublesome static called "gossip." Many women found the talking machine convenient for chatting endlessly with neighbors about a shameful subject, that of a boy and his colored companion. Neighbors shared telephone lines, called "party lines," where one ring, two rings, or three rings indicated which home the call was for. And so, privacy was not assured when the phone rang into three homes.

Noonday and Bookie, realizing the telephone made public their longing to be together, decided to meet despite the gossip and in spite of the weather. They agreed to walk the higher ground of the railroad tracks, and meet where the tracks crossed No-Name Road. The short road from US 10 south, over the railroad tracks, perpendicular to First Street, had never been named. This crossing was a halfway point between their homes.

Noonday arrived first, and for what seemed like a long while, she stood there looking for Bookie. The early evening was very dark due to the massive cover of gray cloud. The rain had stopped, but the heaviness threatened more precipitation. It was a long time before Noonday decided to sit down. She sat in the middle of the track and watched the ground's moisture rise up around her. It moved quickly, suspiciously, like eerie, gigantic ghosts with arms that imprisoned her.

The pensive young girl yelled, "Where the dickens is he?" and looked around, unaware of the approaching train.

Noonday felt the earth move beneath her. She peered through the haze as the fog opened its mouth and unveiled the round light illuminating the short distance in front of her. Her fiercely pounding heart warned her of the danger bearing down the track, a train of massive proportion, and not a ghostly figment of one. Suddenly, the train let out a long, impatient whistle, as it did at all crossings.

"Oh my God!" Noonday leaped into the air, not knowing what peril awaited her beyond the tracks, and at the same time, the giant black phantom rolled by her with a deafening click-a-dee-click, click-a-dee-click, pounding the ground a long way until the sound faded away. Noonday hit the soft earth and then slid down the steep embankment like a greased pig. She floundered wildly, frantically, as the mud rolled over her. The water that gathered at the base of the incline arrested her with a big splash. She gasped and reached for anything that could steady her. Fear reflected in her eyes, the only part of her not covered in mud. She managed to stand, but the slippery slide refused her feet any traction, and she plopped down once again. She slapped the mud in a fit of anger as the wet earth oozed between her fingers and flew in every direction.

"Ahhhhhhh. Ahhhhhhhhh, Book-ie, Bookieeeee!"

Out of the darkness, a hand reached for her. She grabbed it.

"Are you all right, Noonday? What happened?" he asked as he pulled her up out of the muddy ravine.

"I'm not all right, you dumbbell! You're late! Again! You're always late! Look at me! Just look at me!" Noonday sobbed.

Bookie's eyes adjusted to the dark, and he really looked at her for the first time.

"Oh wow, look at you . . . you look . . ." He started to laugh, and laugh he did, and he couldn't stop. He laughed uncontrollably, and while his good sense told him to stop, he could not.

She stood there, dripping, her clothes hanging on her without shape because of their muddy load. Her glorious hair had gobs of mud about her head while some ringlets dangled in her face. She wiped her tears and her dripping nose with the back of her hand, drawing more mud to her face and into her mouth, which she quickly spat on the ground.

"Ugh, I'm eating mud. I'm all mud!" Her every movement caused Bookie to laugh harder. Her fiery eyes, mud dripping from her long, luxurious eyelashes, told it all. She was angry!

"I hate you!—I hate you, Bookie Brenner!"

The remark jolted Bookie out of his laughter. "It's your own fault. You don't know enough to get off the tracks when a train is coming."

"Oh ya, and sit in a hammock I always carry with me, smilin' and a-waitin' for my honey, and maybe have myself a cup of tea."

Bookie didn't laugh. "Couldn't you hear the train coming?"

"If you got here when you were suppose to, before the train, this wouldn't have happened. You're always late!"

"I had to come *after* the train," he said, justifying his tardiness.

"But, what about me? You knew I was here waiting for you," she yelled.

"Don't yell, Noonday. Don't yell," he said uncomfortably.

The couple stood there, and it wasn't funny anymore. They were fighting for the first time, and Bookie didn't like the feeling. It scared him. He didn't know how to handle this sudden shift in their relationship. He could deal with fighting the whole world if they were both on the same side. His thoughts turned to home. Mrs. B. and Olie didn't fight, although he remembered many times when they didn't speak to each other for days. Mrs. B. communicated with Olie using Bookie as her spokesperson, and vice versa. He guessed he didn't like that, either, but there was never yelling. That's all he knew.

Noonday embraced herself, shivering. "I'm cold. What's the matter with you, Bookie? Cat got your tongue? Talk to me!"

She probably wondered why Bookie didn't apologize, then comfort her.

Like an ostrich, he buried himself without any effort to console the one person in his life he had grown to care so much about. He was a young man of few words, like his father. He said nothing, just turned away and started walking down the tracks the way he'd come. She screamed after him, her tears making grotesque streaks of salty mud down her face.

"I hate you, Bookie Brenner! I wish the train ran me over! Then you'd be sorry! Do you hear me! I'd be dead!"

She watched him walk away. "Bookieeee, come back here. Where are you going?"

He just walked on and never looked back. She watched his retreat in disbelief until she couldn't see him anymore. A muddy Noonday started off in the opposite direction, down the railroad tracks, walking on the planks, stumbling and mumbling, and suddenly stopping. "Oh my God, the train. When is another one coming?" She began to run, looking back and ahead, never stopping until she got home.

The party lines quieted down, as it was quite a while before Bookie and Noonday talked on the telephone again. For days, Bookie was an unhappy young man. He was nervous the day he made up his mind to drive over to see Noonday. He couldn't wait any longer. The roads had dried up finally, and he realized how much he missed her. What could he say to make things right?

As it happened, she saw him coming, because each and every day she pulled back the window sheers to look for him. She bolted out of the house, and before he could get a word out of his mouth, she grabbed him and kissed him, and kissed him, and kissed him, and never stopped. "Oh, Bookie, I'm sorry, I'm so sorry. I'm sorry, I'm sorry." She stopped and stared at him. "What took you so long?"

❧

Following the wettest Easter in Mason County history, school resumed and the study sessions continued at the bungalow.

Evening rides for Bookie and Noonday most frequently ended at the Walhalla wooden bridge in one pathway or another that led a short distance into the wooded area. A couple in a vehicle, nestled into trees, desired more than the view that looked out onto the moonlit bridge. Not many knew about this country-style "Lover's Lane," but Bookie and Noonday found it.

"No, no, don't, Bookie," Noonday continually warned.

He loved her so much he had a difficult time pulling away from their passionate embrace. His intelligence told him he couldn't, even though his heart and body ached to, right now, have her completely.

She wanted him just as badly. She was secure in his arms. She loved his touch, on her face, her neck, on her breasts, and beyond. They kissed again and again, wrapping around each other, feeling the hard and soft responses, feeling their hearts beat faster and faster and through the heavy breathing, the spoken words.

"I love you. I want you. I need you so much."

Their love play developed into a building of desire and passion. When the two reached the point of readiness, they instinctively pulled away, breathlessly in pain. Inevitably, Bookie left the vehicle while Noonday adjusted her attire.

Time and again, the two ventured toward the point of no return with their sexual passions. It became a perplexing dilemma within their reasoning, intellectual minds—a problem unsolvable even by a genius so amorously shot with cupid's arrow. The young lovers decided to avoid time alone at the bridge.

So, as a diversion, the couple drove to Idlewild often. One summer evening, they found their way to the famed Flamingo Club. Like driving into a fairyland of lights and sounds, the two were mesmerized by the happiness emanating from the place. They had not traveled far, yet they felt they were in another world. It was a world of joy with beauty and truth, an unadulterated carousel of acceptance with a white horse and a black horse. It didn't matter which you chose. Through music and comedy, this place expressed a kaleidoscope of love and laughter.

Smiles greeted them as a valet parked their car and ushers seated them in the club. Noonday strained to look around, her eyes wide with amazement. Her mother had worked here with a friend. She remembered well the stories Grammama Schreck had told her. Grammama spoke of her mother's friend as the most beautiful woman in the world. Her heart beat faster as she looked at this person and that person wondering, *Could that be her?*

She's gone now, too, Noonday probably thought as she settled down for the show.

As the house lights dimmed, the spots illuminated the stage. A lean, six-foot-tall young man with a wiry frame entered stage right. Applause and whistles welcomed him to stage center. The crowd was most responsive as the young man, without cracking a smile, said, "Roses are red, violets are blue. Grass is green, and dirt is brown."

Saying funny things or saying things funny, he made speech into a memorable, hysterical routine. He just talked and the audience roared with laughter. He moved well, too. He could stretch out jokes, building them into funny bits like the guy with a nervous disorder trying to light a cigarette. Sidesplitting laughter filled the club as the doubled-jointed comic tried to unite a cigarette with a flame. Noonday and Bookie looked at each other, grinning with tear-stained faces.

They, along with others, were in the presence of a new wave of stand-up comics of the 1950s. This young man was a raw, young talent whose name would become a household word in the years to come. Personality encompassed this star, evident in his bit, "Revenge," where Junior Barnes smacks him in the face with a slush ball. The audience, in tears of laughter, watched the comic distort his face to a sorrowful pout and cry out, "What you wanna hit somebody in the face with a slush ball for?"

"You had to be there!" Noonday and Bookie told me later.

I questioned them. "Who was this funny man?"

"Somebody named Kos-be, I think," Noonday answered.

"You don't mean Bing Crosby? He's a singer."

"No, no, C-o-s-b-y, Bill Cosby. That's his name, right Bookie?"

Bookie nodded. "He never sang. He was funny. You had to be there, Maggie."

"I never heard of a Bill Cosby," I said.

"You will," they called out in unison.

Following the thunderous final standing ovation that night, Noonday and Bookie remained in the club.

"Oh, Bookie, it was wonderful. I loved it. I don't want it to be over," Noonday said.

He pulled his chair close, and as he put his arm around her, she laid her head on his shoulder. Watching the others file out the exits, the twosome sat quietly in awe of the wonderful night. When the remaining audience numbered only a few, Noonday and Bookie, having to accept the finality of it, left their table. While passing through the lobby area of the club, Noonday, in a wave of exhilaration, stopped suddenly. She saw a chic black woman, stunningly dressed, leaning over the reception desk pushing papers with authority. Noonday abruptly turned for a better look.

"Trix, telephone. Trix, it's Tremont."

The beautiful woman responded with a commanding but pleasant, "Be right there!"

"Noonday, maybe it's her . . ."

Bookie urged her to follow the woman. Noonday felt a sudden flush in her face, and though she probably didn't realize she was doing it, she did follow the woman into a small cubical off the lobby.

Noonday peered anxiously at the woman who picked up the phone and spoke clearly, loudly, and confidently. "Ya, it was a full house. This Cosby guy puts on a great show. Uh-huh, right. Hope we can keep him coming back."

Noonday stood there, staring at the woman.

Trixie turned and, at once, saw Noonday standing in the doorway. The woman stopped cold and, for a moment, appeared fixated by the young girl.

"Just a minute, Tremont, just . . . just . . . I'll talk to you later." She placed the phone on its receiver. For the longest time, the two faced each other without a word. Noonday turned away. The beautiful woman embarked upon a determined path toward her. Noonday looked up and finally spoke, but her words came out in a quiet quiver. "I'm sorry to bother you, but did you know my mama, Marla Jean?"

Noonday, realizing words were actually coming out of her mouth, spoke again. "Did you, did you know her? Marla Jean?"

Trixie studied the stranger in front of her like she was a ghost. She walked close, put her hand on Noonday's shoulder, and broke into the biggest smile.

"I don't believe it. I can't believe it. You are Marla Jean's daughter? I can't believe it. Yes, yes, I can! I see you are. Yes, you really are Marla Jean's daughter."

Noonday watched the energy rivet around the vivacious, immediately likable woman. She hesitated to tell her that her mother was dead.

"I never knew my mother," Noonday said finally. Trixie abruptly glared at her. Noonday softly declared, "She died when I was born."

Noonday waited, then asked, " I have been trying to find you . . . you knew her, didn't you?"

"Yes, I knew her. Come here, dear. Sit down."

Noonday sat on the bench in the little office, and Trixie sat down beside her.

"Yes, I knew your mother. She was an exceptional woman. We became the best of friends right away. I will never forget her."

"Thank you . . . that means so much to me." As the two settled into each other's arms, Noonday must have felt a great sense of relief. She had found a friend of her mother's, someone from her mother's past, at last.

The two exchanged polite questions and answers while Bookie watched from afar. I think Trixie had to watch what to tell the girl at their first meeting, not knowing what Noonday already knew about her mother.

&

Trixie Siggers now owned and operated the Flamingo Club. Noonday and Bookie met with her often. Mr. Millgard and I had occasion to meet Trixie when the opportunity to take in some of the magnificence of Idlewild was afforded to us as well. Trixie welcomed her new friends into her busy life with gracious, genuine hospitality. Knowing Marla Jean died so young saddened the woman, who relived daily the memories of their shared sisterhood. One solitary night, remembering a special friend, her prayers were such as this:

Oh, my dear friend. I'm so sorry you've been cheated. Before you left, you did good. You brought a beautiful girl into the world. I'm telling you, you must be a-lookin' down and busting up! You gave her your heart.

And God was there, listening.

Trixie filled Noonday in on many pieces of information regarding the earlier days of two young girls' escapades. It was a while before Trixie could tell Noonday of that night when Marla Jean was taken away.

"She never came back here. I looked for her every day. I was sure she would of come back if she could. That's when I got to serious worrying. It took me a while to track down her whereabouts. I asked all 'round, and finally I found her."

"You did? Really? How did you find her? Why, why didn't she come back?" Noonday asked.

Trixie continued. "One day, I started out to find out why. I gather'd up her belongings. She didn't have much, just a bike and some other stuff."

Trixie paused uncomfortably.

"It took some figuring, but, oh ya, I found her. But, my, oh my, she was living in a pitiful place. I'm sorry to tell you, she looked like a rag doll. They had a hold on her. I don't know how or why, but she told me I'd better not stay and—not to come back again."

She looked over at Noonday. Noonday nodded. "Please, go on."

"I was so surprised that she said she was married! She married the younger of the two. I knew him . . . yes, I knew your father. I dated Johnny Flower before Marla Jean had come to Idlewild. I'm sorry to say that Johnny was under the spell of a wicked man, his father. He controlled him. I never understood how or why. I do know that he loved your mother but didn't have the guts to leave his father and take her with him. I had a notion that she liked him, but it was that older man she feared. He was a mean son of a bitch to put such fright in her.

"First time I was there, she kept on lookin' 'round, afraid they might come back while I was still there." Trixie stopped, then started again. Her voice pained, she said, "I grabbed her and said, 'Come on. You're coming home with me.' That beautiful girl—she knew she couldn't. She was married, and besides . . . they'd come after her." Trixie stopped talking, unsure whether to say anymore.

"I did go back one other time with Tremont. That mean old bastard chased us off with a gun. He made me dance for my life. I tell you, Tremont had never started the car that fast to get us outta there. I can still hear JD laughing yet today. I never did go back. I couldn't do nothin'—I shoulda tried again. I shoulda got the police."

Tears flowed as she related what she could remember to the stunned Noonday.

"Where was Marla Jean's mother and father—her family?" Noonday anxiously inquired.

"I don't know, child. I do know Marla Jean's mama died shortly before we met, but she never talked 'bout family. She did say her father made home brew and drank a lot. She come to me quiet, shy as a lost puppy dog, but soon she was a-singing and dancing, and a-laughing with a mile-long smile."

She paused. "She was a good girl, your mama. I sure get to missing her, even after all this time."

Trixie cried as the mysteries surrounding her friend's life and death pained her. Noonday, in tears herself, instantly walked over to her and held her. "Thank you, Trixie. Thank you for telling me all this. I feel better knowing she had you for a friend."

The opportunity to try to find out more about Marla Jean presented itself one summer day when Noonday and Bookie ventured into the area where the black girl's mother had once lived. Following Trixie's directions, the two found the deserted neighborhood of the cavelike dwellings. A great field camouflaged the area, and tall grasses hid whatever remained from years past. Quietly, Noonday walked around, eager to find something but feeling despair when she saw nothing but a cement block here and there. Most dwellings were buried, and finding an entrance was impossible. There were no hills, no trees, no roads, no signs, just a lost community—an Atlantis of Lake County.

Tears burned in Noonday's eyes, and she looked back at Bookie, who, many yards behind her, stood helpless, wanting to absorb her pain.

"Come here," he called.

Slowly, they walked toward each other in the knee-high grass. The wind blew strongly as the sun drew behind ominous clouds. The young man put his mighty arms around his brokenhearted lover. He cherished her, wanted to care for her, and couldn't imagine life without her. His mature love ran deep and revealed itself in his total devotion to this undeniably wonderful young woman. The lovers stood in the middle of nowhere embracing each other like they were embracing their worlds—accepting one another completely, totally, without reservation. The wind pressed against them, but they stood steadfast, rejecting all obstacles, be it a wave of life's disappointments or the fierce wind of prejudice.

Over the next year, Noonday and Bookie became common patrons of Idlewild. They loved the excitement of the little mecca of talent. They grew to love Trixie and the whole aura of the Flamingo Club. Entertainment beyond anyone's expectations was at their fingertips, and they were not without appreciation of that fact. Their love of Idlewild and their love for each other surpassed the dreams of these two young people.

And so it continued. The magic of Idlewild was confined to the woods in the 1950s. The black music was so inviting that Noonday and Bookie reveled in this exciting part of their shared education. The resilience and dedication of the musicians who played in Idlewild shared a message with one and all. Their sound had so many facets that, in time, they attracted a multiracial following. How could race preclude adequate acknowledgment of the input of these black performers?

The early 1950s brought Sarah Vaughan to Idlewild. Sarah Vaughan had started her career, years earlier, with Billy Eckstine and Earl Hines and his Orchestra. A genuinely nice person, Sarah loved Idlewild and, while there, started the practice of staying in private homes as opposed to staying at a motel. She appreciated her privacy, just as she respected the privacy of others.

Iris, one of Trixie's employees and friends, opened her home to Sarah. The little five-foot waitress benefited, since it added to her income and gave her the friendship of a wonderful person. Sarah brought many things to Iris's home, including her pet bird, Sing. She practiced her scales with Sing, and their perfect pitch rang out over the neighborhood.

"It's a bird. It's a plane. No, that's Sarah practicing with Sing," the townspeople would debate.

In time, Iris built a second house behind her original home. She moved into the smaller dwelling while, over the years, many others used her dishes and linens, slept in her beds, and bathed in her bathtub in the larger house. Many times, Iris opened her little house to Noonday and Bookie. She introduced them to Sarah and Sing.

"Maggie, we met Sarah Vaughan. And, Sing, too," they told me one day.

"Wonderful! Yes, I know Sarah Vaughan sings," I responded.

"No, I mean Sing can sing, too. We heard Sing sing."

"You heard Sing Sing? Noonday and Bookie, what do you mean? Sing Sing can't be heard. Sing Sing is a prison."

☙

"Guess! Guess who is coming to Idlewild! You'll never, ever guess!" Noonday squealed. "Trixie has tickets for us. I can't believe I'm actually going to see Lena Horne. Yes—yes, yes, Lena Horne. In person!"

Bookie arrived on time to escort Noonday to the concert. She was stunning in a formfitting black sheath that accented her sensual hourglass figure. She had pulled back her long hair and fastened it up with a soft white-feathered barrette that framed one side of her face. Her dark eyes sparkled with anticipation, and her smile added to her brilliance. Bookie grinned handsomely as he opened the car door for her. Both waved as they drove away. I can honestly say I didn't see the romantic fondness that they had for each other.

On US 10, the traffic chugged along, more traffic than its two lanes had ever seen before. This made the fifteen-mile ride far too slow for the anxious couple. Adding to the fact that they did not want to be late, they became more anxious as the traffic continued to slow ahead. A long, shiny limousine passed by, a sight not common in Mason County. The two gasped, and upon seeing the Michigan seal on its side, one exclaimed aloud, "Wow! I think that's 'Soapy' Williams."

"It is!" said the other.

G. Mennen Williams, the governor of Michigan from 1949 until 1960, was secretly en route from Lansing, Michigan, to attend Lena Horne's show. "Soapy" Williams was a popular politician whose interest in black concerns surpassed many in government during that time. The nickname was appropriate, because his family was connected with the Mennen Company, a soap and pharmaceutical firm.

Bookie continued to follow the important vehicle, and when it became clear that the limo was going to the same place they were going, they exclaimed, "Wow, the governor's going to Idlewild. Same as us!"

The club was filled to capacity. Everyone was there—a diverse group with a singular purpose: to hear music performed by the best. Lena didn't disappoint. Gorgeous, and with a voice box from God's own vocal factory, Lena stood alone, sang, and immediately became a shining star in everyone's eyes. When the show concluded, applause burst forth in thunderous waves, and whistles and shouts of, "We love you, Lena," bounced off the walls of the Flamingo Club.

After the show, the teenagers gathered near the stage with other autograph seekers. Trixie soon joined them, remarking that it wouldn't be long before Lena would be out to sign programs or anything of the like. Lena always appreciated her fans and liked to make personal, after-show appearances if she could.

She soon appeared, humbly gracious, and even more beautiful up close. When Noonday stood in front of the star waiting for her autograph, she told me she couldn't help but stare at her. Lena paused and finally looked at Noonday.

"You sure are a pretty thing. But being pretty isn't enough. Go to school, stay in school, and get an education. Remember, your greatest victory will be in your struggle. Whatever you do, however you do it, once you make it, you will always remember the struggle."

"Yes, ma'am, I will. I want to go to college. Thank you—oh, thank you," Noonday responded.

◈

Despite their diversions outside of school, Noonday and Bookie never lost sight of their future goals. Both remained focused on an education beyond high school. Many evenings were spent with Mr. Millgard and me reviewing Michigan colleges and universities. The time was nearing for submitting applications to these institutes of higher learning. Both young adults, excited to be entering this new phase of their lives, made it perfectly clear they would not go to college without the other. Both needed scholarships to attend college. The likelihood of Noonday and Bookie each receiving a scholarship to the same university or college seemed remote, if not totally unlikely. And as the months passed, anxious times were spent at the mailbox awaiting word of acceptance. In the meantime, high school studies fervently continued.

◈

I received a proposal of marriage from my dear Mr. Millgard. I loved him with my whole heart. It was not the passionate love I had once known with Duggie, but it was a genuine love I could rely on. A stable life with a fine gentleman appealed to me, though I didn't say yes right away.

My patient groom told me, "Don't worry, my love. I will wait for as long as it takes. I love you, Maggie dear. You mean the world to me. I'll wait." He smiled broadly.

"Milly, why do you have to be so understanding? You are too good to me. What am I going to do with you?"

"Marry me, Maggie dear." His eyes lit up behind his spectacles.

I looked into those eyes. "We'll get married—I promise. Someday . . . soon."

The man held me; his arms circled me, endless. I felt loved and cherished, but I felt guilty putting him off. I didn't want to wait, but I felt obligated to finish what I had started with Noonday and Bookie.

I loved Noonday. As she grew older, we often reminisced together. I let her know I loved every minute of our time together. The joys of teaching and loving this special person outweighed all the obstacles and disappointments. I would do it all over again. My prayer was for the education of my gifted daughter to continue.

Their two high school graduations fell on the same day, the first Sunday in June 1947. This fact disturbed the graduates and me especially. Although the times differed, I knew I could not attend both Baldwin's and Custer's commencement ceremonies. The choice was obvious. Bookie would have his family by his side to witness his passing from high school into a new phase of dreams and challenges.

"You know my heart will be with you, Bookie," I explained to him.

"I know it. I'll always have you with me, Maggie. You have given me so much. You'll have to be both of us at Noonday's ceremony."

"I know. You have done as much as I have, probably more, for our Noonday. There were trials and triumphs. Oh yes, we can be proud of our triumphs." A tear sprang from my eye.

I knew that our time together was ending, and all the hard work along the way—the laughter, the tears, but, most assuredly, the shared victories. I hugged the young man standing in front of me. He gratefully accepted the embrace from his teacher.

"Thank you. Thank you," he whispered.

◌

Noonday scurried about the bungalow the day of her graduation from Baldwin High School, frazzled and anxious.

"Where's my hairbrush? Where'd I put it?" she exclaimed.

She didn't dare stop and feel the emotion of the day. She knew she would cry. Likely questioning *Why me?* she sat on the bed, and every bone and muscle of her body surrendered as she put her hands to her face and softly cried.

She finally found everything she needed. She stood in front of the mirror in the bedroom and quickly looked over at her cap and gown.

I have to see how I look in it, she thought.

She grabbed it without hesitation, jumped into the flowing gown, and zipped it up.

Looking at the square, flat hat, she muttered, "How do I wear this thing?" She rested the mortarboard hat on the back of her head.

"No, no, that's not right."

As she tilted it on one side of her head and then the other, she screamed, "I look like a clown! How does this thing stay on?"

She crossed her eyes and was prancing around just as I came into the room to her rescue.

"Oh boy, what do we have here? A Noonday 'heyday' on her graduation day?"

I hugged her. We twirled and fell on the bed, laughing as tears of joy wet our cheeks.

We stopped. I fought for words.

"Noonday—you have earned this honor. You worked hard . . ." I swallowed but then spoke again. "You, my dear Noonday Flower, are going to bloom today. Today is your graduation day. We've had a great journey, but we've made it here."

My smile trembled. The thing caught in my throat and stopped me from saying more. We looked at each other, tears rolling from our eyes. The emotion rendered us still. We lay on the bed withholding sobs yet allowing sundry tears to flow freely. Finally, we stood and tried to brush them away.

I inhaled deeply, shook off the emotion, and said, "Okay, this is the plan. Take the gown off, and you can dress at the gymnasium. We'll take some bobby pins to keep your cap on, okay? I'll help you, don't worry."

The ride over to Baldwin was quiet. Mr. Millgard chatted on and on about the marvelous new suits the store was beginning to sell.

"They're made of wrinkle-free polyester, a new fabric just coming out on the market. I think they will sell very well," he explained.

"That's nice."

"Actually, polyester is a condensation of acid and glycol used in combination with other fibers."

"That's nice."

"Actually, in the condensation process, it looks like cotton candy, and it tastes just as good, too."

"That's nice," I said again.

He smiled, knowing that my mind was as far away from the manufacture of fabrics as it could be. He continued to talk (to himself) as he drove the car, and I nodded and smiled through each mile.

Our history left Noonday and me in deeper thought. We did not often verbally express our feelings for each other. But they were there: the gratitude, the respect, the love. They could not be hidden behind the smiles, the hugs, and our open acceptance of each other.

Before the car stopped in its parking space, Noonday spoke from the back seat. "Thank you, Milly. Thank you, Mother."

I turned to face Noonday just as she got out of the car.

I started to say, "You are welcome, my daughter. . ." but she sped away.

Mr. Millgard and I got out of the car. He held me for a moment, noticing my misting eyes. He smiled and gave me his handkerchief.

We were quickly on Noonday's heels, trying to catch up when she entered the school building. Mr. Millgard sought out seats while I helped Noonday with her cap and gown.

I whispered in her ear, "I'm so proud of you."

I exited the mayhem in the crowded room and went to sit with my fiancé. We watched the graduates file in. I felt Milly's hand grasp mine.

Noonday, the youngest-ever valedictorian of Baldwin High School, rose to speak after the short baccalaureate service and the school-board introductions.

She walked over to the podium and looked everyone in the eye. Her smile radiated with rays of sunshine at noon, but when she opened her mouth, nothing came out. I whispered to myself, "Your notes, Noonday—your notes." I saw her unfold the paper in front of her. Then words came tumbling out, all in the right order, accentuated with gratitude and smiles. Everyone listened. She finished with the poem:

> *A diploma's very special; it's like a golden key*
> *that turns the lock on any door marked*
> *'opportunity.'*
> *But one thing to remember:*
> *If you want to get inside, it's up to you. You must*
> *give the nudge that swings it open wide.*

The entire gymnasium of people clapped as she stood there with the strength of a dream fulfilled. She looked down as if in prayer, then looked up, saying a prayer that had moved her mountain. I beamed with joy, and my heart filled with thanksgiving. I will never forget that day.

One at a time, the graduates filed onto stage center to receive their diplomas. Many in the audience clapped and whistled. It was a proud, joyous occasion for the graduates and their families.

At the conclusion of the ceremony, the tasseled hats flew into the air. Pandemonium filled the room as the graduates tried to reach their loved ones to receive hugs of congratulations. Noonday looked for us as some of her classmates asked her to pose—the Brownie cameras flashing here and there.

In the middle of it all, Noonday felt a tap on her shoulder. She turned to see an older woman next to an elderly gentleman and two younger adult men. It was only a moment before the biggest smile broke out across her face.

"Oh, Vita-Mom. Oh . . . you came—all of you. Thank you for coming!" She hugged the woman who had cared for her, nourished her, and accepted her with a loving heart, without question, ever since she'd saved her life at birth.

"I am so proud of my Noonday!" Vita Mavis said as she looked with tears at the beautiful young woman who, not so long ago, had been a baby and toddler in her arms.

"Here you are all growed up and graduating from high school. It seems you were yea high not long ago. Gosh darn, times flash by like grease lighting." The Mavis men nodded in agreement.

"We wanted to come. You are *our* girl . . ." announced Mr. Mavis as he took out his big handkerchief and blew his nose.

Noonday noticed a tear on his cheek as he quickly brushed it away.

"I love you all," Noonday declared. She reached for Vita's hand. "Thank you, Vita-Mom." She hugged her, then hugged Mr. Mavis.

The big man held her, then exclaimed loudly, "Get on over here, boys. Con-grag-her-late your sister!"

The boys lumbered over; one squeezed Noonday a little too hard, and Gunner lifted her off the ground and twirled her around with a whoop and a holler: "Yippee, you done good, Sister Noonday!"

Noonday squealed with happiness and said, "Do come and help me find Maggie and Mr. Millgard. They are here someplace."

The Mavis family, along with Noonday, Mr. Millgard, and me exchanged memories on the lawn of the school grounds. I could see that Noonday felt special to be the center of attention, and maybe even a bit uncomfortable.

Suddenly, a voice called out, "Yahoo, Noonday! Noonday Flower, Where are ya, girl?"

Then a penetrating whistle captured everyone's attention. Noonday looked around fast and hard. Through the crowd, we spied a great sparkle that captured the sun's rays just right. Noonday squinted. We all did.

It was Trixie, dressed in a stunning sequined gown. Her hair was piled high in a beehive, and she wore spiked high-heeled shoes that kept sinking into the soft ground. She stood like the gala queen of the ball in the grass.

"Noonday, Noonday Flower . . ." And she whistled again. Everyone watched as Noonday joyously rushed to her aid. The young graduate beamed as she embraced the statuesque woman, nearly knocking her down. "Trixie, you're here! Trixie, I'm so happy you're here!"

"There she is! The best dang graduate this school has ever seen! Your mama is beaming from ear to ear. I know it. I just know it! We saw you get that sheepskin . . ."

"Thank you, Trixie. I know Mama's here, too."

Breathless, Trixie declared, "I'm so glad I got here before it was over. I heard you speaking in front of all these people. Man alive, you're good, girl."

Noonday hugged her again, laughing with immense delight.

"Hold on, I gotta take these dang shoes off." They walked arm in arm, one swinging her shoes in the air and screaming hallelujahs and the other laughing and talking whenever she could fit a word in between the "halle" and the "lu-jahs."

෨෨

We spent the rest of this day at a reception at the Brenners' farm, where many gathered to honor the outstanding valedictorian of Custer High School. Many people flowed in and out of the huge house where balloons and ribbons festooned the trees and lawn with color. Scattered tables and chairs invited the crowd to sit, relax, and enjoy the fellowship of lunch with neighboring good friends. Trixie fit right in, and her effervescence and friendliness drew many to her side that beautiful Sunday in June.

And God was there in the midst of many who thanked Him that day. Two who did, on their knees, were Mr. and Mrs. Brenner. Olie and Mrs. B. were proud of their son and were grateful to have been so blessed with beautiful, healthy children. Bookie was the apple of his younger brother's eye, and in the months to come, both brothers would have a sister, the newest member of the Brenner family.

The black girl in the white gown met the white boy in the black gown behind the barn on the south side of the woodpile. They squeezed each other tenderly and whispered congratulations in each other's ears. They sat down on the woodpile and exchanged commencement news from one another's events of the day.

"Trixie came, and the Mavises. I'm the luckiest girl in the world, Bookie." She paused, her manner changed. "Sometimes I wonder why."

"God put you here for Maggie and me. Mostly me." He smiled.

"Oh, Bookie, I get so confused. But right now I feel so good that it scares me."

"There's nothing to be scared of. You just graduated from high school. The 'scary part' is over."

"I know—I know. You're right." Noonday leaned into him and kissed him.

The kiss excited them, and they fondled and caressed and kissed even more. This was their secret.

"Bookie, promise me you'll be with me whenever I'm scared?"

"I promise."

The twosome returned to the party, afraid they might be too obviously missed. And as all days do, it ended, although many would have liked to extend the day's hours because of its many blessings.

ℰ↷

Within a week's time, Noonday received notice in the mail of a full, four-year scholarship to Michigan State University, a fine university located in the middle of the Lower Peninsula of Michigan, about a four-hour drive from Walhalla. She clutched the letter to her bosom. She felt an overwhelming desire to visit her mother's grave—even though she knew her mother lived within her and not among the tall grasses and weeds.

The girl of seventeen, maturing beyond those years, stooped to feel the small cross that once stood at the grave. Noonday tenderly positioned it over the grave. She had been there many times but hadn't visited in the past few years. Guilt grabbed her as she violently pulled the grasses and weeds away.

She sobbed, "I'm sorry, Mama, I'm sorry. God, I'm sorry . . ." She plopped onto the ground. The clouds moved over her while tears rolled down to her ears. She dizzily watched the sky move. She closed her eyes and could still see the sky move behind her lids. Although she lay still, she felt movement above and beyond. The heavens moved over her like a blanket, and she welcomed its soft breeze. She rose, then looked pensively at her mother's grave, despairing at the circumstances that had complicated her mother's life. She bowed in prayer.

"I hope you can hear me, Mama. I know you are not really here. Your spirit is in me, and your soul is with God. I want you to know how much I love you. Thank you, Mama. Thank you for giving me life."

She stopped for a moment to think on that revelation. She looked up into the brightness of the day. "I'm going to college, can you believe it? It is your gift to me. Thank you, Mama. Thank you, God. Amen."

With a tear-stained face, the young girl walked away from her mother's grave for the last time.

When she got back to the bungalow, she told me, "Maggie, I looked around and thought about the Schrecks. I thought about the Mavises, and I thought about you. I'm so lucky. And so lucky that my mother came here to bring me into the world."

In a flash, her thankfulness turned to fright. "But what about Bookie? What if he doesn't get a scholarship to Michigan State University? No, he has to get a scholarship. Just like mine. He has to, Maggie, he has to."

I was shocked by her strong feelings about Bookie and college. Wouldn't she be as happy for Bookie if he received a scholarship to any fine university? I could see then how that would not be the case. Immediately, I felt a somersault in the pit of my stomach as I tried to calm her.

"Minutes ago, you were telling me how happy you were, how lucky you're feeling. Let's wait and see about Bookie's plans. He decides, Noonday, not you."

"I'm not going to college without him, Maggie." She pulled away from me. "I'm not! No, I'm not! I can't."

As much as Noonday was determined to continue her schooling, she was only determined to do so *with* Bookie.

Summer shall come again, but in due time.
In my heart no more her sun will climb
Nor any flower unfold its miracle.
For she is gone whose laughter was a bell,
Whose love made bread and wine of every stone
And kindled stars and moons when there were
  none.
                    —*Daniel Whitehead Hicky*

The flower spreads her petal wings.
                              —*C. Ohse*

CHAPTER FIFTEEN

Life Goes On

August 1947 became the month to remember. The sun shone brightly every day, and the sky shed its tears only at night. Anticipation was high for a perfect growing season with an excellent harvest. I gave thanks for Noonday's opportunity to go to college. The young girl walked on clouds, especially when the same opportunity was awarded to Bookie. Yes, Bookie also got a full scholarship, even with the odds against it. I don't know if it would have happened if they had attended the same high school.

The three of us reviewed their acceptances on the kitchen table at the bungalow.

"Now, a signed agreement must be returned to the university as soon as possible so a place can be reserved just for you. Also, we need to put in a preference for the dormitory where you will live. You can't live in the same place, you know. There are boys' dorms and girls' dorms," I explained.

Noonday and Bookie looked at each other and grimaced.

The excitement built as the two students prepared for college. But summer was in full force, and its perfect days continued to be a time of joy for the tiny communities in Western Michigan near the shores of a big lake. I don't remember a time where I was happier, more content, or so relieved.

"Oh, Bookie, let's live close, as close as we can," Noonday joyously planned. "Let's try to be in the same classes. We'll meet at the library in the evenings. I can't wait!" Bookie smiled in agreement.

૭ઝ

I remember Noonday and me trying our hand at sewing that summer. With Mr. Millgard's help, we purchased yardage of the most beautiful wool plaids. The two of us, first-time seamstresses, were delighted. A straight skirt with a kick pleat on one side with a button-and-zipper closure couldn't be that hard to make, we thought. When finished, we noticed that the skirts had lost all their symmetry. With Mr. Millgard's help, we were able to restitch the skirts. It took us longer than we anticipated, but we were grateful despite the imperfections in our work.

Before the sewing of the skirts was completed, I sent for a cashmere sweater from the Sears catalogue. When it arrived by mail, I was so eager to see how it matched the skirts, I tore open the package. I couldn't wait to present it to Noonday.

"For me!" she exclaimed. Thrilled, she opened it and stared at it, slowly feeling the material. "It's soooo yummy soft." She held it up and squealed, "Oh, oh, I can't believe it's mine." She hugged it to her bosom. "Thank you. Thank you."

She stood and grabbed me. We looked into each other's eyes and, amid the tears, there was love. It was as genuine a love as any affection between a mother and daughter by birth. That moment will remain forever in my mind. The affinity that bound us together was an extension of God's love for all—red, yellow, black, and white.

When alone, the shapely girl put the sweater and skirts on, one at a time. She looked into the mirror and realized how good she looked. She smiled and turned to the right, then to the left, almost twirling 360 degrees to see her back. She held her breasts within her two hands, and then let go, realizing how nicely they stayed in place, filling out the sweater. She smiled at her image in the mirror.

She was a happy, good-looking young woman. She liked herself and didn't know how she could be happier. Every morning brought her the gift of a new day, one with a noonday promise of a dream slowly but assuredly coming to pass—a dream of love in life, and a life of learning through loving.

❦

The Walhalla school had been the center of my life for over ten years by now. I loved teaching and the challenges it presented to me. When the word got around the village that the school would soon close its doors, many became concerned, no one more than I. The rumor bothered me, but I tried not to be troubled. It was just a rumor, after all. I had not received official word. Mr. Millgard was my constant companion, and Noonday was my continual diversion.

I'll face the problem when I need to. I'll not concern myself with "what might be," only what is, I told myself.

The summer months were ending in Walhalla, especially for the farmers in the area. Acres of corn were filling in the fields and growing high. Pollen was in the air, and the appetite of two special young people seemed ardent to receive it. The corn had received the pollen, was growing tall, and starting to tassel out. The new ears of corn were witnesses to the roar of machinery, the song of birds, and the frolic of two happy, sexually ripe teenagers.

Bookie and Noonday loved to run into the maze of corn and, upon finding one another, embrace and topple onto the secluded ground. Once again, passions were ignited after college concerns had been happily resolved. The corn blanketed the activity of the couple, even while standing. They cradled in each other's arms, kissing a forehead, an earlobe, and the nape of a neck. Before long, the gallant Bookie removed his shirt to lay it on the earth. They rolled to the ground, their eyes locked. Feelings of immense proportions erupted. Bookie pressed his lips to hers, pressing hard and harder, and his hands grabbed her torso and lifted her over him. He groaned and quivered uncontrollably.

"I want you so much!" he whispered.

She kissed him gently, but his loving ardor consumed her. She could feel his hardness beneath her and closed her eyes to envision herself with him, flesh to flesh.

"I want you, too," she cried as the startled red-winged black-birds fluttered from their perches on the cornstalks. During the rapid process of undressing, the two suddenly stopped, eyes locked.

He exclaimed, "We can't! We can't! We can't mess this up. We have to wait. Oh God! I don't want to!"

They spoke to each other in frustration, yet with logical reasoning behind their words.

Noonday reasoned, "Quick! Think of something else. Like—like . . ."

"Like what? Seeing tits on top of your head, instead of the ones you have now—under there?" he replied, pointing to her chest.

She teasingly pulled open her unbuttoned blouse. Then, quickly, buttoned it up and turned and ran. The couple ran out of the cornfield, brushing the dirt from their clothing and straightening their posture—Noonday exiting to the right and Bookie whistling to the left.

❧

The summer moved into fall. The Brenners were especially busy with the second cutting of hay and Bookie's last days before departure. Mrs. B. cried every day. She loved her nearly grown son and was going to miss him. He meant more to her than her own needs. She was that way, sacrificing all for her children. Her time was near to bear another child, and this added to her discomfort both physically and emotionally, though she never complained.

Olie didn't think about Bookie leaving. He knew he had to let him go; that was all there was to it. The farm needed him, but the opportunity to excel away from the farm outweighed Olie's need to keep him home. He was proud of his son and wanted him to be the best that he could be, whether it was as a businessman, an honest laborer, or a farmer. Olie never pressured Bookie into farming for his life's work. He guided and directed his son but left the ultimate decision to Bookie, as he would do for Billy.

Olie was hopeful in grooming his second son, Billy, to take over the farm, since Billy was more interested in farming than schoolwork, unlike his older brother, who liked school, too. Olie also had it in his mind to hire someone to help out, especially during the spring planting and fall harvest. The farm was making a decent living for the Brenners, and perhaps, with meals included, the wage of a hired man would be possible. In a month, they would have a new baby, and Olie hoped to spend as much time as he could helping his wife. Bookie, who was so much like his father, worked especially hard that summer. Whether he was feeling guilty about leaving or he was having doubts about leaving at all, it was not clear. He knew he would be leaving during haying season, which preceded the harvest, and all that unfinished work surely bothered him.

Noonday and I would make the arrangements for traveling to East Lansing by Greyhound bus. Noonday and Bookie agreed on their day of departure from Ludington where the nearest bus depot was located, planning to drive there separately so all of Bookie's family could go, too. I was beaming with anticipation—almost as much as Noonday.

"I'll be waving until the bus drives off into the sunset!" I cried, my speech rapid with excitement. "I'm so proud of you and Bookie that I could burst!"

The day finally arrived. Noonday talked with Bookie the night before. Excitement prohibited them both from sleeping that final night upon the beds of the two aspiring scholars. They couldn't wait to get on that bus together and ride off to a new life and a new future.

The twenty-mile drive to Ludington was mentally long. I talked nonstop about the checklist of items needed for long-term passage from one place to another, from one life to another.

"You know my phone number! Please call and give me the phone number of your dorm, okay? And your room number," I instructed. "Is there anything we have forgotten? Well, no matter, I can send it if so."

I pulled into a parking space across the street from the bus depot. Noonday looked up and down the street for the Brenners' car. I opened the trunk, which held Noonday's two suitcases. Again, she looked up and down the street. We carried the bags into the depot. Inside, Noonday stood there, puzzled. She looked around while I stepped up to the window to purchase my college student's ticket to a new place. Then we waited anxiously for the Brenners' arrival.

The time was drawing near for the bus's departure, and still there was no sign of Bookie and his family. We stepped outside, and while the luggage was being loaded into the bowels of the bus, we anxiously looked to the east.

Panicking, Noonday said, "Where is he? What's wrong?"

She looked at me and threw up her hands. "He is always late; he—is always late."

I was becoming concerned as well. This was one time he must not be late.

While many were boarding the bus, anxious Noonday was determined not to cross the threshold of that bus without Bookie. I urged the girl, who had suddenly lost her beautiful smile, to board the bus. I wanted her on that bus.

"You better get on. Bookie will be here any minute. You know him, he'll show up and I won't even have a minute to scold him."

"No, no, I can't! I'm not going if Bookie doesn't come!" she snapped.

The bus started its engines, and still Bookie and his family hadn't arrived.

"I'll call," I shouted as I quickly retreated into the depot.

Noonday wound her arms tightly around herself as tears slowly wet her face. Time passed, perhaps only a couple of minutes. The bus driver kept looking at her, finally opening the door and saying, "Are you boarding, young lady? I can't wait any longer."

I ran out of the building saying, "Get on, Noonday! There was no answer. They're on their way. We'll follow behind. We'll catch up."

Noonday still didn't want to get on, but in the heat of the moment, she felt obligated to do as she was told. She looked at the ticket in her hand, which was now wet with perspiration. Noonday finally got on the bus, turning back intermittently. I chattered on and on about everything being all right. She found a window seat. She placed one hand on the glass, and I could see her unhappy face peering out at me.

The bus moved, and I watched as it became smaller and smaller in the distance. I waved and smiled until the bus turned a corner.

I know Noonday must have scrutinized her doubts on the four-hour trip to a strange new place. She had forgotten what it felt like to be sad, to be scared, and to be alone.

She must have reasoned through her anguish. *Something is wrong, really wrong! Bookie would not have left me alone if he could help it. He'll come. I have to believe that. I just need to get through today. I'll be fine. Don't be a big baby, Noonday. Bookie wouldn't want that!*

෴

Returning to Walhalla, I drove slowly, thinking, *I'll see them soon.* After a mile or two, I started to drive faster. Still, I carefully examined each car going by me in the opposite direction. At one point, I pulled off the road and stared at the cars going by. I pulled back onto the road and continued driving, but upon completing the twenty-mile drive back to Walhalla, I had become extremely concerned.

I headed straight south to First Street and turned west. When I reached the far perimeter of the Brenner farm, my breath stopped momentarily. I could see twirling red lights in the distance and other vehicles. I drove past my own childhood homestead, which had long been sold and reactivated as a working farm. Before I reached the yard of the Brenner farm, wondering how or where I would park, an ambulance passed by me going in the opposite direction. My heart pounded wildly. I strained to look, hoping to examine the ambulance with x-ray vision. I noticed only that the flashing lights were off. I tightened my grip on the steering wheel and bowed my head. "Dear God, let Bookie be all right."

I parked and got out of the car, reluctant to know the truth at the center of the chaos. Neighbors were standing around with unbelieving, hypnotized looks on their faces. *Oh dear God. Oh my God, what's wrong?* I prayed.

Right away, I spied the couple who had bought my parents' farm. I called, "Frank, Frank, what happened?"

Frank had blood all over his clothes. He kept looking at his bloody hands and mumbling, "I can't believe that young man is gone—can't believe it. He didn't have a chance."

I put my head into my hands and sobbed. "Oh no, oh no—no, no, no!" So distraught, I stood there crying until Frank's wife, Louisa, came up to me.

"Oh, Maggie, isn't it awful?"

I screamed, "What happened? Tell me!"

She quickly responded, "The elevator . . . that hay elevator—fell. It collapsed."

The woman started to sob. "It fell and . . . and crushed his skull. He was dead, Maggie, just like that, so quick!"

Again, she wept, unable to talk anymore. I felt faint. I grabbed Louisa to steady myself.

"Where is Olie and—and Mrs. B?" I headed toward the house, not waiting for the woman to answer.

My shaking hands turned the doorknob. Tears shrouded my view as I stumbled through the doorway. Olie sat at the kitchen table with others around him. They were trying, if that were possible, to comfort the man whose head lay on the table, a broken shell of a man who resembled a beaten prize fighter down in the ring, unable to get up. I did not attempt to talk to him. I leaned against the stove and wept. I turned to another room off the kitchen, finding people here and there, seemingly everywhere. Intermittent screams were coming from one bedroom on the first floor. The voice cut through me as I recognized the immense suffering coming from Mrs. B. My heart beat in my throat. A great storm invaded my head. I didn't want to walk in there; I couldn't move. Finally, I did.

Instantaneously, I gasped on a choking sob.

There he was—Bookie.

"Oh, dear God, Bookie. Bookie—you're all right."

He turned from his grieving mother's side and fell into my arms. I'd never seen the manlike boy cry until now. I could hardly hold the pulsating muscular young man.

"He's dead, Maggie. Billy's dead. Billy's dead!"

I instantly realized that it was my young sixth-grader, Billy Brenner, who had been killed. I was torn between relief that Bookie was alive and sorrowful guilt that Billy was dead. Suddenly, I exploded into grief, which created a fountain of sorrow. Tears fell like a waterfall and didn't stop all the way home and into the night. I cried and prayed and cried again. I cried all through my prayers for forgiveness. My night was filled with guilt, as I was relieved that Billy had died, not Bookie.

The day following the tragedy, Mrs. B. went into labor. She never left her bed of sorrows, after having collapsed there twenty-four hours before. The birth was intense and fast. The woman did little to aid in the birth of her daughter—a bright and beautiful Mary, named by the doctor who could not persuade either parent to name her. Mrs. B. withdrew after the easy birth. She remained in a depressed state for days, and worsened for many days thereafter. Olie couldn't look at the baby, so after the doctor and midwife duties were done, Bookie took over caring for the newborn. He knew that he had no choice, and he accepted the responsibility without a word of complaint. The funeral, which lasted for several days, supplied the household with food and helping hands, so the job of tending to Mary didn't overwhelm Bookie until he was left alone with her for the first time. It scared him, but he learned to take one bottle, one diaper, one burp, and one sleepless night at a time. Olie worked the chores outside while Bookie did the more arduous chores within the walls of the home of his now grievously altered family.

Noonday and I often spoke by telephone, although Noonday, who did the calling, could not afford the expense. She continually wanted to come home, at first insisting upon it. I didn't think it was the best thing for her, as she had just started classes.

It was difficult to persuade her, and it became a war of words, but one without disrespect for the other's position.

Bookie pulled away from Noonday. When she called him, he adamantly refused to answer. When he finally did talk to her, he dismissed her offers to come home to the point of being rude to her, revealing a side of him she did not recognize. Their phone calls ceased, so I was the one who called Noonday to report the happenings at the Brenners'. My pretty college coed worried, but her persistence prevailed in her faithful letters to him. Her letters were his salvation, even though he didn't realize it at the time. He, unknowingly, looked forward to the daily arrival of the postman when everything else in life seemed bleak. Separately, they became busy young people, one with books and classroom instruction, the other caring for a newborn, 350 miles apart.

&

The Walhalla school did close, just as it was rumored. It was annexed to the Mason County Central School District in Scottville, the dissolution of many one-room schoolhouses across America becoming a common occurrence. For the first fall in nearly eleven years, I would not be teaching school. Because I was so caught up in the distressing situation at the Brenners', I did not miss the otherwise notable first day of school.

I stopped at the Brenners' almost every day to help care for the baby or, more often, to help with laundry and meals. I knew a little more about that. Both Bookie and I were novices at newborn care, although Bookie took charge of baby Mary surprisingly well. Mrs. B's postpartum depression worsened as Olie dug himself deeper into farm work to the point of unconsciously avoiding reentering the house at the end of the day. Mrs. B. stopped talking, and soon needed to be fed daily and required help with other things of a personal nature. Bookie became overwhelmed with the work, which was like the care of two infants:

one a joyous new sister who knew nothing of the family's hard-
ship, and the other a mother who had seemingly regressed back
to the womb when her own womb refused recovery. Bookie
never complained. His days and nights were so full that he had
no chance to think of what was or what might have been. The
loss of Billy Brenner threw the family into nonstop grieving and
hopelessness no one knew how to fix. There were no tears and
no words asking why. Living from day to day became their sole
function, working, eating, and sleeping without the hope for a
happier time. Many assisted but nothing helped to eliminate the
sorrow that permeated the home of the best farmer in Mason
County.

Noonday held on to the hope that Bookie would be able
to join her at the start of the university's second term after
Christmas. Bookie turned off his feelings, speaking very little
about them. She looked forward to the holidays when she would
be coming home and able to talk to him face-to-face. She was
confident that everything would be fine once she came home.

Noonday adjusted well to the new environment of college life,
thanks to the blessing of two amazing roommates. Clementine,
also relieved to have Noonday for a roommate, became, from
the first day they met, Noonday's best friend. Both students
were dark skinned, and even though Noonday was darker than
Clementine, it didn't matter once their hearts were acquainted.
Paula, in her third year at the university, moved in with them
from another dorm. She turned out to be Noonday's gift from
heaven, as she was the first to stop whatever she was doing to help
her. All three women were tightly packed in room 209, Abbot
Hall, at Moo U, a university that had begun as a renowned agri-
cultural college many years before. The three students unveiled
their appreciation for being there by studying hard and respect-
ing those around them, regardless of skin color or the designer
(or designer-less) clothes covering them. In time, the roommates
became just residents of Abbot Hall, three women who knew

who they were, no one special, and no one different than anyone else. Clementine and Paula set admirable examples that helped Noonday thrive. Clementine and Noonday, both with funny names, did well that fall term, setting the norm for students of all cultures and races to live and learn together.

Early on, Noonday bonded with Clementine, as her roommate helped her accept my (and Bookie's) refusal to let her come home. Clem helped Noonday understand that staying in school was the only answer, despite Noonday's strong desire to be there for the one she loved so completely. Paula also talked with Noonday, often into the early-morning hours, advising her younger roommate.

"I think you should stay here. Bookie will resent you if you go back now. He doesn't want to be the cause of your quitting college. He will hate you and himself for it. You can't make it right for him, no matter how much you love him. He can't make everything right, either, no matter how hard he tries. He can't bring his brother back, or wake up his mother, or talk to his father. The baby needs him; that's all he knows right now. You have to let him work it out by himself."

Noonday tearfully listened and knew they were right. And God was there, speaking to Noonday through two wise and wonderful girls who had come to her to guide and direct.

❧

I gave thanks every day for my Mr. Millgard. He was my shoulder to cry on; he was my ear to listen. He was my eyes to see more clearly, and I loved him dearly. And because the one-room schoolhouse did close its doors, I said yes to marriage and to the "'til death do us part" agreement with the love of my life. I was happy in a contented, comfortable kind of way.

Yes, a small wedding during the Christmas holidays, I thought. Since the decision was made, changes came swiftly to Mr. Millgard and me.

Also during the weeks before Christmas, Bookie finally spoke to his father, convincing him that a live-in nanny was needed. Olie reluctantly agreed. It was time for Mrs. B. to leave her home and enter a hospital program where she could get the professional help needed for a complete recovery. Olie agreed even more reluctantly to that. Bookie started to write to Noonday. His letters were short but always ended with a light-hearted poem, his way of saying he missed her.

> *Like intoxicating wine,*
> *From the sweetening grape vine*
> *My flower bouquet, so ivy fine,*
> *My heart is forever thine.*

She loved the poems, and claimed them as her private jewels, locking them away. Often, she took them out to reread their dazzling declaration.

The healing in the Brenner family had begun, but sadly, for Bookie only. He found immense pleasure in his baby sister, and when she chattered, cooed, kicked, and waved, he smiled. It felt so good. He couldn't help but feel good around her. She was the joy in the middle of the worst time of his life. He wrote of Mary to Noonday; he wrote of the first time she rolled over, of the time she first smiled at him, and even when she graduated to solid food. He bragged of her beauty and brightness, and of her attention to the spoken word, and to the many words he read to her. His words to Noonday spoke clearly of his love for his sister. He never wrote of his dead brother or his lost mother or his work-obsessed father, only Mary.

One day, Noonday received a letter from Bookie with a reference to someone besides little Mary—a woman named Vera.

Vera became the newest member of the broken Brenner family. The twenty-two-year-old was hired in to care for Mary and alleviate Bookie's responsibilities with his sister so he could help his father outside, as fall harvest was nearing its end. Vera fit in well with the hardworking Brenner men. The robust woman didn't do fieldwork, but she could have. She matched them, hour by hour, with a full day's work, cooking, cleaning, and minding Mary.

More and more, Olie lost himself in his work, especially after Mrs. B. left. The giant of a man succumbed to a lost faith in his calling as a husband, a father, and, he feared, as a farmer. Bookie took over each day's decisions and directed the progress of the summation of the year's work. The work was important; it meant income to pay bills and, if luck would have it, enough to set aside for next year's spring beginning.

I continued to stop by, but more often than not, I saw little Mary and Vera.

"Vera? Mary? It's Maggie. Where is that little baby girl?"

"Hi, Maggie, we're in here. I'm giving Mary her bottle."

"I thought I might catch Bookie in the house." I leaned over and patted the baby's head. "Will you tell him I need to talk to him? Sometime soon. It's important."

"I'll tell him. Look at her—falling asleep, and she is not even finished."

I caught glimpses of Bookie in the fields in my comings and goings, but I wanted to speak to him soon. The following week, Mr. Millgard and I stopped by the Brenners' in the evening, purposely to catch Bookie at home. Our knock on the door came just after the supper hour while Vera was finishing the kitchen cleanup. Bookie was holding Mary, trying to read to her from Mother Goose. The infant, though too young to completely understand a nursery rhyme, delighted in the lively narration of her loving brother's tone of voice. Olie sat in his chair, fast asleep, mouth opened wide, looking older than his actual years.

Bookie delighted in seeing us. Vera took the baby from him to put her to bed for the night. Olie awoke with a start. He left the room as if sleepwalking, without speaking to us. With greetings aside, Bookie, Mr. Millgard, and myself remained in the cozy living area where the freestanding wood heater had to be lit that day.

After talk of the cooler weather and other small talk, I took hold of my man's hand and said, "Bookie, we have set our wedding date."

Bookie, a young man who had always been fearful to show feelings, said, "What good news. I am so happy to hear . . . When?"

Instantly, a smile broke across my face. "Soon, over the Christmas holiday—we will finally be married." Mr. Millgard put his arm around me, and kissed my forehead.

Bookie's feelings surfaced and brought tears to his eyes. He seemed openly glad to view our happiness. Though sorrow remained fresh in his past, he could unselfishly put it aside to share in our happiness. Though not yet out of his teen years, the young man displayed a mark of rare maturity beyond those years.

I embraced him. We looked into each other's eyes and understood. We shared a special history that was treasured by both teacher and pupil. Bookie shook Mr. Millgard's hand and expressed congratulatory remarks. It was then that the happy groom-to-be asked the younger man, "In appreciation of our friendship, we would, indeed, be grateful if you could officiate as my best man at our wedding?"

Bookie was surprised. He may have thought: *Doesn't Mr. Millgard have a brother or friend he would rather have serve on his behalf?*

"Thank you. I would be honored, but are you sure you want me?" Bookie replied as he smiled again. He seemed to be thankful to be a part of our happiness, once more feeling like himself. This seemed to be the medicine he needed for his soulful recovery.

He wrote to Noonday more often—not of Mary, or Vera, nor the sadness of his father, not even of the weather. He wrote of his heart, no longer ailing but strong again.

Anticipation filled the weeks preceding the wedding. Bookie knew Noonday would be home, and their letters overflowed with anticipation. Bookie wrote:

> *Forget-me-not, my flower mignonette.*
> *Push my Bachelor's Button, my fair coquette,*
> *My arms will open; my heart's silhouette,*
> *Of you alone; trap me, Venus, my rosette.*

Noonday wrote back:

> *Oh, my silly Bookie, I—in no way—will forget-you-ever. We are joined. Our hearts are one even through this separation. I have so much to tell you. It's wonderful here, a beautiful campus. It will be more beautiful when you are here to share it with me. It seems so long since I've left home and you, my love. I can't wait to hold you, to once again feel your arms around me! xxooooxxxoox Your Noonday Flower, it scents for you.*

Bookie read and reread Noonday's revelation of love. *Maybe. Maybe I can go back with her,* he thought. The university had agreed to keep his scholarship for a year, at which time they would reevaluate it. *Maybe Vera and Father could handle everything, little Mary and the farm work.* He prayed. He hoped. He envisioned the undeniable possibility of it, but put off talking to Olie about it.

The cold weather inevitably moved into Michigan. As the work came to its year's end, Bookie took more trips to Traverse City to visit his mother. Mrs. B. had been transferred to the mental hospital there after all efforts to bring her out of her serious depression were exhausted. The stress of losing her son had triggered the premature birth of her daughter, together creating a pressure from which the woman's body and mind could not readjust. The doctors assured Bookie that his mother might, at any time, rebound or wake up, but they couldn't say for sure.

On a day in mid-December, en route to see his mother, Bookie reminded himself of the hope that she would recover. It had been too long already.

He drove into the far parking lot, got out of the car, and walked to the unadorned, four-story brick building. The cement staircase led to heavy double doors. He walked slowly through them to the reception desk, and signed a paper a woman put in front of him. Soon, he was walking down a stark hallway into the middle of the building. The smell of sickness penetrated his mind and soul. Bookie looked at those who walked the halls, more afraid of their gestures than the words that tumbled out in all the wrong order. Minds in utmost confusion lived here— minds that fled into numerous hiding places, never to be resurrected again.

Upon entering his mother's room, he stood for a moment watching her. He wanted to scream, "Get up! Get up, Mother. Get out of that bed. Come home, we need you. Mary needs you."

He walked closer to her and whispered to himself, "What is this fear that has a hold on you?"

At her side, he spoke kindly to her. "Hello, Mother. It's me, it's Bookie."

She looked at him but didn't see him. Her eye sockets held glassed-over, round objects from which there seemed to be no vision. Her dormant mouth hung there, shapeless.

He took her hand in his, and talked, as difficult as it was, with a prayer that she could hear him. He talked about beautiful little Mary. He talked about my impending marriage. He talked about Vera, the nanny. He talked about Noonday and her excellent progress in college, and he talked about his father and how much Olie missed her. On this day, he talked about himself as well.

"I want to go to the university, Mother. I'm afraid to ask Daddy, he is so sad. He misses you so much. I know he needs me, but with Vera's help, I think he could get along without me." He looked directly at her. "Mother! Please talk to me."

He stopped and looked down. The tears fell without warning. Quickly, he brushed them away, and wiped his nose on his sleeve. "Do you think I should go ahead and leave? I want to go, but I don't know if Daddy can handle the farm without me. Maybe, but I don't know. I just don't know what to do."

The time with his mother seemed to pass slowly, but when Bookie looked at the clock, the time had actually passed by quickly. He had to start the two-hour drive back to the farm for evening chores. When Bookie leaned over to kiss his mother goodbye, he felt something. He remained still, and he couldn't believe what he was feeling, however weak. Her fragile arm reached for him, and her hand barely touched his face. He inched back when he felt her hand fall, and he waited. Again, tears welled in his eyes as he finally rose up and smiled at this beautiful woman whom he so deeply loved.

Gently, he said, "Thank you, Mother."

❧

The snow softly blanketed the ground on my wedding day. The morning sun played upon the snow like a pianist playing concertos on white piano keys. A wedding march filled the air, and sounds of love were everywhere. I, Maggie Dunn, would become Mrs. Theodore F. Millgard before this beautiful day was over.

Preparing for an afternoon wedding was a very busy time for me, and for Noonday, who had arrived on the Greyhound the night before. Noonday woke up smiling, so happy to be home again. She heard me up and about this early morn of my wedding day, but she remained in bed, dreamy-eyed and reflecting on her past. She told me later that she methodically sat up in bed, tucked the pillow behind her, and drank in the room. She thought back to the day when we'd put the little desk in the corner. It seemed so long ago. She looked out the window and spied the old schoolhouse from across the road. It was deserted, empty now. The building that had once symbolized opportunity for all American children, a dream of a people holding the same beliefs of instruction, had served its purpose. How ironic, despite its fancy proclamation, that it had left one American without formal schooling but not untaught.

The beautiful green dress hanging just inside the closet door brought her back to this special day.

She jumped up, saying, "Wow, is this the dress I'm going to wear?"

At that, I stuck my head into the room. "How did my maid of honor sleep? It was really late when we got to bed last night. It worked out well that the bus could drop you off in Walhalla."

Noonday just looked at me. Her eyes danced through her glistening tears of gratitude. "Oh, Maggie, I love you. What a perfect day for a wedding."

We worked feverishly to get to the church with all necessities and accessories to perfectly dress a bride and a maid of honor. The guests numbered few; most of the guests were close friends and family members of the groom. The little Lutheran church was a simple place of worship with wooden pews and an altar, where a statue of Jesus Christ, with hands raised, blessed all who entered in His name. Each pew end was adorned with boughs of evergreen and holly tied with red ribbon. Placed around the altar were many poinsettia plants.

Noonday, dressed in a shimmering winter-green taffeta dress, preceded me down the aisle. She must have been a ravishing vision to the best man, who stood at the altar, finally laying eyes on her after so many months. Her crinolines swished like angel wings as she marched purposely toward the young man she was frantic to see again. At the altar, she turned to her position and winked at Bookie to her left. Bookie's eager heart pounded as he returned her greeting, standing next to nervous Mr. Millgard whose knocking knees barely held him up. My kindly groom's broad, smiling face glistened with perspiration as he awaited me.

After a slight interval, the organ pounded out "Here Comes the Bride." I exhaled deeply and then started down the aisle. My ankle-length gown of white silk with a long, wide veil of white tulle reaching to my feet fashioned me into the bride of my dreams. I carried a wreath of blush roses mixed with deep-red roses and orange blossoms for scent. With my eyes down, I followed my feet to the altar. My beautiful Mr. Millgard stepped to meet me. I could barely look up, and when I did, everything blurred. The exquisite tenderness Mr. Millgard displayed for me on this day marked the true gentleman that I was about to marry. I loved him deeply and embraced his love with my whole heart.

We knelt before God as the clergyman led devotions and joined us in holy matrimony.

And I know, without a doubt, that God was there.

With vows said, the clergyman pronounced us man and wife. We welcomed the love permeating from above, and from those in attendance. We turned and approached our friends and family, walking arm in arm back down the aisle. The small reception, in the church parlor, served my guests with dainty sandwiches and petit fours, along with fruit, coffee, and tea.

Noonday and Bookie put aside their own feelings and turned their attention to my groom and me. We appreciated the congratulatory celebration from our attendants. The honeymoon we planned remained a secret, although we had hinted to Noonday that we would drive south, but not out of Michigan. I was not teaching, but Mr. Millgard had a business, and we needed to be back to the store within a week's time.

Many threw the rice that formed the arch of departure for us. Noonday kissed me as Bookie opened the car door for the detailed adjustment required for sitting down in the seat with all my bridal paraphernalia. The car drove off with streamers and cans, and a "Just Married" sign on its back. Noonday continually threw kisses while Bookie, for the first time, put his arm around my beautiful bridesmaid as I rode away with the dearest person in the world to me.

> *At this point in my novel my prime characters, including myself, become fragmented. My marriage, Noonday's life away from Walhalla, and Bookie's redefined life, inform my conflicts for change. The text following is a narrative of Noonday and Bookie's long-awaited reunion after the wedding and my departure to honeymoon with my groom. For obvious reasons I did not author that loving scene and want to add that other parts of* Noonday Flower *may have been penned by Noonday and Bookie. Those scripts, like their poems and letters, I amended accordingly.*

Bookie saw to Noonday's safe return to the familiar bungalow. She talked continually on the drive there, through the back door, and on into the evening. She had so much to tell Bookie about Michigan State, the classes, the professors, the campus, and the International Club she and Clementine joined. She overflowed with the talk of her new life. He was happy for her, and because the young man's unselfish nature urged his problems aside, he got caught up in her joy and his inescapable love for this girl.

Finally, Noonday looked at Bookie, realizing she was dominating their time together.

"I was happy to see your dad at the wedding. How's he doing? And little Mary? Can't wait to meet her. I'm sorry to be carrying on like this. Gosh darn, I talk too much!"

Bookie shook his head and smiled. "No, no. I love listening to you. I've always loved listening to you."

He looked at her. "You're alive! And I'm alive when I'm with you."

She immediately kissed his cheek, and, with that, Bookie grabbed her and held her firmly. He whispered, "Let's not talk about me, or my family."

She quickly answered, "Oh, Bookie, I've missed you. I can't wait 'til you can join me." They pulled apart and stared at one another intently. Noonday touched his face.

"I've missed your face, your smile, your beautiful blue eyes. Hold me, Bookie, keep holding me. Hold me tight."

Bookie drew her close. He closed his eyes to thank God for the moment. He didn't want to let go. In their embrace, he felt so cherished, so wanted, so loved—the tears fell without warning. Noonday pulled back, wiping his tears with her gentle hands, slowly, tenderly. They looked at each other so powerfully, so intensely, that nothing around them mattered—not the wind outside or the falling snow that moved with the wind.

There was no question. Their love, starved, now hungered for fulfillment. The young lovers walked to the bedroom and slowly removed their clothing without saying a word. This time, they didn't wait to look upon the anatomy of the other. Bookie was overcome by Noonday, and stared at her flawless form, her sheer beauty. She, too, looked at Bookie. His bone structure, encased by taut muscles, entranced her. They walked toward each other.

They touched and caressed each other's softness. Their eyes locked, and without realizing it, they lay upon the bed.

They kissed as though it was the most natural thing in the world. Kissing projected them into a whole new world of emotions. Noonday gasped with joyful shock as his kisses drifted to other parts of her body, giving her unbelievable pleasure. She became like a bride herself, eager for this knowledge of intimate love.

Bookie tenderly caressed her body, kissing her again and again. Noonday slid her arms around him and pressed closer. This level of loving was something neither of them had ever known. Her virgin sweetness, in the way she wanted to give herself to him, made him want her all the more. The touching, the kissing, reached a height of untapped emotions.

"Noonday? Noonday, are you really here?"

"Yes, yes, I'm here. I love you, I love you . . ."

Tenderness welled inside him. He realized that he had never known such pleasure, that he had never known he could give such pleasure. This was the gratification of pure love and the privilege of loving Noonday. She emulated a world of blossoms for the bee. And he, the bee, descended over her tenderly. The exquisite pleasure from the purest, sweetest nectar of Noonday filled him. Again, he kissed her. In sweet reverence, she kissed him back. Back and forth, the kissing progressed. Soon they stopped and listened. Hearts were beating heavily. Then Noonday closed her eyes.

Over her, Bookie memorized her; she was drowning in his eyes. He felt himself upon a wave, flowing onto a dreamy island, a perfect paradise. His heart hardly had time to beat again before a new wave swept over him. He was overcome by his desire. Oh, how he wanted her. He screamed out, "Oh—my—God. I love you!—I love you, Noonday!"

The room echoed his declaration. He listened.

Then, suddenly, ripped from his fleshly desires, he stopped. He felt he had run a mile, every step in slow motion, laboring to the finish line but unable to cross it. His breathing accelerated out of control. He was so breathless, he could hardly speak again. And when he did, it was as if someone else were speaking. "No, no, we can't—we can't—not now—I can't . . ."

He grabbed her as he tried to slow the motion of the earth's waves around him. His body convulsed as the tears flowed with the words: "I love you—I love you—my precious flower." He closed his moist eyes and cried, "I will not—not until—"

Each lover, filled with an intense exhaustion, released the other. Muscles ached, heads throbbed, and breathing finally evened out. The looks on their faces combined desperation with relief. Yet both held their first intimate sharing with the beauty and respect of God's creation of man and woman. All the blessings of their union were collected, all its controversies extracted and excluded.

Time passed with their eyes fixated upon the ceiling, then a smile, remembering their nakedness and looking up at the same ceiling. The afterglow of their time together consumed them; they didn't speak, just felt for the other's hand.

Soon, a whisper: "I love you . . ."

"I love you, too . . ."

And now on the sky I look,
And my heart grows full of weeping;
Each day to me is a sealed and precious book,
A tale of that loved one keeping.
We parted in silence; we parted in tears,
However, the flower did bloom in those by-gone
    years,
And now doth fragrance my heart forever.
                  —Mrs. Crawford

She's gone, Walhalla's flower,
Mid his lingering sorrow.
                  —C. Ohse

CHAPTER SIXTEEN

Over the Coming Years . . .

We returned from our honeymoon earlier than expected. As much as I wanted to be with Milly alone, I felt overwhelmed with what awaited us back home. The holidays concluded quickly, and I moved from my bungalow to the home of my new husband in the little town of Scottville nestled between Custer and Ludington. The time was busy and brief before Noonday boarded the bus to return to school.

Bookie and Noonday, along with Milly and me, talked far into the night about Bookie's college future. Olie, subdued by the circumstances in his life, did not voice his opinion one way or another. He was a man of fewer words since the death of his second son and the loss of the love of his wife. When we contacted the university, we found out that the paperwork that would put Bookie's readmittance in motion was time consuming, and would require more time than we had. Bookie finally decided he had better wait for fall term. He made the practical decision to postpone college despite Noonday's demurring cries.

"No, no, Bookie," Noonday argued. "Come with me now. We can work it out. Please—please."

"There's no time. You'll get behind in your studies. I don't want to have to catch up. No, I'm not going now. Besides, I don't know—about my father."

"Your father has Vera. You said yourself she is working out real well."

"Yes, she takes cares of Mary. We can't ask her to do farm work, too. I don't know if I can get home often enough for spring planting."

"The farm, the farm, *the farm*! I am sick of that farm!" Noonday screamed. Bookie didn't respond. He bowed his head, walked out the door, and headed for home just like he had years ago on the railroad track.

She followed him. "Bookie, come back here! We're not done," Noonday hollered. "Bookie, I'm sorry. Come back." She put her head in her hands and cried, "Please come back . . ."

Tears flowed on and off the day Bookie took Noonday to the bus depot. They tried to be grown up about it, cheerful, too, talking all the while about future plans together.

"This year is over. We have next year. Noonday, please don't cry."

"I know. I know it, but . . ." She could say no more.

She wanted to be held like a small child, a child who soon would be parted from the one she loved. She knew she had the strength to go away alone. The very ones who loved her had given her that. But she wanted Bookie to go with her. That was the plan. What had happened to the plan?

She leaned into Bookie, who took her in his arms and held her without saying a word. Arm in arm, two hearts beat as one. Others rushed around them to board the bus. In tears, Noonday kissed him, then broke away. She started to board the bus, one step up, then she looked back and mouthed the words, "I love you." Seated in the back of the Greyhound, she waved continually until the bus once again took her away.

Bookie stood there even after the bus disappeared. The smell of its exhaust fumes remained with him as he stood in the Greyhound's cloud. He looked at the people around him bundled in scarves and mittens and heading to wherever their lives were leading them—to work, to a meeting, to an appointment, or to school. The despondent young man returned to his car to begin the long twenty-mile trek back to the farm and his life. A life loaded with adult responsibilities and a yearning to be elsewhere.

The winter months gave Bookie too much time to think of Noonday. She was gone—that could not be denied—but her spirit spoke to his heart of a bright future. His mind, on the other hand, dealt with the reality of the situation, not taking an optimistic view but fearing for the future. Still, his telephone conversations with Noonday always lifted his spirits. Noonday always talked with eagerness, like a child bubbling over with the zest of her new life.

"Happy New Year, my love. Just wait until you are here with me."

ℂℂ

Days without sun were many that winter. The months of snow reduced Bookie to a man without hope, a man barren of a love, a love he needed. He became a man deflated of a dream, and no one could deny that he deserved more. By springtime, Bookie's conversations with Noonday were beginning to lose their hopeful expectations. The distance between them had taken its toll on a love that only closeness could nourish. Bookie had a great deal to do to be ready for the approaching planting season, and his conversations with Noonday had been about his present work schedule, not the future. His responsibilities as a young farmer far outweighed his dreams. He became fearful of the loss of his dreams, so he plowed them under, and without tending to them, the invasive weeds choked them. They never came up again.

☙

Then, before anyone knew it, it was the spring of the next year and time to plant crops again. One year after another came and went—expeditiously, but not without heartache and frustration. Noonday's trips home were few. Bookie lost his scholarship, so each year that passed further reduced his opportunity to attend college.

Even beyond the two years that Noonday had been away, his thoughts still sauntered down the road of memory with the one he loved so completely. It was as though a certain person, one in particular, had inhabited his mind so pressingly she would never leave it. Winters were long and hard. Spring work helped Bookie forget, but not completely.

Two more years passed by. Noonday's career at Michigan State University finished, and left her yearning for more. She longed for wise conversations, and in graduate school, she learned to understand the exchange of knowledge and to live it. Throughout her schooling, Noonday exerted an incalculable influence upon many people. Many grew to know and love her.

Noonday thoroughly mastered her four years of undergraduate study. Milly and I visited her often, but because we visited during summer, Bookie couldn't join us. Noonday cultivated her mind while Bookie cultivated his fields. Their choices for independent freedoms became their separated freedoms. Bookie's fate became the business of farming, even though he didn't realize he had already made his choice. Over these years, Bookie busied himself not with books, as he would have preferred, but with knowing the soil and what it could give back with loving care and the knowledge of the land. Silently, he worked hard and found eventual satisfaction in the tillage of the land he loved. Bookie, self-taught, mastered the proficiency of farming. He expanded the farm eighty acres by buying the land he could afford and renting the land he couldn't afford to buy. He was growing more crops, buying and selling more beef cattle, reducing his dairy herd, and thereby making a good living.

Noonday, meanwhile, studied constantly and quickly acquired knowledge about many subjects, majoring in education with a minor in social studies. She, for the sake of people in many communities, black and white, and for the sake of homes in the humble walk of life, wanted to administer to the minds and well-being of others. She wanted to give of herself. She wanted to teach. This was her choice. Farming was not Bookie's conscious choice, although he'd accepted it with a grateful heart.

Word filtered to the Brenner farm by way of the Millgards that Noonday had been awarded a grant to attend Harvard University for continued graduate study in the field of education. I stopped by the Brenners' with the news. "Noonday is so gratefully honored, Bookie. Aren't we proud of her? By the way, she sends her love to you."

"How is she?" Bookie asked.

"Busy. She likes to be busy. I don't think she'll make it home before she moves out East. We'll just have to go there. Let's plan to go after she gets settled," I explained.

But we never did.

❧

When Bookie celebrated his twenty-fifth birthday, he dismissed his inescapable present by recollecting his vanished past, and remembering the magic of it. He knew Noonday would never come home again, especially now when the opportunity to further her education was before her. Her continuing instruction

would take her even farther away from Walhalla, and he feared
farther away from the people in Walhalla—many that she loved.

He wrote to her. He wrote a poem, not a lighthearted poem
like his poems of the past, but a poem of thoughtful and caring
sacrifice. He wanted to free her, and he did, gallantly.

> *You, my flower, express a depth in me; a feeling as*
>   *a poem,*
> *Since first we met; you said, "I am*
> *Black as the stately Ebony Tree,*
> *With roots plagued by shallow hypocrisy."*
> *But you grew strong among the Oak, and Birch*
> *From where the branches of the feathered perch,*
> *They know your laughter was a song,*
> *And, to your smile all of us belong.*
> *But, now my fate allays*
> *A dandelion's spray to windy fields of wheat and*
>   *hay,*
> *And deeply rooted weeds do grow, and choke my*
>   *way.*
> *Bloom, my Flower, climb the Everlasting vine*
> *Of other gardens; leave the weeder behind.*
> *Depart from me, it is the thyme*
> *My budding beauty, my currant starlet.*
> *I wane and wither, my Love Lies Bleeding.*
> *And, though the rose is scarlet,*
> *The willow is weeping, and my love is grieving,*
> *I wound to heal, never ceasing to remember.*
> *The dead leaves dance upon the wind,*
> *As like my heart dismembers.*
> *Awake, my Flower, to meadow's sweetest*
>   *hy-a-cinth.*
> *No pungent yarrow will be tomorrow*
> *A sunbow's heavenly hue colors you*

Farewell, this is the hour,
Goodbye my one and only,
My Lily Rose, my Noonday Flower.

Noonday read and reread the last letter she received from Bookie. She couldn't put it down. She still loved him. She had a hard time accepting the finality of their love. So, she tucked it away as she did with all his poems. This one she placed with the others in her box labeled "Treasures."

Late one evening, the kitchen phone rang at the Brenners'. Olie had retired to bed, as had five-year-old Mary. Vera answered the phone, wondering who was phoning at such a late hour.

"May I speak with Bookie?" the cheerful voice asked.

"Bookie? Oh, you mean Bob. Bob Brenner?" Vera responded.

One of the difficulties of having a past love is that a man has to cope with the memory of her as he goes through life; it's hard to know what to do about that unforgettable person, etched so deeply that nothing can erase the scar. His present circumstances had in due course changed things, unfavorable to both parties, but the love was still there.

"Bookie? Bookie, are you there?" Noonday asked gaily, her voice sprightly. Bookie was surprised to hear her voice. It had been more than a year since they had last spoken.

"Yes, yes, I am. How are you, Noonday?" he asked weakly, somewhat intimidated.

He was surprised. He had thought to never hear from her again. Actually, the sound of her voice excited the farmer. He was immediately drawn back to past days when her talk had brightened his eyes and put a smile on his face. Her engaging dialogue captured the young man as it always had. She was witty, brilliant, and it was easy for Bookie to talk with her, but later in their conversation, he was at a loss to respond to her projections that they get together.

"I got your letter, your poem," she said. She waited. He didn't say anything.

"I have to see you," she continued. "Just say when and where we can meet. Don't you dare say you can't, Bookie."

Bookie became uneasy. He was a practical man, a working man, and a man of few words. He refused her invitation.

"I'm just beginning fall harvest. I just can't get away. I can't meet you. I can't."

She contemplated his reluctance and didn't say any more. He wished her good luck, and like always, he wished her the best of everything and meant it. She hung up the phone and quietly wept. He hung up the phone and knew he was beyond the dream. He was beyond the dream of an educated future with her, the dream of a married life with her, the dream of a family with her, the dream of a long life with her. It was over.

The impression of their conversation, the sense of their past, dwelt within his mind far into the restless night. He couldn't fall asleep. The phone call stirred up feelings he had thought forgotten, though not really. They were always there, buried beneath a subconscious, afraid to come forth, afraid of the pain of loss. His fatigued body won over the activity of his mind, and Bookie finally slept.

The night was quiet. The leftover smell of newly mown hay penetrated the still air. Animals with eyes ablaze roamed their nightly haunts. Vera's bedroom, adjacent to Bookie's room, shared the upstairs with two other bedrooms, one of which was Mary's room. In the early a.m., Vera awakened to a soft but distressing crying she believed was Mary. Her bed, parallel to the wall, moved as she sat upright, bewildered. Realizing it was Bookie who was crying, she threw her cover aside and got out of bed.

She walked barefoot into the hall, where she put her ear to his door. The crying progressed into hysterical sobbing—a release of bottled-up years of heartache and suffering. Vera entered the bedroom. Bookie hadn't realized it until the woman sat on the side of his bed and whispered to him.

"Hush. Hush, it's all right. There . . . there, don't cry. Please, don't cry."

He looked at her, and didn't send her away, but sat up and grabbed her, continuing to sob in her arms. She rocked him back and forth as though he were a child. As the woman comforted him, he calmed down and soon lay back, unembarrassed. Gradually, Vera stood to pull the quilt over him, but he stopped her, and coaxed her to lie by his side. She did so without another thought to the matter. After a quiet moment, she started to run the palms of her hands over the smooth skin of his exposed upper body. He moaned in pleasure under the woman's caresses. Soon, aroused, he started shaking with a deep-seated passion.

Vera had secretly admired Bookie from afar, trying not to let it be known. She wanted him. She had waited long enough for him to want her. To absorb his tingles of expectancy, she unbuttoned her nightshirt and turned within the circle of his arms.

He welcomed the armful; the feel of her flesh to his was more than he could bear. He tightly gripped her thick dark hair, pulling her closer. His desire became obvious to her as the early-morning light revealed his readiness.

She pulled down his briefs and straddled him; all the while, Bookie's intermittent sobs drew him into another dimension, another time, another place. He closed his eyes and explored the softness of the woman over him. Suddenly, her body, along with his, convulsed into a great, aching outpouring of pleasure. He was in a dream as he roughly filled her with his passion. When it was over, she fell to his side, breathless, fulfilled. He turned and held her tight. Throughout his sexual encounter, he hadn't said a word. With his eyes closed, he breathed a sigh of relief for his emotional liberation. But the woman in his bed was realizing another dream, a dream that had come true, and a dream from which she did not want to wake.

Soon, she started to feel his release. She uttered, "Oh please. Don't let go."

The sound of her voice startled him. Jolted fully awake, he looked at her with disbelief. In the newness of the day, he realized what he had done. He'd contaminated the only love he had ever known, defiling his love of Noonday. Suddenly, he felt sick with guilt. With all his dreams adulterated, beyond reconciliation, he cried again, softly, not for himself but for the woman lying next to him whom he did not love.

Over the next weeks, the awkwardness between Vera and Bookie disturbed them to the point of being overly polite to one another. Vera, an animated chatterbox, ordinarily talked endlessly about a wondrous adventure or a past recollection. Now, for the first time in the Brenners' employ, she was at a loss for words. Both were at a loss to know how to deal with their late-night rendezvous, until the next time it happened, and the next time.

One evening, while Vera was drying the supper dishes, she turned to Bookie, who had remained at the kitchen table. "Do you . . . Do you need me, tonight?" she said.

She didn't look at him, just looked at the utensils she was drying and putting away. For the longest time, he didn't answer.

Finally, he stood up. "Yes, I would appreciate it," he said, then walked away.

Vera had grown up in the next county. She and Bookie had known very little of each other until she'd come to live with the family. She'd left school before Bookie entered high school and worked at the canning factory that hired a majority of the locals. She was a hard worker, and hard work paved the way for her debt-free living. That was the way of her family. She never gave a thought to continuing her education. She was content to work and accept her fate as it happened day to day.

Vera was by no means a slender woman. The dessert she made the most often for the family was bread pudding. Mary always asked for more, after the men left the kitchen.

"No, no, Mary dear. One helping, remember. You'll get fat. You don't want to be a duck, do ya? Waddle, waddle . . ." But Vera, more often than not, finished it all herself, licking the pan to savor any sweetness that remained.

There came a time in the middle of the day when Vera kissed Bookie, just like that—no one was around. She placed her arms around his neck and drew him close to her. Her lips, full and red, rested on Bookie's mouth for the longest time. He was conscious of their warmth and softness, and he didn't pull away but just stood there.

After the kiss, she pressed her cheek to his and murmured in his ear, "I know your heart is wounded. Let me help you forget."

She stopped and looked at him with a frisky grin. She walked out of the house and into the yard, looking back with a smile, but continued with the firm tread of the country woman she was—one who liked the feel of the good earth under her feet, and the feel of a good man over her.

Bookie did have some affection for her. She was easy to be with, and he was more than grateful for her care of Mary and the Brenner home. He wished he could love her.

Another time, Vera again approached Bookie in the light of day. Olie had driven into town, taking little Mary along. Bookie, having finished his lunch, was resting on the couch in the sitting room. As though she had been programmed to be his dessert, Vera quietly walked into the room and knelt beside him, embracing him with kisses. She took his hand and held it with pleasure, kissing it again and again. Bookie was soothed by her advances. His resistance to her seemed halted by the trance she put him in. Ultimately, she gazed into his face with her burning eyes, then stood and raised her dress with her rapidly increasing breath. He found his eyes, compass-like, looking directly where she wanted him to look. He resisted the thought of going there, but before he could think otherwise, she, arduously, began to move rhythmically. The seductive dance revealed an immodest Vera, who finally felt comfortable with Bookie, even in seducing him openly. Giggling, she twirled, every time removing an article of clothing. The teasing strip act aroused Bookie's passion easily, wildly, and terribly.

He stood, and without any further thought to the matter, removed his pants and overpowered the woman. In record time, he was done. Apart, the couple lay breathless in the middle of the floor.

Panting, she crawled over to him and looked into his face, whispering, almost in sobs. "I'll make you mine. You'll see, you'll love me. I'll make you love me . . ."

He never answered her. He couldn't even look at her.

There was no doubt that Bookie experienced tumultuous excitement with Vera. It was unquestionably pleasurable during the time of their brief encounters, but hours later, he felt a vague sense of disgust. He had no loving thoughts of her while such sexual scenes lasted, and afterward, he tried to convince himself that he did have a kind of love for her. But it was a love mixed with a kind of hate because he let it happen too often, distorting his moral sense of right and wrong. He knew it was wrong and often begged God for forgiveness in his late-night prayers.

છ૭

Noonday often thought of Bookie. He seemed so far away—not just in distance, but in her thoughts as well. Their time together was so long ago, a generation ago, or so it seemed. She loved him, and always would, but she was beginning to date again, and beginning to feel close to another. She welcomed these new feelings, resigning herself to the fact that she and Bookie would never have a life together. Still, if she spent too much time reminiscing, she could easily find herself back in Michigan in the little village of Walhalla with her beloved Bookie.

She could never dismiss that time of her life—her beginning, her first love. In the last letter she'd written to Bookie, she'd told him of her impending graduation from Harvard, not to brag, but to let him know how much she cared, how much she appreciated him. She wrote with humility, a gratefulness that filled her heart. She thanked him and hoped that all was well with him, signing her letter with her new name, Jean Flower, PhD. She inscribed beneath it, "With Love Always, *Your* Noonday."

☙

Noonday called me often.

"Maggie, I've met someone, Hallet Nouveau. He is a professor here. I think he likes me . . ."

The whole thing was a surprise to me because I thought she was so involved with her studies that she didn't have time to get to know someone so quickly.

She told me, "He is older, and was married. His wife died of cancer."

"Oh my. Are there children?" I asked.

"Yes, two girls . . ."

"Hallet Nouveau is quite a name. It sounds French."

"Yes, it is. He is very French, and intelligent and spiritual. He is a wonderful man, Maggie."

"Is he black?"

Silence.

"I'm sorry, I don't know why I asked."

An awkward silence.

"How's Milly? Give him my love."

"Oh, he is fine. Our new store in Ludington is keeping him very busy—me, too. By the way, Bookie made the front page of the *Ludington Daily News*. Last week, Tuesday, I think it was."

"Oh really? What for?"

"He is Mason County's Farmer of the Year. He even went to Lansing to speak with the senators and representatives. Vera was so proud of him."

"Vera? Oh, the housekeeper . . ."

"Yes. I guess I can tell you, although it isn't official yet."

"Tell me what?"

"Vera and Bookie are going to be married. Well, Bookie hasn't told me himself. Vera confided in me. Anyway, I don't know for sure."

"I guess I'm surprised. She is not—who I imagined he would marry. I'm just surprised."

"Well, no one knows Bookie like we do, but people change. I worry about him, though. He doesn't seem to be happy."

"How so?"

"Remember his smile? It's not there anymore. He works every day, all day. Works too hard. Our Bookie is no more—everyone calls him Bob now."

"Will you send me the article from the paper, please?"

"Of course. Milly and I are looking forward to coming to your graduation. I want to meet this special man."

⌇

Standing well above the middle height of most women, Vera was a woman with large, calm features. Although her face was visibly pitted with acne scars, she had a sort of towering kindness. She was a romantic who dreamed of a life with Bookie, sighing heavily in her daydreams, breathing deeply, and exhaling slowly. Sometimes, a high-pitched hum could be detected from deep within her throat. Mary liked to cuddle with Vera and listen to her inner voice, thinking she had another person hiding inside.

One day, Vera received a package in the mail. Everyone wondered about it because Vera seldom got mail, let alone packages.

In the privacy of her bedroom, she opened it wildly, knowing full well its contents. She found the box within the box and, clutching it to her breast, said, "Thank you, God!"

The label read, "The Parfum Magnet," with full directions that read: "Cleanliness is next to Godliness. Bathe and apply on pressure points, behind the ears, and at the wrists. Watch as you enter a room and cast a compelling spell on all the men there. You can't lose. Marriage or a fling will be yours. Use generously. Money back guarantee."

"Now Bob will be mine," she said to herself.

Vera made the mistake of wearing it in the middle of the day. When Olie caught the scent, unaccustomed to thinking before speaking, he blurted out, "What's that stink? That you, Mary? You mess your pants?"

Mary found the parfum magnet in the trash. She emptied it all around outside, and the family complained for weeks about skunks nesting in the area.

Vera had to rethink her strategy for winning Bookie's heart. She decided a new hairdo might be the answer. Vera's hair was thick and richly brown, her best, most obvious physical attraction. Mary loved to let it down, brush it, spread it out, and play with it during their nightly rituals before bed. This happened often in the sitting room in Bookie's presence. Vera hoped it would entice Bookie to want to play with her hair, and continue to play with her beyond the hair ritual. She envisioned Bookie sending Mary off to bed so they could get started, but it never happened. Mary adored Vera, who became a patient, surrogate mother to the child and a good woman to her brother.

Mary grew to be a well-adjusted, curious, perpetually hungry young girl. Once, alone in the large kitchen, Mary started making her "Dagwood" sandwich. In time, she joined the two halves and admired her composition.

Vera, returning from her trip to the clothesline, found Mary at the enameled kitchen table.

"Mary, what are you doing in here? I thought you went off with Bob and Olie." Vera started to clear off the table. "What are you doing with all this? You just had breakfast." She looked at Mary again. "Well, are you going to answer me?"

At that, Mary ran up and hugged Vera hard. "I love you, Mama-Vera."

Vera, startled with that declaration, answered her. "If ya love me so much, get outta here and let me get my work done. Now, scat!"

Mary flew through the screened door and ran out. Vera turned and, with her apron, wiped away a tear.

When Mary reached the other side of the barn, she pulled down her shorts and retrieved her Dagwood. She carefully peeled the sandwich off her belly, except for what remained there after her Vera hug. Butter and pickle juice left their impression in slippery goo, which was now oozing down her legs. It didn't bother her. A slow, delicious peace came over her as she sat on her woodpile throne and took her first mouthful.

ℰℐ

The next few years passed by uneventfully in Walhalla, Michigan. Olie was becoming an old man rather quickly. He was working less, and Bookie, Vera, and Mary were working more. Mary, like all the Brenners before her, even at her age, learned to appreciate a full day's work, from sunrise to sunset. They were a family of sorts. Mary looked to Bookie as her father and to Olie as a grandfather figure. Vera was Mama-Vera to her, and although Vera and Bookie never married, there were many discussions about it. They got along well with little dissension between them. They worked each day to the point of exhaustion and left the day's intimate questions unresolved. Vera wanted to marry Bookie, but as time passed, Bookie buried the idea so deeply that Vera could not bring it up again.

❧

One hot summer day, a newer, bright, shiny automobile drove into the Brenners' large barnyard. Bookie, with pails of feed in his two hands, stopped to look at someone who he thought had taken a wrong turn. The car kept coming and stopped near the farmer. He slowly lowered the buckets, realizing that the beautiful driver of the car was Noonday. Suddenly, he was whisked back in time, remembering her as she was then, and hardly able to believe she was here now in her midtwenties.

As she bounced from the car, he was stunned by her dazzling presence. His heart pounded as he tried to manage a smile. He felt awkward and spoke as though she were a mere acquaintance.

"Noonday Flower? Is it—is that you?"

She smiled broadly as she approached him. She thought he looked smaller than she remembered and very thin; his head was still covered with fine yellow hair, and though he was not clean-shaven, his skin appeared pale, almost transparent. She wasn't bothered by his embarrassment, as she was so genuinely happy to see him.

"Yes, silly Bookie, it's me. I'm so happy to see you. It's been too long," she said, her voice exquisitely musical.

Her eyes were smiling with that trademark smile, that mischievous, childlike smile he knew so well. She gave of herself as naturally as the noonday sun gives heat and the flowers their perfume. He remembered she was naturally affectionate, and so it didn't surprise him when she immediately, without a second thought, grabbed, hugged, and kissed him. He politely excused his appearance but returned her embrace. Her sweet kindness overwhelmed the self-conscious farmer. She talked on and on like she used to do. The more she talked, the more Bookie smiled, remembering. She was older but still younger than her years. Her vitality danced with her every word, speaking to every beat of his heart. He was overwhelmed by her very presence. They walked over to her rented car and, leaning against it, continued to talk for the longest time. Realizing a lot of time had passed since she'd first driven into the yard, Bookie invited her into the house and, perhaps, to supper.

"Oh, thank you, but no. I promised Maggie I would be back for supper."

Silence filled the air for the first time since she'd arrived. Suddenly, she just said it: "Bookie, I'm—I'm going to be married . . . soon."

Bookie looked at her and then looked away, and thought, *Don't be a fool. Of course she'd marry. Any man would be fool not to want her.*

It hurt so badly, even after all these years. He loved her so much, and seeing her again was more than he could bear. The unselfish man turned to her and, through his reasoning, said, "I hope you know I'm happy for you, Noonday." He paused. "Your happiness is important to me. It always has been."

They faced each other. Not a word was spoken. They couldn't take their eyes off one another. It was as if the shutters of their minds were taking pictures.

"You are my very—special friend, Dr. Jean Flower . . ."

She smiled at the use of her new name. It sounded strange coming from Bookie.

Again, he spoke. "I like your name—but you'll always be Noonday to me."

Awkwardly, they each now looked away, silence prevailing. Finally, he turned and saw tears in her eyes.

He smiled at her and said, "You know—I loves ya. I always will."

Her beautiful mouth quivered and broadened, and then she replied, "And I loves you, my Bookie—forever and ever."

She hugged him and he hugged her back, hard, despite the dust of the years between them. They didn't pull away for the longest time. A hint of desire came flooding back, filling their hearts with the tenderness of love lost. It was too late. They both knew it.

"Goodbye . . ." he said as he gulped back the sound that would have been a sob if it had escaped.

He watched as she got into her car, both so close to tears but smiling for the sake of the other, and the car drove away, taking them out of each other's lives. He watched as the vehicle drove out of sight, and he stood in the dust trail that rolled infinitely behind it. He lingered for another moment to absorb the picture, still in his mind, of the beautiful, soft, and musical woman. His face revealed a man trying to permanently etch in his mind the charm and natural grace of a very special person. He would never forget Noonday. Memories kept pecking at him, from past to present, as he remained cemented in his thoughts.

Later, when Bookie entered the house, his manner changed under the influence of his present life and the reality of another woman in the middle of it. Before the working man had a chance to speak or even wash the dirt of the day's work from his hands and face, Vera spoke up loudly, ignorant of the history behind the visitor and her business.

"What yaw doin' hugging and kissin' a nigger for? Who was that nigger, anyway?"

Bookie stopped in his tracks, stunned, unwilling to accept what he had just heard. Here was a man with a natural dignity and respect for others, a man of patience and attentive manners with women. He bolted toward Vera, and before he had a chance to think, he slapped her face so hard she fell to one side abruptly, the surprising force knocking her to the floor. In the next second, he grabbed her with his two muscular hands and pulled her up. "Don't—I mean, *don't*—you ever call a black person 'nigger' again. Not ever again, not in my house! Do you understand me? Do you?"

Months later, the news reached Bookie that Noonday had married a widower with two children.

I explained to Bookie that her new husband also worked in the field of education. He was a modest man of principle, broadminded and higher-souled than most and thanked the Good Lord for giving her to him. I told Bookie that it sounded like he loved Noonday as simply as she breathed every day.

Bookie took solace in that, but a jealous insistence surfaced whenever he had the time to think on his past for any great length. He could not help but think of how things might have been had they attended university together. But he was wise enough to know one does not live by what might have been.

Bookie continued to be the best farmer he could be, planning the clearing of new land and making it ready for the plow. This was his life, he didn't deny it, and he appreciated it. Father and son worked, raking the hay, planting the corn, spraying the weeds, driving the cattle, and cutting the wood for the next winter's fire. But as Olie's workdays shortened, he watched as his only son worked the hills and flatlands and echoed joy when the labor brought forth the sprouting seed from the soil.

Olie's thoughts often returned to the past, and he'd dream of Lil' Bob by his side in happier days. He'd dream of Mrs. B. with her gentle heart, her hands kneading holiday breads. And he'd dream of Billy farming the fertile ground in heaven's gardens. He'd even dream that Bob might be taken from him as Billy had, though his fear proved unfounded. Slowly, his dreams withered within his aging memory. He never bonded with Mary like he had with his sons. He grew old, unable to account for the years that had passed. In the sum of his life, one thing was true: for his share of sunshine and earth, home and hearth, he was a hard worker and did his very best.

"If anything I did has been worth my time, it is that I had two sons, one measured by his short life and all its possibilities, the other treasured far beyond a father's high regard."

In his final days, that joy and pride was present in the old father's eyes, as his only son worked the land they both loved and respected.

~

The more years that passed, the faster they seemed to go and be gone. Bookie worked hard every day. He didn't wallow in grief or opportunities lost. Patience, humility, and utter forgetfulness of self were the true qualities of this man. He arose every morning to a full day of farming and retired to a full night's slumber.

Mrs. B. and Olie died within a year of each other, and when Mary attended the area community college, Vera ran off with the Maytag repairman. Bookie had noticed that the man came around more often than the old reliable Maytag needed attention, he just hadn't discerned why. It had been years since their last secret indiscretion of the night. And so, at age thirty-nine, Vera left the Brenner home. He felt happy for her in an odd kind of way, and in another way, he felt sad, but one thing was certain: he was genuinely indebted to her for the devotion she had given his family for so many years.

Her last week at the Brenner house, Vera worked like a horse. She washed the windows, all the bedding, cleaned out the refrigerator, all the cupboards, and cooked like a maniac. She waited for Bookie to come home the day she left. He probably would have preferred for her to leave without saying goodbye.

"Bob, remember to use the meat at the bottom of the freezer. Remember, don't let the milk spoil. Even the cats don't like it then."

"Vera, it's okay. We'll be fine."

"Well, I gotta go. Emil is waiting. Maybe I'll get back here, sometime. I'll write, Mary'll write . . ."

"Yes, we'll keep in touch," he said.

She started to cry. "I can't say goodbye to Mary . . . She thinks I'm going tomorrow." She wiped her face and brow with her handkerchief. "Mary's my girl, you know."

"Yes, I know. I'll tell Mary. I'll make sure she understands."

"Okay, then. Well, goodbye." She hesitated and said, "I loved it here, you know."

Bookie shook his head. "I know . . . I'm sorry I didn't show more gratitude for everything you did every day. Forgive me."

She turned and walked away.

"Vera . . ."

Quickly, she turned to face him.

"Uh—you be happy. You're a good woman . . ."

In tears, she walked out the door and out of Bookie's life forever.

Mary corresponded with Vera for years, although Bookie never knew for how long, or even if they ever saw each other again. He surmised that they did. Mary never told him anything about her. He never asked, either.

When Mary transferred to a four-year university for her final two years of college to obtain her degree and teaching certification, Bookie remained in the big farmhouse, alone. He was still working full days, and reading as time allowed him that cherished luxury. He sought out, read, and kept everything written by Jean Flower, PhD. Mary graduated, and, having met the love of her life at college, married and moved to the southeastern part of the state near Detroit. Bookie was truly alone for the first time in his life. He adjusted, as he had with every challenge that destiny had cast his way, with dignity. This man respected people of all races, in all walks of life, whose destiny dealt them a poor hand, turning those cards of life into a winning hand.

The neighbor boys were a help to Bookie; the girls were, too. They came by often to do chores and help with the fieldwork in the summer months. Bookie, with a wonderful twinkle in his eye, always spoke to them on the value of a good education, encouraging them to attend beyond high school, if possible. They wondered if he knew what he was talking about; after all, he was just a farmer and perhaps hadn't even finished high school himself. Still, he became the broken-record advocate for the continuing education of the youth of Mason County.

"'The hearts of men are their books; events are their tutors; great actions are their eloquence,'" he quoted to them from Macaulay.

In time, many came to him with their homework, especially when the youngsters realized this middle-aged farmer's depth of knowledge. The teachers from the area schools also sought out his exceptional skills for tutoring. He had a teacherly obsession to share all he knew, which was a wealth of information few could conceive of anyone maintaining. He understood completely that instruction doesn't always prevent waste of time or mistakes. When his students did waste time or make mistakes, as students do, he told them, "Do not become discouraged; mistakes themselves are often the best teachers of all."

When fixed upon study, or while listening to a serious biography, Bookie's eyes were grave and penetrating. In conversation, they were bright and cheery, and in moments of excitement, they revealed a wonder of discovery. Nothing could have been finer than his facial expression when a student found the answer, the solution, or the conclusion to a question or a problem, leading to an applicable understanding.

"'The habit of reading is one's pass to the greatest, the purest, the most perfect pleasure that has been prepared for human beings,'" he quoted aloud, persuading the children to turn off their television sets. As the years passed, seeing his special students graduate seemed to be the only reward he needed. He always presented them with a sizable check and a wish for the use of the money. "For your books," he would write in the card.

She paused and pondered, and then she fashioned
The scentless camellia proud and cold,
The spicy carnation freaked with passion,
The lily pale for an angel to hold.

All are fair, yet something was wanting,
Of freer perfection, of larger repose,
And again she paused, then in one glad moment
She breathed her whole soul into the rose.
                                        —W. W. Story

Nature declared her a Noonday Flower.
Bookie declared her his Lily Rose.
                                        —C. Ohse

CHAPTER SEVENTEEN

Noonday Flower

In 1981, Bookie entered into the second half of his life, reaching fifty years of age and still farming fourteen-hour days. As long as seedtime and harvest filled most of each year, he was there to do it. He worked hard and felt satisfied in the work he did. Nights were short, but in slumber, with loss of control over his mind, he often dreamed of a lost love.

One early evening, just after a bit of supper, he fell asleep in his recliner. The kindly neighborhood teacher was expecting pupils shortly, so a catnap was routinely needed to energize his body and reasoning mind. In his sleep, he envisioned himself a child frolicking with a special friend. A smile adorned his sleeping face when he heard her laugh in his dream. He saw her beautiful mouth puckered up, a kiss becoming airborne. He received it with great pleasure. She turned with a skip and danced away. He tried to call her back, but his mouth opened with no sound.

Many times, when his pupils walked in on him, they wondered about this unconscious behavior. Often they stood quietly and watched. This only added to their suspicions that he was an odd old farmer, even though they couldn't help but like him.

This time, the knocking at the back door awakened the farmer. Still half asleep, he responded with a sluggish, "Come on. Come on in," knowing his pupils had arrived too soon, for it seemed like he had just closed his eyes.

There she stood—right in front of him. However much he was affected by her presence, he continued to rub his eyes. Surely, he was still asleep. He took great pleasure in what he saw, smiling broadly, so broadly he thought his mouth would break. She was really there, standing before him, straight and lovely. With hair tucked beneath a baseball cap, some flowing out on either side, he searched the face within the cap's shadow. Wearing blue jeans and an oversize shirt whose sleeves reached beyond her hands, he wondered about this apparition. Could it plainly be a farmer's ruse to tease him? Or could it be reality, slowly preparing him so her appearance would be less of a shock? Barely a minute had passed since she'd entered the back screened door.

"Hey there, you ol' cowhand, you need a good wo-man? I can round up the herd, rope up a calf, bale up the hay, rustle the grub, and fry it up in a pan. I'm—a—woo-man . . ." And she laughed, somewhat disconcerted.

It was Noonday, a near-fifties woman, and more beautiful than he had ever imagined her to be. His blue eyes, pale with red eyelids, welled up with tears. He wasn't very old, and yet he looked it. He wiped his sleepy eyes as he stood and embraced the woman with the deepest respect and the long-lost desire to see her once again. He watched her eyes dance in pools of midnight waters while her voice sang to him, "Oh, my silly Bookie! It is so good to see you!"

She threw both arms around his neck and embraced him with the fervor of a bear hug. Bookie was beyond words. He still wondered if she was really here, standing in front of him smiling and hugging him and talking nonstop.

That night, she insisted that the tutoring continue as always. She joined the study group. Never did homework experience more eager participants. The wayward glances between two happy tutors caught their students looking more at them than the lessons applied—and lessons implied as well. Noonday left soon after the students did. She was weary from her long day's journey from Boston, and she promised that she would return in the early morning.

She explained to Bookie, "I told you. I want to help you on the farm. I'll be here at sunup. What's for breakfast? I like bacon and eggs, toast and marmalade, and—coffee with cream. No oatmeal. Got it?" And she exited, as if a dream.

Bookie couldn't discern between waking and sleeping throughout the night. He thought about her. And how he must have looked to her. After all, she was a sophisticated, educated woman, and he was, well—just a farmer. Was she just being friendly, and polite, or was there something else that had brought her here—after all these years? He was hesitant to think on it any further, or any deeper.

The sun peeked through the foliage along the horizon, and soon, the ground mist evaporated over the fields. The dewy morning glistened as he awaited her arrival. When she didn't appear, he feared perhaps he had, indeed, dreamed her up the night before. He started breakfast, just as she had asked, bacon and eggs, and toast. He didn't have marmalade, and he had no cream, only milk, but he always had coffee. As he busied himself, daylight filtered into the room. He loved the mornings, the smells of a new day bringing hope for new beginnings.

He heard the car drive in. Or did he? He stood still. Excitement filled his chest as he anticipated breathing the same air as another—another so exciting he wondered if he would be able to breathe at all. Again, there she was at his door, dressed in the same jeans and shirt. Without the hat and in the morning light, he could see that her coal-black curls were touched with silver, but not much.

She smiled and then laughed heartily as she looked at the set table. "You made breakfast!" She raised a small white bag. "I stopped for donuts, just in case."

They ate and talked, and the morning fled. Together, they left the table, left the dirty dishes on it, and started the chores, later than usual. Noonday appeared serious about helping, although she struggled awkwardly with everything she did. Pretending she knew what she was doing, she whistled a happy tune and followed Bookie's lead. He smiled at her efforts, and felt all warm inside.

Upon completing the chores, Noonday leaned against the fence to rest and immediately felt a steer nudging her. Startled, she screamed, "Ahh, get away, bossy. Get!" She pushed the weighty beast away, and in doing so, got a handful of steer snot, which she quickly wiped on her jeans. She looked over at Bookie and laughed that laugh he remembered and loved so well. Then she threw her head back and laughed uncontrollably. Bookie was mesmerized by her, remembering how easy it was to be with her.

He was glad the corn was planted, which freed him until cultivation had to be started. He wondered again about her visit. How long did she intend to stay? Their conversations on this day were trivial, fun, and he felt young again. A deep enthusiasm overtook him. He had an overpowering desire to know, again, the soft warmth of her soul. He couldn't help but feel a love returning. The love had always been there, lying dormant, waiting to live again. So, unselfishly, he wanted to give his love to her, heedless of his own suffering should she leave him again. But he didn't want to think about that—at least not right now. Today, he was jubilant, and the sun shone indelibly bright.

છે

The couple's days together were numbering nearly fourteen, filled with hours of work and magnificent talks of literature, poetry, and the necessary inquiries into each other's past years.

One summer's eve, sitting on the great porch that encompassed half the farmhouse, Noonday finally spoke of the death of her husband. Bookie had waited patiently for her to tell him, although he had already known. Months ago, Milly and I had driven out to the farm to tell him that Noonday's husband had drowned in Africa when they were on a year's sabbatical from the university. They had been exploring a remote area on horseback when the accident happened. Bookie didn't know any more than that until now.

She began: "The winds were fierce. The sound muffled our communication, dust pelted our eyes, but we went on, almost sightless. Our horses could scarcely move against the wind. Suddenly, a tormenting rain descended upon the whole African Serengeti. The grandeur of it all diminished."

She continued calmly, factually. "We were in the world's cradle of humanity. This was an endless plain of the survival of the fittest among the most abundant animal life on earth. A thousand different forms of life swarmed this bosom of the dusty earth. We had planned on getting a better look at this self-sustaining ecosystem, off the route of other routine safari tours, but had not planned on this . . ." She paused, unsure of her words to continue.

"We went rapidly in one direction and then another. Intermittently, when I was able to see, I saw nothing. The whole scene around us darkened with the rain. Our cries and groans followed us. Hallet kept calling to me, 'Jean, Jean, stay with me. Jean, where are you? Come here, stay with me.' I was. Our horses were close, bumping into each other.

"'Hallet, shouldn't we stop and wait?' I called out.

"As we got to the river's edge, our guides came to a dead stop. They disputed whether we should cross. The river had swollen in a hurry; I heard the wild ripples lapping the river's edge. The Mara River was crocodile infested, everyone knew it. We trusted our guides, but this was not the place to cross. We should have trusted our instincts and not crossed. No . . . no, we shouldn't have crossed. Oh dear God, I have anguished over this, over and over . . ." She stopped. Bookie felt her eternal wish to go back and undo the crossing of the river, but they both knew she couldn't.

She gave a shudder, raising both hands to her face. Then, quickly, she shook it off. Her voice tightened and quivered with her most difficult words. "We were amid the wildest wrath of nature. It was as if we were in a dreadful disturbance of its laws and nature itself lost her way. The dreadful rain did not let up. The waters of the Mara came down in a great brown flow— and—and the wind hurled great sprays of water high into the air. We tasted it."

She looked at Bookie. "The image of crossing that river remains with me—and always will . . ."

She closed her eyes, opened them, and continued. "The noise, a roar, a deafening that filled my brain, I couldn't reason. The blinding wind pounded us as the guides bound us together with rope. The horses couldn't stand still.

"Hallet screamed to me, 'Hold on to your horse, Jean. Hold on tight!' I'll never forget his last words."

She stopped momentarily.

"One guide forced his horse into the river first. I was next. My horse arched his neck as we started down the grassy slope to the river; the horse feared the crossing, too. His legs, and I on his back, sloped straight down until we hit the water. Immediately, I felt the power and full might of the river. The others followed, each with a great splash. Hallet called out, "Hold on tight, Jean! I'm right behind you.'

"The rope between us creaked and strained, but kept us together. We followed one another. There was no turning back.

We seemed to seesaw, down and then up, always trying to straighten our line. Instead of going straight across, the river's current insisted we crisscross, thereby creating the longest distance to cross. The river bottom was not level, of course. Bushes rushed by us, some as big as trees. The undertow was so strong that the horses took each step with great difficulty. It seemed we lacked clear perspective of time and distance. 'Keep moving,' someone yelled. 'Keep moving, don't stop.'"

Perhaps at this point in her telling, agony must have overwhelmed Noonday, just as the river had in the vast Serengeti many months before.

But she continued: "Suddenly—so fast—Hallet's horse stumbled—stepped into a deep hole. Oh my God, it happened so fast. In one split second, he was in the water. I could see his face—the shock, fear in his eyes, and—and he reached for me!"

Noonday stopped, and wept. Her tears fell unchecked, running down her face, dropping onto her lap.

"I felt myself being pulled toward him. I was holding on, but I couldn't hold much longer. My horse neighed and neighed as I was being pulled off him. I grabbed on to his neck and mane. One guide was trying to get to Hallet, but the horses themselves were in survival mode. At once, Hallet realized he was pulling me—me!—he was pulling me off my horse! Oh my God! I don't know how he did it. He threw up his arms and—the rope slid off, he didn't grab it, he released it—and—and he was gone, swept into the wind and the rain. I couldn't see him! Bookie, just like that, he was gone!"

Bookie, spellbound by these tragic happenings, didn't speak. Silence suffered through a second or two.

Her eyes ablaze, she continued, "Letting go of the horse's mane, I screamed and screamed. No one could hear me; my echo flew with the wind. A guide found his way to my side. Indescribable horror shook me as I tried to jump into the river.

He held on to me and wouldn't let go. I wanted to go, too! Oh God, why didn't I? Why didn't I die, too?"

Noonday tossed her head from side to side.

She went on. "A great sense of helplessness consumed me. Uncertain perils surrounded me, and—and suddenly, darkness covered me like a veil. It was impossible to say what happened next. I don't know how I got to the other side . . . how, I don't know."

She stopped, but her whole body started shaking as she recollected the last moments of her late husband's life.

She faced Bookie. "His body was never found. The Maasai tribe kept saying something in Maa, their unwritten language, words that meant, 'in the belly of a crocodile.'"

Noonday wailed with sadness. "I loved him, Bookie . . . I dearly loved him. He was a wonderful man."

She turned away and put her head in her hands and sobbed.

Soon, she felt a delicate, welcoming touch. Bookie turned her to him, pulled her hands from her wet face, and looked into her eyes, red from weeping. Her mouth, usually so full and generous, was uncharacteristically drawn down at the corners. Her frizzed hair pointed in every direction.

"I'm sorry. I'm so very sorry," Bookie painfully declared.

She knew that he was, too.

"I always felt secure with him, and now he's gone. I'm lost. Oh, Bookie, I feel so lost!" She leaned into him and cried. The unselfish man put his arms around her and cried, too.

⁋

Another day, another time, Noonday told Bookie about the girls, now women. "One is married and expecting a child," she said. Bookie listened with wonder, finding it very hard to think of Noonday as a mother, let alone a grandmother.

"The girls became my children, and I was their mother. Me, a mother, just like that! I learned quickly. And I was truly blessed. I *am* truly blessed. Sasha is my married daughter. She is my steady one, tempered by complete honesty, with full devotion to her Maker, like her father. She married her high school sweetheart. They are both working on their degrees in education. And living with me—in Hallet's house.

"Celeste is—well, she's a heavenly wonder. She has the largest, most soulful eyes. Even as a child, those eyes got her what she wanted. We call her CeCe. When she was young, she was quite contrary. She could wind us up, let us go, and—we wouldn't know if we were coming or going. We were always dizzy with our star, CeCe. One week, she'd say, 'I want to be a nuclear physicist,' but the next week, it was a White House chef or a Broadway producer. She's always had a lot of spunk, and still does. She possesses the courage of her father. Presently, she is working on her second degree at Harvard, still brash and sassy and—uncertain where her aspirations lie."

Pensively, Noonday confessed another more intimate detail of her married life—the fact that she felt her husband had never gotten over his first wife.

"I'm not complaining. He showed me every consideration with kindness and devotion. I felt that, as much as he tried, he couldn't forget her. I know he is with her now. That gives me some comfort.

"He placed the Lord in his heart and lived his faith, so I know he is in heaven—with her." Her own words comforted her while Bookie listened and marveled at her strength.

Bookie didn't talk much about his past. When asked, he told Noonday of Mary, now married with young children, teaching high school home economics. Her husband also taught at the same high school and coached the girls' basketball team. Their busy lives kept them from visiting often, but Mary phoned frequently.

જી⊃

On the Sunday following their intimate talks, the farmer rested and the excellent weather beckoned the couple to go walking. Noonday arrived, finding Bookie holding a blanket and wearing his best Sunday attire, except for his shoes. He wore his high-top farmer's boots with his good trousers tucked inside. She smiled, placed her arm in his, and let him lead. They headed through the pasture toward the wooded area at the far perimeter of the farm. The pasture, fertile with shades of green, made their walking wide and serene while the inhabitants stopped chewing their cud and stared, interested in the passersby. They reached the banks of Weldon Creek, where the color of wildflowers covered the water's edge. The bank was dotted with dog violets, wild daffodils, and statuesque tree trunks, the pines and oaks crowned in green. The bright sun dazzled through the leaves, and light bounced in and about. Bookie spread the blanket and gestured for Noonday to sit. She looked about appreciatively, smelled the air, and smiled at Bookie. Together, they felt occupied with the wondrous nature that surrounded them. Their eyes followed each other as if a blink might cause the other to disappear.

As they settled upon the blanket, all the diversities of their separate worlds unexpectedly melted away. Ultimately, their eyes locked on each other. He leaned over and kissed her. They kissed again. The silence of the moment elevated the two into a most intimate and delicate sense of oneness. They embraced, recalling the love flush of their youth. Even upon the threshold of middle age, the magic had returned. They had never felt closer.

The beating of Bookie's heart was felt as Noonday laid her hand upon his chest to calm it. Her cheeks, flushed with the glow of her youth, pressed against his chest. As she unbuttoned his shirt and moved her hand beneath it, she kissed his warm chest and neck, then moved up to kiss the touches of gray at his temples. He held her with reverence, and when their mouths found each other, they kissed long and hard. Upon release, their suspended breath held them motionless. Bookie's blood was pumping through his veins like never before.

Slowly disrobing, they prepared to give their love to one another under the trees, beside the creek waters, and in front of all in nature's sanctuary. Wooing and petting the only woman he had ever loved, Bookie watched as Noonday blossomed for him like the flower she was. He closed his eyes and consumed her fragrance. She led him into a rhapsody like he'd never before experienced, and their music moved the heavens and earth, assuring both that their love, an enduring unity, could withstand the passage of time.

⌘

Noonday and Bookie reveled in their rediscovered love that summer. They opened their hearts to the complete trust of the other, never doubting the giving of it and embracing, totally, the receiving of it. The lovers spent many days and early evenings recapturing the love from their past and grasping the new love of their future.

Bookie paid attention to the exploration of Noonday with sexual courtesy. They shared a desire to give and homed in on each other's deepest longings, generously. They shared affection through touch, which more often than not led to the cultivation of new skills of lovemaking. The dog days of summer were made healingly happy, and the days of rain were made especially creative with more time to express their passion. Bookie and Noonday made their love a journey that never ended.

"'A good summer storm is a rain of riches,'" Bookie recited as he felt the raindrops falling from a dark cloud overhead.

"Ah yes, Henry Ward Beecher . . . 'And blessed be He who watereth the earth and enricheth it for man and beast.'"

She motioned to him. "Come to me, my wild and crazy farmer, and make beastly love to me." With that, she sped away.

The ripple of her voice, a wild tonic in the rain, made him want her all the more. She was endowed with a personality that intrigued him just as her sheer beauty and natural qualities consumed him. Oh, how he loved her. He ran after her as they raced to the house.

It vanished, that thin line between their past lives. Their separate worlds were contained and put in a closed container, or so they thought.

ᘓ

Bookie and Noonday shared the close of each day reading for their own enjoyment or enlightenment. More often than not, it was the local newspaper, the *Wall Street Journal*, or the family Bible, from which they would share a passage for careful examination. They loved challenging each other's viewpoints but always concluded their discussions with a respectful truce.

One evening, Bookie was reading aloud a poem, "The Death of the Flowers" by William Cullen Bryant.

> *Where are the flowers, the fair young flowers that*
> *lately sprang and stood*
> *In brighter light, and softer airs, a beauteous*
> *sisterhood?*
> *Alas! they all are in their graves, the gentle race of*
> *flowers.*

Noonday listened, scrupulously, unsure of its significance, unsure of its message.

> *And then I think of one who in her youthful*
> *beauty died,*

*The fair meek blossom that grew up and faded by
   my side.
In the cold, moist earth we laid her, when the
   forests cast the leaf,
And we wept that one so lovely should have a life
   so brief:
Yet not unmeet it was that one, like that young
   friend of ours,
So gentle and so beautiful, should perish with the
   flowers.*

In conclusion, both reader and the listener who heeded the poignant words were quiet. Both felt the full force of the poet's lamentation.

"I know that poem. I know it, yet its familiarity goes way back—but I can't place where or when. Read it again, Bookie, please." After its second reading, Noonday remained absorbed in thought for some time. She was happy one moment, and troubled the next.

"Let's go over to Idlewild!" Noonday said, breaking the silence. "Let's find Trixie!"

"I don't know, Noonday. It's not the same, not like it was—like you remember it. There are no shows anymore. I haven't driven that way in years."

"I want to go. Oh, let's go." Pleading with him with her beautiful brown eyes, she whined, "Please, go with me?" She had made up her mind, and he knew it.

Every blossom gives a hint
Of some friend we know and cherish
In its grace of mien and tint;
Friends and flowers, alas, must perish.

—*Voltaire*

God makes the blossom whole,
And gives His grace to save the soul.

—*C. Ohse*

CHAPTER EIGHTEEN

The First Black Ghost Town

Into the 1980s, crime had risen, along with unemployment every-where, and especially in Idlewild. A few days later, the couple found themselves driving east on US 10. The drive was shorter than they remembered—probably because cars now went faster than they did thirty years ago.

"Remember when you first got your driver's license? I'll never forget driving around Walhalla. And finding our secret spot at the bridge," Noonday reminisced.

"The bridge is rebuilt now. I miss that old wooden bridge . . ."

"Me, too." She smiled. "Everything is different. Just looks different, not the same." She moved closer to him and put her arm in his. "Remember the light of the moon at the bridge? It was so special . . . I thought it belonged to us. It was *our* Walhalla moon . . ."

"I remember . . ."

"When is the next full moon, Bookie?"

"Soon, I think . . ."

"Let's plan a night at the bridge, okay?"

She must have sounded excited, just like she was fifteen again. He loved requests that she could turn into childlike fun. She could turn the sun into the moon and make the silvery light dance in her eyes. She was his moonbeam, lighting his path. He might have wanted to stop and hold her right there in the middle of US 10. But he continued to drive, looking over at her intermittently. The feeling of her so close to him had been, in years past, only something he'd dreamed of.

All at once she started chatting about a news article that caught her eye because it was about an Idlewild musician and land owner.

"Remember Trixie telling us about the musicians that performed in Idlewild long ago? I was fascinated with her stories of Louis Armstrong and his wife, Lil. It was around 1924 when they started working together. Remember how we laughed when Trixie told us that Lil made him say, 'tweet, tweet,' when he sat at the table?"

"Yes, I guess she wanted him to 'eat like a bird.'"

Noonday continued, "He was unknown back then. But in time, Louis became America's first jazz trumpeter, but his wife, Lil, was a musical talent, too. Trixie said the two got together, impromptu, and put on a great act. Of course, this is what Trixie had heard from Idlewild elders."

Noonday added, "Louis and Lil divorced but remained good friends. Lil still spent a great deal of time in Idlewild because she owned land there."

"Louis Armstrong made Idlewild flourish, that's for sure," Bookie replied.

Noonday responded as if she suddenly remembered what she wanted to tell him. "Oh, this is what I want to tell you. I read that Lil died . . . in 1971, about ten years ago. The news article said she was performing a concert, a memorial for Louis, and in

the middle of her solo, she fell back off the piano bench and died
. . . just like that."

"Really? I didn't know that. I remember everyone's sadness,
even in Walhalla, when Louis Armstrong died."

Noonday added, "It was said that she missed him and always
spoke of him with a sparkle in her eye. Did you know she gave
his old cornet, letters, and photographs to a museum?"

"No, I didn't."

Noonday concluded, "How thoughtful was this woman who
loved and respected one of the most important musicians of all
times . . . all I can say is: 'Here's to you, Lil Armstrong, Idlewild's
one and only Mrs. Louis Armstrong.'"

Without saying another word, the two continued the rest
of the way, each absorbed in their separate thoughts. Bookie
felt that Noonday might be anticipating some of the old
renowned Idlewild, and he worried that a great disappointment awaited her.

"I hope we can find Trixie," he said.

"We will . . . we will."

They turned off US 10 and onto a road that led them into
Idlewild. It wasn't long before Bookie parked the car and got
out. He walked over to the passenger side of the car and opened
it. He wasn't surprised at the look on Noonday's face.

"Maybe we should drive farther. I don't recognize this place,
Bookie."

"It's been many years, Noonday. Let's look around."

After walking through the settlement, they spoke but a few
words. The glare of the reality of the afternoon left the couple
disquieted. One emotion after another crept onto Noonday's
face as she slowly confronted the vaguely familiar surroundings.

From here begins the end of the story of Idlewild as it once
was. Many buildings were empty and unused, and most were
neglected. An unmistakable scent of poverty filled the air. The
nightclubs were gone, as well as the big hotel and the gaily lit

bars. The Flamingo Club had been a shallow shell for years now, and the Paradise Club couldn't make up its mind whether to collapse under its own weight or to let the next winter finish it off. The neon lady above the entranceway to the Flamingo Club no longer danced. The tourist cabins, the "doghouses," designed for carefree summers, couldn't maintain their structures throughout the brutal temperatures of West Michigan winters. The beach houses, still sidled by the lakes, had become victims of time and neglect. Idlewild, once a resort for blacks, had become a gathering ground for the poor and elderly, and in the 1980s, it was designated as one of the ten poorest counties in the nation.

While the village looked hunched and ragged, many of the people Noonday and Bookie met seemed ageless, although they saw very few young adults. They continued to hike the meandering streets only to find a barking dog or an old-timer strolling or rocking on a dilapidated porch. The couple could feel that the village, once a marvelous place, was on the verge of becoming Michigan's first black ghost town.

In the distance, one of them spied what looked like a headstone. Neither said a word as they both headed in the direction of the cemetery. Noonday grabbed on to Bookie's arm. "Look for a Siggers headstone . . ."

"Noonday, most don't have headstones."

With her foot, she pushed away earth. "They are in the ground, nearly covered." She pointed. "Some have handmade markers."

She started to move quickly through the neglected area. "Bookie, do you see anything?" Bookie followed Noonday, both stopping now and then to examine the differing markers. One read, "Ma Buckles, First Lady of Idlewild," although no dates were on it. Soon, Noonday hollered, "Bookie, she's not here, she's not here." She smiled, wildly motioning. "Look, here's her grandmother and grandfather, Siggers, Sam and Queenie. No Trixie Siggers."

"She might have moved away, Noonday. Or she might be buried somewhere else."

"I know, I know, but she's not here. That's good, isn't it?" She looked at Bookie, begging for his support.

He said, "Let's go into Baldwin and check at the courthouse."

The couple drove to the courthouse, a stately brick building centered on a large, grassy plot at the entrance to town. The clerk's office sent them to the registrar of deeds office, which reminded them that if Trixie didn't own land, they couldn't help.

"I know she owns land. Her grandfather owned land in Idlewild long ago."

"She might have sold the land. But let's take a look and see." The woman walked to the back of the spacious room where file cabinets were lined up.

Noonday looked at Bookie and whispered, "Trixie was smart. She was taught early on how important it was to own land. Maybe it is still in her grandfather's name. Do you think?"

"Noonday, we'll find out. We'll find her." He put his arm around her and squeezed her tenderly.

The woman returned to the counter. "Yes, here it is."

Noonday darted to the counter and screamed, "Oh good!"

"Yes, Trixie Siggers does own land in Idlewild. Here's her address."

"I knew it. I knew we'd find her. Thank you so much."

Once again, they drove the three miles back into Idlewild. Up and down the streets of Joy Street and Harmony Lane, they peered at house numbers. Many didn't have numbers on them. They parked and walked, knowing they were on the right street. Finally, they walked up to a house and knocked. No one answered the door. At first, both thought no one was there and that, perhaps, the place was abandoned. But this was the place, they felt sure, finding it from the directions given to them at the courthouse. In one window, the curtains moved. Then a shout: "Who's that?"

"Trixie? Trixie Siggers? It's Noonday Flower. You knew my mother—Marla Jean." No response. "She worked with you years ago." Again, no response. "I met you in 1948. Do you remember? I've come to see you . . . for a visit."

Finally, the door opened. The good-looking older woman sat in a wheelchair and stared up at them. Suddenly, her face brightened and she laughed. "Well, I'll be danged—it's Marla Jean." She motioned for them to enter, saying, "Yahoo, girl! Come on, come on in."

Noonday grabbed Bookie and the two walked in.

"No, no, I'm her daughter, Noonday."

"Noonday?—Huh-uh—Okay, Marla Jean had a daughter, a fine—fine, mighty fine girl." The couple followed the woman into the dwelling, and whether the occupant realized the true identity of her visitors, it didn't matter. Noonday and Bookie sat on an old couch. The springs creaked as they sought comfort. Together, they looked up at Trixie, who had been studying them the whole time. She smiled, and despite her circumstances, the old woman still radiated a stage presence. She spoke lightheartedly, as if on a flight of fancy, laughing often, never lamenting about her poor health and living conditions. She spoke of the past as if it were yesterday, and in doing so, the familiar dancing lights returned to her eyes. Noonday and Bookie delighted in listening to her reminisce about better days. When returning to her present existence, she spoke of her recent house fire, when a pipe from her woodstove had heated the cheap paneling and ignited it.

"Oh, the Good Lord was looking after me. I coulda burned up in this old shack. Now, I'm in an awful fix—with my leaky roof. But I put my pans around when it rains. Least I got a roof . . ."

She deliberately gaped at Noonday. Quietly, she said, "Marla Jean had a daughter. She was born at noon on a September morn. Now I remember . . . you are her."

"Yes, I am Noonday." Noonday got up and went over to her. She hugged the woman, and tears sprung from both their eyes. Noonday pulled a chair close to her and listened as the woman recollected her memories of Marla Jean's past. Bookie watched. His love for Noonday radiated from the quiet corner where he sat.

Just how long Trixie had been living in poverty, they didn't ask. It saddened Noonday to realize the dreary existence of her friend: living with primitive heating, faulty plumbing, and matchstick construction. Despite the grim circumstances of their surroundings, the three friends reveled in their reunion. One thing was certain: Trixie loved the company. She mixed up facts, but it didn't bother Noonday. The contents of their discussion didn't matter. What mattered was the joy she could see in the woman's face when she talked. Trixie didn't mind telling them about her leg, either.

"It was cut off, 'bout seven years now. It got bad—real bad. 'Twas gangrene. I got sugar diabetes," she explained flatly, without a plea for sympathy.

Later, when Noonday and Bookie left with a promise to return, Trixie said, "Don't you wait too long now. He'll be calling me home—the Good Lord. 'Twas fine to see you. Noonday Flower, I remember . . ."

All the way home, Noonday wept copiously. Her deep-soul cry throbbed with sadness. She wept for the *road* of her race, not for its bumpiness but for the fallen trees and boulders that lay in the way.

How did I make it through? she wondered. *It was not because I was raised by whites.*

She thought again. *Books! That's it! Books. They bulldozed the road open and made life passable. The words, one in front of the other, following each other, telling a story, giving instruction, explaining, examining, laughing, crying, living, dying, bound together in considerable length for great recourses.*

Especially the book Hallet read with me. The book of life. The book of peace that surpasses all understanding—the big book, the Bible. Her mind reeled with this revelation.

She loved Idlewild and all that it stood for—freedom for her people, freedom unaffected by the nation's hypocrisy that surrounded it. For years, Idlewild had been a safe haven for middle-class, professional blacks who were barred from going anywhere else in the country. Jim Crow laws kept blacks in social servitude, unable to freely go where whites could go, but now the Civil Rights Act impelled all-white resorts to be opened to blacks. Now able to sample other vacation spots, the blacks had left Idlewild in the dust, and its decline began, ironically, upon the growth of this movement. So, in 1964 when the act was passed, Idlewild's decline began in earnest. Noonday thought it contradictory that racism gave birth to Idlewild's fame and fortune and later *the equal rights for citizens of all races* was the reason it died.

🙠

One day the next week, when Bookie returned to the house after evening chores, he was surprised to see the kitchen table set with a wildflower bouquet and candles on either side. He washed up, returned to the kitchen, and, for a moment, didn't see Noonday. Quickly, he thought, *If she were suddenly gone, what would I do? How could I live without her? I can't lose her again.*

From the corner of the room, he spotted her. She smiled at him. No words, just her smile—the one he always kept within, in a safe place where he could instantly make copies.

Putting away his panicking thoughts, he said, "Your smile fills this room like never before. I still can't believe you're here."

After nourishing the body, the evening meal was soon forgotten. Noonday rattled on, talking about nothing, seemingly, of any importance. He loved her chatter.

"You know why I didn't put fruit in the Jell-O, don't you?" She didn't want him to think she had forgotten. "You've heard the old saying, 'Fruit is gold in the morning, silver at noon, but lead at night.'" She playfully explained, "I don't want you weighted down, my silly Bookie."

Even at her age, the quickness of her wit compelled him to smile. And smile he did, more often than he had ever done before.

Suddenly, with no warning, Noonday blurted out, "Bookie, let's get married! Marry me? Now!" She got down on her knees, looked up at him. She took his hand in hers. "Will you marry me, Bookie Brenner?"

Bookie was stunned. No talk of their future together had been discussed before. From their new beginning, after years of separation, talk of marriage had found its way out in the open. Remembering the promises of long ago, their desires surfaced. But the past was just that—passed and gone. This was now. They probably wondered if their love would be enough at this late date. They knew their love was real because it had endured all this time, but nothing could promise a happy ever after. What about the miles between their lives, not to mention the years lost?

She thought: *He is older, but the very same man I loved in my girlhood. We have a connection I can't explain—it is not the same as I had with Hallet. We have a love that is more than love. It is beyond explanation.*

He thought: *To hold a woman's love, a man must make himself indispensable and be a partner in all things, as a husband, as a lover. Happiness depends wholly upon us, but will our present lives have something to say about it? Will our past separation have a negative bearing on a new beginning? I only know one thing for sure: I will always love her, even beyond the moment my earthly heart departs from me.*

Separately, they both thought: *What is life if it is not saying yes to most things reasonable and doable? Life is taking a deep breath and going forward. Yes, it is a risk. Sometimes we need to do the things we fear. Its cause and effect can lessen the painfulness of life and add to its quality.*

Bookie stood and pulled her to him. "You are serious?" he asked. She nodded, and her eyes boldly answered him.

Abolishing doubt, both of them, bright with the prospect of marrying, finally screamed, "Yes—yes! Of course—definitely yes! Let's do it!"

Two days passed, busy days, filled with plans for a wedding. The purple glens around the countryside echoed a song of summer love. The splendor of the rich-blue sky over fields of corn and grain set up the scene for a perfect wedding day. The whitest clouds tossed themselves into remarkable heaps, and the sun dodged in and out where they were not so deep. The romantic and ever-varying scenery of Michigan became their church— God's great church out-of-doors. Dressed in their Sunday best, Noonday and Bookie headed down the pathway to the creek, just the two of them, just as they had decided. They smelled the honeysuckle along the hedgerow, they picked the oxeye daisies, the red clover, some black-eyed Susans, and the sweet-pea blossoms of the lupine family to form a bridal bouquet. The willow branches overhung the creek almost to the point of touching the stream. The birds, in chorus, flitted over treetops, and the trees themselves became like fair-stature attendants. In one brief moment, a fish jumped up and splashed a blessing upon the scene.

The couple stood among the delicate ferns and pine seedlings, and as they joined hands, they looked at each other. The water mirrored the couple, and they knew the image did not lie.

"I'm ready." The bride winked at her groom.

"And, I, too, am ready, my beautiful bride."

And God was there.

The bride's voice echoed her heart's commitment to her groom. "I take thee, Robert Bookie Brenner, to be my lawful wedded husband. To have and to hold from this day forward, for better, for worse, for richer, for poorer, in sickness, and in health, to love and to cherish—'til death do us part . . ."

With a grateful heart, Bookie's trembling voice replied, "You are the top of my hour, my Noonday sun, the soft rain of my soul, and my heart's most bountiful harvest. I take thee, Noonday Flower, to be my lawful wedded wife . . . to have and to hold . . ."

He wanted to continue, but the words stuck in his throat. In silence and in tears, he forever wed his bride into his soul.

They kissed, and their desire for unity was now realized. They held each other as one would hold a gift, precious and irreplaceable, while the trees swayed their hardy congratulations.

The night fell upon the land, and the angels joined hands and danced the wedding song. If music was lasting like a painting, or a statue, or a book, then their score of promises would be forever.

> *Oh, promise me that some day*
> *You and I will take our love together to the sky.*
> *Where we can be alone and faith renew,*
> *And find the hollows where those flowers grew.*

The couple delighted in the day and forgot all their former lives. Their love reached a most intimate, delicate sense of belonging to one another like they'd never before experienced. It took on the feel of deep appreciation, with the graceful homage of a kiss, slow and deliberate, and a hug, a slow embrace. Dark eyes, light eyes, looked beyond the physical into each other's souls. It could be seen, so clearly, the love each had for the other. They looked into each other's eyes with the far glow of their first love.

They mingled tears with kisses as the unknown forces of life intensified their union. Throughout the night, sleep, alternating with wakefulness, brought forth a touch—a tear—a wink—a hug, or a coming together, perfectly and satisfactorily completed, creating a bond more powerful than life itself.

Morning sunshine announced its arrival, bright and promising, the next day, and all the fiddlers (birds) on the roof celebrated in three-quarter time, the music of a true-love symphony. Faith and trust awoke to the morning song, leaving little doubt that the wedded had done the right thing. Their past separation became just that, the past.

The following days fashioned a very busy groom catching up on the farm work, with no thought of a honeymoon anywhere beyond the perimeter of the home. Milly and I visited, and I didn't know how to interpret their marriage. I accepted it because of the love that bonded us, but within the confines of my aging, forgetful mind, I fought to dismiss the very thought of it.

"Now, tell me again. You got married? How did you get married? When? How come you didn't tell us?"

"Maggie, Milly, we said our vows in the presence of God, down by the creek, just the two of us."

"People don't get married at a creek all by themselves. I love you both, but you are not legally married."

"Maggie, we are married, in our hearts, in God's eyes, we are married."

"Okay, okay . . . I'm trying to understand." I paused. "I remember when you were kids and you talked about getting married. I thought, *How cute.* You were so innocent, lovable, and full of dreams. Your dreams were an important part of who you were. I wanted you both to be happy."

Bookie stepped in. "But not to marry?" He put his arm around me. "Maggie, thank you. Thank you for believing in our dreams. Why is it so hard to see this dream come true?"

"But, Bookie, you love Noonday like you love your sister . . . or—"

"Oh no, Maggie. You're wrong. I love Noonday like I have never loved anyone before in my life. I *love* her, Maggie!" I tilted my head to look at Milly. "Well, Milly, what do you think?"

"If they say they're married, then they're married, Maggie. It's all right with me."

Shaking my head, I said, "I'm sorry, but I just can't accept that you are married without a clergyman officiating. But I guess it's your business, and you can do what you like."

We spent time with Noonday and Bookie, and it took a while, but I could finally *see* that they were married. In reviewing our past together, I concluded that I was blind not to have seen that a *romantic love for one another* had developed over the years. That was unexplainable in my mind, and I don't know why.

I have to say in all honesty that Noonday did her best to be a farmer's wife. She cooked and cleaned and baked and mended. She drove the truck, even without a wisdom of gears. She did the laundry, despite the shrinkage and socks not matching. Upon discerning what should grow and what should not, she weeded the garden. She learned to take phone messages, running to the fields with some. She learned new recipes, hoping for success with one.

When she agreed, wholeheartedly, to can a lug of cherries a neighbor brought by, she thought, *How hard can it be?* Bookie instructed her on how to pit them, put them in jars, and process them in a cooker. She got half of them in jars, and thought to herself, *This pitting is for the birds!* The day's end brought Bookie to the house to find Noonday covered with cherry juice, most of which was dripping from her elbows to her knees.

She gave the rest to the birds, crying out, "Oh, Bookie, I never want to pit another cherry as long as I live. Life is a bowl of cherries, all right. Cherries you don't have to pit!"

He titled his head and smiled. "I love my lady in red. I want to eat you, my love."

"Watch out for the pit, my dear husband!"

"There is not a pit in you. You are perfect."

Angrily, she answered, "I am *not* perfect. Quit thinking I am."

"Whoa, I'm sorry. It's just that I love you so much. Okay, so you've got a few pits—two, actually."

Noonday laughed so hard, she cried. She hit Bookie until he grabbed her and held her.

"I love, love, love you. I don't care about your pits and faults, don't you know that?"

"Bookie, make love to me . . ."

Together, they showered, Bookie wiping cherry residue from Noonday's face and body. The spray of water gently aided them as they slipped their hands over each other. A touch here, a touch there aroused them to come together, close. He held her tenderly and firmly at the same time. His physical energy infected her with energy to match his. Every beat of his heart, every drop of his blood, she knew belonged to her.

Afterward, he turned the shower off. Like a Venus, she stood in the opalescent mist, a woman he loved, a woman he desired. He caressed her with his eyes as he lifted her out of the shower and onto the bed. He toweled her, slowly, meticulously, while her heart swelled to near bursting.

Laying the towel over her, he lay beside her. "I love you, Noonday. I love you . . ." His eyes were moist as he kissed her down to her soul.

∽

On one evening when Bookie got to the house after dark, he found Noonday on her knees in prayer. He quietly walked over to her and knelt beside her. He waited. She finished her prayer but remained on her knees, hands folded, eyes shut. He leaned into her and whispered, "I want to be with you where you are right now. May I join you in knowing God?"

She opened her eyes and looked at him. "Yes, I want that. God loves you, Bookie, my love." That night, Bookie accepted God and His Son as the ultimate truth of life and promise of the afterlife.

The following evening, Bookie got to the house and immediately headed to the mudroom to wash the day's work from his hands and face. He peeked into the kitchen and realized supper wasn't in progress. He loved Noonday so much that her inability to cook a farmer's banquet every day did not bother him. In the back of his mind, he habitually felt guilty for subjecting her to a lifestyle she was not accustomed to, although she never complained and was, always, a willing participant.

He called out, "Noonday, want to go to the Rendezvous for supper?" He turned the water off. "Noonday, did you hear me?" With a towel in his hands, he walked into the kitchen. He looked around. "Noonday . . . Noonday?"

He panicked. Alarm held him captive. Up close, he saw that the kitchen table held a note written in Noonday's hand. He grabbed the note and quickly read the message. He didn't move, just stood there reading and rereading the scribbled message.

CeCe called. Sasha is in labor, too soon, my love.
I must go to her. I'll call . . . Love, Noonday.

The note slipped from his hand. He watched as a draft of air gently landed it on the floor near his feet.

I've wandered to the village and sat beneath the tree
Upon the schoolhouse playground that rejected you,
*   not me.*
None were there to greet me and few are left to
*   know*
Who played with us reluctantly, more than thirty
*   years ago.*

The old schoolhouse is altered now. The bell rings
*   no more,*
To summon fair-haired boys and girls through its
*   hallowed door.*
A shell of past decrees; its walls repeat a blind echo
Of ignorance, accepted more than thirty years ago.

Those early broken ties make salty tears fill my eyes.
To be together, in that schoolyard in the sky,
Brings promise to my soul when we are called to
*   go,*
Forgiving those who played with us, more than
*   thirty years ago.*
*   —Author Unknown*

Bookie remembers, Noonday never forgets.
*   —C. Ohse*

CHAPTER NINETEEN

Robert Olie Brenner

A supply of time may be welcomed or dreaded. For Bookie, the next day was endless. He felt Noonday's presence all over the farm, still invading the air with her vibrant emotions. The hours sneaked through the day until weariness and twilight reminded him of its end. All through the night, Bookie awaited the promised phone call. He lifted the receiver but couldn't bring himself to dial. Throughout the next day, Bookie was thrust into despondency as he went through the motions of his work. Praying for Noonday's return, his mind fled into numerous hiding places. He felt unnaturally selfish when he anguished for her return. He endeavored to take refuge in the memory of their three months together. Naturally tranquil-hearted but haunted by the knowledge that time really does slip by, Bookie resumed his existence, however empty it was. The next day was the longest day of summer, and before it was over, the telephone rang.

"Hello, Bookie? My dear Bookie, forgive me for taking so long to phone you. She's here—our little girl—so tiny. It was frightening for a time, but she is going to be all right. She's so precious."

"I'm so relieved to hear from you—and to hear the baby is fine." He paused. "How are you?"

"Oh, okay. I—uh—I can't come back to Michigan. Not now—you understand. Sasha needs me now, and when the baby comes home, as well."

He was silent.

"I miss you . . ." she said.

"I miss you, too. I really miss you, Noonday. I miss you so much."

ↄ

Two days later:

"Hello, Bookie. How's my farmer husband?" Noonday asked. "The baby's doing well; we are so relieved. Oh, how I wish I were there, with you. I hope the boys are faithfully helping you every day. The old truck running okay?"

"I'm really happy to hear the baby is well." He paused. "Old Squeaker died yesterday."

"Oh no! I'm so sorry. You've had that dog a long time. You'll miss him."

"I miss you, Noonday, so much."

ↄ

A week later:

"Hello, Bookie! I love you—I hope you know that? I love you with all my heart."

"And I love you. It's Noonday in my heart, morning, noon, and night. How is the baby doing?"

"Oh, Bookie, I wish you could see her. She is a doll! Doing better every day—gaining weight."

"I'm glad."

&

Two days later:

"Hello, Noonday?"

"Bookie Brenner! I'm so glad you called. I've tried to get you, but you must be in the fields until dark. It is such a busy time for you. Gosh! I miss the farm—and you, especially when I hear your voice." She paused. "How's everything going?"

"Well—quite well. As a matter of fact, I got over to Trixie's and fixed her roof. She sends her love to Marla Jean's fine daughter."

"Oh, thank you for finding time to get over there and fix her roof. How is she?"

"Trixie is good. She mentioned something about 'pennies from heaven' and 'checks in the mail'?"

"I want to help her, and that is the only way I can right now."

"She appreciates the help, Noonday, I'm sure."

"I can't come back as much as I wish I could. Not now." She paused. "Can you come here—as soon as harvest is completed? Please, *please*, think about it? I know you'll love my daughters, my son-in-law, and my little princess, Haley. They are all dying to meet you!" There was silence for a moment. "Thank you for looking in on Trixie. You're a fine, fine man, Bookie Brenner."

&

A month later:

"Hello. May I speak to Jean Flower, please?" Bookie asked.

"I'm sorry, she is out. Is this the farmer whose name is a book? Well, well, meet Jean's daughter whose name is out of this world. How the heck are you, Bookie?"

"I'm pleased to meet you, CeCe. I hope we will meet in person someday soon. Will you tell your mother I phoned?"

"Will do, Bookie. By the way, you're not one of those boring, stuffy books, are you?"

જ

Christmas 1983:

"Bookie, have you made your reservations? I want you here for the holidays," Noonday asked.

"No, not yet. I'm—a little uneasy about flying. I know—I know that is no excuse . . ."

"I'm keeping my fingers crossed. I want you under my mistletoe. I want to show you off!"

જ

Winter, 1984:

"Bookie, the university has asked me back," Noonday said. "Actually, they need me to fill a position vacated by Professor Bingham, who is retiring. You remember my telling you about him. I've substituted for him many times." She paused. "I'm considering it. I think I'd like to—I want to, I do—I want to take the job."

"Thank you for the books. I've been reading a lot lately. It's been snowing every day." He was silent for a moment. "You should take the job, Noonday. You have so much to give to others . . ."

જ

Spring 1984:

"Bookie, my dear, Haley sends her love along with mine. Honey, say hi to Bookie." Noonday paused. "I'm sorry, I've been so busy. I know, I haven't called. How are you? I haven't forgotten that our first anniversary is around the corner. I need to hold you—so badly."

"And I can't stop thinking about you. I can't believe it's nearly been a year. Can you come to Michigan for the summer?"

❧

Winter 1985:

"My wonderful, Bookie, thank you for coming here. It meant so much to me to say our vows again. This time in a church with my children present."

"I love you, Noonday, you are my wife, my life, my forever after. I am glad we did it, too."

"I am sorry your flight here was bad. Gosh darn it, of all times, turbulence on your first flight."

"It was worth it—to marry you again and meet your family—and see the sights. It is a lot different from here. I see how good your life is and how hard it is to leave . . . for you to come here, even for a short time."

"I'm sorry I got so busy. I was relieved that you didn't have any trouble occupying yourself while I was working. Sasha loved your attention to the baby. I never told her how good you were with babies. It didn't take you long to find the library, either. I bet you touched all seven million books. I'm happy you got to read some of them. Our month together with my family made me the happiest woman in the world . . ."

❧

Spring, 1985:

"Hello, Bookie dear, I hope you are well," Noonday began. "Something has developed since we last talked. CeCe and I are planning a trip to Africa after spring term. She wants me to take her to the Serengeti and the place where I last saw her father. I've thought about this—thought it through—and feel I owe her that. She needs to put her father's death to rest and get on with her life."

Bookie was silent.

"We intend to stay the summer. Africa is so fascinating, much to do and see—the Serengeti especially. I know CeCe will connect with her father there. We will be joined by several scholars from the University of East Africa."

Noonday hesitated.

"Might there be the possibility you could join us? Oh, Bookie, you would love it—absolutely love it! Please come with us."

"How fortunate CeCe is to have you for her mother. But—there is no way I can go. I can't go—my heaviest work is upon me."

"Can't you find someone to tend to the farm for once!"

There was a long silence.

"I'm sorry—I'm sorry. I didn't mean that," Noonday said.

More silence.

"How can I ever understand you and the farm? It has a hold on you."

"I'm sorry. I don't know what else to say."

"Say you'll go. Please think about it. Please?"

"I can't go, Noonday. You and CeCe go . . ."

"Yes. And I hope you realize—it is for me as well as CeCe. I have to face what happened there, and not blame the place. I thought—I thought I had this all behind me until CeCe started asking questions. Too many questions I couldn't answer."

Remembering the death of his brother, the loss of his mother, and the change in his father, Bookie sadly replied, "I understand. I hope you will be able to answer the questions—and accept the answers. Sometimes the answers are not clear. Please take care of yourselves."

"You take care of yourself, too, Bookie."

There was an uncomfortable silence.

"I'll write you from Africa. You work too hard; you're a farming fool and you know it. I love you. You know that, too, don't you?"

"Of course I do. And I love you—for as long as we both shall live. In sickness and in health, in joy and in sorrow, in journey or by my side, you are my wife. Go. You have a vision with wings— my feet still walk a dusty road."

☙

Upon her return from Africa, Noonday found a letter from Bookie in her pile of mail from her long absence. He wrote:

> *My Dear Wife, the Flower Petals of my Heart, the Soft Rain of my Soul, and my Noonday Sun, I welcome you home. I pray your trip was successful and that you are nourished for teaching once again . . .*
>
> *I am feeling the first discomforts of our union. I have seen your life apart from mine . . . It is wonderful, full of wonder and adventure. You have a family and a good position with a university that affords you many opportunities. I envy you, my darling. I understand your reluctance to leave your surroundings, your good wage, and your loved ones. I'm sure you are concerned for your*

*granddaughter's education, as well you should
be, feeling the responsibility to set aside money for
it. I could not bear the thought of you being torn
between your life there and me. I will not let our
marriage, my love for you, be a trap or an obliga-
tion; it never was and never will be. The reason
I love you is because you are free . . . your spirit
and thee. You have been the best times of my life
and, even now, when the clock strikes noon you
are here—beside me—to laugh with me, to cry
with me, to dance with me and dream with me,
to sing with me and breathe with me. You are my
whispering violet, and my most fragrant lily rose.*

Oh, what a rare flower I picked in thee . . .

*I'm so sorry . . . even at our age, I thought we
would have had more time.*

You have my love—for always,

Bookie

Noonday wept. It hurt, cutting far into the essence of her
soul. She loved him so much.

Realizing he was right, she respected his words. She knew
she couldn't leave her home, her children. She had thought she
could—back when she saw him again in Michigan, when it was
just the two of them—living and loving, side by side in a world
of their own, *his* world. And with that, she thought, he couldn't
come to Boston to live, either. Mason County was the land of his
affections, whether he knew it or not, whether she liked it or not.
He was at home with the familiarity of his own universe. The land
responded to his intelligence, and over the many years, he had

grown intimate with the tractor and plow. Bookie communed with nature, and his lifestyle moved with the seasons—spring, summer, and fall. He attempted all tasks with vigor, not settling for anything less than success. Content with a year well farmed, winter was his season for revival through rest and reading. There was no doubt Robert Olie Brenner was a good farmer, but to Noonday, he was more a meditative man who was gentle, generous, and gifted. She knew no other like him, and never would.

She felt her heart break at the prospect of their final separation. Long days without phone calls or letters numbered many. Short nights left little time for memories to surface. She didn't want him to suffer through any more intermittent hopes and dreams. Though she wanted to, and was tempted many times, she never called him. She never saw Bookie again.

☙

Despite his usefulness, Bookie became an old man rather quickly. The many wrinkles on his brow distinguished him beyond his years. He showed a scraggy neck through the many yard-sale shirts he wore. His step was not as lively across the fields any more, and arthritis took its toll on his strength. One night, in his sixty-seventh year, Bookie died; he just sat there in his chair, all night, and for the first time refused the start of his next full day. And as he died, his apparition was such as this: *He felt a delicate motion, fluent and graceful and ambient, soft as a breeze flitting over the flowers. Suddenly,* she *appeared at the gate like a bird, beautiful and free, and as he tumbled off into the noonday sun and into the arms of her feathered embrace, he felt warm and safe. She lifted him over the Earth while it rushed away under them and left the air far behind. He clung to her crest, and without the power of thought, his breath came and went, and he was gone.*

And God was there. I, his teacher, asked God, *Was it Noonday who had posed as a plumed angel to take him home?* I think so.

Your mortal tongue has striven in vain to learn
Lost among the flower path for which you yearned
But, oh the deeply loved are there,
Your books, the attic fair.
Now you have them all, hereafter
To claim them in immortal power.
                              —Author Unknown

To give one's mind a lifetime occupation: read.
                              —C. Ohse

CHAPTER TWENTY

Knowledge comes, but wisdom lingers.
—Tennyson

I spoke with Noonday the day Bookie died. Neither of us knew he'd died, although one had a premonition that he did.

"Have you seen him, Maggie? How is he?" she asked.

"He is fine, Noonday. I don't get out there much anymore, but I'm sure he is well."

"Maggie, something is wrong, I can feel it. I've had this feeling all day. Please call him. Call him now and call me back."

"I will, Noonday. I'll call . . ."

I hung up, pushed the buttons on the telephone, and talked with a stranger, a wrong number. I carefully redialed and got no answer.

I'll call later, I said to myself after lying down. Milly and I napped daily in our later years.

Soon, I was asleep. I remember the dream.

Here he comes, the fair boy, running lightly with his hands in his pockets. And there she comes, a dark beauty with pigtails on her head and a smile as big as her curtsy. They drew close in delightful inquiry. He took her hand. They danced as if they were floating. I could see their faces so well—the glow in their eyes, the laughter, the singing in the wonderment of their time together. Later in my dream, the dark beauty turned into a butterfly. The fair boy watched her fly. In slow motion, he gently caught her and put her under his hat. Often, he took her out to admire her beauty. She remained on his hand, fluttering her wings but never flying away. He thought better of keeping her, so he waved his hand roughly, and she flew. She returned often and rested on his hat, but the boy didn't know it.

It was as if I were in years past with my children around me, when my ears could hear and my eyes could see and my feet could move with ease—when I could stop and listen to the butterflies. From my husband's loins, I was not blessed with children. But, oh, I *was* blessed with children.

Shaking me, Milly called, "Maggie, Maggie, wake up. You're snoring. You're singing, laughing, too. All at the same time, my dear."

I opened my eyes. "Milly, let me snore. Can't I laugh and sing, too? I'm having a good, good dream."

Not easily, Milly sank to his knees, took my hand, and kissed it. I looked at him, and he looked back with a modest smile that lit up his face. I wiped my sleepiness away and valued the pleasure in his eyes. "Now, Milly, what are you up to? You better get up before you can't."

"Maggie dear, this old man with his bad knees remembers . . ."

"And what do you remember, my Milly?"

"One summer noon, I met the most wonderful woman. She spoke to me and I shivered. The stars, bright tingling stars, came out. Even now as she sleeps, and laughs, and talks, and snores, I shiver still. And the stars come out, still . . ."

"Milly, you're going to make me cry. I am an old woman now. There are no stars about me."

"Oh yes. My life has had no richer ornament than you, my beautiful Maggie."

Milly got to his feet and helped me from the couch. I remember our embrace. It comforted me like never before.

I walked to the telephone, remembering a promised phone call. Suddenly, the words of Westwood invaded my mind.

> *So the dreams depart*
> *So the fading phantoms flee,*
> *And the sharp reality*
> *Now must act its part.*

As soon as I knew, I informed Noonday of Bookie's passing. I strained to hear Noonday's voice, wondering if we had been disconnected, and was surprised when she softly said, "I know . . ." and then added, "I heard him when I awoke this morning. He was here beside me."

Later, Noonday called back and told me she would not be attending the funeral.

❧

The Brenner house was a very large, older farmhouse. The upper level was as big as the ground floor with two stairwells leading to it. Upon the untimely death of her brother, Mary swiftly returned to her home. She was inundated with expressions of sympathy and overwhelmed with feelings of loss. She grieved heavily as she tended to matters that had to be done. I was there but could not physically lend a hand, as I was well up in age.

Mary asked with a sense of helplessness, "What am I going to do with the house and the land, Maggie? And everything in the house! What am I going to do with everything in the house? It's full!" She hadn't thought of this day coming so soon. She had a family now, a husband and children who needed her back home.

I calmed the younger woman. "We'll get help, Mary dear, don't worry. I'll see to it."

Just the same, Mary was overburdened with the job of dispersing the contents of her childhood home. Despite all the belongings downstairs, Mary and I were not prepared for the state of affairs upstairs. Mary thought it was empty, after her father and mother had died and Vera had left and she had eventually moved away herself. In fact, she remembered the time she helped her brother move everything downstairs—selling some larger items in the yard.

The day we mounted the wooden stairs, worn lowly smooth in the middle, was a day I will never forget. When we reached the top, I had to sit right away.

We found ourselves in a different world, an athenaeum, a bookroom, a big personal library. Moving from room to room, we saw nothing but books and more books, shelves and piles of hundreds of books. There were books of bright accounts of travels; books of good-humored and witty discussions; books of lively or pathetic storytelling; books of admiration and awe; books of nature and first inventions; books with recipes for cakes and ale, and road maps to find your way as well; biographical and literary books; and books of words as vehicles of thought through essay, prose, and poetry. It was a library of books, with a wealth of knowledge holding a dozen degrees between its covers—degrees in the arts, the sciences, literature, and history, by country or world.

I looked all around, enraptured, and said, with a tear in my eye but a smile on my face, "My dear and precious student, you educated yourself. You did it on your own! I am so proud of you."

I laughed heartily, and with a breathless intensity, I spoke to Bookie again.

"I'm envious, my friend, that you have had an intimate acquaintance with the makers of literature, the makers of history, the makers of books!"

I was old, but at that very moment, I felt youthful and vibrant, saying over and over again, "Bravo! Bravo! Bravo! Here's to you, Robert Olie Brenner."

I clapped my old hands together again and again. "Bravo, bravo . . ."

Mary thought I had lost my mind as she watched me go on and on about her brother and his books. She did not realize the deep connection I'd had with her brother.

"Is this really a time for rejoicing?" she remarked, shaking her head.

Mary retreated to the first floor, leaving me there with my insane celebration. I walked around the room, looking at the rare collection of books, picking up one and then another with incredulous joy.

I sat for a moment, and then I prayed my own prayer, which flowed from a voice within.

"Oh, we walk securely under His guidance, without Whom 'not a sparrow falleth to the ground'! The angels know this man who encountered the mighty 'mantelpiece' of life and put his earthly gifts on it for all to share. The rest of us didn't see, didn't care, and some may say, 'nothing much happened in Bookie Brenner's life, at least nothing of any importance.' Dear Father in heaven, we know otherwise."

My shoulders fell, my chest caved, I sunk farther in the chair. I wept for a student's dream lost, yet found, moreover complicated by an eternal love.

My eyes were held so I did not see. Maybe, I didn't want to see. I know—I know—you loved her, like no other . . .

I looked up and remembered deeply, regretting time lost with Bookie over the past ten years. Solemnly, I stood and wearily walked to the window. As night advanced, the clouds moved onward, and the moon showed its face as it crept across the horizon. I looked out as if the sky were a breath to me, then in one moment, I breathed my whole soul into the air. Inhaling a vibrating sob, I wept.

ের

Back home, I asked Milly not to disturb me while I retreated to the bedroom and my writing desk to reminisce and write some things down. Of course, he replied with a sincere hug, and the words: "If you need time alone, I understand."

I sat for the longest time with a pen in hand but didn't write anything down. My mind flew in all directions over my lifetime, remembering parts and pieces. I had already written a great deal about people I knew, loved, and respected, as well as people who were evil, though I hadn't compiled it all together yet. I recognized the challenges of writing about people because their stories had to be carefully written, chapter by chapter. Reflecting upon my convictions and conclusions, especially of two lifetimes, basically filled up my writing. I felt the stories of Marla Jean's life, and now Bookie Bob Brenner's life, were destined to be told. Adding others to my story, especially the divine sequences of Vita Mavis and Lizzy Schreck, who'd brought Noonday into this world for our delight, could have filled volumes more. That Noonday became a pleasure beyond any of my expectations: I want that to be known. The order of my lifetime with others could not have been more complete and satisfying without that child. There are others; I am feeling blessed to have included passages of these people in my story.

I stopped and finally put my pen to paper to see if I could remember by writing down their names, some of which were not worth the ink.

Sam and Queenie Siggers—Trixie Siggers

Old Black Joe—Moms Atlas—Tremont

Carl and Vita Mavis—Gunner—Norm Camfield—Auggie Has

Henry and Lizzy Schreck—Hank Schreck—William Schreck

Oscar and Sophia Johnson—Duggie Dunn—Theodore Millgard

Olie Brenner—Mrs. B—Billy Brenner—Mary Brenner—Vera

Attie—JD Flower—Johnny Flower—Jack

My lifetime of teaching was very important to me. To reach children and touch them in ways that stay with them, not only verbally, but also with books, was my goal. All children have the privilege to attend school, but some may fail to realize that they can continue their education outside of the school building by reading, too.

I finally stopped writing, oblivious to what I'd written down and what I hadn't.

I bowed my head and prayed, "Dear God, I am weak, but I am Yours. No wave of forgetfulness will wash me away from *You*! Amen."

I called out to Milly, "Come in—come in, Milly. I have finished."

He opened the door and quickly walked over to me. "Are you all right? Is there anything I can help you with, my dear?"

"Nothing at all, my husband." I stood and he tucked me into his embrace.

෴

I had ordered Bookie's headstone upon Mary's request, and one day the mortuary called to inform me that it was done. The man asked me how it should be placed on the grave. I replied, "Facing the Noonday sun."

Noonday came home shortly after that. The evening of her homecoming, she handed me a paper. It was a neatly folded document with names and dates on parchment.

"I want you to know that he was my husband—legally. We were married on his only trip to Boston. It was simple, but my children were there. That was important to me. I'm sorry you and Milly couldn't have been there." She faced me with tears in her eyes. "I loved him, Maggie, ever since I was a little girl, that little girl you took in, who you loved, you nurtured, you taught. I loved him from the beginning. The minute I saw his blue eyes and his hair the color of corn, the minute he spoke to me and touched me, the minute he looked into my eyes and accepted me fully, completely, I loved him." Noonday wiped her tears with a tissue. "I am his wife—I wanted you to know. I loved him, Maggie. I loved him so much."

I stared at the marriage license. "Noonday, forgive me." I looked over the top of my spectacles at her. "I loved you both like a son and daughter, thought of you as brother and sister, but didn't think beyond that." Tears sprang from my eyes. "I'm sorry."

Weakly, I sat down. "I don't know, Noonday. I always felt I was free of any prejudice in word or thought."

"Maggie, my love for Bookie was deep, lasting, real—a passionate true love."

"Yes, I know—I know."

Noonday gathered me in her arms and said, "My dear Maggie, you taught us how to love for real, far beyond superficies. Our love was born because of you."

The next day we drove out to the gravesite. No words were spoken on the drive east to Custer Cemetery. The day was still, and the misty Indian summer morn could have been painted, on canvas and in words. Yet it was autumn, and winter days were on their way.

Noonday helped me out of the car. I pointed, directing our stroll. We found our way along the narrow graveled walk with grass on either side. A breeze whispered, *This way, this way.*

I knew the general area, so it didn't take us long before Noonday called, "Here, Maggie, here . . ." She sauntered ahead of me.

I waited. I walked over to where Noonday stood at the foot of the grave. I expected tears, but instead she smiled at me and took my arm in hers.

With arms around each other, we stood at Bookie's grave. We didn't speak.

Then, Noonday pulled away from me and started to dance. The flowers she carried danced, too. Soon the petals started flying through the air.

"The breath of flowers is far sweeter in the air. Isn't that right, Maggie?"

"Yes, far sweeter."

"Maggie, do you think he can smell them? I think he can—I think so."

She stopped, dropped the flowers, and fell to her knees. "I have no idea how to say goodbye to you, my silly Bookie."

She bowed her head and sobbed. I reached and put my hand on her pulsating shoulder, and felt her pain. I cried, too.

She called out, "Oh, Maggie, why couldn't it have been different? Why couldn't it have worked out for us? Why, why?"

"It could have been different. You could have been born somewhere else." Suddenly, Noonday stopped and wiped her tears with the back of her hands.

She looked up at me and said, "Yes, how lucky I am. How lucky I am to have been loved by this special man—and you, Maggie. But it wasn't luck, was it?"

"No, destiny and luck have no common discourse. God put you here for us."

Noonday turned to face the gravestone again, and spoke directly to it. "You think you can leave me? No way! You have loaded up my heart with so many grand hours that it'll take the rest of my life to put them in my dreams. I'll never let you go . . ."

Noonday tried to speak again but couldn't.

I sought for words to comfort her, and finally said, "No man is born into this world whose work is not born with him. His farm was his life, but his life extended far beyond the farm. He was a man of letters."

"Yes, Maggie, he was a common farmer, and you are right, he was a man of letters. I can see him conversing with authors and scholars, can't you?"

"Oh yes, and with the Good Lord Himself."

Noonday's face brightened. "I have always preferred cheerfulness to crying. Bookie knows that."

She paused and pondered.

Finally, she looked closely at the stone. She wiped her hand over the inscribed words and looked back at me. She got up, and smiled. Then, she hugged me so hard I could scarcely maintain my balance.

"Do you know how much I love you, my mother?"

"Yes, my dear, I do."

"No, you don't."

"Oh yes, I do."

"No, you don't . . ."

We walked away from the grave, and from the words on Bookie's gravestone. They spoke to the world, although only two in the world knew their true meaning.

> *Here lies a beloved farmer,*
> *Embraced by the fields of the earth,*
> *Kissed by the warmth of the sun, and*
> *Truly adorned by a Noonday Flower.*

You are the Noonday Sun
Shining on everyone.
You are the Noonday Sun;
You have only just begun
Honeysuckle frown; Put on your Noonday crown
Believe in you.
Believe in you.

I do . . . I do.

—C. Ohse

Bibliography

Baldwin, James. *School Reading By Grades*. NY-Cincinnati-
Chicago: American Book Company, 1897.

Bartlett, Helen C. "Branch Village and Swedish Settlement in
the Early Days." Mason Memories. Published Quarterly by
Mason County Historical Society and Rose Hawley Museum.
Vol. II, 1974.

Bohy, Ric. "Paradise Laid to Rest." *The Detroit News*. August
19, 1985.

Buckley, Gail Lumet. *The Hornes: An American Family*. NY:
Alfred A. Knoff, 1986.

Collier, James Lincoln. *Louis Armstrong: An American Genius*.
NY: Oxford University Press, 1983.

Dereske, June M. "History of Walhalla." Mason Memories.
Published Quarterly by *Mason County Historical Society and
Rose Hawley Museum*. Parts 1, 2, 3, 4, and 5. 1974–75–77.

Dereske, June M. "Branch Township." Mason Memories.
Published Quarterly by *The Mason County Historical Society
and Rose Hawley Museum*. Vol. VIII, 1980–81.

DeZutter, Hank, and Pamela Little. "Black Eden." *Chicago's
Free Weekly* Vol. 22, No. 35. June 4, 1993.

Eadlen, Iris. Former resident of Idlewild. *Personal Interview.*

1997. ". . .Gentry, Chisholm. "Idlewild: A Resort with a Niche in Local History." *The Kalamazoo Gazette*. September 11, 1985.

Guy, Sara Mae. *Personal Interview.* 1997.

Hardiman, Clayton. "Once a Flourishing Haven for Blacks, Big-Name Stars." *The Grand Rapids Press*. April 26, 1987.

Kotlowitz, Alex. "Idle Awhile in Idlewild." *Michigan: The Magazine of the Detroit News*. 1984.

Mead, Chris. *Champion: Joe Louis, Black Hero in White America*. NY: Charles Scribner's Sons, 1985.

Rose, Phyllis. *Jazz Cleopatra: Josephine Baker in Her Time*. NY: Doubleday, 1989.

Sanders, Ronda S. "Idlewild on the Mend?" *The Flint Journal* B-B 1. January 22, 1996.

Smith, Ronald L. *Cosby: The Life of a Comedy Legend*. NY: St. Martin's Press, 1986.

Stevens, Margaret Fowler. Granddaughter of Adelbert Branch. *Personal Interview.* October, 2001.

Wilson, Ben. "Monday Guest-Ghost Resorts Swing in this Guy's Notes." *The Grand Rapids Press*. February 4, 1987.

Zucchino, David. "Lake County: A Gathering Ground for the Poor and Elderly." *Detroit Free Press*. August 5, 1979.

About the Author

With a lifelong interest in the history of Idlewild, Carla C. Ohse began piecing together the story for *Noonday Flower* in 1994 when her third child graduated from high school. Ohse earned a BA degree from the School of Education at Michigan State University. More than fifteen years after the first publication of *Noonday Flower*, she has brought it back with new content so that readers can rediscover this timeless story. She is also the author of *She Bear Bride* and *Into the Hand of a Woman*. Ohse and her husband, Bob farm 1,800 acres in Mason County, Michigan.

Made in the USA
Coppell, TX
06 October 2022

84157152R00208